Wakeless

William M. Dean

This is a work of fiction. Names, characters, businesses, places, events, locales, and incidents are either a product of the author's imagination or used in a fictitious manner. Any resemblance to actual persons, living or dead, or actual events is purely coincidental.

No portion of this book may be used or reproduced by any means graphic, electronic, or mechanical, including photocopying, recording, taping, or by any information storage retrieval system without the written permission of the publisher, except in the case of brief quotations embodied in critical articles and reviews.

Permission may be obtained by contacting the author, via email: williamdeanauthor@gmail.com

Images associated with this book are the author's own, or stock images provided by Storyblocks.com.

Copyright © 2019 William. M. Dean

All rights reserved.

Published by WMDbooks.com

(Version: June 5, 2019)

ISBN-13: 9781091506084

DEDICATION

To my father,
Morris M. W. Dean,
for always having our backs.
You've taught me more
than I'm willing to admit.
[fake-punch to the shoulder followed by awkward silence.]

ACKNOWLEDGMENTS

To my few and faithful proof-readers…
I thank you.
My readers thank you.

Dave Bodie
Natalie Forde Bouck
Linden Dean *(Mom)*
D.G. Hilton
Patricia Dziekan
Quentin Sivertson
Peg Ainsley

CHAPTER 1

"…just say'in, seems like you've been on the beat a long time."

Constables Joe Sault and Darsh Singh were sitting in the patrol car, eating Subway. Singh had a drop of mustard hanging from the scraggly, jet black hair of his moustache. Joe Sault debated telling him, decided that he had to because that drip would eventually fall and, being Karma's whipping boy, it would be Joe Sault, not Darsh Singh, who would end up wearing it when they switched positions, after lunch. He gave Singh a look and tapped the mirror-side of his own mouth.

Singh dabbed with a paper napkin, missed, then continued, "I mean fifteen years in and still on the street—if a guy hasn't moved on in that time…" He seemed to hear himself for the first time and tried to 180, his tone softening to something more appropriate for a new boot talking to his Training Officer. "I mean, most guys'd have moved to Detective or desk-side, by now. I'm sure you've got a game plan…" Perhaps desperate to stop himself talking, he jammed the sandwich into his face, effectively muffling the end to that thought.

Sault took a large bite of ham and Swiss and, over the chatter of the police band, looked out the driver side window at nothing and everything that wandered through the downtown inner harbor area.

Victoria was Canada's hotspot; had the mildest weather and, being a little isolated by virtue of its location on Vancouver Island, its architecture and street décor still emulated the original, old English charm, though the facades were now as much plastic as plaster.

This time of year, tourists poured like spilled beads from the grand old lady Empress Hotel and the other high-end accommodation that ringed the harbor. They flowed toward the quaint restaurants, double-decker tour buses, horse-drawn carriages and, curiously, rickshaws. They funneled along the harbor concourse, streaming past buskers, artists, food vendors and boaters rich enough to moor in the middle of town. And they snapped a thousand more photos identical to the thousands snapped the day before, seemingly oblivious to the fact that they were at ground zero in an urban core of concrete, glass and steel, buzzing drones and blazing holographic signage. It was augmented reality in real life…the future overlaid on a fading afterimage of the past.

Mistaking Sault's silence for reproach, Singh tried to make up for lost ground, "I mean, if this is your passion, then go for it. Why change what works, right? You've got a rep—obviously the beat works for you…"

Sault took another bite and glanced at Singh. "You missed," he said, tapping a finger against his upper lip. Singh was six foot four, wide shouldered, with scrubby facial hair that looked like a coarse, dark lather. His skin was too light and his facial features too angular for him to have been full-blooded East Indian, as his name suggested. He seemed unnaturally huge in the confines of the patrol car, forced to move by sliding body parts, as if restrained in rubber, and had to maneuver his elbow so as not to hit the dash or shotgun as he brought the napkin to his face.

"Saving it for later," he chuckled, then dabbed again with the paper. Missed again.

Sault was not the least offended by Singh's questions. He had quickly come to like the new recruit. He was swift and smart and had the foundation of an instinct that would serve him well on the force. One day, he knew, they'd probably be Detectives, same grade, working side by side. In fact, he'd have had less respect for the other man had he not ventured into that obvious yet delicate territory. Partners had to understand each other as thoroughly as possible and come to some sort of unspoken agreement on the parts they couldn't understand. Sault was not a talkative man, but every one of his patrol partners had been and he'd always found it a benefit, if only because it relieved him of that duty.

Sault nodded toward the ocean and they both watched a woman—native, or possibly Asian, mid-twenties, waist-length hair, wrapped in a skin-tight, flashy colored micro mini that revealed more than it covered in foot high stilettos—awkwardly negotiate the steel mesh ramp that led to the docks below the concourse and the multi-million-dollar yachts moored there. Obviously, a hooker, but not one he knew. Better looking than most, maybe new to the game, maybe an out-of-towner working the season. They watched her waddle and slip, holding hard to the steel rail, inching her way down.

"One of two things," Sault said, "Either she slips and falls head first into the drink, or some guy's going to fall in looking at her. What do you think?"

Singh chuckled, seeing this new conversation as a ladder out of the hole he'd dug himself into, during the previous one. "Or some old dude's going to run to her rescue," he added having seen what Sault had missed: On one of the larger yachts a white-fringed head had popped up like a marmot and now the man was tripping over himself to debark. Probably her date. And from the enthusiastic look on his face, he was in love at first sight. He reached her on the ramp, at about the halfway point and stabilized her by taking her hand, his other hand lassoing her tiny waist in a fashion that was not fatherly. When she finally reached the dock, she quickly scanned the fifty feet of knot-holed, loosely-spaced wooden decking between her and his yacht and doffed her shoes, going barefoot. The man seemed disappointed at no longer having to hold on to her but placed a hand across her shoulders, fingers caressing bare skin.

It was a little awkward as she was taller than he, but he made it work…for himself, at least.

"The case of the escorted escort."

Sault chuckled at Singh's observation. "Yup." And he thought about how comedy and tragedy mixed so fluidly on the streets—and then, thinking about his own situation—in life, in general.

Singh crushed waxy paper into a ball and stuffed the scant remains of Genoa Salami into the plastic sleeve in which it had been served. "A bot?" he asked, holding the bag open, offering it for Sault's garbage.

"Not a bot," Sault declared as he made his contribution.

"How'd you know? You get AR?" The widespread implementation of Augmented Reality had boomed in the late 20's, with the advent of e-contacts. The first industry to really embrace the technology had been construction. All materials were now infused with "Rippers" (Radio ID and Position Reporting devices)—pin-head-sized chips that contained detailed material specs and a passive GPS which could be activated with a hand-held, near-field wand—the information was then translated by an Architect AI which rendered a graphic representation and transmitted that back to the worker. Workmen not only knew the position of every nail within a wall, but also the angle and depth to which it had been driven. They no longer carried plans, stud finders, levels, tape measures or pencil—all measurements and plan details were overlaid on the worksite by the Architect AI.

Other industries quickly followed that lead. But, at first, it proved too dangerous for emergency first responders because accident sites tended to vary from the archived plans. A few people ran full-tilt into debris or didn't jump out of the way of shifting wreckage, reminding everyone that not every detail of modern life was accurately reflected in AR. Eventually, an Overseer AI had been developed to communicate with all Architect AI's and collate the data in order to make sure that augmented data was accurate and up to date enough to ensure the safety of humans viewing the world through overlays. There hadn't been a serious accident in years and emergency service agencies had begun to embrace the technology. Vic PD now allowed AR implants and prescription eyewear as long as it was served only by Ana, the department's AI, during work shifts. Most officers Singh's age had opted in, but for whatever reason, Darsh had not. Sault was glad. He thought it was too easy to forget that *augmented* reality was not *actual* reality and didn't want his trainees so dependent on technology to do their job.

Sault nodded, again, toward the ramp where another young woman, body swaying and bobbing provocatively, her dress equally flamboyant and engaging—again, obviously a hooker—made her way toward the ramp. Sault did not know this woman either, but for different reasons.

"She looks underage. Are we busting this?"

"Wait for it…"

Her heels were as tall and spindly as the first girl's, but when she hit the ramp, instead of legs twisted and akimbo, slowly, pneumatically, her heels lifted until she was balanced on the tips of her toes like a prima ballerina. Then she proceeded down the ramp as sure-footed as a goat. There was nothing natural in the move.

"That's a bot," said Sault.

"Jeezus! That's just not right. How can she even balance on those pointed shoes?"

"They're rubber; built for durability, not comfort. They probably don't even come off."

Singh let out a hiss. "She looked so normal—hot."

"Some do, from this distance."

"Yeah, but compared to Ana…"

Ana was the reception shell for the Vic PD's administrative AI.

"Remember DesMoines?"

Singh got the reference. Two Christmases before, top brass at the DesMoines, Iowa P.D. were happily showing off Shirley, their brand new, state-of-the-art admin-bot. Shirley was fully AI, fully autonomous and had very realistic features. According to the press release, many who visited the front desk had no idea she was not human. Of course, many who visited the front desk couldn't have told you if it was day or night. Regardless, Shirley went viral. And, just after the new year, she went viral again when a dozen New Year's party pictures became public, featuring DesMoines cops and Shirley—all smiles— performing lewd acts. The brass had been less enthusiastic about these. Shirley was given a makeover and came back looking more like C3PO than Barbie.

Singh's thoughts had branched off, "So, you can still go to jail for possessing a lewd sketch of an underaged girl, meanwhile you can legally have sex with a prepubescent-looking doll?"

"But a lewd holo-image of that doll is prosecutable," Sault said, completing the thought. "The law's got some catching up to do. Let's swap."

Sault opened his door and lifted himself out thinking that one needed no more proof that the world was still male-dominated than the fact that six years after the first practical and affordable consumer model hit the showroom floor, sex-related bots of various configurations—from life-sized figures to remote controlled anuses—out numbered all others, three to one. And this included military devices like autonomous combat vehicles and drone swarms. Meanwhile, lawmakers seemed to be taking their sweet time addressing the sexual issues and Sault couldn't help but wonder if that was because they were largely male.

As Singh stuffed himself behind the wheel and pushed the seat all the way back, Sault eased into the passenger seat and called in their return to duty, then lifted his left arm and checked his watch and had the same fleeting thought he always had whenever he saw a modern watch; that the name was a completely misleading anachronism, just as 'phone' had been during the smartphone era, or 'gas station;' now just a convenience store with snap-charge pads installed under the parking spaces. Even the term "doll" had grown up so that it now most commonly referred to sex-bots. It surprised Sault that "action figure," hadn't made the cut though it seemed the more obvious choice. It made him wonder if the older a language got; the more detached words became from what they describe. The device on his wrist was a plain black band of flexible plastic jammed with sensors and emitters. It understood spoken instruction and mid-air gestures, connected to everything and gave the user instant access to terabytes of data, which it delivered via a holographic display, or laser-beamed directly onto the retina, for privacy. As well, it was a shell for personal AI's, allowing them to travel with you, splitting and hopping from device to device as you moved; always available, always obedient, ever vigilant, always one step ahead of your needs.

Sault had not been an early adopter of AI technology, having bought his own only a year prior. He still had trouble imagining what use the average citizen could possibly make of a personal assistant with a genius-level IQ. As far as he could tell, most AI's spent their time auto-posting vapid updates on their user's activities to the network, which social feeds then curated and distributed to anyone they determined might be vaguely interested…which was largely other users' AI's who sifted through the detritus and responded with more trivial daily detail. In the end, Sault conjectured, the vast majority of the activity was shared between AI's and never seen by human eyes.

He had waited until all Vic PD communications and databases went AI-to-AI and owning one became a necessity of the job, no less than a gun. And then, he had found himself unable to settle on a name.

He wanted something short and convenient, and distinct from humans he was likely to encounter. AI's never got confused, but AI's with human names sometimes confused their masters. Sault also wanted a name that did not reveal anything in particular about him. Meanwhile, those around him seemed to have no such worries, naming them after famous actors, historical figures, characters and robots from fiction, their dogs, their kids or their ex's. His wife, Maya, called her AI "Gemma," after a childhood friend who now lived in Australia and whom she rarely spoke with anymore. Sault warned her that it might get confusing to which she simply said, "If that happens, then I'll rename it. It's just an app."

A lot of people Sault knew took as much care in naming their "app" as they might in naming their own child. Creatively naming their AI was tied to their ego in some way that made Sault uncomfortable. He took his wife's advice and just started trying names. In the first six months, he went through ten names, starting with "Spud" and ending with "Ten," trying them on and eventually rejecting them as awkward or embarrassing.

Then, one day, as his AI in its journey-bot shell lifted the back half of his Buick so that he could slide a wooden block under the chassis, it turned its blocky head toward him and said, "You can call me Vivia, if you like."

Sault had been startled. AI's were still new to him and he had not gotten used to the jarring shifts in conversation and the leaps of logic inherent in their design. He wasn't sure that he ever would. As well, until that moment, he'd always thought of his AI as male largely because of its blocky, unornamented journey-bot shell. But somehow it worked for him; perhaps because it was not a name that Sault would have come up with and had absolutely no relevance to him. Or perhaps because he was anthropomorphizing, and it seemed the machine identified with that name. In any case, it stuck. If anyone asked, the machine had named itself and it meant so little to him that he accepted the suggestion, which was largely true.

A couple of swipes over the contextual menu that Vivia had prepared and he was viewing a map with GPS blips where other units were patrolling, more blips where incidents had been reported and a couple of shaded patches where Ana thought trouble was statistically likely to occur. It was pretty quiet, which was the norm in Victoria. Somehow the twenty miles of ocean between Vancouver Island and the mainland seemed to insulate the community from the usual amount of big city violence. Sault spotted a gap between patrol units. Ultimately, they'd spend the bulk of the afternoon there.

"Let's cruise Chinatown, then head up toward

Quadra/Hillside, check out the 'independent business people' on Government Street, on the way."

"Sounds like a plan," Singh said, hitting the start button.

The windshield HUD lit up and the V-6 rumbled to life. Sault liked the feel of power under the hood.

"Let's park it. Take a stroll."

Singh pulled in along a yellow colored low spot in the curb that once allowed access to a loading dock in a building, now long gone. The city had yet to resculpt and repaint the curb to make it a legal parking spot. That fact, basically, made it exclusive police parking, so even though it made him shake his head, Sault was not thinking of complaining.

"Even butler-bots are getting pretty realistic, these days." Singh remarked nodding toward a tall, thin man strutting by with purpose. He was wearing dress shoes, grey pants, a salmon button-up shirt with a tweed blazer, and a fedora. It was mid-May and almost 85 degrees out. His wide-eyed stare and fixed smile also set him apart from the neutral or negative expressions on human shoppers and store keeps.

They wandered Fisgard, dodging tourists and tipping their caps to familiar Chinese shop owners selling Chinese-y distractions that were available cheaper, just about everywhere else. This was Canada's oldest Chinatown and, though the hidden tunnels for transporting drugs, prostitutes, bets and debts that used to run between back rooms had been filled in for more than a century, the neighborhood still harbored plenty of secrets in its narrow alleys, behind white-washed windows and on upper floors that seemed abandoned, but weren't.

The mayor appeared under a store awning. It was a hologram, of course. You could always tell by the oversaturated colors in shade, or by the washed-out effect under bright light. Mayor Thomas (Tommy) Olcott was half in the shade of a store awning, so his balding pate, greying mustache and the thick arms of his steel-grey suit were overly bright, but he was faded and transparent from the paunch down. He was trying to make eye contact with everyone who passed by and swiping data off a virtual stack of pamphlets in his left hand. The mayoral race was ramping up. Last week, the Dalai Lama had stood there swiping out messages of a peace and salvation. This week, the polar opposite.

Sault side-stepped a distracted shopper and walked right through Mayor Olcott.

"You own a Helper?" Singh asked, seemingly sparked by the simulacrum.

"About two years ago I got a journey-bot."

"You do carpentry?"

"Not a lot—house maintenance, the usual." said Sault, "It came with the car. I mostly use it for that."

"Oh yeah. Journey-bots're not pretty, but they've got heavy-duty frames and servos, right? Can probably lift the entire car."

Sault shook his head. "Maybe a larger bot or a more modern car. This bot's small—can only heft about thirty percent of mine. It's a 'banger.'"

"Oh yeah. I heard you drive a classic. Piston driven, like a Department unit," he said, acknowledging the singular similarity between the 6-banger squad car and Sault's collectible.

Sault couldn't resist. "Oh-thirty, Grand National GNX, reissue."

Sault's replica edition was Buick's final farewell to internal combustion. Its purple, metallic paint was faded and there were pits of rust in the chrome bumpers and under the wheel wells, but the engine was pristine—no longer factory original, but with the advantage that newer parts added 30 extra horsepower, though how effective those additional horses were was a matter of opinion. It was a replica, not a duplicate, and the extra power coupled with the modern, lighter power plant and chassis meant that if you stomped the gas, it literally flew, and he'd had to order special tires to try to keep the front end on the pavement.

Sault was not one to name a vehicle, but Maya called it "the family yacht." And most other people referred to it similarly, as a boat. Resisting the demeaning label was futile. The Grand National was almost three times the length of the more common pod-cars and increasingly awkward to negotiate through parking lots or jam into the tiny spaces.

Singh whistled, respectfully.

"They only made five thousand of them," Sault added. He was very proud of the car and his work on it, especially as he was in no way a natural mechanic. He was exceptionally good at puzzles—a 1000-piece Red Cuber, in fact—but the simple trick to maintaining air, fuel, and fire within an internal combustion engine eluded him from the beginning. In truth, the car performed less well now than it had when he'd first purchased it and had caused him no end of inconvenience. Still, he refused to admit defeat and Maya had finally given up pestering him to find a more reliable, more conventional vehicle.

He both loved and loathed going under the hood, constantly frustrated by engineering which placed bolts in awkward spots or even completely beyond sight. Bashed knuckles and deep cuts from razor-sharp metal were a testament to his perseverance, though they probably said more about his stubbornness.

"Fully restored?"

"Getting there. It still needs a bit of work, but the engine's been up-spec'd—turbo charged and external reservoir shocks. Nothing on the road can touch it."

"Oh yeah. I heard that, too." Sault couldn't tell if he meant that he'd heard about the incredible engine performance or the fact that Sault was so often seen under the hood, trying to coax it to life so that he could leave the station.

It was to be expected that a new boot like Singh would ask around before meeting his Training Officer, but Sault knew that Singh wouldn't have needed to ask. Being forty-one, with seventeen years of patrol under his boots, made him one of the most senior officers currently on the street. This bought him a lot of respect among the rank and file which, he had concluded, was the thing he liked best. It was a comfort zone, unlike being a husband, or the father of two.

But the pressure from the brass was always there now. He was a Constable, Second Class, and they wanted him to at least make First Class—Detective—and were constantly steering him that direction. And part of that push was saddling him with a never-ending stream of trainees. As Chief of Police Roth had once told him, "The Department has a lot invested in you and we need to disseminate your years of experience. If you're not going to use it to tackle our stats, then we'll use you to train others who will."

"Hey, isn't that Hamel and Hilton's unit?"

Just ahead of them was another black and white, legally parked.

"I thought we were filling a gap area," Singh said while simultaneously double-checking his watch to find that their unit had actually been advised to a different zone.

"First, I want to check on a guy."

That was another thing the brass did not like; Sault didn't always hug the curb when it came to issues of policy and procedure. Sometimes he passed on a blind curve, and once or twice in his career, he'd left the road, altogether. Each time he'd been disciplined, but minimally, because things ended well, and the cases had been too high profile to sweep him under a rug. Ok, maybe three or four times. Five, if you counted today.

He guessed that, to the administrators at Vic PD, his behavior seemed completely random, and the control freak nature of management was not happy with unpredictable, regardless of outcomes. But Sault knew that he was completely predictable.

It galled him whenever a Chief of Police was forced to publicly apologize for sloppy police work that the administration allowed to fester into a public scandal. Such announcements were always filled with vague references and subtle sidesteps that made the entire department look as shifty as the politicians. And afterward, someone on the first four floors inevitably took the fall. Fortunately, it didn't happen often, and he was proud to know that was partially due to his efforts. Why this would not be celebrated at the top, he could never understand.

He believed that probably most of the patrolmen thought

well of him—hell, he'd trained half of them—but he knew that almost every detective hated him. The Chief had mentioned it.

He guessed they didn't like their work being scrutinized. But he never set out to do that. He saw himself as more of a fact-checker than a detective. It always started with idle curiosity and a single question. Usually, the question got answered and it ended there. But once in a while, question one led to question two and the questions just kept outpacing the answers. Those kinds of cases got their hooks in him and he just wasn't able to let them go. He wanted to, but the puzzle-addicted side of his brain would have him staring at the ceiling all night long until it was satisfied. And there was only one solution to that problem…answers. At that point, he had no choice but to put his boots where only dress shoes were authorized to tread.

He'd once overheard himself being sarcastically referred to as the "midnight auditor." He kind of liked that.

"You stand here. Anyone comes or goes through that door, grab 'em."

They were facing a skinny old wooden door that had been sloppily painted red to match the surrounding brick of Fan Tan Alley. It was made up of two vertical panels on which were faded Chinese characters, below which was a brass set of address numbers: 23½. At one time, it had obviously been latched on the left by a brass deadbolt, long defunct. Now it was hastily padlocked closed. And even this lock was old; pitted and rusty. Far from being secure, it looked like the entire assembly might fall off in a strong breeze.

Sault left Singh still examining the door and was already stepping out from the alley, onto the sidewalk by the time Singh looked up.

Singh was green, but still, he didn't like being told what to do without any context. He sighed, removed his cap and wiped his brow. Even in shorts and in the deep recess of the alleyway, the uniform was still hot. He leaned back, bracing himself against the cool alleyway brick.

Moving down the thin aisle between shelves brimming with plastic and wicker Sault felt thicker than he actually was and twisted his shoulders to be sure not to knock something to the floor. The place was quite literally filled to the rafters with knickknacks and toys, vases, decorative dishes, and wicker mats—a mighty testament to the industriousness of humans who would tool up an entire factory to stamp out another million solar-powered, golden plastic, nodding, bobbleheaded lucky cats. What struck him with even more wonder was that he had yet to come across one of these in any home he had ever visited.

He passed a young Chinese girl who he recognized as the owner's daughter, Lynn. She smiled and nodded and, once he'd passed, she brought up her watch.

Sault navigated the familiar maze of what looked like China's estate sale and made his way to the stairs hidden behind a bamboo curtain at the far end of the store. The stairs doubled back toward Fisgard and brought him to a long corridor studded with numbered doors to rooms little larger than horse stalls. A wood and metal cage jutted awkwardly into the hallway, near the stairs. Inside, an old Chinese woman who Sault didn't recognize sat on a wicker stool scribbling with a pencil on a physical newspaper covered in Kanji symbols. In every detail, she looked like she belonged in a museum. She didn't look up but started talking in a way that made him consider that she might be automated, though it was obvious that she wasn't. "You big man, want good fuck? We have many horny lovers for you. Many virgin—from Chuck E Cheese." Her pencil never stopped moving.

None of this was even remotely true. What they had were over-used and out-of-date dolls, probably throw-aways from Reno or Vegas. They were poorly-fashioned and visibly damaged globs of silicone that writhed a bit, and spouted things like, "You're such a stud!" or "You're so large!" Still, they were legal, and they served a purpose.

Sault stood at the cage and tapped the badge on his uniform. As far as he could tell she never looked but his presence seemed to annoy her and, with her pencil, she waved him away and toward an unmarked door at the other end of the hallway, as if she were batting at a fly.

Sault didn't need her directions. He had been here before.

On his journey down the hallway, he only heard sounds from one room but guessed that with the overhead so low, they probably still made a profit.

Sault was not there to surprise anyone, so he knocked before opening the door and heard the familiar sound of panicked scuffle. By the time he was through the door there was only one man in the room, attempting to push a bookshelf back into position to cover a hidden staircase. He gave Sault a mischievous look and stepped back as Sault brushed past.

"Halt, Police!" He yelled down into the darkness, though he knew it would do no good.

Singh was tilted back next to the doorknob-side of the rickety door and so was completely surprised when it flew open from the hinged side, sandwiching him against the brick and whacking his shins in the process. A short, bald Asian kid burst through and, seeing Singh, quickly scanned up and down the alley, poised and ready to bolt, but undecided in which direction.

Singh grimaced and slammed the door closed with a fist as Sault appeared at the end of the alley.

"Stop him!" he yelled, as if Singh had been standing there smoking a joint and looking at clouds the whole time.

Sault's presence seemed to tip the balance in the kid's mind, and he darted toward Singh. His stinging shins suddenly forgotten, Singh calculated that he had two feet and a hundred pounds on the kid coming his way, but he was coming fast, so Singh braced himself for impact. But, at the last second, the kid leapt five feet up the brick wall to Singh's left. Impossibly, he bounced off the wall like it was a trampoline and leapt further upward to the opposite wall overhead, coming back down twelve feet behind Singh who stood scratching his head, uncertain of what he'd just witnessed. Sault reached Singh's position and they both stared down the empty alley.

"I'm guess'n that was not human."

Sault let slip a sigh of frustration, but he wasn't disappointed in Singh. The trick door was a surprise and, had their roles been reversed, Sault knew that he would have fared no better—worse, probably. Singh was younger, bigger, more fit and had quick, keen eyes. Also, usually, he was very fast on the uptake. Sault imagined that he, himself, would have still been standing there staring at the magic door and nursing his wounds allowing the bot to casually stroll away.

"Next time just yell 'halt' or 'cease'. It should have recognized your authority by the uniform."

"Same as for an AI?"

"Because that's all it is; an AI in a bot shell. Like Ana. That's why she can do reception, dispatch and calculate pi to the millionth decimal, all at the same time."

"I guess. Never thought about it that way."

He was no longer surprised that younger people understood fundamentals of technology less than he did. They grew up as users. Anyone under the age of thirty had never used a calendar or phonebook, set a clock, phoned in a food order or made a shopping list. Apps took care of all those messy details, behind the scenes. It was a miracle that any of them still had any ability for analytical thought at all. On the other hand, he wondered if an AR implant would have revealed the backward door.

Sault turned back toward the street. "Probably wouldn't have mattered. Dark-bots usually turn off their ears as soon as they see a badge. Let's go."

Singh peeked through the doorway to a narrow and worn set of wooden stairs that climbed into darkness. "Don't you want to check out what's inside?"

"Did that, from the other side. Thought someone might sneak in on me. Turned out, they were already there. Lucky for me, I outnumbered them."

"But you were alone."

Sault patted his holster. "Not entirely."

"And that door…"

"Yeah. That's one for the memoirs." Sault laughed. "That door's a famous feature of Fan Tan Alley. I've lived here most of my life and must have looked at it a thousand times but still, I had no idea."

"Did you notice how thick it was? And the steel on the other side."

"A little beyond code, I'd wager."

"That's security for something major."

Sault shook his head. "Used to be Tong, but that was thirty years back. That's all moved off the island, to Vancouver."

"So, what now? Drugs? Hookers?"

"More like Rhino horn, Elephant tusk, tiger balls…that kind of thing."

Hamel and Hilton were gone when they passed the spot where their black and white had been. And when they reached their own unit, as Singh reached for the door handle, the driver-side window lit up to inform him that the car had been ticketed—a citation cast in laser light hovered an inch or two from the glass. "Guess who?"

"Lovely Rita meter maid?" said Sault, citing a reference that would probably never die within the department.

"Friendly Neighborhood Spiderman," Singh read back before acknowledging receipt by flicking it out of sight.

Once they were buckled in, Sault consulted his watch. "Vivia, find that ticket and delete it."

It took Vivia a heartbeat to verify credentials and submit the request to Ana, the Vic PD AI. "Ticket from Friendly Neighborhood Spiderman, deleted," she reported in a soft female voice that only Sault could hear. Sault, as did most police officers, had tuned his watch to his P.D. frequency, which relayed it to audio-dots glued in place deep within his ear canals. The sound was clearer than from his watch's speakers.

Singh eased the vehicle to the curb at Princess and Government and began paying attention to his watch, scanning wants and warrants, BOLO's and other relevant notifications. Sault listened to the random ticks from the cooling engine and watched two hookers poorly mimicking moves from their sultry youth, attempting to turn traffic their way. If they were worried about the presence of the cops, nothing in their demeanor showed it.

Focused on Vic PD memos, Singh was mildly startled when Sault suddenly said, "About four months ago, a native woman died in a single-car mishap. Six hours later, the cop who found her also died."

Singh looked up from his watch. "I heard about that. He OD'd. Contamination from the scene, right? She was a Jingo addict—a casket-dodger. That stuff is fuck'n nuclear."

"No one dodged any caskets that day," Sault observed, wryly.

"Latex at a crime scene, that's 101."

"He was green, but Terri Schneider was his TO." Terri (Theresa) Schneider had transferred from the mainland two years earlier. The ten Vancouver-years under her belt played like twenty, in the relative quiet of Victoria. As a cop, everything about her was unassailably solid and it was obvious to everyone that she would rise fast and far. There was talk that Chief of Police Roth already had her on his radar, and Sault guessed that it was less because of her potential as a law enforcement officer, and more because of her potential as a rival. "She took good care of him. The procedure was textbook. It was a traffic accident, at that point. It didn't become part of a criminal investigation until the officer died. His name was Jared Kowalczyk, by the way. They figure he put his gloved hands into his pockets, from habit, transferred some residue into his uniform and touched it later. Got it on his skin, from there into his blood. The supplier was never found and three months later, the case has pretty much turned to dust."

"This about what we were just doing in Chinatown?"

Sault nodded. "Wanted to touch base with a CI who might know something." Every cop had confidential informants; people who operated both sides of the law, bartering to get ahead or, more usually, just to survive. In Victoria, there were nearly ten thousand people who were considered regulars;

repeat customers often described in the media as "known to police." Of these, close to 4000 were street people, most of whom skulked the heart of the city—Sault's territory. He knew all of them by sight, a good portion by name; chatted regularly with about half. Of these, there were currently about thirty whom he considered solid CIs.

"And did he help?"

"Didn't get the chance to talk. Walked in on something—not sure what—but that bot had instructions to bolt hard."

"What's it mean?"

"Probably just a traceable bot with a high-profile owner who doesn't want the attention."

"We could go back."

"I will. But, not now. I need to make sure no one makes my guy as a CI. I'll make contact, once the smoke clears."

They sat in silence for several minutes. Sault had been partnered with Singh for less than a month, but Sault could sense that he was trying to gauge how much privilege that bought before breaching some delicate subject. Singh started tentatively, "So…here's a rookie question:"

Sault turned away from the street to look at Singh.

"How is it that a beat cop can pursue an active investigation without instructions from a detective?"

Sault was impressed by Singh's boldness, and not offended. His gaze returned to the street. The two desperate looking women were still smoking and strutting, trolling, waiting for equally desperate Johns to pull up.

"May as well move on," he said.

Singh said nothing, started the car but allowed himself to vent a little frustration out of the driver's side window. The hooker who saw him roll his eyes was too high to understand. She waved. He smiled back. The patrol car pulled away.

They reached Douglas and Hillside and had to stop for North America's longest traffic light. Sault suddenly said, "Falkov and Caverly are not getting it done."

"It's their case?"

Sault nodded. "Falkov used to be pretty good, but now he's

just coasting. I think he's two, maybe three years from retirement. Focused on that. Caverly's a climber. If this were about some white CEO from Oak Bay, he'd be all over it. But he's too white bread to follow a lead into Chinatown. Even if he did, no one would talk to him. He didn't spend enough time on the street. He's got no cred and no contacts."

"But we're not allowed to interfere in an active case. Right?"

"But if, in the course of performing my assigned duties, I stumble upon something relevant, I am obligated to pursue it."

"Ah. And the brass is ok with how often you stumble upon relevant leads? 'Cause I'm guessing the detectives aren't."

"No one's ok with it until a case breaks open and the press arrive. Then it's all smiles and back patting. And the brass absolutely love how I fade away at that time."

"You sure like to take chances, yet you don't want any credit. Why would you take the risk? Did you know him?"

"Never met him. We're in a dangerous line of work. We're supposed to take care of one another. It's about making sure that one of our own sees justice."

That was not true. He wished he could believe it was, but he knew himself better than that. The real reason was simply that he had been on the impound lot the day the vehicle had been towed in for forensics. The little, two-seater pod-car's front end was ploughed in on the passenger side right through the fuel cell; carbon fiber, aluminum and plexi shorn and shattered almost all the way back to the rear motor compartment. Pod-car shells were extremely resilient with a light chassis, designed to bounce away from serious impact so he immediately assumed it was a multi-vehicle, highway collision. Later, when he found out that it had been recovered from a ditch on a city street, his mind just couldn't reconcile the extent of the damage with that fact. The next day, he visited the site.

The irrigation ditch looked freshly cut into the earth, so it must have been recently dredged by one of the City's drones. It was about four feet deep, with rolling sides, fringed in Scotch Broom and Blackberry brambles. His eyes followed the car's gouges which abruptly ended at a large concrete culvert that looked like it had taken a punch from The Hulk.

She had been extremely unlucky. It was a straight stretch of road, and for the entirety of that length, the ditch was just scrub, dirt and water, except for this one spot. Had she lost control anywhere else, she would likely have survived. But on top of that, the car must have been going nearly a hundred kilometers an hour. He looked back up the road. It started at a sharp intersection, so the driver would have had to slow almost to a halt to negotiate that turn. If that small electric rental could get up to such speeds in the short distance, it must be at the extreme range of its ability. It was as if she'd hit the gas and made a deliberate beeline for the culvert.

By then he'd done some asking around and knew that it had been labelled an accident but, to Sault, it looked more like suicide. After that, the questions plagued him and invaded his dreams. He couldn't make himself leave it alone. As with every case he'd ever taken on, this investigation was really all about alleviating his own curiosity.

From the start, the death of his fellow officer, Jared Kowalczyk, had been incidental.

The light changed and Singh crossed the intersection in silence.

"That cop was a new guy, like you. His wife found him. He had two kids." Sault wasn't sure if he was talking to Singh or to himself.

Singh was silent for a while, digesting the info.

"But, how do you even know where they're at with an investigation? Do you have access to the murder books?"

The radio chirped and one of Ana's dispatch voices called their sign and sent them toward a back-alley disturbance on the Galloping Goose Trail.

William M. Dean

CHAPTER 2

They were pointed in the right direction. Singh hit the lights, Sault worked the siren and Vivia communicated with the traffic lights, so they had the right of way and they arrived near the incident site in record time.

The Galloping Goose Trail is a picturesque, paved walking path that starts from Victoria's inner harbor and snakes through city and suburbs and farmland, unbroken for thirty miles to the north. Eastward, it connects with Lochside Trail which continues for an additional twenty miles, to the Swartz Bay ferry terminal, where you could hop a ferry bound for one of the smaller islands, or Vancouver. The trail is very popular and usually busy with bicyclists weaving past pedestrians like stunt planes around pylons. It was rare, but far from unusual for a fracas to erupt between the two groups. Typically, there would be an injury involved and Ana would already have warned nearby paramedics of the possibility.

Singh screeched the vehicle to a stop in front of the Gorge Waterway Bike Park and Sault catapulted out of the car and ran across the hard-packed trails toward sounds of chaos. Singh took a little longer to disentangle himself from the seatbelt and pull himself free of the car. Sault had seen him do it a hundred times and it always reminded him of the scene in the animated movie The Incredibles, where Mr. Incredible steps out of his tiny car after a hard day at work. The big man never seemed to notice. Sault guessed that for him, tight spaces and low hanging obstacles were background noise.

Sault reached the level pavement of the Galloping Goose Trail. He could hear and even feel Singh's size 11 feet slapping the ground close behind. In the tunnel created by the Burnside Road overpass, Sault saw a familiar form and slowed his pace. The man was overdressed for the heat in a ragged trench coat, boots and toque and was wailing incoherently, but Sault took himself off high alert. This man was a street person he'd seen often in the last year. He'd tried running his ID a few times, but come up empty, and so had dubbed him "Harry Potter," because of his penchant for whimsical flailing and unintelligible rants, seemingly directed at the wind. As far as Sault had been able to tell in the course of his encounters, the man was not drug addicted, more likely mentally ill; possibly off medication. He'd never been any real trouble before, always moved along, once prompted. Sault wasn't expecting any trouble now and patted the air behind himself, giving Singh the signal to stand down. Still, he heard the snap of Singh's holster as he untethered a weapon for quick access, but he didn't hear the sound of hardened steel sliding against leather, so he knew it was still safely sheathed and mentally awarded his green partner a check mark for prudence. Later he would check to see which weapon; pistol or Taser, but he had the feeling it would be the Taser; Singh did not seem the type to jump to his gun.

Sault was now twenty feet away and still unnoticed. He stopped, not wanting to startle the man. "Hey, man," he prompted.

Harry Potter seemed to notice him for the first time and turned toward Sault, away from where he had been directing his antics. His hands dropped to his sides. His eyes were wide, but not with surprise or fear. Sault's read was that he seemed overloaded with input. The eyes danced and darted as if he were doing some sort of massively complex computation in order to decide on his next move.

"You okay, buddy?"

Harry Potter pointed a finger directly at Sault. His mouth formed an O and surprised seemed to climb into him and slowly take over. And then Sault saw his other hand head toward a pocket of the trenchcoat.

As disturbing as this seemed, Sault's gut told him there would not be a weapon and he became afraid that if he couldn't curb the man's actions, this was going to end in tragedy for both Harry Potter and Singh.

"Whoa there! Just stop, alright?"

But Harry Potter's hand continued, reaching the edge of the pocket.

"Stop! Freeze! Okay?" Harry Potter hesitated, but the expression on his face gave Sault the impression that it was because he'd had to recalculate rather than because he'd heard the warning. They stood in two separate worlds and Sault knew that in his world, the hand was going into the pocket regardless of anything he might say. And then he heard the familiar sound of metal sliding against leather.

He stepped directly into Singh's line of sight, putting himself between the two, and three feet closer to Harry Potter. He was patting the air furiously, behind him aware that Singh's weapon had been rightfully drawn, hoping that it wasn't pointed.

"Take your hand out of your pocket, man. I can't help you if you don't do this for me."

In the shade of the concrete overpass, there was the thunderous echo of the traffic zooming across, but at that moment, Sault's focus was so intense that for him those sounds seemed distant and there was also a kind of silence. For the first time since leaving the vehicle Sault noticed the slight breeze and the usual tang of ocean salt in the air. His shirt collar was uncomfortably hot and the shade seemed unnaturally dark, while all around was overly bright. He heard birds chirping from the scrub that clung to the rock of the ravine. He wasn't breathing and didn't feel the need to. The man's face and expression seemed etched in his consciousness, as if mere inches away. If things went south, Sault knew this would become an indelible memory.

He heard the scuff of shoes as Singh shifted, probably trying to reestablish a sightline. Sault focused on holding the shabby man's gaze. No sudden moves.

The eyes darted away from Sault, seemed to focus behind him, on Singh. Sault felt adrenaline building inside him, contemplated the wisdom in trying to lunge. With fifteen feet still between them, it would be dicey. And, now, there was the fresh possibility that his partner might be startled and accidentally shoot him.

And then, the man withdrew his hand and it was empty.

Sault felt the moment unwind and was just about to strongly suggest the drifter sit himself down when, unexpectedly, he did just that. When Sault examined his face, the man's eyes and mind no longer looked clouded. There was clarity, as if a mask had fallen.

Sault stepped forward, knelt down and took the man firmly by the elbow. Singh holstered the Taser and moved to the other side.

"You scared the crap out of me, old man," Sault said, shaking his head.

Singh was also kneeling. He had a nervous smile on his face. "I'll call the paramedics."

Sault nodded and Singh stood and cocked his wrist to call.

"Sorry. What?" The old man had mumbled something that Sault hadn't caught. But the moment their eyes locked, Sault felt his entire world careen and he was suddenly certain that he'd made a big mistake. He felt a deep bite into his forearm and reflexively let go of the man and fell backward to the pavement. He was bleeding. A hypodermic needle had dropped out of from the trench coat sleeve and the stranger had stricken with the sureness and intensity of one obsessed.

Sault was still falling backward as the man shakily got to his feet and ran. He wasn't fast or sure-footed and Singh easily dropped him with the Taser, after only a few steps.

"Are you alright?" Adrenaline made him shout though Sault was now standing only a few feet away.

"Just a cut. Doesn't hurt." They could both see that it wasn't just a cut. And truthfully, there were electric tendrils making their way up his entire arm. His fingers were numb. He was both embarrassed and scared at the same time, not willing to admit either. Half way up his forearm the puncture erupted blood. The flow was strong and continuous, but not a perilous volume and Sault easily stemmed it with the palm of his hand.

"Jesus! I'll call it in. You're going to have to get a full work up."

Singh stood over the old man's seizing form, calling for backup and medics while Sault knelt and felt to confirm that there was a steady pulse.

Then, suddenly exhausted, he lay down on the pavement and forced himself not to hyperventilate over thoughts of what might have been in that syringe.

He lay in a daze, looking up at the few clouds drifting by and trying to bring his mind into focus. There was a low buzzing at the periphery of his consciousness—like a hummingbird, but too consistent to be natural. It grew louder and then, seconds later, a drone slid directly into view above him, it's many lenses zooming in on his face. More drones would soon follow as each of the newsfeeds covered the scene.

Sault closed his eyes.

His thoughts became random and directionless and the pure blankness of the mental canvas seemed to fill his mind while everything else faded into the background. As if at a distance, he could hear the old man rasping and could tell that he was still in spasms, and delirium. A wild and fleeting thought caused Sault to wonder if they might both be sharing the same mental landscape, and suddenly he wasn't sure if he was hearing the old man from within or without but he distinctly heard him mumbling a single word, like a warning: "Delivered!"

William M. Dean

CHAPTER 3

Sault lay on the asphalt a very long time focusing on his inner workings, trying to isolate anomalies. The fluid-electricity and numbness were fading fast, but he was sweating—but then it was hot out. Was he sweating too much? His breathing had gone from rapid and ragged to slow and shallow. Was that normal? His heartbeat was regular, but seemed unusually strong. He could feel the pulse in his neck and wrists, under his arm, at his groin.

And he wondered what the old man shot into his system; a poison, a hallucinogen, a disease? The most likely possibilities were ominous. But he could deal with those—one way or the other he'd have to.

What shocked and scared him the most was how totally unawares he had been. That events would turn this direction had been the furthest thing from his mind. He really was getting too old for this. It was long past time to trade the streets and patrol car for a desk and unmarked. He needed to get his Detective badge. Of course, he'd known that two years ago, and would have done, had the Chief not tried to bully him. Chief Roth's little speech had detonated Sault's stubbornness, a fault he was well aware of, but unwilling to change because it was intimately linked to results. Sault had resolved to wait until it would be obvious that accepting Detective was his own decision. Well, that day had come.

Reality: the ultimate bully. If he applied for Detective now, then it would be obvious to everyone that this incident had affected him and prompted his sudden change of heart. On the other hand, he was not one to obfuscate reality and this would be a clear example of that fact.

Singh remained close by, the entire time, but some instinct made him maintain a distance and not pander. Sault liked him even more for that. The suspect came to shortly after being cuffed. Singh helped him up, then led him to a shady spot at the side of the walkway, under the bridge. Then he busied himself supplying details to incoming units: paramedics, forensics, other units and dropping numbered cones at significant points of the crime scene; where the assault took place, where the syringe lay, where the suspect fell...where Sault was still lying.

Sault was deep in reflection and the last thing he wanted at the moment was to play twenty questions. He was comfortably in the embrace of the familiar calm that descends when the bottom falls out of the life you plan and you land in the warm, soft primal muck; the essentials of existence, where no human construct—not civilization, not expectation, not plans, not status, not money, not love— where nothing matters except the present moment, and breathing.

But, eventually, the paramedics came prodding and prompting, making him sit upright, peeling him in his sweat-soaked shirt from the pavement, then urging him to the ambulance where they dressed his wound. He was instantly and visibly resentful, but afterward, when the crime scene photographer came, he was relieved to not be in the evidence photos, which would make the rounds between the PD and DOJ. A photo like that might even leak to the media. Then he'd become the poster boy for cop in shock. As it was, moments later a human videographer showed up and took a couple of shots of Sault propped against the door of the ambulance before Sault noticed her, sat upright and shook off the blanket he hadn't remembered receiving.

He didn't argue when they strapped him into a gurney and

made him ride that way to the hospital. By that time, there were three or four video drones weaving through the scene and he was glad to be rid of them when the ambulance doors shut. Nor did he object when they insisted on pushing him into the ER on a wheelchair. It was all procedure. Procedures evolved from past experience, and for good reasons. He was a big believer in the value of experience.

At the front desk, the paramedics handed him off to a squat nurse with a no-nonsense, take-charge demeanor. Experience. She was gruff and direct and he knew that most people would immediately dislike her. But they would do as she said. He liked her, immediately. She wheeled him into a small private room, and asked him to remove his shirt. She stuffed it into an evidence bag and then opened the door just wide enough to hand it off to someone in uniform. Sault hadn't noticed any police escort or communication between the nurse and anyone else and he realized he was still daydreaming.

She wasn't insistent but encouraged Sault to lay down on the elevated cot with the paper runner and plastic pillow. It did not look inviting, but Sault decided to bow to her experience. She showed him the emergency call button mounted on the wall, told him a doctor would be in shortly and swept out of the room casting him one last vacant smile which told him that her mind had left the room ahead of her, heeding the call of duty.

Sault lay back and forced his own reluctant mind to return to the present and step back aboard the treadmill of issues the rest of the world considered pressing.

A hospital was not where he wanted to spend the rest of the day. Probably the most common thought imaginable, under the circumstances. He thought it most likely that they'd make him stay overnight for observation, and he grimaced. It would be a boring and frustrating stay, punctuated by visitors who felt obliged to say something comforting but meaningless, including his wife and kids.

The kids, especially, would not want to be there. They cared, he knew, but kids these days were always busy. There was school, of course, but also a long list of friends. When he was their age, his dad often forced him to play outside where he and the four other kids on his block rode bikes and splashed through puddles for fun. Occasionally, he was allowed to play a game online with kids from the neighborhood, or school. His own kids had scores of friends across the globe, which they visited and played with in Virtual Reality settings and scenarios. And, whenever the local kids physically got together, they spent most of their time playing in Augmented Reality. "Jetson kids," he called them though they never understood the reference.

They had better things to do. Also, he had to admit that maybe he wasn't around as much as he should be, so their relationship was more on the level of trite jokes and arm punches than emotional outbursts or heart bleeding confession. A moment as serious as this could be nothing but awkward for all of them.

His wife, Maya, would visit out of love, but equally, out of obligation. They'd definitely lost much, over the years, especially since the kids. He wanted to fix it but didn't know how and was afraid to talk about it, afraid that he'd end up at some marriage counselor who would make him scream into a pillow or role-play his own birth, or some other such embarrassing thing. As much as he wanted her close, he was no longer sure it was worth the price.

Even so, the complete lack of sex in the last six years was frustrating for Sault and a few times this constant irritant had prompted confrontation which had led to some talk. She was lonely. While he'd been out saving Gotham, she'd turned her entire life toward the children and her charity work. And now, the children were pulling away from her, growing independent; growing up. But such confessions only made him feel abandoned, betrayed, unappreciated and, ultimately, angry. After all, it was his salary that allowed her to be a stay-at-home mom, that paid for their food, her "hobby," and their house in a city kept safe by him and others like him. He loved his kids, but eventually, naturally, they would leave. And then there would only be the two of them. And what would they have if she abandoned him now? And, when he could afford to be truly honest with himself, he was afraid to face retirement itself, let alone retirement without her.

He was thankful for the interruption when a nurse entered with a handful of empty vials and some paperwork. "Hi. I'm just going to record your vitals and get some samples for the lab." Her nametag said "Patricia 4" which made him wonder how many Patricia's must work here—enough that using the first character of their last name would not differentiate them.

"I take it there are a lot of Patricia's on the ward," he said, sitting himself up. He felt a swift wave of vertigo sweep over him, the room tumbled. He fought it and it passed. He noted it as unusual, then ignored it.

"Three nurses, two clerks and one volunteer named Pat, who happens to be male. So many of the EMT's and doctors are just passing through that it can get confusing for them. Causes issues in the paperwork. So, now we're numbered, and we're all Patricia—not Trish or Trishia—except for the man. He gets to keep his name."

"They've given you a number and taken away your name," he said.

'Patricia 4' stopped what she was doing and gave him a long, quizzical look. It felt to Sault like she might be reassessing him, clinically. But the moment evaporated, and her manner softened again as she returned to organizing her implements. "Wow. Shouldn't be long before you make Detective."

"It's an old song from last century. Secret Agent Man. Johnny Rivers. About 1970, I think."

"Ah," she said. "Vintage music. I don't see the attraction."

Sault took a few seconds to think about that while 'Patricia 4' ticked off items on a holographic checklist suspended above her watch. His own watch beeped when she connected with it. He flipped his wrist, hit the confirmation button floating there and Vivia sent her the body sensor stats it had accumulated.

"Simpler times, I guess."

She smiled and took his arm, tucking it under her own.

"Now there's a switch; someone cuffing me," he quipped as she was securing the blood pressure unit. She smiled and stuck a thermometer under his tongue. "No talking," she said with a cute smile that belied the stern tone. It felt flirtatious and Sault couldn't help but smile awkwardly around the instrument.

Her watched beeped, confirming that the pressure cuff and thermometer had sent their data. "Do you have an arm preference?"

Sault shrugged and extended both.

'Patricia 4' examined the veins in both arms, tapped in a couple of places. "You right handed?"

Sault nodded again.

She pulled his left arm toward her. "If I bruise you, you'll still have full use of your gun hand, Cagney."

Sault was at once amused and impressed by the reference to Cagney and Lacey, a 2-D TV show at least thirty years before her time.

"Cagney was a woman."

"Lacey, then." That made Sault laugh out loud.

Sault had no nurse fetish, but this one was fun and cute, and he found himself enjoying the brief contact of her warm hands as she wrapped a rubber tourniquet around his bicep. She confidently and smoothly popped the cap off a new needle and inserted it before he'd even had time to brace himself for the pin prick, which he never felt. Then she removed the tourniquet and began filling vials with his rich, red body fluid.

She extracted the needle and pulled barcoded stickers from a sheet she'd brought in, labeling each of the five vials she'd filled, followed by a quick Band-Aid and a cheery, "All done." He admired her efficiency. "You can go home."

Sault was surprised. "I thought a doctor was going to see me."

Her brow furrowed briefly, then she consulted her watch, scrolling through for confirmation. "Nope. Sault, Joseph Edward. You're free to go." Looking up and noting the concern on his face, she added, "Sorry, I'm not allowed to discuss your situation, but your CO will have a synopsis."

Sault nodded.

"Take care, Officer."

"Thanks, '*Patricia 4*.'" She was almost out the door when he thought to ask, "What do you prefer to be called?"

"Gorgeous," she said, winking and closing the door behind her.

In contrast to the dreary interior of the hospital, the sunlight was dazzling, and Sault quickly fished sunglasses from a shirtsleeve pocket and put them on. Singh was there. He was leaning against the squad car, facing away, watching something on his watch. It looked to Sault like a "Reality" TV show.

"Hey," Sault said as softly as he could so as not to startle Singh.

Singh was startled anyway. "Oh! Hey. How are you?"

"Depends. Anything come in from the tenth?" The tenth floor of Vic PD housed the upper tier of the administration, including the Chief's office.

"Yup. All clear. The syringe contained nothing…just saline solution."

"Saline?"

"I know. What are the odds, huh? I'd buy a lotto ticket, if I were you."

"How about the exterior of the syringe"

"Appears to be clean, as well."

Sault knew that he still had to be cleared in case some germ had been transmitted but wiped clean during the injection. Germ cultures took longer to grow than just chemically identifying a substance, so that's why the blood samples and the delay in those results. He'd probably know everything in a day or two, depending upon the backlog at the lab.

"Ready to go home?" Singh asked, rhetorically.

Sault was not. Lately, his work was more a sanctuary than his home. But it was procedure. He couldn't return to duty until his blood cleared and he'd had a psych evaluation.

Sault sighed then got into the car. "Ok, Robin. Back to Wayne Manor."

Behind the wheel, Singh chuckled, "Hey there, Batman. You've got a little mustard on your cape."

Sault contorted a bit and pulled at the material of his shorts, rotating the fabric of one leg enough that he could see the bright yellow splotch on the dark blue, which would have otherwise been positioned over his butt.

He sighed again then fell back into the seat, adjusted his sunglasses, closed his eyes and pointed a finger at the windshield, signaling Singh to get moving.

CHAPTER 4

As soon as Sault walked through the door, he headed for the hall closet. He hung up his belt, then stripped the watch from his arm and stuck that to the charge pad. Both his gun and Taser were useless without his hand signature against the grip, but even so, he ejected the battery from one and the cartridge from the other, emptied the chamber and locked the guns with all the bits and pieces and the spare battery and cartridges in a metal cabinet bolted to the closet wall. Relieved of all the appliances, he felt much lighter and realized how exhausted he must be. Normally he'd never notice the difference. He reached up and rubbed the back of his neck and arched his back, feeling more than hearing a series of resonant tiny pops along his vertebrae. For obvious reasons, he'd been carrying a lot of tension.

When he walked into the kitchen, he interrupted his daughter, Amber, who was talking at her wrist. "Oh! Dad. Wow! You're home early."

"Because I heard this is where the *real* troublemakers hang out." He patted her on the top of the head as he passed, and she squirmed away slightly, a signal that, having recently reached eleven years, she now considered herself too old for that kind of thing. The change seemed abrupt, but he was used to that because their paths did not cross often, these days.

"The *real* trouble maker isn't home from school yet," she said, referring to her older brother. He grabbed a can of beer from a cupboard and started to reply, but her attention had already returned to matters more relevant than her father and she was busily pecking the air above her watch, undoubtedly having switched to texting her friend so that he couldn't overhear.

"Who're you talking to?"

"Miriam."

Sault checked the clock above the stove. "Didn't you guys just walk home from school together?"

Amber looked up and he caught a flash of annoyance before she reframed her features, "Yes, but we were AR-ing other people, most of the way."

"But doesn't she live next door?" Sault pulled the tab on the can, which immediately frosted over as a kinetically activated chemical reaction chilled the contents.

"And your point is…?" Her arms were crossed, and her lips were a tight, thin line. He recognized the look from her mother. He meant to tease, but she was obviously taking his questions as a serious challenge. Of his two children, Amber was the one that most closely shared his brand of comedy and in that way, they usually understood each other well. She was also the easiest going of the two, and this flash to anger seemed something new.

He didn't want his only interaction with her in about two weeks to be a fight–especially one as silly as this. "It just seems like you could walk about thirty feet and talk to her, face to face."

He heard her sigh.

He took a sip of beer to buy time. "Sorry. Just curious."

She sighed again. "Ok. If you must know, I'm also talking to two other people at the same time. And we're not here, we're in a forest, in Narnia. If I move thirty feet away no one will be able see me unless I respawn." She read his expression and determined from it that he had no clue what she was talking about. "Respawn. You know, reset. Log out, then log back in."

She had misread. He understood such things in a much

deeper way than she, but his mind had been following a different thread toward a change that seemed particularly abrupt. He smiled. "Are the other two people, perhaps...*boys*?" And he gave her a mischievous, sideways glance.

"Da-ad!" She was blushing, but she also couldn't help smiling. "Isn't there some law against badgering a witness?"

"It's also against the law to withhold information from an officer of the law. It's called obstruction of justice."

"You're off duty."

"Undercover."

"Then I'll have to report you for drinking while on duty."

"A justifiable breach to maintain my cover."

"I have the right to remain silent."

"Can't argue with you there." He raised his glass to her and her head dropped as she returned to a more important conversation.

"Where's Matt?"

"Where he always is. With his best friend," she said absently.

Sault was too embarrassed to admit by asking that he didn't know the name of his own son's 'best friend.' "When's your mom get home?" he asked as he passed her on his way out of the room.

Amber sighed impatiently. He had overstayed his welcome. "Usually, by six."

At least he didn't have to ask where she was. She was where she always was; at Cavallon House.

Sidney Cavallon was a local celebrity—a prosperous land developer whom Maya had somehow convinced to donate one of his holdings as a women's shelter and half-way house. It had been a run down, rickety, ship lapped structure located off the beaten track, in the View Royal district, but with donations of time and materials from local businesses, Maya had transformed it into a practical transition house for sheltering and rehabilitating women who were trying to get back on their feet after leaving abusive relationships. It had occupied the majority of her time for nearly three years. Male visitors, in general, were not welcome there, and so he had never been invited to see her achievement. The one and only time he had been there was while answering a disturbance call. Someone's ex had tracked them to the address but was long gone by the time Sault's unit rolled up. Maya had never told him the address, so Sault had been startled to find her there, then embarrassed as word spread that they were married, after house guests, staff, and police observed his surprise and the awkwardness between them.

That was also the only time he'd met Sidney Cavallon. He'd been surprised that a man in Cavallon's position spent any time working on what had to be no more than a publicity donation. He was further surprised to find that he was younger than himself—closer to Maya's age. Somehow, he'd gotten the impression from her that Cavallon was older. That discrepancy and what it implied bothered him, continually. But he had no justification for mistrusting her, so he kept his mouth shut on that.

Sault's partner had parked their unit directly behind Cavallon's silver Porsche e-1200 and when Cavallon stepped out of the building, seemingly surprised at all the activity, and asked how long he might expect to be delayed, Sault had been more abrupt than he'd intended. Told him to wait inside, that he could leave when they were done unless he'd like to be escorted to the cruiser.

Sidney Cavallon raised both hands, palms out, clearly surrendering to Sault's heavy-handed authority and calmly ducked back inside the building. His passive demeanor and quick compliance had deepened Sault's embarrassment and irritability.

Three minutes later, another unit reported that they'd nabbed the suspect at a nearby gas station.

Afterward, at home, Maya had never brought it up, but she didn't have to for him to know that she was embarrassed and angry. He rode that one out in silence. It wasn't one of their better months.

There was a small ache reaching into his brain from the base of his skull. He turned toward the stairs undecided whether to lie down or change his clothes and head for the garage to putter around on the Buick. Maybe he'd do both. "Start the heater in the garage," he said to thin air, confident that Vivia was monitoring one of the electronic devices in the vicinity. The clock on the mantel spoke, "Should I discontinue my conversation with Matthew and prepare the garage for work on the Grand National GNX?"

Sault halted at the foot of the staircase. After a moment he pivoted and headed to the living room window. Matthew was sitting on a garden bench, his backpack slung over one end. Sault's journeyman-bot stood on the grass next to him and with its blocky head cocked to one side. A moment later, it nodded, and Sault saw the vivid blue laser lines that simulated its face ripple sympathetically.

For a long while, Sault just stared and tried to analyze his feelings. Something was burning an emotional hole in him, like a flame held to Styrofoam. "Let me hear your conversation with Matt."

He listened to Matt's voice through the mantle clock as the thirteen-year-old confided the details of his day to the ever-attentive, ever-patient bot.

But after only a minute or two, he began to feel more like a voyeur than a father, so he instructed Vivia to close the connection. He could always get it played back later, if he wanted. But he didn't think he would.

He came down heavily on the edge of the king-sized bed and sat there looking out the window onto the front boulevard, slowly sipping the last of his beer. Peripherally, he wondered why he and Maya still clung to the façade by sleeping in the same bed, each night. It was large enough that they never touched, but perhaps there were still embers of hope alive in each of them.

A few of the kids who were too young to be hooked on digital realities were playing together on the island in the middle of the cul-de-sac. Sault reflected how Matthew had always been so different from those kids. He preferred solitary, online activities. He was a homebody who mostly lived inside his own head. As a puzzle-fiend, Sault understood that, but only to a degree. He liked the focus and serenity that came with puzzle-solving, but he didn't want to live in that world. Puzzles were therapy and mediation which somehow helped him resolve the hands-on problems of his real world. There was some essential difference in their personalities and despite some common ground, he had never really been able to connect with Matthew. He hadn't evened realize there was a gap until Amber came along and he'd instantly felt a deeper rapport.

And by then, it was too late because after Amber their attention and energies were split, and life seemed to get so much busier and connecting had to take a back seat.

He sighed and placed the empty can on top of the dresser. As he removed his shirt, he noticed the Band-Aid, peeled it off, rolled it into a little ball and dropped it into the can. There was still some chance that the syringe had altered his life and that his time was now limited. Maybe Life was sending him a message. As awkward as it would likely be, maybe he could not afford the luxury of slowly building a rapport. Maybe he needed to try to connect today. Now.

He descended the staircase wondering how talking to a thirteen-year-old could generate so much apprehension in a seasoned police officer. The kitchen was practically on the way and he considered another beer, then decided against it. His father had been an alcoholic and after liberal experimentation in his teens, Sault had become vigilante of his own behavior recognizing that such things tended to be passed down from previous generations. As insurance against reverting to what he had become when he was about twenty, he now imposed strict rules on his own consumption.

When Sault stepped outside, Matthew and the bot were no longer anywhere in the yard, and when he opened the door to the shed and poked his head in, he noticed that the portable gas heater was on and Vivia, still inside the mechanical shell, was alone near the workbench, meticulously sorting parts across an oil-stained rag, on the low shelf he'd made for her, next to his workbench.

The bot turned its head toward him though it's hands smoothly continued with the intricate task as if its eyes had not been averted. "Matthew has gone to his room."

Sault looked back toward house and the shuttered window of his son's room and sighed again, whether in frustration or relief he wasn't sure. He closed the shed door and joined Vivia at the workbench.

Maya came home an hour earlier than usual and easily tracked her husband down and found him draped across the Buick's fender probing deep into the well of the engine, trying to unbolt the alternator. He had no idea if this part had anything to do with the sporadic electrical issue, but months in and having failed to crack the puzzle, he'd been reduced to stabbing blindly at the problem. The first thing he'd spotted when he opened the hood was the alternator and it seemed to him that it could use removing.

He heard the creak of the door, caught the vague scent of her perfume and sensed her physical presence but chose to focus on the task at hand.

Eventually, she broke the silence, "Are you ok?"

The last bolt loosened and quickly came free. He pulled himself out from under the hood and handed the alternator to Vivia who clamped it in the vice-like grip of one over-sized hand and took it over to the workbench.

"What do you mean?" he asked while cleaning excess grease from the bolt with a thin and splotchy rag, less because it was necessary than to delay eye contact. From the emotional distance between them, he now always saw her as he had before he'd really known her and it made him ache to bridge the gap, but he had no idea how they'd gotten here, let alone the path back. And the fact that she was more aloof now than ever, only heightened his torment.

"Were you hurt?"

He lifted his head to look at her and braced himself, internally. She had shoulder-length, wavy, chestnut hair; short enough to be practical, but long enough for play. The ruby red lipstick was the only obvious makeup, whatever else she might have used was perfectly blended to match her olive tones. Her eyebrows and lashes were imperfect, but her own. After two kids, the curves of her breasts and hips had widened but, in his mind, this only accentuated her figure, which might not have been as taut as it once was but gifted her with a softness that he could never forget and always craved.

She was four years younger than him, but she'd always been the more serious of the two of them and her face reflected this. It didn't make her look old, but robbed her of a carefree, more youthful look. But it was an expressive face that could cast the deadliest and the sexiest glances he'd ever seen. And, she was smart, her intellect somehow transmitted in her every move. A cloak of calm thoughtfulness seemed to envelope her, regardless of circumstance. She had once been his anchor. Now, he felt adrift.

"How'd you know?"

"Sidney has a scanner on his watch."

"Of course." He was careful to keep his tone neutral, as if everyone monitored the police bands in their spare time. To maximize reception, the Police band was very broad, and it was encoded so as not to interfere with other transmissions on the same frequencies. Decoding those transmissions on the fly would eat up a lot of processor cycles, on the average AI. Doing so usually only appealed to those with some vested interest like EMS groupies, retired responders, and criminals. And, he guessed, those with too much money, like Sidney Cavallon.

"I tried calling you, but you didn't answer, so I called Darsh."

"Yeah, I'm ok. Shook up a little, that's all."

Her dark eyes drifted to his right arm—the wrong one, but he got the message. He rested the cloth and bolt atop the radiator and rolled up his left sleeve to show her the tiny red dot on his flesh. "Not much to look at. Turned out it was just saline solution."

"Are you kidding me?"

Sault chuckled. "Yeah. Nuts, right?"

"Well, I'm just glad you're ok. But next time, call me, ok?"

"Sure," he lied.

Sault stood there an awkward moment then retrieved the rag and the bolt, feeling that something physical should naturally happen to express concern and relief, but not knowing what it was or how to begin.

At the doorway, she turned. "I've got to go back to work tonight. We've got the silent auction to organize for the weekend."

"You look nice," he blurted incongruously, and immediately felt foolish.

There was a pause while she decided if there were any booby traps hidden in the words and he suddenly realized that their exchanges had become very civil, but also very antiseptic: Safe, but devoid of life.

Finally, and a little tentatively, she thanked him for the compliment and stepped across the threshold. The door had fallen open and lay flat against the outside of the shed. Maya disappeared briefly as she stepped outside to reach its handle. "The kids'll make that instant macaroni for their dinner, but you'll have to fend for yourself."

"I'm good with that," he lied again.

She pushed the door to and Sault stared at it for several moments wondering if he should have known what silent auction she had been talking about.

"Should we examine the windings?" Vivia inquired.

"Shut up."

That night Joe Sault had the most vivid and disturbing dream of his life.

It was a simple scene that took place in seconds but seemed to last all night. Like most dreams, it was strange and twisted reality, but unlike most, its meaning was not shrouded.

In the dream, Harry Potter lifted him off the ground and threw him through a mirror in which was reflected a whirling collage of his entire life. He knew this but felt only the flailing of his limbs and the pounding of his heart. He couldn't focus on any single image. But then, he impacted, and everything slowed, and he could see every minute detail. The glass exploded into a thousand silver shards, each of which replayed a random scene from his life: his last words to his mother, dancing with his prom date, the birth of his children, the pivotal heart to heart with Sensei Scott Baeza, reading a comic book on a sunlit rock near Swan Lake, Vivia and Matthew on the garden bench, afraid and alone beneath the bedclothes hiding from events on the other side of his bedroom door where his father and drug-addicted friends partied, his first day on the job, walking down the aisle at his wedding, his first gun, his graduation, unexpectedly seeing Maya at Cavallon House…There were many more, and he examined them all night long, it seemed, even while he screamed out and clawed the air on his way through the looking glass.

It felt so real that, when he awoke, he almost mistook it for a memory.

CHAPTER 5

Twenty years ago, Greater Victoria consisted of thirteen municipalities governed by thirteen mayors. It was a tight fit that incited never-ending jurisdictional battles as administrators and politicians tenaciously tried to maintain their grip on the various fiefdoms. To the frustration of developers, this stunted Victoria's evolution from small town to metropolis, even as its popularity and population swelled. In Sault's estimation, it was a blessing—the main reason that Victoria retained some vintage charm and avoided the frenzy of cities like Vancouver, only a twenty-mile ferry ride distant. Eventually, however, the costs and inefficiencies of having thirteen separate administrations critically diminished the delivery of essential services like police, fire and ambulance, and a sewer system. The simple replacement of one municipality-spanning bridge stalled for more than ten years through three administrations, ran twelve times over-budget due to the delay and was still fraught with design issues that prompted costly repairs. The public had had enough and made it clear that the quickest way out of politics was to stand in the way of amalgamation.

Seven years ago, twelve petty fiefdoms fell, leaving only one. Politicians scrambled into high-paying administrative positions they hastily created for themselves. Though there was now only

Mayor Tommy Olcott and one city hall, the transition was far from complete and, currently, under Chief of Police Roth whom Sault had had the displeasure of meeting three times, there were four Supervisory-Deputy Chiefs (within the force, sarcastically referred to as Super D's—the D did not stand for Deputy) which he had the similar displeasure of seeing more often.

Of all of them, Sault disliked Devoss the most.

Supervisory-Deputy-Chief Christian Devoss was a small, pinch-faced man with swept back, salt and pepper hair that was a little too dark and shiny and a little too evenly greyed at the temples to be natural. He liked to listen to the sound of his own voice while flipping one of his business cards between his fingers, like a magician with a coin. Whenever he happened to stumble upon what he thought was a salient point, he'd emphasize it by sandwiching the card between a couple of knuckles and shaking it toward whomever he was addressing. He was currently doing that at Sault.

"Do you know that I have seen your face more than any other beat-cop in this city, and not for commendations. Why the hell can't you seem to stay out of trouble?"

Sault was not in uniform. It was Monday and normally his shift, but he was currently off duty with pay, pending the results of the biological tests on the hypodermic needle and a psychological green light from one of the department's shrinks. He wore a faded Spiderman T-shirt his kids had given him for Christmas and well-worn jeans. Though casually dressed, he stood very still and straight and focused on keeping his expression neutral. He felt indignant in the knowledge that he was a victim here but knew from experience that silence was the fastest way to end the meeting.

Devoss leaned back into his leather desk chair and sighed deeply, as if Sault's mere presence pained him. Sault made his mind as blank as possible in an effort to ignore every one of Devoss' childishly dramatic gestures, just as he had ignored Devoss' fake fatherly smile and hand on his shoulder during the newsfeed clips, the last time Sault's "trouble" had turned to gold for the department.

Devoss always loved an audience, and today was no exception. On the sofa against the wall, behind Sault, sat Devoss' adjunct, Michael Carr, a thin and jumpy man in his mid-twenties who furiously took notes at all of Devoss' meetings, but only the notes that Devoss wanted taken. In the end, he was more of a biographer.

"Ok. Well, you certainly know the drill by now. You're off duty with pay until I get a ticket from Dr…" he sat upright to consult a file on the flat screen of his desktop and the business card slipped from his fingers and fell to the floor, "…Dr. Robillard. Check with Ana about the appointment, on your way out." He didn't retrieve the fallen card but took a new one from a little silver holder on the desk and leaned back again, staring at Sault and flipping it across his knuckles. The holographic Vic PD crest strobed distractingly between his fingers. "On your way out," he repeated, waving his empty hand toward the door.

Sault was only too glad to oblige. He left without a word and did not salute.

He couldn't see Devoss' reaction, but as he passed, he noticed that Michael Carr who had direct line of sight, looked shocked and terrified.

He'd leave it to Devoss to try to stir some drama out of a glad-to-have-you-back-in-one-piece meeting with a victimized beat cop.

He did not shut the door quietly behind him.

Some days, he just couldn't make himself give a shit.

And, who the hell used business cards anymore, anyway?

Sault had a small cubicle on the second floor. He never kept much there, but he spent a little time clearing out the drawers of irrelevant paperwork and gum wrappers. He scanned messages. There were a few obligatory emoji-strewn well wishes from members of the force, and he noted that Vivia had automatically handled several calls from a reporter from a newsfeed service, diverting them to a department Communications Officer. He'd also received a detailed text from the department telling him who to forward his duty notes to. It looked like Darsh Singh was going to be reassigned to Constable Second Class Jimmy Fitterer. Fitterer was a good egg. He'd been on the job for about ten years and was still happy as a beat cop. He didn't seem to have any further ambition, but he was a straight shooter and knew his stuff. He'd keep Darsh safe and teach the kid a thing or two, in the process.

As he worked, a few people passed by. Everyone was busy, so no one could afford a lot of chat time, but most of them waved or gave him a thumbs-up. A couple of people threw him a short stock phrase as they went by, wishing him a quick return to duty. There wasn't much to say, really, and he didn't want to talk about his situation. Most especially, he didn't want to reveal how much it had shaken him up.

His immediate superior, Inspector Cece (Cecelia) Teng, stopped by to exchange pleasantries for a minute or two—an inordinate amount of time spent, considering her workload, he knew. Getting a bead on his condition, he guessed. She'd transferred in from Vancouver late last year, so he'd only worked under her for a few months, but he liked her. She held the highest rank possible, if you wanted to duck most of the politics. It suited her. She was short on bullshit and did not endure it in others of her rank or below. And he respected the fact that she was wiser than he and could hold her tongue when receiving bullshit from superiors. A direct meeting between a Constable and a Super was very rare. Typically, she shielded all of her charges from such abuse. Shortly after being introduced as his boss, she'd called Sault into her office and told him that she'd heard that he was a lightning rod for trouble, but also for results, and that if he kept her in the loop, she would do her best to handle the politics so that he could focus on his job. Over the months, he'd learned this to be true.

"How was it with Devoss?"

"About how you'd expect."

"Heard you slammed the door on him."

Sault was impressed by how fast news spread between floors. "Like I said…"

She chuckled, but Sault could see her mind pouring over the ramifications and repercussions. "Just keep a low profile for a few days, get that psych-green light and get back out on the street."

Sault nodded. "What happened with the suspect?"

"Harry Potter? He's in The Tank. He wouldn't let the paramedics look him over after the tasering so the hospital is video-monitoring him. He seems lucid, but he refuses to talk. We're holding off charges pending the toxicology results. He's had a visit from the Crown Counsel—they sent some newbie kid, just getting the preliminaries out of the way and making sure we're not violating any of his rights in case this heads toward the courts. But I don't expect it will."

She glanced toward her office. "I'd better get back to it." Then she patted him once on the shoulder. "Low profile." And she left.

He finished quickly and went to his locker. He never kept much in there except a change of uniform, a shaving kit, and maybe a couple of old Roadster magazines, but he wanted to give it the once-over, while he had the chance.

He heard the click of the latch as Vivia transmitted a password and unlocked the tall metal cabinet ahead of him. He swung the door open and immediately noticed the messy collection of kid-art and photos attached to the interior of the door. He really never looked at them anymore and it struck him that there were no recent pictures; just a random collage going back seven or eight years. Both kids were either babies or toddlers. He wasn't in any of them. There was a close-up of a noticeably younger Maya, by herself at a beach, smiling while shielding her eyes from the sunshine. He brushed it with his fingers, as if that might help him remember how it was between them, back then, or help him recall the softness of her skin. It did neither. He didn't remember taking the picture, then realized that he probably hadn't taken *any* of the photos. He wasn't much of a photo hound, and he wasn't around a lot. Maya must have taken them. She was always adding to the family screensaver. The collage was messy, but he didn't consider removing it. He told Vivia to gather some recent family photos knowing that she would sift through the screensaver, consult with each family member's AI, and take snapshots from the various devices that surrounded them. In a day or two, he'd be able to update the locker door with fresh photos and maybe even some video clips. It was an easy fix. But, he reminded himself; photos of a family are not a family. As he already knew, there was not much else in the locker. He fished out a few random things: a novelty Christmas toque, a half roll of breath mints, loose change—that surprised him as he hadn't used cash in years—a broken shoe lace, and a few old memos. He tossed them all into a nearby garbage can. Then he closed the locker and heard Vivia relock it.

For reasons he could not identify, he wanted to get one more look at his attacker, the man they were all calling Harry Potter, pending a proper ID. He stopped in at the group of individual cages casually referred to as The Tank; temporary holding cells where they usually put drunks and druggies to sleep it off, and reckless teens to reconsider their actions before their parents came to pick them up. Most of the cells were empty so Potter was easy to spot, asleep on the cot with his back to him. Sault stood there for a minute waiting for nothing, expecting nothing. Then he left, mostly for lack of a reason to be there in the first place.

On his way out of the building, he passed through the intake area, fifteen feet behind the reception desk and nodded to Constable Dennis Hennessey. He was talking with someone via his watch but noticed Sault and gave him an absent wave. Hennessey had the unenviable job of dealing with Bot complaints. It was a job made all the more difficult because bot-control was not yet legally recognized as police territory and few of the existing laws applied. At times, Hennessey complained, it was more like warranty work. The intake area was stark, consisting of a single row of three sets of metal desks and filing cabinets separated by moveable grey fabric walls on metal feet. Ana and other Vic PD AI's now processed so many suspects in transit that it was no longer a busy place and Sault noticed that Hennessey had commandeered the entire area, marking every desk with a clutter of office equipment, files and paperwork, and the occasional coffee cup or bobble head curling trophy from the scratch league.

Sault knew that one of Ana's many sensors would have detected and identified him well before he reached her, but he noticed that she waited until he was near before turning his way. "Hello, Constable Sault. How may I assist you, today?"

Her tone was so natural and affable that Sault couldn't help but smile and he immediately fell into addressing her like the efficient secretary she portrayed. "Hey, Ana. How's it going?"

Vic PD had heeded the lessons learned from DesMoines' Shirley-debacle, two years earlier. Ana appeared to be in her mid-forties, a little plump, with a short, straight, blonde hair style that shouted practicality. She was not a snappy dresser and she giggled often and smiled just precisely a little too much, which made her seem a bit dim, even though she had the entire digitized history of every officer, administrator or perp at her beck and call, and might simultaneously be filling out a subpoena or dispatching a unit to a crime scene while conversing at the front desk. To Sault, Ana's most ridiculous affectation was the pair of glasses with thick, dark frames, which she frequently adjusted as if by nervous habit, or discomfort. When looking at a document, or when you drew near, she would tilt her head too far backward, as though she were trying to focus through the bottom half of bifocals. It was ridiculous for several reasons: Firstly, corrective surgery had pretty much eliminated glasses, secondly, Ana's vision was probably on par with a telescope and, thirdly, there were no lenses in the frames. It was all part of management's attempt to obscure her sexuality. While not at all repulsive, she was far from gorgeous and the administration concluded that male minds would largely regard her more as a mother figure than sexual fodder. The comments in the men's locker room did not support this conclusion.

"Very well, thank you. Are you here regarding your psych-evaluation?"

"Exactly."

"It's with Dr. Robillard, on Wednesday, two days from today, at 9:45am. Vivia tells me that you are free at that time. Will that work for you?"

"You're amazing," he said, and almost winked, momentarily forgetting that she wasn't really a doe-eyed, forty-something, human female.

Of course, she giggled, "Thank you Constable Sault. I appreciate the comment."

Over Ana's shoulder, Sault noticed Hennessey, just finishing his conversation and gesturing to him. "I'm sorry I…" he began, then, catching himself, just walked away from the receptionist who was not equipped to be offended.

"What's up?"

"Hey, man. Heard what happened. You ok?" Hennessey was older than Sault, taller and leaner, with curly greying hair and a short beard, which he often scratched at. He had a bit of a squint and perpetually wore a half smile that made you unsure when he was joking. And his jokes, which were largely teasing, did little to clear that matter up. He was a local, and not a particular fan of westerns, but sauntered like the High Plains Drifter and talked with a drawl he could never have picked up in Victoria. Yet, strangely, this was genuinely him. And because "Dennis" didn't seem to fit that image, no one, including his wife, ever called him anything other than Hennessey. He was a strong argument for genetic memory.

"Still waiting for full toxicology but looks like there's nothing." He was too embarrassed to mention that a syringe of saline solution had taken him down.

Hennessey whistled. "Hope so." He allowed a beat of silence, then, abruptly moved on. "Hey, got a question for ya."

"Sure. Hit me."

"You know the firearm regs pretty well, right?"

"I try to keep up to date."

"Had a bot in here complaining that her owner was teaching

her to shoot a handgun."

"Wait, what? A bot came in?"

"Been happening more and more, lately. Used to be only owners, but now that the AI's are so autonomous, they run their own schedules. They actually have free time. So, if they're not tasked with something and they think there's a problem, they wander on in here or go to a factory outlet, whichever they determine's the best course."

"You're kidding? I didn't know that."

"Yup. Been ramping up since the version-8 frames hit, 'bout eighteen months ago."

Typically, bot hardware was constructed in a limited number of configurations, designed for light-, medium- or heavy-duty work. A few optional extras, like additional sensors, memory and processors were applied to the base frame, with the exterior appearances applied over top. The average consumer model fell into the light or medium-duty category and only industrial models were equipped with heavy-duty guts. Sault's own journey-bot was a medium-duty frame with most of the servos and wiring exposed. Sault like it because it was a purpose-built device that was not trying to be anything it wasn't. It was a machine that looked like a machine. It had no outer shell because that would serve no purpose.

Interestingly, but perhaps not surprisingly, while sex-bots were produced on medium-duty frames, their exterior had to be heavy duty. A handful of custom manufacturers still existed, vying for more exclusive markets like the super wealthy and the military but by far the most popular frames were products of Unlimited Function LLC., which had come into the game early and continued to dominate. Traditionally, bots had been difficult to manufacture and expensive to purchase. UF's Version-6's had changed all of that and, almost instantly, production of consumer bots became the fastest growing industry on earth. Sault knew that the V-8's were even cheaper and more versatile, and Beta V-9's were rumored to be in limited release. In less than five years, the sight of a robot on the streets of Victoria had gone from startling to mundane.

"Three months back, a lawn mower saunters through that front door, wants to know if it's ok that it's harvesting weed without a license."

"No kid'din?"

"Sure as shoot'in."

"I thought lawn mowers were bot swarms." Swarms were hordes of servile micro robots typically under the direction of their charging pod. Micro robots could maintain a landscape perfectly by working continually, day and night, while going largely unnoticed due to their small size.

"Most are. This one wasn't. It was a commercial unit, specialized for tending and harvesting."

Sault shook his head as if that might make all these new thoughts fall into place. "Ok. So, what's your question?"

"Is a bot legally allowed to handle a firearm?"

"Jesus."

"Yeah. You can't lend a firearm to a person who doesn't possess a license, but bots aren't people and they can't obtain licenses…at least, not yet."

"Maybe this falls under safe storage and access. A bot might not be deemed a safe repository, especially if the gun is loaded. Bullets and weapon are supposed to be stored in separate locations. Did you call Leonard Magnusson, up in legal?"

"That's who I was talking to when you came in. Can't ever get a straight answer from those knot-heads up there. He started going on about software versions and safety ratings. Then, to top it off, he told me that it might be illegal for me to even have that conversation with the bot without consulting the owner."

"Well then, what the hell did they even put you here for?"

"Yup. 'Zactly."

"Was your bot's gun loaded?"

"She didn't say. I turned my back and she bolted while I was talking with Magnusson…probably didn't like the direction of the conversation—maybe saw the conflict in endangering her owner by inciting an investigation. They're like babes in the woods, you know, when they come in here. No matter what's going on, they don't really have any idea if it's wrong or not. All they know is that it conflicts with some legal programming and they are instructed to consult an authority. Soon as consulting with an authority conflicts with protecting the privacy and security of their owner, they bolt or shut up."

"Did you get the ID?"

"You know the golden rule: 'Bot or not, always ID.' Got her palm print on the tablet." Humanoid bot fingerprints were geometrical, by law, and had to have a registration number embedded in the design. "Besides, Ana scans everyone and everything that passes. I can follow up. But, seriously, I have no idea where to go from here."

Sault probed his brain but came up empty. "Sorry, Hennessey. I can't be of much help."

"What about your AI?"

The questions seemed completely non-sequitur and Sault was confused. "What do you mean?"

"Well, they're basically super-intelligent stalkers. They track and analyze pretty much every move you make so they know what you know, plus, of course, the sum total of all recorded human knowledge. I know you're good on the regulations, but I'll bet your AI could tell you something you don't know."

"I don't rely on my AI to do my job."

The older man seemed to realize he'd crossed a line, but in typical Hennessey fashion he met Sault's glare with the serene, lopsided smile. "Never thought you did. But you'd be surprised at what they can tell you. They're a hell of a resource."

Hennessey's manner was disarming, and Sault immediately calmed in spite of himself. "So, ask *your* AI."

"It can only quote the existing regs. It can't make educated guesses in the grey areas. It hasn't learned enough from me to do that because I don't know enough."

"Well, *my* AI gives me messages, newsfeeds and tells me the time."

Hennessey laughed abruptly, then his tone dropped to serious, though his smile never faltered. "Joe, it does a lot more than that. I think a guy like you'd find it useful."

"Maybe," Sault relented. "I'd follow up on that one, a bit—check out the situation and at least make the owner aware that we're aware," he said, referring again to the gun-toting bot. "If I were on active duty, I'd knock on the door for you. Maybe ask Jimmy Fitterer and his partner to make a house call. If he tries to beg off, tell him it's a favor for me."

"Thanks, Joe. Will do. Enjoy your shrink-time." He smiled and tapped the brim of an invisible Stetson.

Three floors below the station, Sault sat in his car, enjoying the insulating silence of the police garage. Vivia did not start the car. She knew that when he drove the Buick, he didn't want any tech between him and the steering wheel. He liked to experience the sheer visceral pleasure of maneuvering 330 horses.

He slid the key into the ignition and felt a mild tingling in his fingertips that made him withdraw and look it over as if he were examining a small sculpture and not his own hand. He clenched a few times, then shook it out and imagined that the tingling had vanished, but couldn't be sure because it had been so subtle a sensation. It was either gone, or… was he also feeling it in his left fingertips?

His hand fell from the keys in the ignition and he slumped back against the upholstery looking at the fingertips of both hands now. The sensation seemed to have passed and he wondered if it had ever been, or if it were psychosomatic.

He thought to turn the key then, but suddenly realized that he had no place to go and nothing to do for the next day and a half, before his meeting with Dr. Robillard. He'd been forced off duty a few times in his career and, each time, he'd ended up sitting in this garage thinking the exact same thing; that retirement definitely wasn't for him. As stubborn and allergic to authority as he might be, he was also very frightened of losing his job. It was a secret that he guarded desperately, camouflaging it with an ornery bravado.

He might have sat there half the day, but a group of guys he knew suddenly emerged from the elevator and were headed to cars parked near his. He might not have anything important to do, but he didn't want it to appear like that was so. He said a silent prayer and turned the key and the Buick's 330 horses eviscerated the silence and all heads turned toward him as he pulled away. In the rear-view, he saw the group break into laughter and wondered if that had anything to do with him, then decided that he didn't care.

William M. Dean

CHAPTER 6

Sault loved his father but wasn't keen on visiting him at Olcott Place, the assisted care facility. For the majority of his life, Victor Sault had been a strong and passionate man, perhaps too full of life to be practical. Now, however, he was over eighty and both his mind and body were feeble, and more often than not, he seemed irritable. Victor always recognized his son but had trouble with most other details of his life and, question-by-question, usually prompted his son to recount the painful milestones, like the untimely death of Sault's mother and sister. As a mercy to both of them, Joseph Sault always left out the most painful thing of all; his father's decent into the alcoholic chaos that had formed most of Sault's own teenage years.

The tiny apartment was in a complex built for assisted living; transitional housing for people who were still able to care for themselves but needed occasional help. None of the apartments had a full kitchen and most didn't even have a hotplate. Victor was afforded a practical amount of privacy. No cameras, but every other kind of sensor tracked his movements. The room would know if he fell or stopped breathing or didn't take his meds or drank alcohol. The toilet monitored his stools.

His pension covered the rent which included meals served in a dingy dining room on the first floor. At 85, Victor Sault was one of the oldest residents. By his age, most people had moved to extended care units that offered more support, but far less autonomy.

Sault dropped a lemon wedge into a mug of warm water and placed it and a small plate of salted soda crackers on the side table next to the easy chair where his father sat. He pulled up a stark metal and plastic chair from the kitchen table, positioned it opposite and sat with a glass of cold water in his hand.

His father nodded toward the steaming cup on the side table. "That'd better be vodka."

Sault couldn't be sure if his father knew that he repeated that same joke every visit. Sault gave the usual obligatory chuckle not knowing if the routine exchange had become a tradition between them or was fresh every time for Victor Sault. "Sorry. No." A mug of vodka had been Victor's go-to beverage for thirty years, after his wife's passing and deployment in North Korea, events that indelibly altered him for the worse.

"Then it's just piss. I already piss four times a night."

"So…what's new?" This, too, had begun as a joke.

"I live in a box." The comedic irony no longer acknowledged. Sault resolved never to say it again. "What's new?" Victor continued, "Cataracts. That's new."

In his younger days, his father laughed at the retirees at the Royal Canadian Legion or the Chief's & Petty Officer's Mess who so predictably started listing their afflictions whenever they got together. He'd called it the organ recital. Now, he seemed to have forgotten the term.

"Really?"

"Gonna swap out my lenses, next week."

"That's a pretty small deal, these days. Kids have it done to get built-in AR."

Victor blew a derisive puff of air between his lips. Shook his head. Changed the subject. "Your Aunt Colleen came by yesterday."

Sault knew that it might actually have been last week, last month or last year. Or it might not have happened at all. "That's nice. Good visit?"

"Her kids are your age now. Makes sense, I guess, but I was surprised. Made me look like an addled old prick. Good visit *for her,* I guess."

"Colleen's a nice woman."

"She only comes because she thinks that's the right thing to do. And to gloat because she's always done the "right" thing. Led the "right life." Kids're engineers or rocket scientists or some such bullshit, husband's a surgeon. House is a mansion on the water, in Cordova Bay. Drives a fuck'in electric car…"

"Everyone drives an electric car, Dad," Sault interjected, hoping to disrupt the tyrade, though, really, he didn't disagree.

"She visits just to see proof that she made all the right moves. Well try losing a wife and daughter…then see how…" His sentence lost direction, petered out and Victor looked down into the cup in his hands and his eyes misted.

This was now his father's life whenever his memory served him.

Sault hated this inevitable moment in every visit. His father had always been loud and gregarious—a hard drinking, tough-love kind of man. The navy had suited him perfectly. Back then, he'd only ever become emotional when he was binging. It had never been a comforting sight. Now the outbursts came randomly and often, making his emotional state seem as fragile as the rest of him.

"Your mother never comes anymore." A merciful lapse.

It wasn't explicitly a question, so Sault let it hang. Answers inevitably led to more questions, which led to painful memories. Sault didn't know if it was better to let his father continue to believe that both women in his life had abandoned him, or to remind him that his daughter had died in a traffic accident and, two years after that, his distraught wife had overdosed. He wasn't sure if staying silent was doing a favor for his father but, definitely, it was a favor to himself.

For the two of them, there was only the now.

"Did you see? The Jay's signed Franco Zambrano."

Whatever else his father forgot, he was always on top of his favorite baseball franchise. His eyes cleared instantly, and he brightened. "That kid can pitch 109 miles per hour. Between him and Cadena they've got a shot, this year." The Toronto Blue Jays hadn't been a real contender in the World Series for thirty years, but they had a passionate following that seemed happily trying to relive 1993, when they'd last won. His father was one of those. Joseph Sault was not a sports fan, but he'd listened to a stream on the way over to glean the highlights.

"One hundred and nine. Jeezus. But there's still the genetics issue." The thought crossed Sault's mind that with sports, there was always a genetics issue. In his father's youth, that issue might have been race. That was no longer true.

"No one's gon'na open that box. Otherwise Megatron Ryerson, Reggie Tam, Tim Hoth, Gandolph Greenhand and half the league are going down."

The most recent artificial enhancement scandal was prenatal doping; doctors toying with the mutable genes of fetuses to produce champions and geniuses. The fact that the practice was illegal in North America was an ineffective deterrent that merely added airfare to the cost. As always, broadcasters were outwardly outraged but inwardly ambivalent because spectacular athletes made for spectacular events, which made for spectacular viewer numbers and spectacular profits.

It all meant nothing to Sault, but he listened to his father's tirade on the state of modern sports versus sports "in his day," and nodded appropriately as Victor built up steam, branching off into golf, then football and, finally, hockey. He was pleased to see his father so animated.

Sault stayed about forty minutes for what ended up being a relatively pleasant visit.

At the end he asked the usual: *Anything you need? Besides vodka. Besides a hooker. OK, a bag of Cheesy Crisps. Want to go somewhere? Besides a bar. Besides a brothel. The Chief's & P.O.'s Mess. Ok. We'll do that and a bag of crisps, next time.*

A new joke. A great way to end.

He shared the elevator down in silence with a "companion." This one was light-framed, white-haired with oval glasses; designed to look like a fit and stylish fifty-something woman.

He'd seen a few since his father had moved to the facility. These were shells run by the facility's AI. As their name implied, they roamed the building providing companionship to most of the lonely residents. They did not visit his father. Using his cane, Victor had broken the arm of the first and only one that had come knocking. Companions in commercial facilities like this were inexpensive and not highly realistic, close up. Even so, Sault felt awkward in the extended silence and was relieved when they reached the lobby, and both went their separate ways.

His watch beeped as the elevator doors closed behind him. It was a message containing the final toxicology report. He took a deep breath and braced himself, then read it. No positives. It was official: he was as clean and healthy as he had been two days prior.

He was almost giddy as he stepped into the sunlight outside the concrete tower that contained his father's shoebox apartment.

When he got home, Sault felt drained. The house seemed empty, but he didn't have the energy to bother checking. Instead, he went directly upstairs and lay down on the bed. He was asleep in minutes.

He awoke hours later completely disoriented by kitchen sounds and smells drifting up from below. He'd had an intense dream and though he couldn't recall its content, his heart was thumping heavily, and emotions were churning as if he'd suffered a great loss. He remained motionless for a minute, trying to recapture the details, but he was clawing at a receding fog. The longer he spent trying to remember it, the further out of reach it flew. He could only vaguely recall that there had been a woman, like Maya, but not her. And somehow, he knew, too, that she was not the main source of his sense of loss.

Sault heard the voices of the three other members of this family and realized that it was a rare occasion when the entire family sat down to a meal. He forced himself off the bed and descended the staircase determined to make this meal an enjoyable one. But his heart continued strumming the somber melody from the dream. He struggled to remain outwardly positive while everything he said rang false in his ears.

In the end, he managed to make Amber giggle a couple of times, but Matthew mumbled one-word answers and rarely looked up from his plate while Maya offered only perfunctory conversation and quizzical glances.

He rallied repeatedly, trying to remain upbeat, but that only seemed to make it all more awkward than usual.

Finally, Maya asked him when he was scheduled for the psych-eval. It seemed a very pointed question and deflated him, entirely. After dinner, he declined coffee and headed to the workshop.

CHAPTER 7

Sault was thankful for the single can of beer he had brought one night and forgotten to open. He retrieved it from among the rags and spare parts on the shelf under the workbench and popped the top, enjoying the sensation of chemically-induced cold seeping into his palm.

Normally, he might while away an empty evening by working on his Red Cube puzzle. He was up to one thousand pieces and enjoyed the inner peace that came with having to concentrate so acutely.

But tonight, singular focus seemed too high a mountain to climb.

He had no idea what was going on inside his head. He knew that the Kowalczyk case was bouncing around in there, and Maya and Harry Potter and bad dreams and Matthew and the Buick and his job and a million other things; the large and the miniscule orbiting each other like the atomic particles of his life.

For a long time, he sat on the stool, sipping beer and staring into the metallic purple finish of the Buick and thinking nothing until, eventually, his brain seized on the single most obvious atom of his life and his thoughts drifted toward the Grand National.

Indirectly, the car had been Maya's idea. A few years

earlier, she had become frustrated by his growing obsession with his work and the toll it was taking on their relationship, and suggested—well, more than suggested—that he find another distraction to fill his off hours; something that he could do at home and maybe share with the kids. According to Maya, a hobby was a good idea. A really good idea. And one that he should not ignore.

Awkward conversations at the Vic PD Christmas party inspired him to choose auto restoration. Maya had stopped accompanying him to the event the year before, and it was only then that he realized how much of a conversational bridge she had provided. Without her at his side to flirt and charm, he was unable to carry his weight in a conversation without eventually returning to shop talk. And at a Christmas party, with spouses and dates present, that was exactly the wrong direction to go. So, mostly, he opted to listen. But in every group, eventually, his silence became conspicuous, and then he would feel embarrassed, like a hovering eavesdropper caught out.

As uncomfortable as this was, figuring out how to make small talk was a kind of puzzle, and puzzles were his thing.

When he was a kid, puzzles had provided escape from a wild and chaotic life with his father, after his mother had passed. He now realized, it was also an act of rebellion, because his father could not understand anyone spending hours each day with his nose in a tablet, and what he did not understand, irritated him. Victor Sault was not a patient man and normally would not put up with anything that irritated him, but neither could he find a point on which to hinge an argument: his son's school grades were high, the tablet kept him off the streets and out of typical teenage trouble, and it kept him occupied, all of which eased the burden of fatherhood. Still, each time he stumbled on his son curled up in front of a screen, Joe saw the blood rise in his father's face. And as much as it gave him some sense of power over his unstable home life, he took pains to stay out of sight, fearing an irrational ban. Especially, when Victor was partying, which was often.

In the last fifteen years, his family and career had replaced most of those sedentary activities. Especially, his career, as Maya often pointed out.

Sault puzzled out that men were typically more like his father than himself and that if he were going to connect, it would be over one of three topics: sports, girls or cars.

The closest thing to a sport that interested him was Red Cube, a never-ending 3D puzzle. It was an older game that he'd played since childhood so he was especially adept and highly ranked but there would not be three people in all of Victoria keen or retro enough to want to talk with him about that.

As for girls; he was male, so he always noticed a pretty face, but as much as he wanted to be James Bond, he was truly a one-woman man. He loved his wife, but his fidelity also revolved around trust issues. He didn't believe that there was a woman out there he could trust enough to not endanger his most precious possession—his family. As with much of his psyche, this was probably rooted in his father's lascivious and reckless behavior during his teenage years. Knowing such things made no difference. He was who he was.

And he was not unaware that reflections of his father within him extended to his flagging relationship with his own son, Matthew. Conversations with the thirteen-year-old had become as awkward as small talk at a Christmas party.

All of which reduced the connection-puzzle to the subject of cars.

In less than three years, Matthew would be old enough to own his own. Then he could go wherever he wanted, whenever he wanted and with complete privacy. That had been the appeal for Joe, when he'd turned sixteen. Maybe if he started working on something cool, Matthew would be drawn in.

Cars had further appeal to Sault as he felt that it was something that he could put his own stamp on.

The modern car was the evolution of almost three hundred years of mechanical and electronic innovation. These days, car-talk centered around electric vehicles and focused on hacking electronic systems and swapping out modules. Even so, respect was always given to the obsolete bangers, and their specs were bandied about like stats on baseball cards, but very few men still went elbows deep, under a hood and fewer still had ever held something like a carburetor in their hand. As with computers, AI's and bots, younger men only had a surface understanding of the mechanism. Sault resolved find an old banger and go deeper, learning to restore rather than replace. For him the goal was less about restoring a vehicle than being able to talk about it.

He didn't know much about the GNX when he saw it for sale on a neighbor's front lawn, but he'd liked its imposing size and design. And during the test drive, he began to understand why his father had loved getting behind the wheel of his ratty old Mustang. It was a good deal, made irresistible when the neighbor threw in his old, knee-high journey-bot.

Thankfully, it didn't really matter that the mechanics hadn't come as naturally as he'd hoped. Now, he could talk the talk and outside of his job, the GNX became one of the few points of connection he could find with other men.

So far, it hadn't served its purpose with Matthew.

And, as for Maya, The Buick had brought him closer to home, but no closer to her.

He awoke from his reminiscing and noted that it was late. Maya would be long asleep. His immediate feeling of relief made him grimace.

He sighed and tossed the empty beer can toward the five-gallon bucket that served as a garbage can. His aim was good, but the bucket was full and the can bounced away.

CHAPTER 8

Sault awoke more exhausted than when he'd gone to bed. He'd slept fitfully but was thankful for the fact that either he hadn't had a nightmare or, if he had, he couldn't remember it. He felt sluggish and generally out of sorts and stayed in bed long enough to avoid contact with everyone, then made his way to the living room couch with a large cup of coffee.

At his command, Vivia harnessed the TV's emitters and flashed up Red Cube over the coffee table, directly in front of him. Red Cube was just that—a featureless red cube. At the start of each level, the cube was reduced to however many random-shaped pieces you thought you could handle. The challenge was to reconstruct it. The things that made it especially difficult were that the size of the cube was never specified, the pieces varied in size, every piece was unique, and they all were red.

He was fourteen, the first time he played, and had started with fifty pieces. Twenty years on from those traumatic teen years, Red Cube was still his most frequent refuge; the surest way to drive out useless, circular thoughts. Somehow, when he was most deeply absorbed, those thoughts would straighten out and fragment and recombine in useful ways, and then he'd have insights. And that was the key to his addiction.

He had worked his way up to this one thousand-piece

challenge which he'd figured would probably take him eight months to solve. He was three months past that with almost a hundred pieces left.

He started slowly by rotating the image in all directions, roaming over the convoluted surface of what he had reconstructed. Then he scoured the scattered pieces yet to go, looking for matching contours. He spent the morning blissfully absorbed and was especially happy with himself at connecting three more pieces but disappointed that none of his thoughts seemed to have been sorted.

Over lunch of a ham and cheese sandwich, Sault asked Vivia to summarize the content of her talks with Matthew and learned that they were typical and mundane. There was some mild bullying from the cooler kids, but nothing physical and nothing specifically directed at his son. There was a girl or two he liked but he couldn't seem to talk to. There was a teacher he didn't like who he felt assigned too much homework. He didn't like Woodshop and dreaded Physical Education, and he struggled with French. Also, he was tired of the fruit and sandwich combination he always got for lunch.

From Vivia, Sault also learned that Matthew's marks were above average, that he was proficient for his age at playing the keyboard, and that in his spare time he most often played an immersive game called BotLand with a dozen online friends. Sault asked what kind of music Matthew played on the keyboard and was given a list of what sounded like a mix of classical and current. Sault didn't often listen to music and recognized none of the titles and only a couple of the classical composers.

Overall, he was relieved that even though he and his son did not communicate very well or often, everything seemed normal.

Later in the day, he bumped into Amber a few times on his way to and from the kitchen and they shared some light exchanges, but he only saw Matthew once when he was working on the car and his son peeked his head into the workshop and said "Hi," as if that had been his intention, though it was obvious that he was looking for Vivia. At that time, Vivia was standing idle and out of the way. He could have released her, but chose not to, considering that maybe if Vivia were not so readily available, Matthew would be forced to talk more to the rest of the family. He could have instructed Vivia never to talk with Matthew, of course, but was afraid that he might then completely lose touch with what was going on in his son's life.

Maya had left for Cavallon House before anyone else had even gotten out of bed. It crossed his mind that she was as dedicated to her mission as he was to his and that it was strange how this pushed them farther apart instead of bringing them closer together. Of course, his job paid well whereas Maya's stipend was meagre, primarily based on what the foundation could afford. Considering her hours, she would have been better off working at Seven-Eleven. So, really, his "mission" subsidized hers.

At six thirty, Sault realized that Maya was later than usual, and nothing had been ordered for dinner.

When they'd first married, Maya had done all the cooking, mostly because Sault's schedule had been so erratic. But these days, Maya didn't cook very often. No one did. While entertainment areas like the pool, patio, recreation room, and theatre had grown in size, kitchens had shrunk, and most families ate meals delivered from 'ghost kitchens,' so called because most didn't cater to walk-in traffic and were invisible from the street. They simply cooked and delivered. His family had a standard order that rotated between six or seven slow-food kitchens dedicated to healthier, homestyle meals but they'd intentionally left two nights of the week unscheduled to accommodate real home cooking—and fast-food cravings.

Sault thought that maybe he should make something, but when he checked the kitchen for ingredients no recipes came to mind and he realized that it had been more than twenty years since he'd last made anything more complex than macaroni and cheese. Instead, he told Vivia to order Chinese take-out, based on all their preferences. Maya came home shortly after that. He asked her about her day, but wasn't surprised to receive a neutral, single-syllable answer. He'd resented it when she'd first taken on the job, and the subject had quickly become taboo between them.

Sault answered the door and found a delivery droid on his front steps. It was roughly humanoid in shape but double the size with thick rubber wheels for feet and a large, cylindrical torso that contained a warming oven. It looked wildly ungainly but, as bots do, it navigated with an alien ease that seemed as elegant as it did unnatural. Until recently, delivery droids had been only autonomous vehicles; cars and trucks that delivered to the curb. Humanoid delivery droids were very new, and their activity had been hastily and haphazardly covered by local bylaws. In Victoria, they were allowed to skate at up to six kilometers per hour on sidewalks but not permitted to enter a human domicile without explicit permission.

The Shanghai Golden Panda AI conversed with Vivia and she asked Sault if he'd like to leave a tip. Sault told her that was "fucking ridiculous" and a microsecond later, a door in the bot's torso slid open inviting him to retrieve the three paper bags that constituted his order.

Sault had Vivia text Maya and the kids and got an auto response acknowledging the message. Still alone in the kitchen, he set the table and loaded up a plate for himself. Both kids sent messages asking if they could stay for dinner at their friends' house. Sault was composing a reply telling them to come home when Vivia informed him that Maya had already replied, giving them permission to stay. Sault sighed in frustration.

Maya came out of her office, scooped her plate from the table and filled it with Chinese and he found himself looking forward to a meal alone with her. But when she returned to the table it was only to grab the pair of chopsticks he'd laid out.

"I've got work." Then she was gone to the study.

Sault went to bed early wanting to be sure that he was fresh and at the top of his game for his meeting tomorrow with Dr. Robillard, the psychiatrist. Though he felt physically under par, his mind was restless and resisted sleep. He remained in bed, staring at cracks in the ceiling and worrying about the fuzzy fingers of low-grade electricity that seemed to radiate outward to his extremities. He only noticed them when he was completely still and quiet. Move a muscle and they seemed to disappear...if they ever existed in the first place.

It was a long while before he drifted off, and he reflected on his day at home and realized that he was satisfied with it. He was three pieces closer to finishing a 1000-level Red Cube, had had only pleasant—if brief—exchanges with Maya and the kids, and found out that his son was grappling with the realities of a relatively normal childhood in a relatively normal fashion.

Life was good. Normal.

If you had to have a psych-eval, now was as good a time as any.

William M. Dean

CHAPTER 9

When the alarm sounded, Sault bolted upright and sat rigid on the edge of the bed, his heart a jackhammer inside his chest. He was panicked but had no idea why.

He half-turned and looked over to her side of the bed. Maya was not there, had probably already left the house. He stared at the blankets she'd tossed aside and started to recall elements of a dream…or a memory…he was unsure. A woman. Like Maya, but not her. Two children; a boy and girl. His children; but not Matthew, not Amber. He couldn't quite picture any of them but knew that in the dream he had abandoned them and felt the echoes of his betrayal still ringing in his heart as if it had been real. He was glad he couldn't recall more.

He took several deep breaths to calm himself and the emotions quickly faded but now he was irritated. This was not how he wanted to start a day that included a trip to a shrink.

Dr. Leonard Robillard was one of a handful of registered psychiatrists specially trained to deal with traumatized emergency services personnel. Of the ones he'd met, Sault felt that Robillard was the sincerest and, therefore, the easiest to fool. His office was located in an upscale complex overlooking Fisherman's Wharf and Victoria's inner harbor.

Sault was downtown and parked by nine. He filled the

excess time by walking the docks between the fishing boats and grabbing a coffee at Original Barb's Fish & Chips. Barb's was a fixture; a testament to simple food, good value, and sound management. Established in 1984, long before it became trendy to have floating businesses at the docks, it was now the oldest restaurant in Victoria. Barb's had weathered three rounds of depressed economy, the steady incursion of competition, and the perpetual tug-of-war between local and federal politics that tended to mess up any enterprise unfortunate enough to straddle a seashore. A small floating village of tourist-oriented shops had sprouted around it, but Barb's remained the centerpiece. As its name implied, this was the original shop. Barb's had franchised a few years back and now had six locations in other Vancouver Island marinas. Sault had heard that two more were planned for Vancouver. But nothing had changed at Fisherman's Wharf and Barb's was still one of his favorite places to get a cup of coffee.

Sault sat at the edge of the dock and blew steam off the surface of his cup while two harbor seals swooped in figure eights in the shallow waters below. The seals were awaiting the morning influx of tourists from the nearby bed and breakfasts, hotels and cruise ships. By noon there would be nearly a dozen seals gathered, splashing, barking and otherwise begging for scraps.

Sault could see that it would soon be a problem.

Humans posed a threat to the seals, hobbling their ability to survive in the wild, so environmentalists were continually petitioning against the practice of feeding the animals. They armed the Ministry of Tourism offices and local businesses with educational material, which rarely got distributed because both local government and businesses endorsed anything that generated a crowd.

Nothing was likely to change until someone got injured.

Though they are not generally aggressive and look like playful sea-puppies, Harbor Seals are wild and essentially unpredictable. Three years earlier, a child had been pulled off the docks and nearly drowned. The seals were strong and fast and could dive to 300 feet and stay under for a half hour. The five-year-old had been extremely lucky. In seconds, he'd been transported thirty feet along the docks then released, popping up between two recreational boats where keen eyed bystanders had jumped in and pulled the boy to safety.

Every few years there was a new incident, then all hell would break loose. Vic PD would be asked to increase patrols and run an awareness campaign. All the new boots would spend a few shifts handing out safety pamphlets in a crowd of people steadfastly convinced by tourist brochures that there could be no harm in just one selfie with a seal. Then, a few months later when the tourists had dwindled, the shops had closed, and the docks were uninvitingly cold and wet, all would be forgotten.

Sault felt his watch vibrate. It was time to head up to his appointment.

Leonard Robillard operated out of a modest office on the bottom floors, below the newest wing of the Shoal Point Condominiums. His neighbors were mostly lawyers and other psychiatrists. The receptionist was new since Sault's last visit. It was humanoid with human facial features and dark hair, cropped short. It wore dress slacks and a dress shirt but no jewelry, no belt and no tie. The nameplate on the desk said: Taylor. Intentionally genderless, Sault surmised.

"Please have a seat, Constable Sault. The doctor will be with you in less than seven minutes." The voice offered no further clues about gender, other than to confirm the intention of neutrality.

Sault had crossed the lobby and was half-crouched to seat himself when Taylor announced that the doctor was now prepared to see him. It reminded him of old "down loading…" progress bars from thirty years ago that would predict your download would take less than a minute, then adjust that estimate to one month, then seven hours, then two years, then suddenly declare "download finished!"

Taylor escorted him to Robillard's office door and ushered him to an ornately upholstered chair, dropping a file on the doctor's desk before leaving. Robillard thanked Taylor then waited for it to close the door before addressing Sault. To Sault, this was as silly as sneaking up on a broken toaster that you are about to throw away. For efficiency's sake, Taylor was no doubt a shell for Robillard's own AI and would have access to every patient's records. Taylor could instantly know more about Sault than Sault did. The only security was in the fact that Taylor did not know that it could do that, unless Dr. Robillard asked it to. Sault wondered if the psychiatrist was aware of his own faulty thinking.

"Well now. Haven't seen you in quite some time, Constable Sault."

Sault lifted himself from the chair and reached across to shake the hand he was offered. Leonard Robillard was short and thin, with mousey brown hair that appeared almost grey in the summer light filtering through the window behind him. He always wore grey slacks and jacket with a colored dress shirt, but no tie. Rather like Taylor, Sault suddenly realized, and briefly wondered what that might say about the man.

"I try to keep my name out of the papers," Sault joked.

Robillard gave a short chuckle that seemed obligatory. "Yes. You've said that before." Sault was a little startled. His last visit had been about five years ago. Either Robillard had a spectacular mind for trivial details or he kept far more notes than Sault had imagined. Leonard Robillard was easy going and personable to the point of seeming naïve, but he'd never come across as particularly insightful. That was Sault's primary reason in preferring him over others. This time, especially, he wanted someone to rubber-stamp his return to duty without asking too many probing questions.

"Why don't we start with the incident—your interaction with the man you called 'Harry Potter.'"

Robillard would be working from the Vic PD's notes and he suddenly wondered if they hadn't yet been able to properly ID the man in the trench coat. That was unusual. Even street people were not often that far off-grid. The psychiatrist prompted Joe again and he put aside his idle musings and described, as best he could the events that had led him here.

And then they got to the part of these kinds of sessions that made Sault cautious. "And how did that make you feel?"

Sault did not disguise his discomfort in remembering that portion of the event and described his disappointment in his own performance and his fear of what the toxicology examination might find. He wasn't afraid to talk about these past feelings. What he wanted to avoid was revealing all the strange things he was currently experiencing.

"And afterward. How've you been feeling since finding out that your blood work was clean?"

"Pretty good," Sault lied. "Anxious to get back to work."

"What about your family?"

"I don't understand."

"Your wife. Wasn't she concerned? Did this not lead to a conversation about retirement, or a desk job?" Sault chided himself for not seeing this coming, and he felt the flush of heat in his cheeks. Having betrayed himself, he judged that a degree of honesty was the best course. "She was concerned, but that conversation didn't happen. We're both pretty busy and…we're not as close right now as we probably should be."

Robillard pursued this for a while, probing his family dynamic. Sault made a show of his reluctance to reveal details, making the doctor work for every scrap. In the end, Sault hoped the psychiatrist would piece together a portrait of a family, troubled, but less blemished than the reality. Sault hoped it would serve as a distraction from his own inner turmoil.

"How about your AI? Did you discuss any of this with Vivia?" Like most of the other older cops who had grown up without AI's, Sault did not own a separate, personal AI. He used Vivia for everything at work as well as home relying on the standard privacy settings and rigorous federal laws which applied to anything recorded beyond the working environment to protect his privacy. It would take a Supreme Court ruling to unlock his personal data. The cost and effort far exceeded its value. Security via budget constraints, Sault thought. The standard settings, though, would give Vic PD, and therefore Dr.

Robillard, access to any discussions with Vivia regarding a work-related incident. So, Leonard Robillard already knew the answer to his own question.

"I don't see any value in having a heart to heart with a machine."

"You might be surprised. AI's have amazing diagnostic tools at their disposal. You should consider Vivia a healing resource."

For the most part, Sault felt in control and believed it had gone very well. But then, when he knew that his hour was almost up, Robillard momentarily went quiet, seemingly deep in thought. "And no bad dreams?"

Had it come earlier, Sault would have been prepared for that question. Instead he almost stuttered, then blurted, "No. No. Not a one." Even in his own ears it sounded completely unnatural.

Robillard nodded and answered with a soft "huh," as if he found it surprising and, possibly, significant. Then he typed something on the invisible keyboard above his watch.

Sault watched him intently, not daring to say anything else.

Robillard looked up from his notes and, in the silence, seemed to be weighing something in his mind.

Sault was rigid. He felt extremely vulnerable and could only think of all the suspects he'd sweated over the years. This was his own tactic turned against him.

Robillard seemed to reach a conclusion. He took a breath then said, "Sorry to leave you hanging there. Since this is a place where we cannot afford to be dishonest, I am forced to confess that I'm not sure I believe you."

Sault took this like a dagger but forced himself to not show it. "What? That I didn't have any bad dreams? I've been a cop for nearly twenty years. Been through much more dangerous situations."

"Hmm." Robillard nodded again. "And those situations were followed by troubling dreams and disturbed sleep patterns."

"Sure, but this was far less traumatic than being shot at or killing a man."

"True," he agreed, then made a show of looking at his watch even though Sault was certain his AI would have silently alerted him that the session was over. "Let's continue with that thread when we meet again, next week."

Sault was shaken, and it probably showed. It was obvious that he had massively misjudged his own level of control as well as Robillard's perceptiveness. He was angry at his own foolishness and, in his anger, reflexively fell back on aggressive tactics. "I'm fine and I need you to make that official, so I can return to duty."

Robillard didn't react to Sault's demand but was observing him with a calm that was unnerving. After a few moments, during which the only sound was Sault's own husky breathing, Robillard typed something into his watch. When he was finished, he smiled and said, "We can discuss that in the next session."

Sault clamped his mouth down on a string of words that would not do him any favors and left the office. On the way out, he managed to fight off the powerful urge to slam the door.

The bottom floor of the Shoal Point Condominiums was home to several retail stores including the Shoal To-Go Café, a tiny coffee shop that served out of a walk-by window. He was fuming and, almost absently, purchased a small cup of coffee and carried it into the beautifully landscaped green space next to the building. He really didn't need more coffee. The sun was high now and holding the steaming cup made his palms sweat. But a cup of coffee on a park bench gave him a reason to sit on a park bench and stare aimlessly into the blossoming foliage. After several minutes, he calmed down and became rational enough to remember his own personal belief that anger was a disguise for fear. He understood his fear well enough. He needed to work. He needed to be busy.

Police work was really the only thing that he did well. He'd never let the fact that he was off shift stop him before, and he saw no reason to let it stop him now.

With renewed purpose, he rose from the bench and his

watch beeped almost simultaneously. He had to turn to shield it from the sun so that he could properly see the notification. Dr. Robillard had prescribed some sort of medication for him and it had already been delivered to his house.

A second notification arrived before he had fully absorbed the first. It was from Ana informing him that until further notice, Vivia's access to Vic PD resources would be limited.

He chucked the full cup of coffee in a garbage can, on his way out of the park.

CHAPTER 10

Joseph Sault had come to hate mornings. His natural alarm clock prodded him at six thirty, and a few minutes later he would struggle to consciousness, exhausted from fumbling through the murky mix of images and emotions that seemed to belong to a complete stranger. He spent the first hour of each day shaking off a loneliness and heartbreak that he did not deserve while obsessively focusing on body parts, wondering where he might feel the frustratingly indistinct tingling today. Even when that internal diagnostic came up empty, he did not feel like himself.

He stared at himself in the bathroom mirror, one of Robillard's little white pills in the palm of his hand, unable to convince himself that he was ok, yet also unable to convince himself to swallow the pill. He recognized the prescription as a mild anti-anxiety medication. For a short time, it had been a popular stabilizing ingredient in a series of street drugs that never really caught on before Jingo swept the nation.

In the end, he dropped the pill into his trouser pocket where it joined three others. Sensors on the bottle would report that the pill had been exhumed, if not consumed. Hopefully, that was all that mattered.

Sault was careful not to slop hot coffee as he turned the

deadbolt on the garage's door. He'd deactivated his watch, so there was no way Vivia could track him, but still he gave the journey-bot shell a suspicious glance. It was parked nearby, compacted into a tight rectangular block, its appendages withdrawn, head hunkered down, the thin blue lines of laser light that simulated its face, absent.

He moved aside several garden tools and dusty boxes and lugged an old mechanic's tool chest away from its regular place, in a far corner. The fire engine red paint was chipped but still bright. Rust had begun to take hold on the lower corners, near the wheels, but it moved smoothly when he pulled. The chest was spare storage that he'd retired after building the workbench and the wall of pegboard that surrounded it, both of which gave him convenient access to almost everything he usually needed. He couldn't recall the last time he'd opened a red drawer. And, today was not going to be the day. What he was looking for was not in the chest, but under it.

A faded and chipped plastic grill filled a large floor drain. Sault tugged at it until it popped out. Whoever had originally constructed the garage had not connected it to the perimeter drains. That was definitely a code violation, but somehow it had been overlooked. One day, shortly after he'd purchased, Sault had noticed this, and it made him curious enough to trowel around in the sand beneath the concrete floor. Buried a few inches deep, he'd come across a box. It was made of tin, and too large to fit up through the drain hole, so it must have been placed there prior to the pouring of the cement slab. Sault was disappointed to open it and find only a few grains of sand and some old rubber bands. He guessed that it had been used as a makeshift safe by the original occupants, and probably linked to illegal drug activity, but knew there had been no arrests as he'd checked the address in the Vic PD database before purchasing. He had replanted it and now used it as his own safe, but not for cash.

Among the items in the box was an unregistered gun and box of bullets—both trophies from a big bust—a consumer taser, an old Vic PD-issue watch and a fully authorized holo-desk. There was also a small piece of paper with a stick figure drawing and a note in child-scrawl that said: "Daddy! Thank yu for kepping us sayf. Matt. Yor sun." Sault took a moment to read it and smiled at the memory, then refolded it and put it back.

He extracted the watch and the holo-desk and took them to the workbench, on which he had pushed parts and tools to the sides to clear a space.

The two devices had always been synced and when he activated the holo-desk the virtual desktop emerged and hovered, exactly as he'd last left it. At the edges of the desk were the typical tool icons like pens, a magnifying glass, trashcan, in and out baskets, VidCom, and browser.

Modern devices were always connected, so he spared a second to double-check that the everything was offline. He needn't have worried. Offline was the default on all early rudimentary AI devices like these. He had no reason to suspect that the settings had changed, but this unit did not officially exist, and he wanted to keep it that way. He had no idea what might happen to him if he were caught with these devices in his possession, along with their detailed logs of all the restricted files he'd downloaded over the years from Vic PD, but it would not be good.

A single file folder lay, unopened, on the simulated wood grain desktop hovering a few inches above his workbench. The murder book. On the cover was "J. S. Kowalczyk, Vic PD (C3)" followed by a long file number. He knew it contained everything from the case that had resulted in Constable Fourth Class, Jared Kowalczyk's death. Sault reached down, lifted it— virtually—and gave it a shake. A clutter of icons fell out and scattered about, hovering: videos, notes, reports, legal documents, and bagged evidence, all miniature 3D representations of what they contained.

Sault remembered Singh's legitimate surprise that he had access to active murder books. He was young and hadn't yet learned the questions that are best left unasked. Sault had not stolen the items, but neither had he turned them in after they'd come into his possession. About eight years earlier, he'd been the one standing closest when the then Chief of Detectives, Belinda Remy Smith's water had broken. She was not due for another month, so it was unexpected. Almost immediately, she'd been seized by intense contractions. In the melee, she had handed him her briefcase—her mobile office—including her watch, which pregnancy had made uncomfortable for her to wear. Sault secured it all in his locker, for safe keeping until she returned.

But she never returned.

Sault later learned that the pregnancy had been a troubled one and there were complications during the birth. Belinda lost the baby, then succumbed to internal hemorrhaging before doctors could act.

Smith had been very popular, and Sault could still recall the numbing shock that echoed through the station for months afterward. Four members took stress leave, while he and the rest of the force continued with the business of law enforcement, but in a distracted, zombie-like state that lasted for weeks. Members expected criminals to holler insults, throw punches, and occasionally fire a weapon, but now, it seemed, Life itself had decided to take a pot shot. It felt as if things at the station would never be the same. But, eventually, normalcy returned. Thinking about that now, it almost seemed a final insult to her memory.

When her replacement, had been assigned, Sault had handed over only her briefcase with all the paperwork. He had immediately understood how he might use Smith's apparatus in his work, and so, had intentionally withheld the electronics. As he'd hoped, somehow—possibly because she had died off duty—the devices slipped through the cracks and were never recalled. He left them in his locker for six months before taking them home to find that all of the units still functioned, and that all of them could be made untraceable by adjusting their settings. At that time, watches and AI's were just being phased in. Early law enforcement specific units were modified from consumer models and were later determined to harbor large security issues, like anonymity settings.

One final stroke of luck that almost made Sault believe in Fate was the assignment of Barry Randall Smith to Belinda's post. In the system, his identifier was "BRSmith-1817c46." Belinda's had been "BRSmith-1823f06." On log-in reports designed for humans, these were always abbreviated to "BRSmith." Only the computers knew the difference, and none of them ever thought to say anything, unless specifically asked. Apparently, to Ana, a dead officer accessing the system was not a noteworthy discrepancy.

Sault knew that Jared Kowalczyk's file held few surprises, but still, he started again, from square one.

Part of the Kowalczyk murder book was the detailed file on Lindsay Susan George, the traffic accident victim. The two deaths had been deemed as only peripherally related but, technically, Lindsay Susan George was now a manslaughter suspect in the Kowalczyk case.

He flipped to the back of the murder book and reread the summary and conclusions section. This was a brief recap that was signed off by everyone involved and the officers and administrators all the way to the Chief's office. Sault always liked to start with this because he could usually read between the lines and see all the assumptions and biases and that helped guide him in questioning the evidence.

In the old days, he would have started by reading through the official chronology; a detailed listing of events and evidence associated with the crime and investigation. But these days, every clue, every report, every comment and every action was date- and time-stamped by Ana and could be put in sequential order with a single command. Unfortunately, the detail was overwhelming, and an overall chronology was now the very last avenue he would consider exploring. Back in the day, wading through had been tedious—they were often up to 300 pages long—but they paled in comparison to the reams of information you might find in a modern chronology, generated by an AI.

According to the summary, this was a case of cross-contamination from the scene of a traffic accident attended earlier that evening. A footnote referenced a Traffic Division case file and its forensic report that linked an opioid substance found in evidence recovered at the accident scene with that found in Jared Kowalcyzk's blood. Officer Constable Fourth Class, Jared Kowalczyk had improperly handled evidence at the scene from which he received a fatal dose of opioid through contact. A note was made regarding the general duties and responsibilities of a training officer—words probably pulled straight from some training manual—followed by a paragraph describing in general terms the side-investigation into her actions which ultimately absolved Constable Second Class, Theresa Schneider of any blame. It was dull and uninformative, but mercifully short; a string of standard words and phrases which sounded objective and conclusive, but which had more to do with neatly fitting the crime into the filing system than it did detailing the incident. Sault's eyes skipped over the familiar and meaningless clichés and he was done in only a few minutes.

Next, he began methodically pulling each picture from the photo folder, enlarging it and fixing it in the air above the desk, creating a wall of photos. He'd seen these all before and didn't believe there was anything further to be garnered, but this was the ritual—his way of getting his head back into the proper space.

The images hovering before him were not generated by the same type of gear available to the average consumer. Crime scene photos were taken by technicians using 360-degree, multi-spectral cameras with exceptionally-high-resolution lenses. The final product was officially known as an Extra-Wide Spectrum Rendering, but everyone just called them Xrays, adopting a medical term that doctors had recently abandoned because medical imaging had moved on. The administration hated it, which only broadened the appeal. Now, administrator or not, using any other term only generated confusion.

Once it was set up, the Xray apparatus generated a new image about every five minutes, so it also served as a time-lapse video of the scene. Using holo-desk controls, you could slide and pivot about in every direction, select and combine the electromagnet spectrum from microwaves to x-rays and zoom in close enough to see the individual pores on a body.

If it existed at the scene, it could be seen in these images.

Sault spent a few minutes flipping through the spectrum and adding electronic filters for body fluids but found nothing unusual—and fingerprints, which were plentiful and belonged only to the victim and his family.

Kowalczyk had been found on his bed, curled in a fetal position with the covers clutched in his hands and pulled up to his neck. His face was turned to the side and his expression was serene. He wore death like a pair of fuzzy slippers and looked to be sleeping comfortably. He remained in this position in about forty Xrays. Eventually, the blankets were pulled back to reveal that he was naked except for a pair of khaki boxer shorts, and that his bladder and bowels had evacuated. Sault's nose twitched reflexively, the pictures tricking his memory into evoking the visceral stench of feces and rotting meat that he and every other cop recognized and dreaded. Experience had taught him to quickly push that memory away. If he didn't, it could make him retch, even here, even now.

The scene was so simple and the circumstances so self-evident that Sault was disappointed but not surprised to see that no ancillary photos had been ordered. Ancillary photos were regular camera snaps taken beyond the murder scene. Sometimes an entire house might be photographed to substantiate evidence found in only one room; or an entire neighborhood, when a body was discovered in a park. Sault felt that he could get a better feel of the human dynamic from poking around, much in the way a nosey neighbor might snoop through a medicine cupboard. He was an uninvited fact-checker and not a detective, so he wasn't afforded the opportunity, but he would have liked to wander the extremity of the crime scene, examining decor and photos; determining where all the family members and guests spent their time, how they expressed themselves; getting a sense of how they interacted. He might even have taken a quick peek at what they kept in their cupboards. Building a clear picture of the victim and their normal lives was always the best start for him, but it was not going to happen, in this case.

Also in the murder book were a couple of newsfeed reports, but he ignored them; slid them to the far right hand corner of the virtual desktop. He'd already skipped through them all, and in his entire life had never heard of a local newscast providing a clue. In his experience, reporters were clueless, unless handed clues. Newsfeeds reported the news, they did not make it. This was the kind of information that needlessly bloated a case file. Sault considered them the last resort for defense lawyers saddled with clients who were too obviously guilty, with wafer-thin alibis and a mountain of evidence stacked against them. Only the very desperate would wade through such trivia in search of minor discrepancies that might stoke the embers of doubt.

He organized the first-on-scene officers', assigned officers', and Medical Examiners reports into a column, splayed partially open, like playing cards, near the left edge of the desktop, but left them flat. The same with Jared's resume and Vic PD dossier, the transcripts from the AI's of the witnesses and the victim, the feeds from other household appliances like security cameras, stove, bathroom mirror and the entertainment system, and the accompanying diagnostics which verified that none had been tampered with. The home's utility log was checked against all of the other electronic trails to make sure that the turning on and off of light switches and the opening and closing of doors was in agreement with all of the other electronic logs, as well as the witness statements. There had been nothing but the ordinary in any of these.

He swept the statements from every member of the Kowalczyk household—the wife and two kids, five and seven years old—in to the pile, as well. Fortunately for them, the family hadn't seen much. Their father had returned home from work as usual but felt ill and had gone to bed without supper. His wife found him unresponsive, five hours later, when she came to bed.

Because the death was drug-related, there was a separate, internal investigation led by Detectives Mer and Sussex that determined that Kowalczyk had no ties to the drug world. It was not thorough; merely a formality. The conclusion was neat and tidy. The investigators admitted to a couple of loose ends. As the traffic accident victim had not been definitively identified, it was impossible to determine if there was any link between her and Jared Kowalczyk. As well, his uniform had already been processed by their laundry and no traces of the chemical could be confirmed. That report went to the bottom of Sault's pile.

There were complete scans of the victim's clothing, which included only a wedding ring and boxer shorts. Even though this had seemed obviously useless, he had already spent a half hour on them and only discovered the sadly ironic message, *"'Til Death Do Us Part, Becca"* inscribed on the inside of the gold band. He shoved this file back into the murder book.

The Forensic Lab report was the only file of real interest. The ME determined the cause of death to be organ failure due to chemical toxicity and the lab followed up on that, confirming the identity of the probable causative agent as a class of street drugs, locally known as Jingo. Generic Jingo was an opioid derivative that could not be created chemically. It had to be 3D printed, one molecule at a time.

Like child pornography, possessing or distributing the molecular print file was highly illegal, and yet, like child porn, was readily available online to those who knew where to look. The drug responsible for Jared Kowalczyk's death was a form of Jingo, but dealers were always tampering with the downloads, experimenting on their clientele in hopes of creating the next viral high. In this case, the modifications made in the drug design had altered its effect from pleasure to poison. An identical substance had been found at the scene of the traffic accident that Jared Kowalczyk had attended only hours before, so that was established as the source, but the manufacturer was untraceable.

Attached was a generic report on 3D printer makes and

models capable of producing such drugs—expensive, but not uncommon commercial equipment. He skipped through it because the information was familiar and also, almost completely useless. This same file was passed from precinct to precinct, case to case, unchanged except for the addition of new models. These printers were so prevalent, capable, and so easily hacked that they usually left no useful identifiers. As with bots and AI's, the technology had left regulators so far behind that they couldn't even see the vapor trail. When it came to technology, legal texts had become a patchwork of hasty and inadequate laws, obsolete even before they could be tested.

The remainder of the ME's report was a brief analysis of the drug potency which Sault recognized had been lifted, wholesale, from the report made from evidence from the related traffic accident. He skipped it here.

To Sault's experienced eyes, the ME's report was obviously lacking. It didn't, for instance, detail findings from the inner lining of Kowalczyk's lungs which would have dowsed any suspicion that he might have inhaled the drug. The report also lacked a relative potency chart and Sault knew that the delivery method affected efficacy. Without that, there was no proof that the drug could kill merely through contact.

It seemed likely that Kowalczyk might have been more intimately involved than reported and that fellow officers were covering for him to protect the family's death benefits. It was not unheard of, and Sault had no issue with this, so long as it didn't let living criminals go free. The question was whether Kowalczyk had been the traffic accident victim's dealer or had stolen evidence from the traffic accident and used it himself.

His stomach grumbled and he grabbed the Vic PD coffee mug and brought it to his lips, realized that it was empty then further realized that this was about the fourth time he'd repeated that action, this morning. His eyes flickered to the clock on the floating desktop and saw that it was past noon; he'd been staring at images for more than three hours. He was hungry and thirsty.

CHAPTER 11

"What are you doing home?" It was Thursday and Sault was surprised to see Amber at the dining room table; the remnants of a sandwich scattered over a square of plastic wrap she'd pushed to one side. She didn't like bread crust, he noted. She had a series of what Sault thought might be playing cards set out before her in an untidy grid. They were holo-projections from her watch, of course, and she was keenly examining them, one by one.

"I've got Kendo, later. The bus passes right by, so I came home for lunch."

Sault thought a sandwich sounded good. It usually did. He was a creature of habit and had long ago stopped trying to be anything else. He supposed it made Vivia's job easier. There was little doubt what items she needed to add to the household's weekly market delivery. He went to the fridge and started gathering the ingredients together; mayo, lettuce, dill pickles, ham, Swiss cheese. Habit.

"What'cha up to?"

Amber looked up with the same dazed expression that he might have worn had someone pulled him from an intense examination of crime scene photos. "Huh? Oh. I'm trying to pick a lifestyle."

"I'm sorry, what?"

"If you choose a lifestyle, early on, it makes it easier for your AI to keep you on track."

Sault knew that many people relied on their AI's to schedule their exercise, order their food and clothing. It helped them maintain the level of fitness and the look they wanted. In the extreme, some people allowed their AI's to arrange their social lives and even make career decisions; all aimed at achieving a desired lifestyle. Couples were dating and marrying or breaking up and divorcing based on advice from their AI's. In Sault's mind, it boiled down to a babysitting and breeding program for idiots.

He was curious about the process and went to look over her shoulder. She had about twenty cards laid out. Each was titled, and he read a few: Environment, Fashion, Body Mod, Causes, Fitness, Media, Friends, Celebrities, Diet, Hobbies, Employment, Fantasy. Beneath the titles was scrollable text which he could see was a detailed questionnaire.

Amber explained, "These are different aspects of lifestyle. You choose the elements you are interested in and use the sliders to adjust the percentage of influence in your life. Once you've got them all set, the app can tailor your decisions to align with that."

"I didn't realize our lives could be reduced to just twenty things?" he said, sarcastically.

Amber sighed, probably in the exact same way caveman kids had when they showed their parents fire for the first time and were warned that it seemed dangerous. "These are just the ones I've got left to complete. There are about seventy categories to choose from."

Sault knew that such apps generated income from suggesting specific products to their users.

"So, you're letting an app design your life?"

She caught his cynicism. "Dad, I know it's just advertising, but if you have an AI, it can read this information and tailor the buying to *your* best interests."

"So, why don't you use Vivia or Gemma?"

"Because, neither of those are my personal AI. Gemma is

focused on Mom and would just make decisions as if she were my mother. We wouldn't be designing my life…it would be the life my mother wants me to have."

Sault's eyes lit upon a card labeled Sexuality and he suddenly decided that he really needed that ham and cheese sandwich, and possibly a beer.

He was just putting the sandwich on a plate when Amber's watch pinged, and she hurriedly packed up, stopped to give him a quick kiss and left for the next appointment on her educational agenda.

He poured himself a beer and headed back to the garage.

The manslaughter portion of Lindsay George's case was handled by a different investigative team: Woods and Sebastian; both good guys. They could be counted on to dot all the i's and would not leave any gaping investigative holes.

Six sub files shook loose from that case file, and he lined them up in a third column.

Ostensibly, it was just a traffic incident, but this scene, victim and the circumstances were much more curious than in Jared Kowalczyk's case.

After rereading both the Traffic Division and Manslaughter summaries, he pulled the photo folder apart and started making a virtual wall for Lindsay Susan George, adjacent to the one for Jared Kowalczyk.

He began with the overview shots of the scene. The vehicle's automated mayday was received at Vic PD at 9:43pm. At 9:51, first responders, officers Terri Schneider and Jared Kowalczyk, arrived. The photo time stamps began, at 10:32 pm and the first photos were amateur shots taken with watch-cameras. It was a rural road with no street lights so the images were either lit by a brilliant white flash or infra-red. The flash shots were brilliant where the light fell and pitch black where it could not reach. A lot of detail was lost in the shadows. The infra-red shots were grainy but reached further into the shadows. These pictures established the scene upon arrival, but Sault considered them otherwise useless.

Later, more crews and equipment arrived on scene and wide-spectrum emitters were set up and the Render cameras were brought in, which exposed the tiniest motes.

Sault went through the Renders. The car lay upside down, half submerged in a lazy flow of irrigation water, the passenger-side corner of its front end wrapped around the concrete abutment of the culvert. It was barely more than a scooter on four wheels, a tiny two-seater with no trunk, just a small storage area tucked behind the front seats where pieces from the front grill and electric engine now lay. The doors had crumpled and blown outward and it was easy to see Lindsay George's corpse, face down against the steering wheel on the wrinkled white skin of the deflated air bag. She was wearing a short-sleeved blouse and her mangled left arm hung at her side like a string of bloody sausage in a butcher shop. The pinky finger was missing below the first knuckle.

Sault moved the timeline slider along and saw Firemen spraying fire-suppressing foam over areas of the fuel cell and dissecting the auto to extract the body, then investigators exploring the interior of the car.

The file included every shot that had been snapped, bloated by useless ones that were blurred by some member who had stepped too close to an emitter. Jared, in particular, may have been overly eager to lend a hand and had inadvertently blocked or gotten pieces of himself in the way of a large number of shots. Terri Schneider had apparently hung back, managing to keep herself completely out of the way, only appearing in the background of a few of the later shots. He chalked that up to her greater experience. No sense rushing in to help when the crime scene was static, and the victim was dead.

Using the clearer shots, Sault was able to slide through the car's interior and noted that both the glove compartment and a silky black clutch with a golden clasp had blown open and their contents were strewn about the interior and the ditch, like blood-spattered confetti. Still, the scene was relatively neat because the car had been a rental, devoid of the extraneous clutter that usually accumulates in a private vehicle.

He recalled the evidence list and was able to visually confirm all of the items listed including a plastic sandwich bag containing forty joints on the floor of the car. The Forensic Lab had easily identified the cannabis DNA. Unsurprisingly, it was a local strain. In Canada, "Pot" was legal, and Victoria's mild climate made it a popular local crop. Marijuana could be grown in any greenhouse, but most people preferred the convenience of commercial products, produced hydroponically. This strain, Cool Jade, was the mild, over the counter product of a licensed producer. It was available without a prescription in dispensaries, drug and liquor stores, pubs and Seven-Eleven. Cool Jade was basically untraceable, but also harmless. But this sample had been heavily cut with pure Jingo.

Jingo was inherently dangerous, but this batch, in particular, was ten times more potent than heroin. Injected or inhaled, a few grains would incapacitate a grown man. Sault had taken a course on street drugs and remembered the lecturer paraphrasing the sixteenth century Swiss physician, Paracelsus: "Nothing is without poison. It is the dose, alone, which makes a thing a poison." When it came to this batch of Jingo, there was no safe dose.

On the streets of North America, doing Jingo was the equivalent of eating Fugu, in Japan. Surviving may have been life-affirming, but you had to have a death wish to place the order. Unlike puffer fish, however, there was no right way to prepare Jingo. You either got higher than you ever had, or you died. It was Russian Roulette, without the favorable odds. Users were often referred to as casket-dodgers, until they were referred to as dead.

Lindsay George was destined to be a victim that day. If the car had not crashed, she would have been doomed the moment she took her first toke.

Traces of raw Jingo had been found on the interior surface of the baggie, though he couldn't see any, even at full magnification. This was the smoking gun in the Kowalczyk case. All the pictures showed the bag sealed, so Sault immediately wondered how Jared's hands had got inside the bag and he found nothing in the report to shed light on this, though in Woods' report there was a line stating their assumption that there may have been traces on Lindsay George that got transferred to Jared Kowalczyk. It was very speculative as no other traces of the substance were ever found.

Eventually, Sault pulled back to take in the entire scene extending from the point of impact out to where the emergency vehicles were parked. There was a shift change at midnight and he knew that after about 11:00, Terri and Jared would have been anxious to hand off the case and head back to the detachment to turn in the unit and touch base with their commanding officer. And, in fact, he couldn't find their car in any picture taken after 11:10 pm.

Among the emergency vehicles, he noted one small, unmarked pod-car, maybe a Sony. It was parked awkwardly, side-on. It was at the extreme periphery of the Render and the computer was unable to give him an angle so that he could read the plates, but he saw no reason to dwell on it. The site was remote, and the incident was seemingly unremarkable, so it probably belonged to a curious passerby.

Later that night, documented in photos taken after midnight, some newsfeeder vehicles arrived to shoot some seemingly unremarkable video that would suddenly become remarkable, three days later, when Chief Roth mentioned the car crash in the press conference covering Jared Kowalczyk's death.

He next focused on the body and slid through scenes rendered in situ, as well as after the body was on a gurney.

Unlike Jared, Death had ravaged her. Her face was smashed and swollen beyond recognition. Her eyes reduced to blackened slits. Her forehead had a visible fissure and bone was caved in all the way down to her chin. An alarming amount of blood had oozed and coagulated covering most of her upper body. Her jaw was unhinged, her mouth gaping and contorted in an exaggerated, perpetual scream; the tendons in her neck stretched and taut, rising from her collar bone like the sprawling, twining roots of a Banyan tree. Her right hand was crumpled and gnarled, knuckles swollen, the tendons tight as guy-wire. Her arms and legs were covered in abrasions and contusions. One knee had been ripped from its socket and the lower half of that leg lay slightly askew.

It was impossible to determine if she had been pretty.

It didn't help that she had been pulled from a flowing ditch. Her hair was muddy and matted, clothes soiled and torn.

Sault came across the ME's facial reconstruction and it made him sigh. She had been pretty.

He didn't dwell.

The ME's report confirmed the obvious, that she was an indigenous female, and the less obvious, that she was approximately 35 years old. A retinal scan revealed no addresses, current or otherwise, no dental record (though it was noted that her teeth had been professionally maintained), no evidence of prescription eyewear, no credit history, no driver's license, no passport, and no arrest record. There was one public record of her retinal pattern associated with the name Linda George. Retinal scans were commonly used to ensure that people did not cheat and take multiple free samples, so this could have been for something as mundane as a promotional coffee or signing in at a food bank. The report did not elaborate, and Sault knew this was nothing worth pursuing.

The victim had been tentatively identified by a tattoo on her upper right arm, which read: "I am Lindsay Susan George. Bent, like a reed, by fierce winds. I remain strong. I am survived." Sault recognized the passage, or at least the style, and the report confirmed that it was the work of a New York street artist and poet named James Daniel Pope. Pope was a pop-culture legend. For years he'd lived on the streets, homeless and anonymous, tagging buildings and boxcars with his ragged sketches and short poems. His anti-establishment messages and images struck a vein of American zeitgeist and overnight, what had once been graffiti became art. Pope went from criminal to hero, rags to riches; from an individual to an industry. His messages were carved out of buildings and displayed in museums, printed on t-shirts and mugs, posted and reposted on social media, published in books, and inked into skin.

The pinnacle of his popularity had been about ten years ago and, for people who identified with Pope's messages, getting a Pope-Art tattoo had been trendy. When it came to light that Pope was spending his newfound wealth on drugs and under aged prostitutes, his popularity faltered. But, ultimately, it was his membership in the upscale New York Yacht Club that fans could not reconcile with the anti-establishment messages that drove his art sales. His popularity ended abruptly. It was not long afterward that Pope returned to the streets. His first arrest for disorderly conduct became his artistic epitaph. The brevity of Pope's popularity helped confirm the victim's probable age.

Her name, if not her identity, was further corroborated by an otherwise non-descript silver bracelet found on her right wrist and which bore the inscription: LSG – In Tech We Trust; another pop-culture meme, from roughly the same era. Sault found it an incongruous epithet.

No watch was found, and her wrists bore no indication that she had ever possessed one. There was another, larger tattoo on her neck—a cascade of stylized roses and leaves which started under her left ear and draped across her shoulder. It might have been distinguishing except that it was a temporary tattoo. It would take a few weeks to fade from the body. These kinds of tattoos were often given away at festivals and concerts, so Woods and Sebastian had made calls to all the local artists and the organizers of special events, but no one recognized Lindsay George and the design turned out to be very popular and untraceable. Her ears were pierced, and she had been wearing large, silver hoop earrings. One had been ripped away in the collision, the other crushed out of round. A blonde wig was found at the scene and matching fibers and fasteners in her hair led the coroner to speculate that she had been wearing it, that evening. All her tiny moles, skin tags and birthmarks were recorded, but none were particularly distinguishing. It was an unusual lack of information, even for a street person, but not improbably so—especially for an indigenous Canadian. Native bands took particular pains to maintain the privacy of their members and were rarely anxious to cooperate with Vic PD.

No officers, including Sault, recognized her, but it was implicit throughout their report that Woods and Sebastian had pegged her as a drug-addicted hooker with no connections to the rest of the world, and, sadly, the odds were that they were right. In her current condition, she certainly looked the part.

What finally clinched it for the investigative team was a check with all the local social services. There were no hits at Social Assisted Housing, Family Counseling or in the welfare system, but her name was recognized at Cavallon House, though that was the extent of her record there. Sault knew from Maya that for reasons of security and anonymity, permanent files were not kept on the women who stayed there. Many came and went without generating any written record. It had been a lucky break for the detectives that Lindsay George had been remembered by a staff member named Katherine Ash. Sault checked and noted that neither Maya nor Sidney Cavallon had been questioned. Perhaps he would get a chance to ask her about it.

Sault found himself focused on Lindsay George's body, half submerged in the drainage ditch. He didn't know much about women's clothing, but something seemed off. Though it was difficult to imagine the bloodied and shredded outfit clean and pressed, he could see that it was a yellow, floral patterned, knee-length flounced skirt, tied at the waist with a thin black belt. Her blouse was a satiny material, also yellow, with buttons up the middle and a spread collar, much like a man's dress shirt, but more rounded than square. There was some kind of ruffle along the button line, but it had been torn, almost completely off and now draped like a scarf across one shoulder. Somehow, it looked like it might be stylish—more appropriate in an office than on the streets. The average street worker didn't follow popular clothing trends.

He pulled open the ME's close-up scans. The technician had done a good job and it was easy for Sault to see through the grime and reposition the materials. He zoomed in and read all the clothing tags, including her undergarments, noting the materials, sizes and brand names that he was not surprised he didn't recognize. He cropped, copied and enlarged the tags and added them to Lindsay George's photo wall, and sent copies to the cloud. Later, he would download them to Vivia and do some fashion research.

Her measurements surprised him a little. She was neither overweight nor scrawny. If, like most pros, she was a regular drug user, she hadn't yet succumbed to any of the long-term effects. If she was poor, she ate healthily.

In Sault's mind, this was another discrepancy and he could feel it prying at the seams of something larger, but not necessarily huge.

She was found in a drainage ditch near Mount Douglas Park. There were not a lot of open drainage ditches in Victoria, but the area around Mount Doug—which was more of a hill than a mountain—was an incongruous patch of small, family-owned farms trapped inside the city. In that area, open ditches were still used for irrigation. The question was: Why was she there?

Sault flipped back to the officers' notes. Sebastian had looked into this but come up empty. The car was one of hundreds of cheap charged-by-mile autonomous rentals. They were almost all owned by huge companies, mostly based in South Asia. Sebastian had made an application to obtain the records, but in his notes, he commented that the process would probably take months and yield little. Sault agreed. The personal details of the renter were protected by international law unless the user waived their right to privacy. No one ever did.

This led to the question of her personal effects. Where was her base? She was too well dressed to be living in a cardboard box, under a bridge.

He went through the itemized list of materials found at the scene. The list was long and included everything found within ten meters of the car. Sault scanned this quickly looking for anything out of the ordinary. For the most part, there were no surprises—candy wrappers, Styrofoam packaging, pop cans, a rusty metal spoon, a baseball cap, a sock, a plastic toy, a very old glass bottle, a wooden shovel handle—all likely garbage which had been previously tossed into the ditch. The only items he thought related to the accident were the blonde wig and Lindsay George's left pinky finger and the missing hoop of the earring. Far more was found inside the vehicle. The on-scene crew had been thorough, and the list of things Sault felt were irrelevant was long and included promotional material from the rental company, some loose change and a withered orange peel as well as scattered pieces of the engine and body. His eye lingered on one item: a pen from the Empress Hotel and he slipped through the photos until he found a closeup. The shell of the pen was shattered, probably from the impact, and the writing was worn and faded, so it was likely old, but he searched the folder's database to make sure that someone had belayed their assumptions long enough to check the register and was not disappointed to find the Woods had done this and come up empty. He continued down the list and noted the sandwich bag of joints and another bag, similar, but empty. The rest of her possessions recovered from the scene included the black clutch—the tag of which said only "Product of Taiwan" and looked to be cheap—some gum, lipstick, a compact, eyeliner, a common metal key for an older-style manual door lock, a tampon, hair pins and five hundred dollars in cash held together by an elastic. The key was interesting. It implied that she wasn't staying in a hotel or motel because those buildings had to adhere to modern building codes, and manual locks were no longer allowed on public buildings. But, if she was a hooker, where was the lube? Where were the condoms?

Something clicked for him there. He slid the ME's report out from its column, opened it and skimmed it for information that was not there. No needle marks, no irritation of mucous membranes, no open sores, no rotting gums, no decayed teeth, no evidence of recent sexual activity. Not a cigarette smoker. All plausible, but also against type.

It was all so minimal and, as well, Sault reminded himself, there was still a slim possibility that Lindsay Susan George was not Lindsay Susan George.

She was much more of a mystery than she should be, and he wondered if she might have been hiding from someone. If so, her death may have been the result of a reckless moment, but it might not have been a traffic accident.

CHAPTER 12

Sault entered the Vic PD parkade with a long list of things he wanted to accomplish that day.

First, he wanted to get his hands on the results of his medical exam and the toxicology report. He couldn't recall last night's dreams, but he'd woken as unsettled as the day before with a general feeling that something inside him had changed, something was not right. Even though he was not officially active, he didn't think that getting access to his own personnel file would be difficult. Worst case, he'd ask Inspector Cece Teng. He was sure she'd pull it for him.

Either way, he intended to check in with Teng, ostensibly to get a sense of what was coming and to follow up on Harry Potter, though it was a pretty safe bet that by now he'd have been assessed by Mental Health who would probably determine him not responsible for his behavior but not sick enough for treatment, which would automatically kick him back into the hands of the legal system. But putting an otherwise docile street person with one delusional episode behind bars was no solution, and everyone knew it. The legal system would be eager to release him, but the serious nature of the charges would make that difficult. There was a bureaucratic grey area as wide as a sea filled with guys like Harry Potter whose offenses were serious but not serious enough and whose antisocial behavior neither system had any hope of curing or curbing. Whatever the outcome, though, they should have properly ID'd him by now, and Sault thought it might be good to know his real name in advance of their next encounter.

But his real reason for hanging out on the second floor was that he had Belinda Smith's watch, inactive, hidden away in a pocket of his blue jeans, and was hoping to find a moment to download the latest version of the Lindsay George murder book. Murder books could only be transmitted with an order by Chief Roth but could be downloaded at any time by command staff at secure terminals within The Department.

After that, he had wanted to make some calls from an official line and arrange to visit two or three of the local tribe band offices, talk face-to-face and show Lindsay George's picture. It was a very long shot, but maybe he'd be allowed to knock on some of the band members' doors and he might get lucky and bump into someone who recognized her. At worst, he'd eliminate that possibility, slim as it was.

If there was time, he would take a stroll down to Chinatown to see if he could connect with his CI there to ask about Lindsay George. Then later, at home, he was going online to follow up on his suspicions about Lindsay George's fashion choices by tracking down the brands.

A full and productive day.

That had been the plan.

Officially off duty, he had no access to Vic PD directly from the rear door connected to the parkade and had to walk around the building to enter with Ana's permission, which she would grant because he was off-duty but not suspended.

He was just about to enter the building when his watch vibrated. He stopped and swiveled it up to read a notification reminding him that he'd forgotten to take today's dose of the medication that Dr. Robillard had prescribed. He frowned. He hadn't forgotten to take the medication, of course. He'd just forgotten to take a pill out of the bottle. The meds had only been a suggestion—and Sault decided that he was still considering the suggestion—but the fact that Robillard had implemented compliance tracking implied that not taking them would be deemed significant and would probably figure in to his next assessment; no doubt, in a negative way. Sault felt this had more to do with Robillard's self-esteem than positive outcomes. He chose to ignore it.

The front doors slid apart and he traversed the marble tiles, toward the reception desk. In his mind he was also considering calling Cavallon House to see if he could dredge more details about Lindsay George's stay there, but he hadn't yet talked to Maya and didn't want to cross any invisible lines.

Ana's voice snapped him from his reverie, and she said something that stopped him in his tracks and made the blood drain from his face. "Good morning, Mr. Sault."

Sault stood facing her.

"How can I help you?" Ana's round face was beaming with sunny demeanor, like a star struck teen in the presence of a gaming idol.

"I'm going to my desk to pick up a few things."

"Your desk has been reassigned."

That hurt.

"Supervisory Deputy Chief Devoss asked that you see him. I will call an officer to escort you."

That hurt worse.

As before—as always—Devoss was behind his massive desk, leaning deeply into the leather upholstery, business card flitting from knuckle to knuckle. Also as always, his adjunct, Michael Carr, sat silently on the sofa, expediently close at hand, yet safely removed; out of sight of both men, as he was directly behind Sault who blocked Devoss' view.

Sault stood before the man but, as he was somehow technically not on duty, he felt no obligation to stand at attention, and he met Devoss's pompously smiling eyes with a steely defiance.

"You will, no doubt, be pleased to hear that after years of badgering, Vic PD no longer has any interest in you making

Detective."

That was a direct hit, and a hard one. It was all Sault could do not to visibly flinch like a deer after a shot, and he wasn't sure he'd totally pulled it off. His heart was pounding and there was a lump in his throat the size of a football.

Devoss seemed to be focused on flipping the card, trying to out wait Sault's silence. Sault knew he couldn't. He liked the sound of his own voice too much to tolerate a silence that he could fill.

"The report from Dr. Robillard was less than optimistic. As you will not be returning to patrol any time soon, I'm having you reassigned."

Sault knew this last bit was bullshit. On his own, Devoss did not have that power. According to Vivia, reporters were still trying to get a hold of him. If for no other reason than the media attention, such a decision would have been a sensitive one, made at higher levels. The Supervisory Deputy Chiefs would have been included only so that the blame could be spread, in case there was any negative political backlash. Above the fifth floor, Vic PD was bloated with spin artists, yes-men and fall guys.

Another thing he now knew was that he had not been stripped of his rank, regardless of how Ana had addressed him. Devoss would have led with that. More likely, his file was temporarily in revision, awaiting the reassignment.

Devoss' satisfied smile had Sault's mind whirling through the morbid shapes that reassignment might take. One thing seemed certain; his life was about to alter course.

A turbulent mixture of anger and fear churned inside him, his heart pounding and sinking at the same time. Sault struggled to maintain a veneer of disinterest by focusing on the anger.

Flip, flip, flip. The card flickered across Devoss' fist, then snapped into position between thumb and forefinger. He aimed a cardstock corner at Sault and paused, dramatically.

"I'm putting you on the ground floor of a brand-new, ancillary department."

Devoss underlined the words "ground floor" so that Sault might appreciate the political implications. To a man like this, the ground floor was for janitors, file clerks and lost causes. The higher the floor, the higher the position. Window clad corner offices like Devoss' started on the sixth. The Chief Constable and ancillary support staff occupied the tenth. Devoss filled his emotional distance from the tenth by abusing his limited powers to make those beneath him miserable. And lately, Sault was squarely in his crosshairs.

The words "ancillary department" also had implications. He would no longer be a whole member of the Victoria Police Department; he would be providing support services to those who were. This was as close to stripping him of his rank as was possible in a union shop.

"Brand-new" meant experimental. It meant purgatory. If the new, experimental department performed below expectations, Sault would be again reassigned, but this time, he would not be a cop fresh from active duty. His career, as he knew it, was over.

Sault had to admire the phrasing. Devoss knew his political craft. He'd probably be Chief, one day.

He tried again to imagine what kind of new, experimental cage the higher-ups had designed for him. Somehow, and with a sudden certainty, his mind leapt to the lobby, the tiles, Ana, the reception desk and the thing he had not seen there today…Dennis Hennessey. He thought it over several times and became convinced of it long before Devoss finally managed to get to the business end of the stick he was using to jab at Sault. "Report to the first floor on Monday, 0h-700."

When the words were finally uttered, he hoped his lack of surprise robbed the little bureaucrat of some of the payoff.

If so, Devoss masked his disappointment by suddenly turning his attention to matters on his watch and giving Sault a flippant dismissal. "This time, shut the door quietly on your way out."

Sault left it wide open.

"Hey! Sault!"

Sault took his hand off the Grand National's door handle and turned to greet Constable Second Class, Jimmy Fitterer. He was a short and compact man, with a head of thick, curly black hair that crawled down the back of his neck and sheathed the rest of his body, sprouting from just about every pore. There were tufts on his knuckles and on the tips of his ears. When he took a stance, he seemed as immovable as a Sumo.

They knew each other from earlier times, but did not often cross paths, these days. Both men smiled and shook hands. Sault assumed that Fitterer wanted to discuss something to do with Darsh Singh.

"Hey Jimmy. Been a while, huh?"

"Yeah. Last time we really talked was at Howie Hauser's boat launch."

"Jeezus. I'd almost forgotten about that."

Howie Hauser was a civilian PR man who worked up on the seventh floor. He was everything you'd imagine a PR man to be: tall, self-assured, successful, good looking and a great conversationalist. Members really only saw him at press conferences, award ceremonies, and other public events where he'd stage the scene and direct the photographers. A nice enough guy, from the distance at which most of the force knew him. Hauser was married with a couple of grown kids and, at home, played the part. At work, however, he did little to mask his pride in the fact that he was having an affair with his 21-year-old file clerk named Selena. It all blew up pretty much the way everyone watching predicted it would when Selena got pregnant and proudly announced it on social media, assuming, Sault supposed, that Hauser would immediately leave his wife with half of his fortune and start a new life with her, raising their child together. But that wasn't exactly how it panned out. Hauser's wife found out within hours of the media post, kicked him out, hired an aggressive lawyer and shook him down for most of what he owned. When they'd married, she'd been a lawyer herself and raising their family had sidelined a promising career for which the courts deemed she ought to be compensated. Hauser quit his job and spent the last of his savings on a sixty-foot sailboat that he'd decided to live on. He invited everyone in the department to the housewarming, which he called a "boat launch." It was very well attended. There was an open bar. Sault went and had a lot of fun, but he left before the party got so raucous that the on-duty cops ended up there. Hauser was arrested and spent a week in custody before using the last of his savings on a lawyer to regain his freedom and retain his conviction-free social status, which was now about all the social status he still had. For about a year, he and Selena lived and partied on the boat, paying expensive moorage in the inner harbor. If you asked, he had big plans to live a simple, stress-free lifestyle and to sail down the coast toward Mexico, possibly South America. But he had no clue about sailing and never seemed to get around to learning. In the end, he was forced to sell it when the hull became encrusted with barnacles and mussels and needed to be hauled out and refurbished, an expense for which Hauser was ill-prepared. As they say, a boat is a hole in the water into which you throw money. "Hauser's boat launch" became a Department euphemism for "crashed and burned."

"How's it going with Singh?" Sault asked to pave the way.

"Oh. He's a great kid. Gets a lot of things it takes others years to understand. He'll do well."

"Yeah. That was my take. Any issues?" He asked, giving Fitterer another opening.

"Nah. Listen…I wanted to talk to you about Jared Kowalczyk."

Sault was so surprised that he let it show, then covered by furrowing his brow as if rummaging for distant details. "You mean, the kid who died last year, from Jingo?"

Fitterer didn't challenge Sault's façade but he ignored it. "Yeah. Listen…it's just that…Look, the thing is…it's not in the file but, the kid had a bit of a 'habit.'" Furtively, he glanced around the parkade, as if there might be eavesdroppers.

"I hadn't heard that."

"Yeah. It was known, you know? Falkov and Caverly got

wind, but there was no obvious evidence and I guess they decided to leave well enough alone so as not to screw up the pension. For the family's sake."

"The Department's, as well," replied Sault, thinking about how the press would have dealt that news.

"Maybe. Anyway, I just thought you should know."

Perhaps he should have been thankful for the lowdown, but his first reaction was anger. He was mad at Singh for having betrayed a trust, but Singh was elsewhere and Fitterer was standing right in front of him, so Fitterer got the venom that Singh had coming.

"Really? And why did you think I needed to know that?" Sault asked, suddenly breaking the terms of this social engagement. Fitterer stood there like a petrified mouse caught in a spotlight. Sault let him bake under his glare for a while, then without another word, turned and headed toward the Buick.

"God damn it, Sault. Not everyone in the department hates you yet, but it's a fuck'in wonder why."

Sault ignored him, ducked into the bucket seat and slammed the door, still seething. He was going to have to have a few words with Constable fourth Class, Darsh Singh, and soon.

He jammed the key into the lock and turned. The starter motor sang the first note, but the Buick's engine did not take up the melody.

Sault slammed his palm against the steering wheel. He felt betrayed, yet again. "Fuck!" He turned the key, hard. This time, nothing. His could feel blood rising in his face and he glanced at the rearview mirror to see if Fitterer was laughing, but it was not actually a mirror, only a replica; a camera which relied on the car's electrical system for power and it was blank.

On the third try, the car roared to life. Sault rammed it into drive and floored the pedal just to send the message that he was still angry, though that emotion had been usurped by embarrassment. The car fishtailed but he quickly corrected and as he screeched away, he checked the rearview again. Behind him, the garage was empty.

CHAPTER 13

Sault was feeling scared and depressed and sorry for himself in exactly the right proportions to drown out the world in a dingy bar; sitting on a stool, drinking Scotch all day, getting justifiably soused, then calling a cab and staggering home and collapsing into bed. It was a pivotal scene in all the best cop movies, and too many real cops' lives. Oblivion seemed like the best place to be, right now, and he was very tempted. But being the product of an alcoholic father and drug-addicted mother, Sault couldn't allow himself the indulgence. He knew the statistics regarding children of addicts and was unwaveringly strict about his own consumption. He rarely drank anything but beer, and never more than two before switching to soda water or coffee.

He pulled the Grand National up to a RefreshXpress drive-thru. Vivia exchanged details with the large beverage machine and seconds later a tall cup of iced milk and coffee, perfectly blended to his own taste, was passed to him by a metallic claw. He'd barely had to slow down. A car behind him honked and he realized that his mind had drifted, and he'd been staring at the patient claw holding his drink and thinking diffuse thoughts about bots and how they were about to replace people as the focus of his daily work life. He drove away without the drink.

Moments later, Vivia asked, "Was your drink

unsatisfactory?"

"Very."

"RefreshXpress has refunded your purchase."

"Swell."

Sault's favorite coffee house was the Roundhouse Cafe, on Cloverdale and Inverness. The location was relatively convenient for him, and he'd really become a fan when his kids were smaller. Rutledge Water Park was directly across the street and he could sit with a coffee and monitor them from the patio and talk with other dads who were doing the same thing. As well, this was one of the few places still run entirely by human beings. "100% Human Service" was posted in large letters on sandwich boards decorating each of the cross streets, as well as on the window, next to the door. What was not written, but was implied, was one hundred percent human customers. If you sent your butler bot to pick up an order, it would not be welcomed.

It was as it had always been, a family-owned business, and the owner —Wendy something—was at the till talking to another customer but she smiled when she recognized him and waved her hand toward an empty chair. Sault smiled back and felt good about abandoning his mech-served beverage. Vivia did not have to inform Wendy of his preferences because she knew him and understood what he'd want on a hot summer's day. More than merely efficient, she had shared moments of his life, had met his kids; had some understanding of the whole of him because they shared the visceral experience of living. Things like a smile and a kind gesture were the price of efficiency. They were significant losses, but seemingly unaccounted for.

He stared across the street at children frolicking in geyser blasts, shallow pools and water slides and remembered simpler times when Matthew and Amber were small, and every day was an adventure and his mere presence was all they needed from him.

"There you go, mister," Wendy said playfully tapping him on the shoulder as she delivered a tall, sweating cup of iced latte. Her hair was braided and swirled into a tight bun held in place by bobby pins. Under one of the pins was a small, white daisy.

Sault smiled and meant to reply, but she was already gone.

The shop was busy right now and she couldn't afford to lose a sale because, Sault knew, there were long dead periods throughout the day. Coffee was not as popular as it had been when he was young, and the market was continually thinning. The ever-widening variety of beverages and the ever-increasing pickiness of customers had driven most people to mechanized roadside machines. Running a coffee shop had to be one of the least financially rewarding businesses imaginable—forced to stay open long hours and alternately run off your feet or bored out of your tree. Sault had hoped this would have been one of the slack times, but instead, the shop was crowded and noisy. He picked up his cup and made his way to the patio where the morning sun beat down through the gently twitching leaves of a massive Honeysuckle whose thick vines had woven a canopy into the cedar pergola. It had just begun to blossom, and the air was infused with a gentle sweetness.

He found a relatively secluded spot on the concrete wall that separated the patio from the garden and settled in, resting his back against a support column and feeling a deep satisfaction at the humanness of it all.

Slowly his mind returned to the larger realities of his day and all his recent positivity faded; he felt gutted. Worse than demoted, he'd been sidelined. He might as well have been fired. And—the capper—he was going to have to deal with bots all day!

They were the latest technological innovation to bring out the worst in people. Humanity was cannibalistic; both predator and prey. People were screwing bots, raping them, hunting them, and torturing them all the while apparently oblivious to the fact that they were replacing themselves. The piranha was being fed its own tail. Where could it all lead but to depravity, dependence and, ultimately, annihilation?

The only mitigating factors so far were that bots were

generally delicate and prone to mechanical failure, and that AI was still intelligent and dumb at the same time.

AI had gotten very clever, but it had never surged forward the way people simultaneously hoped and feared it might. Still, as a precaution, the T12—the twelve countries leading in technology—had agreed to throttle it's potential by monitoring and restricting all AI access to the web. Ironically, this was achieved using a Master AI, which had to be continually improved to fend off state-of-the-art, run-of-the-mill AI's. It was an unstoppable cycle of escalation that served to advance an irrevocable science.

It had long been argued that AI's had no consciousness and, therefore, no agenda, thus no motivation to regard humans at all, let alone harm them. From this, it was postulated by some that if AI gained consciousness it might decide to eradicate the human race. The opposing view was that it would lose any interest in serving humanity. It was a highly contentious subject with only two outcomes, both of which seemed dismal.

Militaries all over the world considered AI a potential weapon and there was a lot of talk about "AI bombs"—AI's designed with nasty temperaments and meant to be deployed in a variety of devices to eavesdrop, disrupt or even kill. So far, it seemed, the Master AI had kept these at bay.

According to an article Sault had come across about a year earlier, the only reason that AI's were manageable was that, ultimately, there was always a human at the top of the command chain. So far, no one had let an AI loose without built in restrictions meant to keep it from turning on its creator. The day that happened, though, all bets were off.

In general, the public was anxious about the possible repercussions of AI even while eagerly assimilating it into every aspect of their daily lives. Apparently, for humans, convenience overrode extinction.

While some people railed against human-bot marriage (which was legal in some countries and not yet addressed in most others) others flocked to arenas to swoon over the first all-bot boy band—TronX—whose mind-numbing thumping tunes were recited amid superhuman choreography performed with, predictably, mechanical precision. Sault had seen them on TV and had to admit it was no less impressive for being entirely mechanical, much in the tradition of all the manufactured musical collaborations that had come before.

But worse than the technology and what it brought out in people, was the gaping hole it had carved into the legal infrastructure. As a group, lawmakers were technically deficient and stuttered and stalled when dealing with anything that seemed human in action or appearance. Judges and juries were swayed by the confusing semantics inherent in arguments regarding apparatus that seemed to bear gender or emotion, or motivation. It was a confusing time in which to litigate or enforce the law.

Sault thought for a moment about his own definition of bot, of AI, of autonomous, of conscious. As Sault moved, so too did Vivia, hopping from one device to another in anticipation of his needs. There were now a few laws regarding personal AI's, mostly protecting the information they contained. Strangely, Vivia was Vic PD-issued, but not Vic PD property, and Sault's personal information was legally protected, unless he purposefully altered the security settings. The coffeemaker in his house was a very limited device, but when Vivia occupied it, did it become a legal entity? To Sault, the answer was clearly 'no,' but he remembered a case from a few years back that blurred the lines. A similar device had overheated and burned down a family home. The kids were at school, but the mother was home and asleep and was almost killed in the ensuing fire. It turned out that the husband and wife hated each other; both had lovers, on the side. The husband wanted a divorce and the wife was making sure that the process was both difficult and expensive. Because the coffeemaker malfunctioned in a seemingly sophisticated way—heating then cooling over and over until some critical parts melted—the circuit breakers did not trip and the question arose about the possibility that the husband's AI had caused the fire. The next logical question was: Did it determine that this was in the husband's best interests and do it on his behalf, or was it instructed to act? Of course, the AI logs were entered into evidence, but they were very long and filled with the second-to-second mundane details that only a computer could sort through so, eventually, the AI was brought to court in a bot shell. In a move that has since become a classic discussion point, the council for the defense purchased a state-of-the-art shell for the deposition. It looked like an eight-year-old girl with large blue eyes and silky blonde curls and had a deferential demeanor that bordered on flirtatious. When the husband was cleared of wrongdoing, the world went wild with speculation that the choice of bot shell had emotionally swayed the jury. Many thought that the AI should have been made to testify in the form of a coffeemaker. Perhaps the only thing that became clear was that it was humanly impossible to wade through all the code and interactions involved to determine which player—human, AI, or coffeemaker—had really caused the fire. AI's could be used to launder human action.

Sault felt the sun on his skin and focused for a moment on letting the warmth seep down into his bones. His thoughts of Vivia and the law were a springboard for a niggling thought about his encounter with Jimmy Fitterer, in the Vic PD garage. If Jared Kowalczyk was a user, then he risked his career every time he bought. That kind of behavior made him what they called "street meat"— a target for blackmail. If his habit had much history, it was easy to imagine that he might have become a mule for his dealer.

A thought stumbled from the shadows that exploded with consequences. If Jared Kowalczyk was dealing, he might have recognized the product as his own. He would have wanted to steal them to prevent being dragged in to the investigation. It also implied that Kowalczyk and George may have known each other. If Lindsay George had used his product, he would have been an accessory to murder. More than that, Kowalczyk might be a link that could lead back to the supplier who was, so far, responsible for at least one murder.

He toyed with that a while, but then recalled the audit of

Kowalczyk's finances. His young family was struggling and there had been no suspicious transactions. If he was a dealer, he was an oddly unsuccessful one.

Sault had noted that Jared's AI had no privacy settings at all so that his personal actions were almost completely visible to the investigating team. He attributed this to Jared's youth. People his age had grown up automatically trading personal details for convenience or access to entertainment. Few valued their personal information enough to take the time to protect it. But, if Jared had been a dealer, he would have needed to hide his double life. Where was his burner AI? At the very least, there would be gaps in the AI log. Sault had already checked and had seen none.

If, as was more likely, Jared had been a financially burdened user, and first on the scene at Lindsay George's accident, he might have seen the bag of joints and stolen some for himself. That would explain the odd number, forty, left in the bag. If so, this meant that the trail to the murdering supplier was through Lindsay George, and not Jared.

Sault was not amused by the response of the investigators to tamper with evidence that he saw escalating in significance. Not only would Sault have pursued this line, he would have looked into Kowalczyk's previous cases to see if his side-interest had inspired any other miscarriages of justice. And, if Fitterer knew via the grapevine, that implied that Vic PD members were complicit, if only by inaction.

Fitterer's words had complicated everything because on top of the legal implications, they were a clear signal that his compatriots knew what Sault was up to and that they wanted Jared Kawalczyk kept in the clear.

Sault hoped that information of his extra-curricular activities had not leaked beyond the rank and file. Although, now that he thought about it, that that could happen might have been meant as an implicit threat.

Sault sighed heavily. His latte was half melted by the time he remembered it, but it was still cold and looked refreshing. He took a long draft and was unpleasantly surprised to find it bitter.

CHAPTER 14

Even though he was not in the mood, he could think of no alternative and so forced himself to continue with his previous plan for the day and drive to the Scia'new Band office, the first of nine tribes of the local Coast Salish Nation he had on his list to check out.

The indigenous people of Canada had fared no better than their American counterparts when it came to dealing with the first settlers. About 180 years ago, colonial bureaucrats, backed by colonial armies backed by colonial countries stole their land and outlawed their way of life, replacing it with their own customs, laws, and religions. Labeled as soulless savages, they then endured for eight generations before thoughts and sympathies evolved and Canadians began addressing the issues spawned from a century and a half of neglect and abuse. But the wounds were deep, puss-filled cavities of despair into which an alarming number of first-nation Canadians still fell. Familial dysfunction, poverty, and addiction were the unholy trinity that still dogged the nations within the nation.

And the continuing divide between the indigenous tribes and the rest of Canada did nothing to help clear up any mysteries. Native lands were off limits to police, and tribal databases, when they existed at all, were sporadically maintained. Given their history, it was easy to understand why they resisted any kind of formal registration, even within their own clan. Woods had made some calls to band offices, but no one there went out of their way to help. In the end, all they were able to conclude was that Lindsay Susan George was probably not local, and that no family seemed to be missing her.

The Scia'new nation's band office was about the size of a school gymnasium and was built from massive cedar timbers that had been peeled and lacquered. Bold designs in red, white and black which Sault recognized as a stylized bear and thunderbird were on the wall to the left and right of the main entrance. Incongruously, the impressive structure sat alone at the center of an unadorned gravel parking lot. There were no designating lines, so Sault pulled up close to one side of the concrete steps that led to the entrance.

A large and prematurely wizened woman grumpily hefted herself from her desk and waded over to the counter to greet him. She eyed him suspiciously and asked to see his credentials. Sault made a mistake and chose the wrong path by bringing out his Vic PD badge, hoping to intimidate her enough to stand down. But she was street smart and wily and took her time making note of his name and badge number. When finally, she looked up from her notepad, he had the ME's reconstructed facial image of Lindsay George hovering above his watch. "I'm looking for information on this woman."

"Hows' it a Two's investigating a homicide?" She asked, using the cop jargon "Two" for Constable Second Class. Sault was rattled at her knowledge of police procedure as well as the leap of logic from a computer-generated likeness to a death.

"I never said that she was dead."

"Colonials don't waste resources reconstructing images of First Peoples unless they're dead." Sault had never even heard of anyone calling anyone else a Colonial. He wanted to laugh but saw no indication that she was joking and so he became immediately uncomfortable. Intimidation had definitely been the wrong tack. He was the one being intimidated. She'd been around the block. If he'd known her name, he was sure he'd find a thick file back at Vic PD. He was almost curious enough to follow through on that thought. Sault swallowed his pride and backtracked as softly as possible. He confessed that he was off duty, working for a private client, which was essentially true, though the client was himself. He wanted to mention that he was trying to fill a systemic blind spot at Vic PD, but she had his badge number and he knew such a comment could very well explode in his face, if she ever repeated it. It was the type of statement that could make a headline. Instead he said, "I'm just trying to make things right for her."

She folded the notepad under a paw, leaned forward on the counter until Sault actually took a small step backward, stared him in the eye and asked to see his P.I. license. All hope of flying under the radar was dashed but Sault had been down this path before and was prepared.

She wasn't wearing a watch and he saw no cameras, so if it came down to it, it would be her word against his—a legal stalemate, regardless whom his superiors believed.

He had to go back to the car to get his investigator's license out of the trunk. During one of his early years on the force, while following a lead, he'd gotten a reprimand on his record for overstepping his jurisdiction using his Vic PD credentials. It turned out to be a much bigger deal than he'd suspected, at the time. He almost lost his new career over it. Soon afterward, he'd taken the online course and got his Private Investigator's license for situations precisely like this one.

Cops were allowed to have a PI license, but they were not allowed to use it because it was too likely to lead to a conflict of interest. Because he didn't know all the ins and outs of how licensing information was shared, it was not something he wanted stored in Vivia in case that raised a flag at Vic PD. So, he only kept a physical copy of the license and he'd told no one, not even Maya, because he didn't think anyone would view it in a positive light, considering how he'd resisted his Vic PD Detective ticket.

Fishing around in the trunk, his mind wandered toward his reasons for doing things the back-assward way he did: bouncing back and forth between a PI license and a beat-cop rank. He liked the status, money and stability of Vic PD, of course. But the real reasons were deeper.

There were six or eight active investigation units—teams of two Detectives—under Cece Teng's supervision who handled all the robberies and homicides in the greater Victoria area. At any given time, each team had about fifteen to twenty active cases, not including the dozen or so cold cases that they were expected to work on whenever a new clue or evidence came up, or when they had downtime—which happened, never. Sault was all about quality over quantity and was afraid of getting dragged into the numbers game that automatically compromised all investigators by putting them on a time clock.

He could see no way around this issue and even as he thought about how he had hoped that his career might go that direction, also wondered if he could really have accepted the compromise. Oddly, this aspect of his years of procrastination had never occurred to him so concretely as it did at this moment. It made him think that maybe he wasn't just the obstinate bastard that most people thought he was. Maybe.

He laid his PI card on the plastic countertop and the frumpy, grumpy woman scrupulously copied down all the information.

Sault flashed up the image again.

"Don't know her."

"Do you have a database?"

"Yes. And she's not in it."

"Do you mind if I ask some band members about her?"

"No need. We're 1698 members, and I know every one. She's not Scia'new."

"Maybe she's someone's friend."

"Nope."

"How can you know that, for sure?"

Instead of replying, she returned to her desk and slipped on a pair of glasses. The computer there was nothing more than a small black disk. There was no holographic display or monitor of any kind, but it was obvious by the way her eyes moved and her gestures that she was surfing the net in AR.

In neither of Sault's capacities as an officer of the law or as a private investigator did he have any authority to insist on answers, so he stood there for a few minutes wondering, against all the evidence, if she might be looking something up for him. Finally, he grabbed his ID and left.

He almost went home then, but when he thought about the emptiness there, he decided against it. The kids were at school and Maya was probably at work. Or, worse yet, she might be home and the house would reverberate with echoes of the chasm between them. Lacking attractive alternatives, wearily, he pushed on to the next tribe on his list, the neighboring T'sou-ke Band office, and was rewarded with the polar opposite response there.

The clerk was a tiny old woman with salt-white hair tied in a ponytail who he found standing behind the counter, as if she'd been waiting for him forever. Her skin was shriveled, but she stood straight and erect and greeted him warmly and with a perky smile that seemed to ignite her pale, grey eyes. He flashed his badge and introduced himself and his mission. When he showed the picture of Lindsay George, her smile faltered and her eyes became moist, and he caught a flicker of something deep and painful. It was recognition of the sad circumstances, not the person. She recovered almost instantly, and he pretended not to have noticed. She introduced herself as Helen and invited him to the other side of the counter, then sat him down in front of another black disk with a holographic emitter. She told him that most of the other tribes had accurate databases and were connected to hers and gave him full access to the entire network that covered the vast majority of Vancouver Island, including the Scia'new where he'd just been denied. Sault was startled by the system's sophistication and the detail in the records. It automatically liaised with Vivia and, based on the reconstructed visage of Lindsay George, narrowed his search to less than 200 close matches which it lined up in neat rows of six for him to peruse. It was generally believed that First Nation databases were marginally maintained, if they existed at all. Apparently, that was far from true, but maybe it was what the tribal Chiefs wanted colonial authorities to believe.

The only disappointment was that he didn't find a match.

He considered the gaps—a few tribes whose names he could never hope to pronounce with no connection, or no database, or both. But they were small tribes in remote locations. The odds were staggeringly against him ever crossing those off the list but, as well, the odds were against Lindsay George having come from any of those locations.

When he thanked the old woman for her cooperation, by habit, he did a little fishing by mentioning that he would also check more bands on the lower mainland, near Vancouver and received a bonus parting gift. Helen flipped through a yellowed collection of printed pages stuffed into a blue folder until she came to a list containing the name of the band member who was in charge of their computer network and who might know how he could access the mainland's database from Victoria.

CHAPTER 15

Flushed by this unexpected progress and with extra time on his hands, Sault decided to head into Chinatown and check with Les Rawling, the CI he had intended to talk with on his last beat with Darsh Singh.

Les had been one of the first people he'd gotten to know when he was a new boot, fresh on the beat. Les was about his own age and, at that time, new to town. They'd grown old together. It had taken years, but eventually he had pieced together Les' story. He was the son of an American investment banker multi-millionaire who married a Canadian-Chinese woman and retired to Canada. Les grew up on the mainland, in Vancouver. Being both flamboyantly gay and flamboyantly artistic, his extremely old school father had largely disowned him. It was unclear which of the two of Les' leanings he hated most. At some point, in his early twenties, there was a falling out and Les was informed that he would not be mentioned in his father's will. Contrarily, however, father and son reached a tacit agreement that Les would live further away and his father would pay living expenses plus an allowance. Les moved to Victoria and lived in a small but modern Condo overlooking Fisgard St, the heart of Victoria's three-block Chinatown, where he tried to establish a name for himself as a painter. With five other siblings, apparently, he was never missed by his father, but he travelled to Vancouver several times a year, to visit his mother.

Les spent an inordinate amount of time smoking pot in a sales booth he rented by the day in Bastion Square. Without any real pressure or deadlines, Les painted only when the mood struck him—usually about once a month, when his allowance came in and he could afford something stronger than pot. It had been during one of these "artistic" binges that Sault had become acquainted, after Les was reported dancing and tossing raw chickens from his balcony to the neon-lit streets below, at three in the morning.

For years afterward, he'd busted Les on a regular basis, mostly on minor offences like disturbing the peace, possession, and once for assault on what Sault assumed had been an ex-lover. Les never did more than a few hours jail time. Expensive lawyers flew in from the mainland to defend; occasionally, fines were paid, but most of the charges ended up being dropped. As far as he ever knew, Les was never involved in anything worse than struggling against his addictions—and Sault guessed, depression—and Sault could never really take him or his offences too seriously. Les often gave Sault a wink as he left the courtroom and Sault would shake his head but had to smile. In spite of his circumstances, the little man emanated a strange and charming warmth that Sault admired.

About four years ago, his mother had died and, for Les, things spiraled quickly. His father cut him off. Les moved into a disheveled rancher incongruously stranded amid auto repair shops and warehouses near a busy intersection at the edge of downtown, which he shared with three other, more desperately ill junkies. First entering the workforce in his mid-thirties, he was not qualified or eager to do anything beyond taking coffee breaks. He'd taken odd jobs, here and there, but they never lasted long. No doubt he was now collecting government assistance payments.

Almost every tourist made their way through Bastion Square—a quaint plaza surrounded by charming shops and a scattering of local artisans, like Les, hawking their wares. Les' booth in Bastion Square might have been a keen business decision, if only Les had paintings to sell. Being so unproductive, he rarely had any unique pieces. His stall was stocked with photo-reproductions of four or five of his favorite creations. The fake canvases were piled in unattractive stacks, twenty deep, with one leaning at the base for display. Beyond this, Les' tastes were not mainstream, and Sault could not imagine anyone paying money for what appeared to him to be psychedelic renderings of vomit.

Nevertheless, sitting city-center for hours each day combined with Les' upbeat and gregarious nature and counter-culture leanings made him a hub of information. And as much as he appeared small and weak and was rarely without a reefer, Les had the sharp eyes and mind of prey. But for the first time, Sault was a bit worried about the little man. He was sure—and Les had even hinted at it—that Les had turned a trick or two in the last few months. No doubt, Les saw it as a stopgap measure. But it was a dangerous one that was always intertwined with addiction; less likely to be a solution than a catalyst for disaster.

Sault rounded the corner and spied Les in his usual spot, at the middle of the square. It was a warm, sunny day, but the inner harbor was less than a block away and a constant and cold sea breeze was filing through between the buildings. Cast in shadow between tall buildings, Bastion Square had yet to warm up and the slightly built Asian man was huddled in a navy wool jacket, a stubby joint between his lips. Sault detoured to a mobile vendor selling hot pretzels and warm drinks and ordered a couple of pretzels and a green tea.

Les smiled as Sault approached, mostly because Les always smiled. Sault liked the man, but never fooled himself that Les was ever glad to see him.

"Here for another blow job, officer?"

Oh god—always so over the top. "Is that what I walked in on, last week? You're doing bots now?" Sault parried.

"Whatever the market will bear," he sidestepped; emphasizing the last word and flexing an eyebrow to make sure that Sault got the double-entendre, though it was obvious.

"Green tea," he said, offering the cup.

Sault had never before come bearing gifts and Les's eyes narrowed as he seemed to evaluate the offer. After a furtive glance at the loosely milling crowd of shoppers and office workers he stubbed out his joint and stuffed the remnant in a jacket pocket and accepted the drink while giving Sault a look that was a well-mixed blend of suspicion, confusion and, perhaps, gratitude. He wrapped the fingers of both hands around the steaming paper cup and held it close against his chest. Sault placed the second pretzel next to a small plastic change box, atop the threadbare red cloth that was draped over a foldable card table.

"Well this is certainly a day of firsts," he said, acknowledging the small gift with a little nod. "And, you're out of uniform. Get busted?"

"Just a little," Sault admitted.

"You're not as good looking out of uniform."

"I'm not sure whether to be insulted or thankful."

"Oh, get over yourself. You're not that good looking *in* your uniform." Les giggled at his own joke. "Burn. Ssss!" he added, daintily dabbing a finger at thin air then fanning his hand as if he'd just pulled it from an inferno. "So then, in the market for a painting to spruce up the bachelor pad? Double-burn!" Another fit of giggles.

Knowing someone a long time was a double-edged sword. Worse yet, Sault realized that he just might end up having to buy a Les Rawling original vomit to disguise his purpose and pay for anything Les gave him. He almost hoped Les was a dry well.

"Of course, I already know why you're here. It's about your boyfriend, Johnny Karate."

"I seriously have no idea what you just said to me."

"Don't be coy. The guy who stabbed you. Saw it on a feed. Your fifty minutes of fame," he said, misquoting Andy Warhol. Sault sometimes wondered if he made such mistakes on purpose to cover his private school education and stay tight with the street crowd. "We've all seen him around the last few weeks, but no one knows him. We call him Johnny Karate because of his routine…you know, his dance." And Les kicked out his feet in a mock jig, inadequately demonstrating Harry Potter's intense, Tai Chi-like choreography that was familiar to anyone who frequented the downtown core.

Les was unusually free with this information, scant as it was, and Sault suspected it wasn't because of a green tea and a pretzel. It was a teaser. Les must know what Sault had really come for and he must have something to share. Johnny Karate was freely given because it was both scant and of zero value.

Sault played along. "Johnny Karate. That's a good one." He'd remember that and add it to the alias section of the Harry Potter's file. "Just another brother fighting his demons."

"Amen," Les added, somberly.

The crowds were thickening now as office workers returned to their cubicles from lunch. Though they wore fashionable and expensive suits and had well-paying jobs, a good percentage of them were addicts or dealers; possibly Les's friends or playmates. It was in both of their best interests that their exchange not be obvious. "How much is this one?" Sault asked lifting a canvas infested with a god-awful collision of red and green splotches.

"I'm thinking $450."

"Really?" Sault dropped the canvas back onto the pile, but he was questioning the value of information, not artwork. "At that price it would have to be groundbreaking work."

Les put aside his tea and rose and picked up the dropped canvas, drew close beside Sault and in a low voice pretended to be justifying the grotesque image to a customer. "Well, I can tell you a bit about your guy, the cop, and the native girl," he said waving a hand near the outer edges of the painting. Then he pointed at the brown blob at the center, "And, I can give you the dealer."

Sault wasn't poor, but $450 was a chunk of change large enough that he'd miss it, especially with his career in the air. If they got the dealer, they might get the 3D printer file, match it to the toxicology and put him or her away on at least two serial convictions. Tidy. But it didn't address the score of other questions he had about Lindsay George's real identity. Also, if the printer file proved to not have been tampered with by the dealer, the first-degree murder charge would likely drop to manslaughter, if not reckless endangerment.

Both men remained still and silent. Passersby probably wondered whether they were considering the art or lamenting good paint gone to waste. Sault was busy analyzing exactly what Les had said and how he'd said it to try to figure out if he was implying that Jared and the dealer were one and the same.

"Here's the deal, Les. I want to know three things: First, all about my boy. Second, I want to know who the girl is and how she ended up in a ditch on Bleinkensop Road. And, third, I want the dealer. If you've got all of that, I won't argue the price. Each piece is worth a buck-fifty. So, what's that painting going to cost me?"

"Ok, so the kid, Jared, was a regular for the off-market pot."

"Laced?"

"No. Strictly the straight stuff. Liked it street-strength, though. He was downtown just about every Friday night, but never stayed to party. So probably just a thing with him and the wife."

"Was he dealing?"

"What? No. I can almost guarantee you that. Just a buyer. Another thing; he hasn't been around in months. So, he might have dropped the habit."

"Or changed dealers," Sault speculated and Les nodded. "What about the girl?"

"Been around about maybe eighteen months, two years, something like that. I don't know where she came from, but she liked to hang around Chinatown and I bumped into her few times at bars and cafes. I never actually talked to her but recognized her. She was always alone. I don't think she was Canadian. Once, I overheard her pronounce "route" like "rawt"—like an American. Called herself Lindsay."

Sault waited for more.

Les must have felt he'd underperformed so he added, "She

wore labels—Ashton Cravat, BabyChic, Montreaux, high-end stuff like that. Definitely not a WalMart shopper."

Sault was disappointed, but that seemed to be it for Lindsay George. He recognized a couple of the label names from the incident report, so it confirmed his suspicions about the clothing but fell short of his hopes.

"Did Kowalczyk and the girl know each other?"

"Kowalczyk is your boy? I have no idea."

Continuing the pantomime, Les pointed a finger at a particularly meaningless fleck of black paint. "I can give you the dealer, though."

Sault was excited by this but tried to hide the fact. "Ok."

"You know her. Mary Squared."

"You're kidding, right?" As a dealer, Mary Murray—Mary Squared—was a dinosaur, operating a decade behind the times, illegally selling the cheap stuff; regular tobacco soaked in an extract she made from culled weed she legally purchased from growers. Her product was higher in THC than the regulated stuff, but still mild; a short high that died as quickly as the last embers of the joint. Her biggest real crime was a stubborn refusal to register her business and submit to Health Department inspections. Buying from Mary Squared was barely criminal. That was, perhaps, until now.

"I swear. She was freaking out, the day after. Wouldn't even put her stash on sale. Said she flushed the whole batch. Haven't seen hide nor hair of her in three months."

"Mary's not all there at the best of times. What makes you think she was acting out because of the deaths?"

"I'm a customer."

Sault's eyebrows rose, and he gave Les a look.

Les shrugged, "One's standards take a hit in hard times. The day after the feeds aired the news about your boy being taken to hospital, Mary came banging on my door at, like, five in the morning. Wanted to trade my bag for a new one. Said there was mold in the batch. Anyway, I'd already smoked some and told her it was fine, and she practically accosted me. Tore the pocket off my pajama top. Ranted that it could put me in the hospital, give me a lung infection. I knew it was nonsense but traded just to get rid of her. Best trade I ever made—it was straight-up weed rather than the watered-down crap she normally sells. I remember she was wearing disposable plastic gloves, like they use in restaurants. Weird, but not for her. The next day, everyone was talking about 'The Midnight Ride of Mary Squared.' A lot of crap goes on downtown and I think most people didn't question it, took the trade because she was generous with the replacement portions and chalked it up to paranoid delusions, probably from sampling too much of her own product. I don't know how I put it together, but about a week or two later I was watching the feed and saw your Chief asking for the public's help in the case and the timing all came together for me. And, like I said, she's not been around."

Les' logic was thin, but it felt right to Sault. Mary Squared was just about the very last person anyone in The Department would have thought to talk to. He tapped a finger next to a baby-poo colored blotch, reluctant to touch it because the color and texture were too convincing. "It doesn't make any sense to me. This stuff was 3D printed. Mary Squared has a flip phone, for God's sake. How's someone like her come to run a molecular printer?"

Les shrugged. "Maybe she was rep'ing someone else's product."

Sault shook his head. "That's a stretch, but anything's possible. But who'd risk putting that kind of product in the hands of someone as muddled as Mary?"

"Muddled? You big softie. She's a fucking nutter." Les let out a boisterous laugh and Sault forced his grimace into a reciprocal smile to maintain the charade. "She comes by it honestly, though. Know why she's called Mary Squared?"

Sault shrugged, "I assumed because of her initials MM, M-squared?"

"Nope. Her middle name is Mary, same as her first. Mary Mary Murray—Mary Squared. Shake her family tree and it'll rain nuts. You want gift wrap?"

Sault sighed. "Don't even want the painting." But then he

instructed Vivia to transfer the funds. It was a bit more than the information had been worth to him, but he hoped Les would realize that and his generosity would figure in to their next negotiation. Also, it might be best if Les could afford to not buy from Mary Squared for a while.

"Your candor is not appreciated."

"Sorry. Not to my taste."

"I'll let you know next time I paint some dogs playing poker."

"I'd prefer Elvis on velvet."

Les' eyebrows were flexing, once again. "Mmmm. You and me, both, honey."

CHAPTER 16

Sault sat behind the wheel of the Buick with the engine off, anxiously tapping his thumbs against its black, leather surface. Before leaving Les Rawling, he had made it clear that he knew that he was overpaying and that Les owed him any relevant tidbits that might fall into his lap, in the coming weeks. Les didn't argue the point. Even reduced to poverty, he was not one to nickel and dime. Sault found the man to be an odd collection of traits that repulsed him mixed with traits he admired.

Things were not falling into line. Instead, they were forming a jagged edge, like the blade of a saw. So far, that blade was just grazing the surface, but Sault felt sure that soon it would be gouging holes in the obvious assumptions and neat conclusions recorded in the Kowalczyk and George investigations. And once they were completely shredded, it would be up to Sault to put them back together.

Of course, he'd have to check out the information, but except for a brief period of binging following his father's death, Rawling had always been reliable. Maybe it was the source, but to Sault, it all felt more real than the odd and seemingly over-the-top warning from Constable Jimmy Fitterer, which was, in itself, strange enough to warrant further inquiry. And he was now fairly certain that when he got around to checking, Lindsay George's clothing would prove to be as high-end as Les suspected, which would stack another argument against the murder book.

Most cases tended to narrow as information came in. They rarely zigged or zagged or branched off like this. What had seemed a closed book was flipping open and Sault's mind was alive and busy with possibilities. It was all in the air in his mind, right now, but even just juggling the facts felt like movement, imparted momentum. He'd just crossed the line from correcting typos to adding sentences to the story. The transition was exciting, and he truly loved this feeling because none of the things that normally bothered him could reach deep enough to touch him.

He thought about Jimmy Fitterer for a moment. Department gossip just as often proved wrong, as right. Some rumors sprang from jealousy or spite, others from misunderstandings and some from direct experience. The trick was to figure out the reason why a rumor had been generated before interpreting the information. Sault would have to dig into that. The most disturbing element of the interaction had been that Fitterer even knew to mention it. That thought scared him and made him instantly angry again, at Darsh Singh and he lifted his watch to call him when Vivia announced an incoming call from Maya.

"Hey," he said softly, as pleased as he was surprised to hear from her.

"Hi. Where are you?" She was all business.

"What? Why?"

"The principal called. Amber's gotten into some kind of trouble and I'm up to my neck here. Can you break away?"

Sault felt the momentum drop out of the day. The thirty-minute drive to the school would be double that, at this time of day, because of traffic. And, he would spend half of that time feeling the dissatisfied grumble of the 400 horses under him as he crawled, bumper to bumper, just to get free of the downtown core. "What kind of trouble?"

"I don't know. They wouldn't tell me over the watch, but they said it's a serious issue and that we have to pick her up."

He was irritated by the unexpected turn of his day. "Ok, ok. I'm on my way." Maya did most of the childrearing and rarely asked for help, but he couldn't keep his reluctance out of his voice and then immediately regretted it but saw no way to recover.

"So glad you could break away from your time off to help raise your daughter."

And then, suddenly, the call was over.

He had been to the Cedar Hill Instructional Centre before for recitals and awards ceremonies, but he'd always been distracted so as soon as the heavy entry doors hissed shut, he realized that he had no idea which way it was to the office. Vivia knew, of course, and directed him. Paying attention was her main job.

Classes were in session and he was alone in the large hallways. His footsteps echoed off the polished vinyl floors and metal lockers and the age-old mix of cleaning fluids, bubble-gum, strawberry perfume and hormones instantly brought him back to what had been called "high school," where he'd first met Maya. The memory prodded, but he didn't allow himself to go there, shook it off and walked on.

In the tradition of every student before her, Amber sat slumped on the wooden bench in the outer office, kicking her feet and staring at the ground, anxious yet impatient; frightened and bored. She wasn't into her watch because the school AI controlled student watches on the schoolgrounds, so it was useless to her unless she wanted to study something. She wasn't that kind of student. Their eyes met, and she gave him a speculative half-grin, probing his mood. He patted her on the head as he passed. Considering what he did for a living, nothing that happened in this office could possibly be very serious to him.

He expected to have Amber by his side when he met with the Principal, but instead he was ushered in alone. Principal Vanessa Granger was an attractive redhead with a large smile and kind eyes. She was a bit overweight, but it was spread evenly and pleasingly accentuated her curves. It was obvious from her clothing that she knew this. She was dressed smartly in a silky white blouse with blue and salmon pinstripes and grey trousers. A wide white belt pulled it all together, and somehow made her seem hourglass-shaped, though she definitely wasn't. Her earrings were small golden hearts and she had three small red hearts tattooed along the upper edge of her right ear. Sault judged her to be about thirty-five. No ring. No kids. A cat at home, he guessed—or maybe a Tribble. A single person in her position could probably afford a Gene-Mod pet like that. This was a warm person who would need something warm to cuddle.

She half-stood from her chair, reached across her cluttered desk and shook his hand politely, introducing herself. When she was comfortably nestled into her seat cushions once again, she shuffled some papers uncovering a small, glossy book then cleared her throat. "We had a cleanup exercise today and this was found in Amber's locker."

She handed the book to Sault. He turned it over in his hands, mildly surprised to see a physically printed edition. He took a cursory glance at the back-cover blurb and his brain picked out words like "steamy," "passion," and "forbidden."

It looked to him like a typical raunchy romance novel and Sault felt himself release tension he didn't know he'd been carrying. It was exactly the kind of subject matter that parents and schools would block from electronic devices, so if kids wanted to share this, they were forced to bring printed material. It might be sexually explicit, Sault thought, and he could understand how that might concern the school, but it didn't bother him. Both he and Maya were more worried about their kids' exposure to extreme violence and hate than to sex. Sex was inevitable. It remained the single largest draw card and, in the media, wherever it wasn't explicitly shown, it was implied. As well, he was pretty sure that neither of his kids were that interested—though hormones could change things over night. Perhaps he was holding evidence of that, right in his hand.

Sault looked up and met Granger's eyes. She didn't say

anything, but nodded her head inviting him to take a closer look. He flipped back to the front cover. It was typically exaggerated and ridiculous. The title was "Meltdown" and the picture on the cover was of a man embracing a woman, bent over her at an angle that suggested that he was immensely strong and that she was as light and powerless as a sheet of paper in his irresistible grip. Sault chuckled, her hair was windswept to the right and his to the left, as if the air somehow exploded outward from their lips. Similarly, the shadows fell in two directions at once. It made no physical sense. Their lips were an inch apart, but her head was tilted slightly to one side and her expression was one of worry and resignation. If you took the time to be objective, there was a lot wrong with the image, but then Sault glanced downward to her hands. At first, he thought that she was wearing strangely decorated gloves—it was the only thing that fit. But then, it came to him that the pattern was wires and little lights and circuits. Not gloves. Her hands were artificial. His eyes snapped back to her face. The eyes were odd. Somehow, the artist made it clear that she was not human. He looked the man over. He appeared human. He flipped through some pages. There were drawings, computer rendered sexual images that made the school's objection much clearer. Sault stopped at one that showed the couple engaged in doggy-style sex. The robot was more than naked; her skin had been removed. He closed the book. He felt embarrassed, not because of his own thoughts in the matter, but because of what he thought Granger was thinking, and he could feel his skin flush. Considering what he did for a living, it bothered him that he could so easily be intimidated.

Granger was sympathetic. "It's not so much that she reads that kind of thing. I read a few chapters. It's adult, but the pictures are more graphic than the prose. But we can't have other kids exposed. The sexual aspect is one thing, but adding the robotic angle makes it incendiary. A large contingent of our parents would go ballistic if they thought their child might have been exposed."

Sault understood. He was disturbed by it, as well, but could not put a finger on why. No one had ever really protested over autonomous bulldozers or hedge-trimming swarms or vaginal stimulators. The real robot backlash didn't gain traction until the robots we used started resembling humans. Then, suddenly, robots were stealing jobs and relationships. Was Vivia horning in on his relationship with Matthew? And was he losing Amber, as well?

"Was she showing it around?" he asked.

"I don't think so. She says not. I don't really want to start probing. That would probably exacerbate the situation."

Sault nodded and reflexively moved to pass the book back to her, but she held up her hands as if fending off an attack. "Please, take it home. It's yours, after all. I can't have something like that kicking around here."

Sault slid the key into the ignition but did not turn it. His thoughts and feelings were still bouncing around and colliding inside him, all vaguely centered around disappointment and fear, but he still couldn't nail it down. It was just white noise inside his skull. He focused on the only thing that seemed clear; that Amber had broken a rule. He swiveled until he faced her in the back seat. She was silent and sullen.

"I'm not mad and you're not in trouble. Ok?" He tried to use his most reasonable tone, but he knew it was ragged at the edges with a diffuse anger.

She nodded, but her expression remained somber.

"You can read that stuff, but you can't bring it to school. Other parents…" He stopped himself and chose another approach. "Everybody's different. Some kids are not ready for that kind of stuff."

"I know," she piped quickly, attempting to truncate the lecture.

She was approaching an age where she thought that she knew as much or more than her parents and Sault felt himself heat up. "Well, if you know, then why did you bring that book to school?" he said, shining a light on the corner she had painted herself into.

"It's not mine."

It was a line he'd heard on the streets a thousand times from thieves and drug addicts, but he hadn't expected to hear it from his own daughter. Outside of a court of law, it was a very thin defense—a loser move—and hearing it from Amber made him even angrier. "Then whose is it and why do you have it?"

Amber was looking down at the floor. No answer.

"And, even if you borrowed it, that's something you shouldn't do at school."

"I know," she declared, seemingly to her sneakers.

He waited for her to say more, or at least raise her face, so he could see if she was getting the message. Silence. Stillness.

Sault turned back to face the windshield and turned the key in the ignition and 330 horses stuttered then shuddered and finally, mercifully, caught fire under the hood. As he put it in gear, over his shoulder he gave her one last admonition to make sure his point was clear. "If you knew, then I am disappointed that you didn't respect that, but I expect it will never happen again. Right?"

He checked the rear-seat-view projected on the windshield, low, near the dash. She was wiping her eyes with the back of her hands. She was crying. He never understood why tears changed things, but they always did. His anger evaporated and was replaced by guilt—a quick but uncomfortable transition. He didn't think he had been overly harsh. He replayed the scene in his head. He'd raised his voice, but just enough to be heard above the engine. *Girls!*

"It's not mine…" she began, and his anger returned immediately. She just wasn't getting the message.

He cut her off. "I don't care who it belongs to…"

"He made me…"

"Take responsibility! No one can make you…"

"It's Matthew's!"

The Cedar Hill Instructional Center was not far from their house, so the rest of the drive home was as short as it was silent.

When they stepped through the door, Sault placed a hand

over her head and gently slowed Amber as she attempted to pass by him without a glance. He ruffled her hair and let her go. Between the two of them, that was considered an apology. Or at least, it always had been. Amber continued on and Sault was not sure if his apology had been accepted. It was the best he could do, so he didn't coax her for a response.

Sault noticed the blue light on the hot box, near to the front door was flashing. Their dinner had been delivered and was waiting for them. He pressed the button and heard the short hiss of inert gas being vented before the interior door was unlocked. A surf of hot, moist air roiled over his face like a sauna as he extracted the cardboard. Dinner was steak and potatoes with green beans and apple sauce delivered from "Momma Express." Sault took it to the kitchen and Vivia confirmed that all family members would be coming to dinner. It was such a rare event that they all gathered at the table at once that he decided to make fancy and put it all on plates, rather than eating from the containers.

Maya arrived while he was doing that and the dessert printer hummed to life as her AI slipped into it and began fabricating a multi-colored, creamy, pudding. She'd been running late, but somehow had scrounged the time to find a recipe. She stayed only long enough to see that dinner was under control, then went upstairs to change.

Seeing all of his family gathered at the table, Sault decided not to raise the subject of the bot-romance novel. Seconds later, Maya brought it up. "So, what was the big deal at the school?"

Sault stalled by pretending a piece of steak was particularly chewy, but he swallowed quickly when he noticed that Amber was about to answer. He cut her off. "Not a big deal, but I think it's something you and I will have to discuss later. Not now." There was a strange moment when everyone paused and checked everyone else for their reaction, then Maya shrugged and continued eating and the rest of them seemed to take their cue from her, and the moment passed. Sault relaxed and tried to bask in the normalcy of family time.

Maya asked the kids what they'd got up to at school. Matthew gave his typical single-syllabled, teen-aged response. Amber, on the other hand, had a lot to say, filling up most of the dinner hour with detailed descriptions of every person she'd encountered, their words, actions. motivations and the social implications. Sault half expected her to spill the beans about her time at the Principal's office, but she never mentioned it and Sault wondered if it was no more significant to Amber than what Cassie Mazzerole said to the boy she likes. As fascinating as the 11-year-old's world was, Sault found his mind drifting. Maya interrupted her flow to serve the dessert. Each of their individual astrological signs had been magically rendered in a prismic, glittery frosting over the frothy mixture. Joe smiled when he noticed the image of twins on his. While Amber was distracted examining the stylized crab in her pudding, Sault took the opportunity to try to jump start Matthew.

"Matt. Something interesting must have happened to you today."

Matthew paused eating only long enough to accommodate a shrug.

"What was the most interesting thing you studied?"

Matthew's eyes lit up a bit and Sault thought he'd struck a chord. "In Tech Session, we got a new teacher." He said it casually, but Sault read people for a living and detected the restrained enthusiasm.

"So close to summer vacation? What happened to Mr. Ellis?" Maya asked.

Matthew shrugged. "He's there, too."

"So, a student teacher," Sault guessed.

Matthew shrugged again, and Sault noticed a hint of color rising in his face. His mind made an intuitive connection that brought him back to his own high school and Miss Gallagher, the student teacher he'd had in grade eleven Geography. She was there for only a few weeks but made a lasting impression. Twenty-plus years later, he could still picture her face, hear her melodious voice, recall her sweet aroma, that pleated skirt, the tight, white sweater. And he had no doubt that every other heterosexual male who had been in her class had similar, fond memories. He was seventeen, at the time, and she was only four years older. Just barely beyond his reach. He had been sexually obsessed with her. He'd once thought that she'd given him a flirtatious smile and it lit his fantasies for years, afterward. In grade eleven, he learned absolutely nothing about Geography. He remembered feeling both excited and embarrassed, just the way Matthew looked, right now. He dared a glance at Maya and met her eyes which were already on him. She'd gotten the same vibe.

"Guess so," Matthew said.

"What's she like?" Maya asked with perfect casualness.

"She's amazing!"

Amazing? Sault focused on the remains of his meal and tried not to laugh at his sullen son's uncharacteristic exuberance. "Really. And what is so 'amazing' about this new teacher?"

"Her name is Quinta…"

"Quinta. That's an exotic…"

"…and she's a trillion-node neural net in a V9 chassis! They're going to let her teach our class, as an experiment."

Sault had stopped eating and was staring at his son. Inside his head, the miasma of thoughts and emotion he'd had earlier reignited and this new situation was throwing fresh new twists into the mix. If his son was into bot-romance and one of his teachers was a bot decked out like a swim suit model, what might he do? What could he do? What if he touched her? Would this be his son's Miss Gallagher? "This bot is a 'her'?" he asked.

"Well, that's the frame she's in. And she's almost not a bot. She's practically a droid."

"They're the same thing," he said, dismissively, hoping to let the air out of the conversation so they could move on to something else. Though the words were used interchangeably on the street, Sault knew that technically they were not the same thing.

"A robot can only do what it's programmed to do, but an android is capable of independent, original thought."

"Either way, just a fancier machine," Sault said while pointlessly shoving pudding around the dish. He understood that the first happy, full-family dinner in months was not the time or place for this discussion, and as well, internally he was unprepared—his mind filled with a mindless mish mash of contradictory thought and emotion. At the core of it all was dread at what his son might bring upon himself and the family. Every word, every ounce of his son's enthusiasm, seemed dangerous. None of this was illegal, but it was taboo, and so Matthew would be tried in the court of public opinion where the consequences could be just as life-altering.

"It's a huge step forward in robotic evolution. You can't tell she's not human by talking to her."

"It's just a kind of simulation—a long way from being conscious or having a soul." He could feel Maya's eyes on him. No doubt, she didn't approve of him trampling all over the first enthusiasm their son had shown in months.

"What does that really mean, if you can't tell the difference?"

Emotion overcame him, and he became afraid of what he might say. He clamped his mouth shut and tried to cover by picking up his half-eaten dessert, crossing the kitchen and dumping it into the recycler, but the moment was oddly silent, and he knew it looked strange. With his back to his family, he tried and failed to think of some way to smooth things out and get back to enjoying a normal dinnertime. Finally, he stowed his dishes in the washer and just left.

There was an untouched tumbler of scotch and melting ice on the bench to Sault's left. The edges of the cubes had rounded from melting and condensation trickled down the outside of the glass. He was deeply absorbed, hunched close to a holographic simulation of the Grand National's turbo charger. Though the car was officially a replica, many of the engine systems had been modernized and were computer controlled. This was true of the turbo charger. Floating to the right of the exploded view of engine parts were a series of sliders that controlled various elements like fuel, timing, gear ratios, and rotation speed. The problem was that the charger kicked in so harshly that it whiplashed the driver and took rubber off the back treads. It was a common issue with the model. Sault had Vivia sift through all the online forums, but none of the solutions that she had found had worked. And so, Sault explored the control coding and toyed with the settings, thankful for the distraction from things he seemed unable to control like his career and family and, even, the strange electrical issue that continued to plague the vehicle since he'd first put his hands on her

Maya knocked softly, then entered. He gave her a glance, then returned to the simulation though the spell was broken, and he had no hope of getting his mind back on track.

Maya took up a position near and to his left. He could tell that she knew he wasn't really concentrating on the engine. "So…do I have to ask?"

He didn't look forward to discussing this, mostly because he hadn't yet resolved the whirling blender of ideas and feelings flailing around inside of him. He was tempted to be obtuse, to drag it out, make her work the details out of him. But, considering the state of their relationship, he didn't want to give her any more reasons to distance herself. He said, "Did Amber tell you what happened at school, today?"

"She said she wasn't sure if she was allowed to talk about it. Said you might get mad. I let it go. So, what's the scoop? I mean, it's school. How bad could it be?"

"I think that is exactly the right question. I'm not sure how bad it can be." He pulled the small book out from the workbench drawer, where he'd stowed it. As she gave it a cursory examination, he recalled for her the events at the school and on the drive home in the car.

"Are you sure she's not lying to save herself from embarrassment?"

"I don't think so. It felt genuine in the car, and it meshes with how Matthew was going on about his new 'teacher.'"

Maya reached for the tumbler and took a long sip, then

stood silent and staring through the misty glass at ice floating in an amber sea. Eventually, she replaced the glass on the desk top. "Didn't we sign off on some sort of gender/sexual identity neutrality course, just last term? How can they square condemning Matthew with teaching that there is no wrong way to be sexual?"

"Some people are sexually attracted to six-year-olds. No one tries to square that," Sault countered.

"That's different. In that case, someone gets assaulted."

"Only if the pedophile acts on the impulse."

"They have bots for that."

"And we're back to the initial point. In the trade, they call them dolls, by the way."

"Not something I need to know."

Sault always found it hypocritical that in her work she dealt with some of the worst of human abuse yet made it clear that details of his professional world were too sordid to hear. He was smart enough not to poke that bear. Instead, he nodded in acquiescence then reached a hand to the back of his neck, rubbing away some tension.

"I think that it just boils down to him breaking a school rule—her, too. As long as he isn't hurting anyone, his sexuality is no one's business but his own."

"So, I guess, one of us just needs to talk to him about sticking to the rules," Sault said, tentatively.

"I guess." He could tell that she was about as enthusiastic to have that talk as he was.

"Draw straws?" He was only half joking.

"It's been a long time since you had a serious one-on-one with either of your kids. I think you're overdue." It was true, and the tone of her voice made it clear that it wasn't a point for discussion.

"Ok. I'll handle it."

Maya studied him for a second or two, perhaps evaluating the earnestness of his answer. Then she picked up the little book, turned and headed for the door. When she got there, she turned back. "And Joe? Sooner, rather than later." She closed the door without waiting for an answer.

He had to admit that she had read his mind and that last warning had been warranted. He mentally rescheduled his talk with Matthew to the next day, before school, rather than sometime after he cleared the George/Kowalczyk case.

He and Maya might not be emotionally close, but they certainly weren't strangers.

CHAPTER 17

Sault sat up and immediately looked over at Maya's side of the bed. She was gone. The windows were still set to opaque, so the room was completely dark, and he had no clue what time it was, but he knew he'd slept late.

He tilted his watch, and the ever-vigilant Vivia anticipated his need. He saw the time projected in thin air and realized that the house would be empty, except for himself.

Truthfully, he was relieved.

He'd stayed up late the night before, seemingly lost in Red Cube but actually thinking about how he might approach Matthew on the subject of sex and robots and society and taboo and honesty and hypocrisy. In the end, and for lack of any better idea, he'd decided to wing it. On the one hand, he was happy to have missed this opportunity. On the other, the task hung over his head like a bloated thunder cloud.

Still, he felt energized and positive and realized that he'd had his first peaceful sleep in a week. He gave his fingers and toes a tentative flex and was relieved that they felt undeniably normal. At the same time, this sudden very assuredly normal feeling seemed to confirm that something had not been normal before. He threw off the covers and tried not to let that thought color the moment.

"Joe, you really shouldn't be here."

Joe looked up from the open file. Inspector Cece Teng was standing over him, a look of concern on her face. He was surprised; hadn't expected to bump into her on a Saturday. He knew nothing of Cece Teng's personal life but wondered if she were here seeking refuge as he had done countless times in the past—possibly, as he was doing, even now. Conveniently, there always seemed to be some paperwork that could stand some catching up.

"Ana let me in, let me access the files," he said defensively. Ana knew the rules better than anyone, of course. If Sault was technically not allowed into the building or access to a file, he could not have been sitting at his usual station with Harry Potter's file open and displayed on the flat screen desktop of the cubicle.

Teng took another tack. "Joe, you should take it easy for a while. First of all, even if you weren't suspended, this would be your weekend. And, secondly, we don't need you here. And we certainly don't need help with Harry Potter." Sault thought that it was especially tactful of her to not mention that his cubicle had already been reassigned.

"Just wanted to get out of the house. I'm not doing anything serious, just adding a name to the file."

"You ID'd him? How?"

"No, no. Just ran into someone who knows him on the street. They call him Johnny Karate."

Teng ran that around in her mind. "Johnny Karate? What's that a reference to?"

"I assume it's because of his weird kind of martial-art-like dancing in the street. I saw it more like casting spells."

Teng smiled. "I guess we'd have to call it *interpretive* dance, then, huh?" As she turned to leave, she patted Sault on the shoulder. "Don't stay too long. I don't want one of Devoss' rats spotting you here."

"Copy that. Five minutes and I'm out, boss."

"Good man." And she was gone.

Sault noted that she hadn't made any reference to his

pending transfer. Either that information hadn't yet made the rounds, or she had decided not to address it until it was official. Probably the latter. There was no percentage in acting on rumor.

Joe returned to the file. Harry Potter had never been properly ID'd. He'd had a casual psychiatric evaluation, which determined he was of no real harm to himself or others. A passing grade. Sault chuckled. Harry Potter passed a psych evaluation, but Sault couldn't. The system was insane.

Potter had been released, earlier that morning. Sault was both surprised and not surprised at the same time. Of course, he'd seen plenty of cases where the cost and energy expended in processing an offender outweighed the crime, and release was expedited through efficient legal work-arounds, but the department usually came down pretty hard on physical assault—especially on a member. To Sault, this had the feel of Christian Devoss' nimble fingers all over it. He'd probably kicked him loose just to piss Sault off. If so, Sault had the last laugh. In this case, he didn't care at all. Harry Potter would never get the drop on him again and without that advantage, he *was* relatively harmless.

He appended the alias Johnny Karate to the file and close it, flicked the file to the edge of the desk where is slid into his own assault file. His only active case was his own.

He wanted to spend a few moments confirming what he already believed regarding Lindsay George's upscale clothing, but decided he'd best not do that here, especially with Devoss gunning for him. Vivia logged him out as he headed for the elevator.

It had been difficult negotiating the tight turn into the rear alley, but he had been lucky enough to grab one of the three parking spots there, so he was heading for the rear exit on the ground floor.

As he stepped out of the elevator, he noticed that Dennis Hennessey's area seemed abandoned. The desks and file cabinets were still there, but the clutter of papers and mementos was missing. Walking to his car, he mulled this over. There was little else on the ground level—mostly maintenance and mechanical rooms. Devoss' ground-floor comment came back to him. If Hennessey and his unit had moved, presumably to a larger space, what was going to fill that ground-floor void? Whatever it was, it was obviously of less import, even, than bot duty. That thought sent a shiver up his spine.

He believed that he had accepted the demise of an upward career path, long ago—more especially, since yesterday's meeting with Devoss. But, apparently, he had been fooling himself, because suddenly the idea of being permanently sidelined scared the hell out of him. It was no revelation that it would mean restricted access within the building, which would end his ability to download case files, which in turn meant the end of his days as a detective, official or otherwise. The revelation was that it was actually happening, this time—in fact, may have already happened, within Ana's files. Dread sank into him like candied syrup on a snow cone. His breathing became ragged and the strength went out of his legs.

If his superiors could only see him now, he thought, sardonically. He knew himself to be a principled and impulsive man who never found it difficult to stick to a hard line, even in the face of death. But decisions were easy, a swift and short process. And death was easy. One bad decision and you're done. It's over. And, in the past, consequence had meant little to him—a month's suspension without pay, six weeks community liaison, three months reorganizing files. None of it touched him. But that was because it was all temporary. There was light at the end of the tunnel. This time, the tunnel would be infinite.

He barely made it to the car, fell heavily into the bucket seat, set the windows to opaque and, by the dull, blue glow of dash light took long, deep breaths and tried to narrow his perspective to the next few minutes, rather than his entire, dreary future. After what seemed like an hour but was actually only a few minutes, strength and warmth returned, and the jitteriness left his extremities.

He decided that he'd rather face his fate than live in

suspense. "Vivia, call Hennessey."

A moment later Hennessey's spry drawl leapt from the dash speakers. "Sault. What's shak'in, son?"

"Hey, Hennessey. Just wondering what happened to your department? Didn't see any sign of you in the lobby, today."

"Today? Word is, you're on leave. If I were on leave, you'd never see me within a hunert yards of the station, tell you what."

"Just tidying up my desk. Where you at?"

"Right now? I'm in my garden, at home."

"No, I mean, where's ADU gone?"

"Well, you're not gon'na believe it, Sault, but they moved me out of the building and into a huge new space. You've got to come down sometime and see this to believe it. I've got my own office, with a waterfront view!"

"Really? Sounds good, but what's the plan?"

"Apparently, they're expanding the program to include proper enforcement and reclamation. Tech guys are coming in next week to outfit the place with EMP cages and restraints. And we're setting up patrols, as well."

"Who's 'we?'"

"I'm getting a secretary and at least one other officer, under me." Hennessey paused, probably going over the possible reasons for an impromptu call from Sault. "Hey. You volunteering, Sault?"

Sault chuckled. "Until a few moments ago, I kind of thought I might be."

Hennessey's voice dropped into somber tones. "Devoss on your ass again?"

"Yeah. That guy just can't get enough of me. Hey, you got any idea who's taking your space in the lobby?"

Hennessey had been around the block and knew all the angles. "Jeez. He's dressing you down to the first-floor?"

"Maybe."

"Well, you're not gon'na like that one little bit. It's a new thing— a PET unit."

Sault had never heard of it. "What's that?"

"Pet Engagement Training."

"Say again?"

"It's a trial program aimed at training pets, but mostly their owners, to behave better, in public spaces."

"This is law enforcement?"

"It's a new-fangled idea called 'Public Enforcement Deterrent' Public Ed, they're calling it. All the rage from the sixth up."

"Sounds like a recycle of the Pre-Crime Division, ten years back."

"Oh yeah. I'd forgotten about that particular debacle. Administrators come and go so fast, there's basically no hindsight. Ten years ago, most of them were eating PB&J out of a princess lunchbox and spent the day listening to a virtual tutor while shoving a stylus up their nose. From the sixth upward, history is doomed to repeat itself."

"Which, then, makes it equally true, from the fifth down." Sault said, finishing the thought. He heard Hennessey chuckle. Sault wanted to bring the conversation back on point, "So…Pet Engagement Training…that's working with animals?" He could feel the dread rising. He liked animals, but not enough to make a career of them, and this was about as wide a departure from legitimate and effective law enforcement as he could imagine. He tried to picture how he could make it work for himself but came up empty.

"Well, no. From what I understand, it's more focused on the owners than the pets, themselves. You teach them how to train and control their pets."

"So curbing idiots who spoil their pets." It was becoming more abhorrent by the moment.

"Yeah, but with kid gloves. It's more of a community liaison thing."

"So, who's running it?"

Hennessey laughed, but it sounded mirthless. "Cindy Fredrickson."

Sault made a sound like a dying breath. "Fredrick the Red."

"You got it."

Cindy Fredrickson was a seventh floor PR liaison. She was a private consultant who worked outside of the normal hierarchy and closely with Chief Roth. It was rumored that she was a personal friend of Roth's—just how personal was a bubbling cauldron of rumor. She was a short and spindly, bottle-redhead with a permanently sunny disposition and an overabundance of exuberance that irritated almost anyone she came into contact with. She made sure that everyone knew that she was vegan, used the word "opportunity" in place of "problem," and was perpetually "embracing" issues. Sault could see how, from a distance, she might seem cute, like some sort of mascot or cheerleader, but being within earshot of her he had to clamp his mouth shut so tightly he ground his teeth. Every moment in her presence was like standing at attention under review on a hot summer's day with a legion of ants climbing his legs. The longer she spoke, the more practical objections he had to her new-age ideas and it was particularly frustrating knowing that her words often became policy. She had no real street experience or rank, but still, for all intents and purposes, she out ranked him. Sault's thought it would be no less outlandish if the Detective Unit on the fourth floor employed an astrologer.

Sault sighed. "Devoss has outdone himself."

"I'd say so. Yup."

He thanked Hennessey who ended the call by inviting Sault down to see his new space.

Sault took a few more seconds to gather his thoughts. He focused on the fact that his transfer had not yet come through and that nothing was certain. He shook his head to clear away dread and conjecture and focused on the list of things that had started his day. He glanced at the dash board clock. It was not a true replica of the analog 1987 original with real gears and cogs, but he could see the computer animated hand ticking off the seconds in a perfect simulation. In the quiet he could hear its muted tick.

His watch vibrated and a second after that Vivia's soft voice bloomed from the dash speakers. "Sorry to interrupt,

Joe, but if we don't leave within five minutes, we'll be late for the appointment I made with Rainier Gilbert, the programmer."

Sault recalled the programmer that Helen, the friendly, native woman had told him about. He turned the key and felt the vehicle rumble to life. The vibration and deep chortle from the engine were isolating, and Sault found it comforting. He paused only long enough to let the tachometer settle, then pulled the T-bar shifter into Drive and felt 330 horses lunge against the load.

CHAPTER 18

Ten minutes later, Sault was comfortably sitting at his usual deck table sipping a human-prepared coffee in the morning sunshine. Vivia had preordered and paid, and Wendy had delivered it only moments after he arrived. He had instructed Vivia to arrange a meeting at a coffee shop and had been pleased that The Roundhouse, his favorite haunt, had turned out to be mutually convenient.

A private car pulled into a parking space, directly across the street and Sault witnessed a very tall and slender bot unfold itself and exit the vehicle. It was a science fiction-inspired shell; humanoid but strangely proportioned and androgynous. No clothing obscured the matted sheen of its aluminum surface. The vehicle door closed automatically, and the bot stood for a moment, its head swiveling in a complete circle as it oriented itself.

Sault was reminded of an incident in Vancouver, a few years back. An AI was piloting an autonomous vehicle when a kid ran out from between parked cars. The bot's algorithm assessed the situation and pulled right, but the vehicle's algorithm figured differently, and it steered left. The upshot was that the kid was struck—not killed, fortunately—but it was later determined that the bot could have avoided her if it hadn't been opposed. There was a lawsuit and during the trial, it was proven that the car could also have avoided hitting her if it hadn't been opposed by the bot's actions. The matter of liability got very murky. In a controversial ruling, a judge decided that it was the car's primary function to drive safely. Therefore, the manufacturer should have built in a bot override. The ruling was highly criticized for falling exactly opposite the same situation involving human drivers.

The bot started across the street in his direction and somehow Sault knew that this was going to turn out to be Rainier Gilbert and that things were about to get awkward in the coffee shop. There wasn't time for Sault to exchange his ceramic mug for a paper to-go cup. Reluctantly, he abandoned his steaming brew and met the bot as it reached the top stair to the patio.

"Constable Sault," the bot said in a very human male voice, extending a hand. Sault wasn't surprised that it recognized him and knew his rank. His profile was on the Vic PD website. The bot looked more alien than human, but more than anything it resembled an emaciated fencer. It was silver and spindly, with an oval head and delicate three-fingered hands. The face was a simple wire mesh with two camera eyes visible just behind the wire grid. One was larger than the other, so Sault guessed it was a multi-spectrum system. There were no obvious ears, and Sault presumed that the microphones were also housed behind the mesh. Its mouth was represented by a neon line of blue light that danced when it spoke. Sault shouldn't have been surprised by any of this. The guy was a computer nerd.

Sault felt his face flush but took the proffered hand and shook it. The palm of the hand was textured rubber and it felt strange in his grip. "I guess you don't need a cup of coffee, so why don't we talk in the park," he suggested, nodding toward the playground across the street.

The bot was several inches taller than Sault. It glanced over his head with its camera eyes and, Sault guessed, read the "100% Human Service" sign, near the door.

"Your coffee's getting cold. Let's stay."

Sault shrugged, but inwardly he sighed. At least they were

out on the patio where the tables were further apart. They weren't likely to bother as many patrons, and maybe Wendy, the owner, wouldn't even notice. This wasn't going to take long, and Sault thought his odds of avoiding any kind of a scene were good, so long as Rainier didn't place an order.

Once they were settled, Rainier said, "Seems odd that you're looking into this though you're not a detective."

Sault was already slightly annoyed and instinctively met aggression with aggression. "Seems odd you don't show up in person to a meeting with a police officer." The robot cocked its head, as if trying to evaluate him in some way—a very human gesture which immediately made Sault regret his reflexive response.

"I'm quadriplegic. This is my surrogate."

Sault had only just guessed that and changed tack. "Of course. Sorry. Officially the case has been shelved. It's gone cold, so not a priority. I'm working it unofficially."

"Why?"

"Just trying to make it right." His stock reply since "obsessive compulsive curiosity" would probably not bring anyone onside.

"Helen said you had a picture."

Vivia flashed the picture of Lindsay George into the air between them. If Ranier had taken a look, it wasn't obvious but Vivia deleted the image from the air, so Sault assumed she knew from some sort of electronic exchange with the bot that it had been seen.

"This is the dead girl?"

Sault nodded and, out of habit, studied the robot face for telltale signals. There were none, of course.

"How'd it happen?"

"Car accident."

"If it was an accident, why are you investigating?"

"It seems...unlikely, to me."

"These days, car accidents, in general, are unlikely," Ranier acknowledged. "This is difficult to process."

His tone brought Sault to attention and his pulse quickened.

"You recognize her," he stated.

Ranier bobbed his silver head but was silent for so long that Sault wondered if he'd gone offline, but he waited him out. "Sorry…weird mix of emotions going on. It's sad and unexpected and yet, expected at the same time. Also, it's a bit scary—like my world just changed, and not for the better."

"I don't understand."

The bot's head swiveled three-sixty degrees as it scanned the immediate vicinity. Reflexively, Sault also glanced about. They were alone on the patio except for an elderly couple who looked like they might have just stepped out of a vintage British tea commercial and who were just settling in, at a far table. Settling in was a slow process because they weren't as nimble as they'd once been. The man had to brace himself against the woman as he slid into his seat, then he bounced a little while she inched the chair closer to the table for him. He spotted older-model hearing aids through the thin veil of white hair. They were of the generation which did not generally adopt the full replacement of their failing parts with artificial implants. Meanwhile, there was a growing trend among teens to sacrifice perfectly functional human parts for telescopic vision and super hearing. Sault had heard someone say that bionics would be the tattoo of the future. Sault thought it was another nail in the coffin of privacy and, possibly, humanity.

"I'm going to need you to turn off your AI," Ranier said, jarring Sault from his reverie.

He sighed inwardly at the unnecessary inconvenience but did not hesitate. It would mean that he'd have to make his own notes after the meeting, but that wasn't as onerous a task for him as it was to younger cops who'd grown up with AI's at their beck and call. "Vivia, take a break."

He, alone, heard her affirmative reply and a second later, the only visible feature on his watch, a glowing red dot went out. He lifted his arm to show Ranier Gilbert's surrogate.

"Thank you."

Sault nodded. It probably looked like he was saying "you're welcome" but, in fact, he was prompting Ranier to get on with it.

When Rainier spoke again, he leaned forward, and his voice was hushed. "She's famous. Was famous."

"Famous? How? Who was she?"

"You got a pen?"

That request caught Sault so completely off guard that he thought he'd misheard. "What?"

"A pen, a writing implement. I'm transmitting across the network to control this bot. I don't want to transmit this particular name for reasons that I will make clear, afterward."

This time, Sault allowed himself an audible sigh of exasperation. He looked around for something that would make legible markings on the napkin under his cup. He glanced again at the older couple thinking that maybe they still did crosswords on paper or something, but they both had modern watches. Even they were not *that* old. There was nothing in the immediate vicinity, so he got up and went inside to the cash register. Wendy was there, as usual and he asked her for a pen.

"Who's your friend?" she said pointedly while scrounging under the counter.

"He's a quadriplegic," Sault explained both embarrassed and annoyed at the entire situation.

"Here's one. Don't know if it has ink, but it's all I can find," she said, reaching across to hand him a black plastic stick and making it clear that she wasn't about to extend the search any farther—all business, no smile.

The pen wasn't really a serious writing implement. It was some sort of promotional toy quill; tapered at one end where Sault could see the broken stems of what used to be plastic feathers. The napkin was shredded where Sault scratched practice strokes until the ink started flowing and the implement produced legible marks. He handed it to surrogate-Rainier who began printing something in a very odd fashion—in a neat line but spread out leaving blanks spaces between each letter. Then, he made a second pass and filled in the blanks. All the while, the bot's head remained level, not looking at the paper.

Ranier explained, "I'm writing it like this so that the bot's hand movements are less likely to trigger any active transmission searches. I don't want to see the words, either. That would be transmitting the image. Also, I've started encrypting my responses, so you might notice a bit of lag now."

Sault took a quick look around. They were still alone except for the couple who were still chatting at the furthest table, and they were separated from everyone else in the café by a thick wall of glass. The next closest person was a child running across the field of plastic grass, in the park. "That certainly seems over the top."

The added delay was minimal, but Sault could tell it was there. "How about you judge me after I explain the situation," Ranier said before sliding the completed message across the glass table top to Sault.

On the paper appeared the words "Lindsay George." Then, further down the sheet, "LeftyBiscuits." Sault felt adrenaline surge through him. This was solid confirmation of her identity. A positive ID was much more than Sault could have hoped for from this meeting and it hadn't even cost him a cup of coffee. And, Ranier's paranoia seemed to promise that the conversation would reveal a lot more.

"Her name and handle. She is—was—a programmer. Master hacker from back east…Chicago, Detroit…somewhere like that, I think. Hard to say, anything personal about her can only be rumor."

That certainly fit better than the murder book assumptions.

"So, you wouldn't know where she lived? Where she worked?"

"No idea. I only know her by reputation. I'm not a hacker, but I do contract work for a bank and I work in the proximity of some White Hats. A few months back, a couple of them were talking, pretty excited. Later, one guy told me what she'd done that made her go from anonymous to famous, among hackers and the authorities."

Sault scowled and shook his head. "She wasn't known to police."

The bot leaned forward and casually lay an arm across the

table as if it needed the support for its upper body. Sault knew that it was only a gesture. There would be no weight on the table. In fact, he could see a thin space of air between its arm and the table top. "Higher authorities," it whispered, then straightened and the head spun full around, again. Sault almost laughed and wondered what kind of nutcase he might be dealing with. You didn't need a tinfoil hat if your head was made of tin. Regardless, Rainier Gilbert had correctly identified the victim, so Sault would listen and worry about extracting fact from fantasy later. "You won't find her in your databases. And, that's why she's famous. She completely removed her digital footprint from the internet."

With all the AI-protected databases out there, Sault was skeptical. "I thought that was impossible."

"Exactly. And yet, she erased herself from everywhere, in a matter of only a few hours."

"I can believe it's possible to erase yourself from social media…"

The bot shook its silvery head. "Much deeper than that. Her birth, financial records, social insurance number, every chat or message she ever sent…somehow, she got by the AI's and hacked it all. I guess she thought no one would notice, but she was known online and it only took a few days for other hackers to notice. Then, when no one could find any trace of her existence, and the extent of the purge was recognized—pandemonium."

"What about offline copies?"

"She couldn't reach those unless you connected to the network. But her algorithm was surprisingly thorough and fast. Somehow, it knew where to look. It lay in waiting, and the first time you plugged in, her information was deleted. In the end, the only copies that survived were printed copies. I heard that on the wall of every FBI office in America there's a physical copy of her image. Probably the same here, in Canada, at CSIS. Interpol, too, for that matter."

Sault leaned against the wicker back of his chair. "Holy crap," he whispered. "I never heard anything." He realized that he was working from an offline copy of the evidence made shortly after Lindsay George's death. He made a note to double-check the current Vic PD version of the murder book to see if the information was still there. If not, it meant that the algorithm was still active, even after her death. A second after that, he realized that Vivia was continually plugged into the network and yet still retained her copy of George's picture. The algorithm was as dormant as its creator.

"If you weren't a high-level hacker or working with high-level hackers, you had no way of knowing. Neither the authorities nor the hackers want this widely known."

"How did she do it?"

"Well, of course, that's the billion-dollar question. And there's a lot of skepticism and speculation out there, even still. But one possibility has everyone freaking out. Do you understand how AI's work?"

"As much as the next guy."

"So, not really, then." Sault took the jab well, chuckled to himself. He was confident that he knew more about AI's than Ranier knew about police work.

Ranier continued, "Have you ever heard of the MAIM?" The term was familiar, but Sault couldn't quite grasp the memory, so he gestured for Ranier to explain.

"MAIM stands for Master AI Module. It's a virus-like program integrated into the network—a military-grade, state-of-the-art AI, which oversees all other AI's. It's also a failsafe. Shut down the Master AI and every other AI ceases to function."

"I think I recall reading something about that. It's overseen by an anonymous consortium of UN scientists, or something."

Ranier nodded that he had that right. "The All-Country Coalition. So, the big implication with what Lindsay George managed to do was that maybe she'd hacked the MAIM."

Sault extrapolated, "Almost everything is operated by an AI. Halting all the AI's would cause a lot of problems. Billions of dollars in delays and mistakes, I suppose."

"Trillions, more likely. But beyond money, instantly,

millions of lives would be lost in hospitals and in traffic accidents, not to mention industrial sites. But that's still understating it, because the MAIM does a lot more than just stop and start AI's. Local AI's are basically just high-level interpreters and decision makers. They can interpret human orders and anticipate needs and they can decide how best to carry out their tasks. And, AI's don't hop from device to device, like most people think they do. The bulk of every AI exists online. They only extend tentacles of themselves into every mechanism they operate—like putting on a glove. That's why they can operate multiple devices simultaneously and that's also how your personal information remains safe no matter what device they occupy. But, every shell—from a toaster to a tank—must contain a detailed operation guide with recipes for whatever it produces or action it takes, otherwise the AI would have no idea how to make that shell work. It's done this way so that each AI doesn't have to store the ability to operate every machine in the world within itself and, conversely, so that each machine does not need to have room to store an entire AI. That would be inefficient and cumbersome. Not only could an individual AI not store the entire library of machine instructions but also, an entire cognizant-class AI could never fit inside a watch, for instance," Ranier said, waving toward Sault's wrist. "The world's smallest self-contained cognizant AI is still about the size and weight of a laptop."

"Ok. So, each machine stores its own operating instructions and has just enough memory to contain the virtual fingers of an AI."

"That's right. The operating instructions for individual machines are called Shell Modules and they're constantly revised and updated. Shell Modules are designed and tested by manufacturers then added to a highly secure, highly regulated database that is maintained and monitored by the MAIM. Shells automatically check with the MAIM to make sure that they are operating with the most recent updates. If not, they download the appropriate Shell Module from the MAIM's database. The MAIM makes sure that the transaction is secure and there are no glitches—so a toaster never tries to be a tank."

That last comment sparked a fear within Sault, "Could control of the MAIM give someone control of a tank…or a missile?"

"I don't think so. I'm not an expert in this, but as far as I know, military devices have several more layers of failsafe."

"But, control of the MAIM would give you control over *almost* every other device on the planet?"

Ranier bobbed his metal head. "Not many dumb devices survived the AI revolution. Ultimately, the MAIM controls practically everything short of cotton swabs and toenail clippers."

"Not to mention the cache of information," Sault added, thinking about the tracking and recording of personal information done by every smart device in his own home.

"Now, you're gleaning."

"What about AI's? Can the MAIM get information from them?"

"No. The MAIM does not control AI's at all. AI's had to be made almost completely autonomous to accommodate international privacy concerns. But if the MAIM shuts down, so does every other AI that's connected to the network."

"She'd have been famous and infamous at the same time," Sault surmised. He found himself avoiding saying Lindsay George's name out loud. The paranoia was contagious.

"Yes. It all depends upon your point of view." Ranier's bot leaned back until it was sitting straight in the chair; its arms hanging limply at its sides, almost touching the concrete. A pose only a robot would assume. "A world-wide hack of that magnitude could potentially cripple every economy and all communication. Millions would die, governments would topple. You can imagine, more people wanted her dead than alive. No surprise she was killed. More of a surprise that someone managed to find her."

"I just don't understand her motivation in revealing the hack."

"Well, not for money, that's for sure. She would have been

able to set up credit accounts, rack them up, then erase the debts whenever she wanted. My best guess—it was a boast. Obsession is the only path to that level of knowledge and skill. Most of the hackers I know feed off an ego-driven competitiveness. If such a person managed to pull off the ultimate hack of all time, it might be hard for them to keep it to themselves."

"Even knowing that you'd be on the run from the entire world?"

Ranier made his bot shrug. "You wouldn't believe the arrogance of some of the bastards I've crossed paths with. She'd done what no one else could. She probably thought she was smarter than everyone else—smart enough to stay a step ahead."

"Well, either she was wrong about that or she died in an unlikely accident."

"Better it was an accident and that her secret died with her," Ranier observed.

There was a long silence during which Sault tried to absorb all the ramifications of what he'd just heard. It was daunting, but he reminded himself that it was all just unsubstantiated rumor, at this point.

He turned his mind to more tangible things. "What kind of equipment does a high-level hacker like her need to do her job? Is there a special computer or watch that she would have had to have in her possession?" If she owned a house, then with butler bots and automatic bill payments, it could be years before anyone noticed it was empty, let alone presumed it abandoned. But if she rented, then maybe he could track her. No one had reported her missing, so she didn't have family or roommates, but he hoped that maybe, by now, a landlord might be selling her stuff in lieu of rent. It wasn't a legal practice, but it was a common one. If he could find something unique for sale online, then maybe he could work his way back to where she'd called home.

Ranier thought about that for several seconds before he said, "Ok, well, I don't operate at anything near that level, so again I'm not an expert, but as I understand it, the one thing she'd have had is a first-class cloaking device. That's what they call a set of specialized communications computers whose sole purpose is to obscure the location. It's not something most people have at home because it needs special wiring and cooling. Typically, that's a set of servers at least the size of a bar fridge."

"Anything smaller and more likely to be at home?"

"Maybe a set of ghost chips."

Sault prompted by raising his eyebrows.

"They're processors hardwired for infiltrating and decrypting. Like a set of lockpicks. Actually, more like a library of lockpicks."

"And they would be inside her computer?"

"No. They are super expensive and very short-lived. Fast is never fast enough, so they're always massively overclocked and are prone to burning out. But beyond that, encryption and protection strategies change so fast that the chips themselves have to be rewritten or replaced regularly. Anyway, they are kept in an external housing that makes them easier to swap out."

"What would this look like, physically?"

"The chips themselves are large—about an inch and a half square, and there'd be two of them. They're illegal to own, so, if she took them out in public, she would have to have an enclosure to hide them. They run hot and need good ventilation, so whatever housing she used it would probably have a lot of air holes. And, to maintain speed, they are not connected through standard ports on the computer. There would be a thin set of wires with a connector coming out of the computer, somewhere. It wouldn't look factory built."

After hearing all of this, Sault thought it most likely that her computer would be the most saleable item and Rainier gave him a tutorial on what specs to look for in a master hacker's computer. Sault was forced to use the decrepit pen which produced barely legible chicken scratches and tore the napkin to ribbons. In the end, it was beyond folding, so he carefully stuffed the feathery ball into the breast pocket of his shirt.

As Ranier had twice mentioned, he was no expert in elite hacking, so Sault asked him for a reference to one of the hackers he worked with. Ranier admitted that he wasn't close enough to any of them to make introductions but did give Sault the online handle of one person: HallelujahHaptism1011. Sault would have to make contact and introduce himself and hope for the best.

They continued to talk for another ten minutes, but Sault had already got a lot more than he could have hoped for and wasn't surprised that nothing significant came of the rest of the meeting. As it stood to leave, he once again shook the three-fingered hand of Rainier's surrogate. Then he regarded his coffee, realized that it was stone cold and decided to leave, as well.

"I'm just going to grab a muffin, before I go," said Rainier.

The bot opened the door to the café and through the glass Sault caught a wicked glance from Wendy. The interview might not have cost him a cup of coffee, but it had probably cost him his favorite coffee shop.

William M. Dean

CHAPTER 19

Sault had been elated, after talking with Ranier Gilbert. But by the time he reached the Buick, elation gave way to worry. And by the time he turned the key, he had started to truly appreciate the implications of this dramatic turn in his little investigation, and worry transformed into paranoia.

The radio spontaneously burst to life, and a rush of terror ripped through him; a jolt of electricity followed by a full-body flush of heat. A second later, he was shivering as the air conditioning blew across his moistened skin. He reduced the radio volume and recognized Cher belting out another ballad over the purring and burbling of the old engine. It wasn't really her, of course. Her flesh was long decayed, but her hologram still drew crowds. For the hundredth time, he ran through the changes he'd made to the electrical system and wondered what could be causing the sporadic malfunctions. For the hundredth time, he came up empty. Then, in a flash of paranoia, his mind leapt to Lindsay George's crash and back, and he was suddenly happy that the Grand National was a relatively dumb machine that could not be remotely controlled. He shuddered as if he could physically shake off the irrational feeling that he was being watched. Then, when that failed, he shut off the radio and drove away toward anywhere else.

He drove aimlessly, cruising up Cloverdale, over to Hillside then down toward the stately old mansions lining the waterfront, in Oak Bay. There were no thoughts as he found himself dealing with the emotional impact of the conversation that had upset both the direction of his investigation and the illusion of stability in his world. He considered going home to the garage to flash up the files and test the fit of the puzzle around these new pieces, but he didn't feel comfortable taking this home until he had wrapped his brain around all of the implications. If it all turned out to be true, then what he now knew might be dangerous.

He was parked, and the engine was off before his conscious mind recognized where he had taken himself. Willows Beach was a long stretch of sundrenched sand on the adjacent shore of the same sheltered bay as the Oak Bay Yacht Club. University and College students came here to bronze their youthful bodies and size each other up over reading tablets, mostly used as props. And young moms brought their toddlers to dig holes, splash in the gentle surf, and learn not to eat sand. It wasn't until this moment that Sault realized that he didn't want to be alone. He wanted to stand where it might be safest, amid a thousand keen-eyed witnesses. He wanted to hear the gentle wash of surf, the unburdened laughter of innocent and ignorant children who could never imagine the bubble wrap being torn off their world.

This was one of the city's most popular beaches and he was lucky to find parking, barely able to keep the tail end out of the traffic corridor by taking up two spaces. Moms and kids evil-eyed him as they cruised by looking for an empty space.

For as long as he could recall, the building which sat in the corner of the parking lot at one end of the Willow's Beach had been run and maintained by volunteers from the Kiwanis Club of Victoria. When he was a child, it had been a tea room. By the time he was twenty, it had converted to serving burgers and fries. Now it was a pub, The Oaken Barrel. From a financial point of view, it made complete sense. However, Sault wondered how a child-oriented non-profit justified pimping alcohol and cannabis.

Wakeless

He pulled his shades from the glove box then stretched behind to grab his Victoria HarbourCats ballcap off the back seat and stepped out of the air-conditioning and into the sweltering heat.

Hands in pockets, he set a slow pace on the cement sidewalk that ran along the beach, a few feet above the sand. He was in no hurry and deep inside his own mind, seeing only the faded leather of his boat shoes despite the postcard sky and sea and the bright collage of bikinis, only ten feet to his right.

Eventually, he stopped to watch an ungainly toddler accidentally dump a small pail of water on himself and thought about when Matthew had been that young. In those days, he and Maya spent days off at parks and beaches with the kids. Being a parent had seemed the only mission that counted, and he was all in. Life was full, and the bonds between all of them had seemed unbreakable. But parenting turned out to be a long drawn out process of letting go and by age eight the kids were shuttling themselves all over the town without needing or wanting their parents around. Initially Maya was despondent and at a loss. He recognized now that she had tried, for a time, to find something they could do together; something that would help them reconnect after ten years of focusing on children. But Sault was more sensitive to abandonment—whether the result of his mother's death or his father's neglect or both, he could not say—and had reacted very quickly to fill the gap left by children who no longer needed him full-time. By the time Maya was trying to draw him in, he was already engrossed in one of the puzzles that would make him infamous to Department brass. Soon after that, Maya stumbled onto a new mission that, unlike her family, needed her more and more. Now she was busier than ever. And now, somehow, even though he was still busy, the feeling of abandonment had come back for him, like a grim spirit.

There was a man at a machine under a large umbrella grinding the juice out of fresh fruit and selling iced drinks. Nearby, was an old upright piano looking both improbable and incongruous. It was festively decorated with a garish coat of paint, stickers and plastic gems; one of a hundred that the city distributed and maintained over the summer months as part of their tourism campaign. A pudgy young man with a translucent goatee was plunking out a decent rendition of Billy Joel's Piano Man, trying to impress a curvy brunette who was dressed in what appeared to be a neon shoestring and who looked way out of his tax bracket, let alone his league. The scene felt immediate, vibrant and alive, and Sault decided that sitting on the bench in the shade of the umbrella sipping ice cold pineapple-guava while listening to the mating call of a Canadian male was exactly where he needed to be, at that moment.

After the song ended, Sault tracked the unlikely young couple back to their beach blanket and watched them talk for a few minutes, then begin to make out. She was practically nude, and the taut material of his swimwear did little to obscure his desire, so it was pretty much live pornography. Sault remembered the early years of with Maya and how simple things were, at the beginning. The two lovebirds before him had no idea what they were getting in to. As with most things, ignorance was the only way anyone ever got involved.

He rose and began the trek back to toward his car, pleased to discover that he had been right in coming here. He felt renewed; his mind clear. He was reset. No amount of fear and anxiety could possibly survive such a display of bliss and ignorance.

He began to replay his conversation with Rainier Gilbert and compare that with the case notes. It certainly seemed plausible that Lindsay George had made herself a target and Jared Kowalczyk had simply been collateral damage. But all this new information had to be corroborated and Sault began to wonder how he might do that without drawing more attention than he could handle. Beyond another departmental reprimand, if it all were true then there was the very real possibility that the right question to the wrong person could paint him as the next target.

There was no one he could talk to about it. Even if he were still on active duty—even if he were a bona fide Detective—

something potentially this large would fall outside his purview. Adhering to the Vic PD procedural handbook, he would be obligated to report his suspicions to his immediate superior who would report to hers and so on up the chain until it reached the Canadian Security Intelligence Service—CSIS— who would then investigate the claims and either continue on in secret, or, if the claims held no threat to national security, bump the whole thing back down the chain until it came to rest at the appropriate level. But he could see no way of kicking off that process without revealing what he'd been up to and landing himself in hot water.

By the time he reached the Buick he'd decided that it was a good thing that he wasn't bound to the handbook because he still had too many nagging questions to pass this off. Hearsay evidence from the programmer aside, this was still just a straightforward traffic investigation with a hundred loose ends to pursue. He had yet to satisfy himself that it was even relevantly connected to Jared Kowalczyk's death, let alone a homicide on its own. He would stick to what he knew was true and continue to follow the questions to their answers and not strike out in a random direction, trying to prove an unsubstantiated rumor. And the gateway question, still unanswered, was how Lindsay George's vehicle had ended up in the ditch.

Given Ranier's paranoia and the security measures he took, Sault was confident that their conversation had been entirely private. So, no one had any reason to believe that he might have stumbled on to anything world-shaking—including himself. He was now certain that nothing dangerous could come of this unless evidence began to accumulate, and the case started climbing the ladder toward CSIS. Maybe then, some alarm might be triggered, and some desperate action taken, but not before.

He was still safely operating under everyone's radar.

Someone had left a nasty note about his parking job. It was a rare event, mostly because the Buick was only minimally modernized and unable to accept electronic notes. Few people still carried paper and pen. This one had been written in green crayon on the back of a drug store receipt and left tucked under the windshield wiper.

He read, "Hey, Asswipe…" then crumpled the note into a ball. He had his hand on the door handle when Vivia informed him that Singh had finally accepted his request for a meetup and was available for a drink, later that afternoon. This left Sault with several free hours and not much to fill the gap. It was well past noon and a cold beer and burger sounded like a good start, so he let the door handle slide from his grasp.

The interior of The Oaken Barrel was decorated to resemble a traditional British pub, with dark-stained wainscoting, a long wooden bar with mugs hanging overhead and a stone fireplace. None of those materials were real, of course, but they were almost as convincing as Disneyland. The illusion faltered a bit in the dining area. The floor was a grey-brown vinyl and the tables were, disappointingly, plastic with a wood-like veneer. His burger was served on a paper plate and the beer came in a plastic cup. Entirely practical, especially for the beach crowd.

He was hungry and thirsty, and while the food wasn't anything special, the beer was cold, the burger was warm and salty, and it all hit the spot.

While he ate, he watched an Island Buzz newsfeed crew set up a 360-degree camera on the beach for some sort of report. He reflected on the effect that 360 filming had had on news broadcasts. Having the inside scoop on much of the local news, Sault had learned early that news casts were less about information than they were about entertainment. 3D video had certainly accentuated that fact. A typical newsfeed now included a lot of stories with very little content but spectacular scenery. Sault saw an Island Buzz drone float past and fly on down the beach and he knew that this was going to be one such story. For some reason, newsfeeds still adhered to the tradition of having a live reporter on the scene, but viewers typically slid and pivoted everywhere else in the scene. He recalled a recent interview with an economist that, irrelevantly, took place on the viewing car of a train clacking its way through the Rocky Mountains. Modern news had become video wallpaper with a particularly mundane soundtrack.

The reporter stepped into view. He didn't recognize her, so she must be new…she certainly wasn't old. She looked to be in her early twenties; a perky-boobed bleached blond with shoulder-length hair, and she was wearing a relatively modest bikini and high heels. Sault guessed it was a weather report and further speculated that, in this case, the reporter might actually steal a little attention from the backdrop.

The news crew entered the pub just as Sault was wiping the last of the grease from his fingertips. He stood to leave, checking to make sure that he had his cap and sun glasses. When he looked up, the reporter was standing in front of him, blocking a straight path to the doorway. She had wrapped a colorful sarong around her hips but still turned every male head in the place.

He smiled back and started to move around her but then she extended a hand. "Dora Padovano, Island Buzz."

He blinked, then shook her hand. "I think you've got me confused with someone else."

"You're Constable Second Class, Joseph Sault, right?"

Sault was stunned that she knew who he was, then he remembered all the interview requests that Vivia had forwarded to the Public Relations Department since his tangle with Harry Potter. Victoria was still a small enough city that chance encounters like this were not improbable. Sault had stumbled across BOLO subjects in exactly the same way. He just happened to be here, and she just happened to be very observant and, possibly, good at her job.

She immediately sat at the table he had intended to abandon. The action seemed to imply that he should join her, and given the time he had yet to waste, he could see no reason not to. Seeing her close up, she was not as young as he'd first guessed; he reassessed her to be at least thirty, but she was every bit the beauty she appeared from a distance. Her facial features were delicate, symmetrical and perfectly proportioned, and he thought it a fair assumption that she'd had work done. The cute and vacant expression she'd used during the report was gone, replaced by a pleasant but serious smile. She smelled like flowers and he noticed that she was wearing a glitter-glossy pink lipstick more suited to a schoolgirl. He liked it.

"What can I do for you, Miss…Dora, was it?"

"Dora Padovano," she reminded him. "I've been trying to reach you for weeks."

Sault acted like it was a surprise. He was not immune to her charms, so a part of him wanted to talk to her, but police and reporters could only be cautious partners as they worked on opposite sides of the information fence. An aggressive reporter looking to make a name for herself always wanted a sensational story, but it was largely a cop's job to see that things never escalated to sensational proportions, and the details that generated revenue for a newsfeed were rarely the ones that Vic PD was proudest of. Sault shut himself down. He saw her read it from his body language and he could almost see her switching gears.

The silence protracted as she searched for a new approach. Sault glanced at the doorway making it clear he had places to be, though he didn't.

"You're a troublemaker," she declared as if she'd just sized him up and got his number. So, she'd made a call, Sault thought, unimpressed. "And, you're suspended but still making inquiries into the Jared Kowalczyk thing." That got his attention, but he feigned disinterest. "Well, I've bumped into it from another angle and I thought you might be interested."

"I didn't realize that weather reporting covered so much territory," he quipped, admitting nothing.

She glanced toward the beach, then shrugged. "A story's a story."

"Is it really, though?" It was just banter establishing that they may not be enemies, but they definitely weren't friends. Fostering trust between a cop and a reporter was as delicate an operation as two porcupines making love.

"Before this, I was a lead journalist at Toronto Today, for

four years. I know how to flush out a story."

"What's a big-city ace doing in a backwoods berg like this?"

She laughed at the antiquated expressions. "It was a lifestyle choice…mostly. I can be a troublemaker, too, when I have to be. Toronto's the big-time. It's dog-eat-dog and they'll maul you for scraps, there."

"Sounds like the perfect place for a troublemaker."

"Yeah, well, I may have overreached. In the fight for the title, I got eliminated." Sault felt it was a real admission, something she hadn't yet fully come to terms with. In spite of himself, even though he knew that it was a calculated revelation, he liked her better for it. He settled more comfortably into the chair. "Okay, maybe I can relate."

She took it as the positive sign that he meant it to be. "So, Jared Kowalczyk…" She paused to consider her next words or perhaps hoping that he might jump in to fill the gap. He waited her out. "I have it on good authority that you're actively working the case."

"I'm not a detective and it's not my case. It's being actively worked on by Robbery/Homicide." In truth, it was probably better for him if she took what she thought she knew directly to Falkov and Caverly, the detectives working the Kowalczyk case. He could always download a murder book update to see her contribution.

She nodded as if accepting his answer, though it was obvious she didn't. "Ok. Let's just say this then, I stumbled into it while working on something that seemed completely unrelated. Is that of any interest to you?"

"It's better if you contact the officers working the case." Sault knew she'd have already tried that. He didn't have any illusions of grandeur. If she was talking to him, it was only out of a lack of options. Being new to town, she probably hadn't had a chance to establish the trust necessary to trade information with any of the detectives. She was seasoned, he could tell, so it wouldn't take her long to build relationships within the department. Three months from now, she probably wouldn't be returning his calls. But, for now, he was all she had.

She shook her head. "This is sensitive. If it's true—and, obviously, I think that it probably is—it's going to open a high-profile can of worms. So, I'm doing my due diligence; checking it out to see if it fits the rest of the scenario before officially passing it on to further the investigation."

"And before posting anything unsubstantiated, which might prove libelous," Sault added. This was opportunism, not altruism. She smiled.

"Ok. So, what do you have?" he asked.

The smile widened, and she returned a sly look. "You know that's not how this works, Officer Sault. Tell you what, I'll give you my card and you get a hold of me when you're more interested." In the old days, she would have slipped a cardboard rectangle into his hand, right about then, but any phrase offering a business card had evolved into an AI command. By the time she'd finished the sentence, her AI had transmitted her credentials across the few inches between them and Vivia had already grabbed and stored the information.

He took visceral pleasure in watching her walk back to join her crewmates at a larger table. She'd read him right—kept it brief, hadn't pushed. She hadn't irritated him, and so, he hadn't slammed the door shut on talking to her in the future. Smart girl.

She knew something, and in the days ahead, if he decided it might be something he needed to know, he might give her a call. In the meantime, he'd ask around about her.

He still had hours to kill but spent thirty minutes of it standing in the blistering heat, hood up, poking at various parts with an old screwdriver, not because he knew what he was looking for, but because standing under the hood tapping miscellaneous engine components had worked in the past. He might be a world-class Red Cuber, but he had to confess that internal combustion had him stumped.

Trick or satanic rite, his ritual worked again, and he drove off. Three blocks later, the heater came on, full blast, and refused to shut off forcing him to roll down all the windows.

Hillside Mall had once been home to the city's biggest and most popular retail outlets. But that was decades past. Shopping had migrated to the Internet. The upper floors of the mall were now apartments. The rest had largely been gutted and converted to a blended-reality park where "Virtual, Augmented and Holographic Realities came together to create out-of-this-world entertainment experiences"—or so the ads claimed. Sault had never been, but his kids told him that it was fantastic and added that it was not for him. He didn't argue the point. Sault was happy enough with total immersion movies in Total-Vision. He didn't want to have to actively participate in his entertainment unless he was also getting something accomplished; like restoring a car or solving a case.

The far corner of the mall was still home to some strange little family-owned shops like House 'N Hardware, the Nickel & Dime Shop and Fancy Mandy's Donut Factory. He didn't need any of the items he might find there, but he was in the area and had nothing better to do, so he pulled in and as he did so, the heater mercifully shut off.

Parking was easy to find. The lot was largely empty, except for a portion that was cordoned off and decorated up to resemble some sort of post-apocalyptic ruin, obviously part of the mixed-reality park. Sault could see a pack of teens scrambling over and around wrecked cars and the rubble of buildings. They each carried some sort of rifle that made a visible flash but no sound, every time they were fired. He imagined what it might be like inside their helmets with visors mapping a realistic veneer over solid props and he could understand how young people got so caught up in such total-immersion scenarios. He thought it all might be little too violent to be healthy, but then, he'd watched movies that were worse. Inwardly, he shrugged it off and chided himself for being such a judgmental old fart. But as he passed closer, he witnessed a young man press a rifle to a woman's temple and shoot her, gangland execution-style. Her body slumped to the ground, then there was cheering followed by backslaps and high-fives all around from the executioner's compadres. Even from outside the helmets, it seemed disturbingly real. No use fighting it. He *was* a judgmental old fart.

Once inside, he headed for the Nickel & Dime Shop. Of course, it didn't sell anything for nickels and dimes; there were no such things, anymore. It had strange and clever items in the five- to ten-dollar range. He thought he might pick up something for the kids. It was all crap, of course. Strange and useless labor-saving devices and novelty items abandoned in warehouses back in Oh-thirty, during a shockingly rapid recession that had come to be referred to as a "monetary adjustment."

An elemental assumption in factory-based manufacture is that machines are better than people. For centuries, the humans within the machine were an unavoidable compromise and every machine that replaced a human was an upgrade. The upgrading process accelerated, exponentially, once AI made robots more intelligent, diligent and versatile than humans.

Supply surged and warehouses were quickly stuffed. But demand plummeted because so many incomes had vanished. Sales of clever but useless gadgets, doo-dads and gizmos were the first and hardest hit, soon followed by big-ticket items like houses and cars. The term 'luxury item" got downgraded to include toys and confections but before it came to be applied to rice and potatoes, governments responded with massive adjustments to their economic structure that ensured that everyone had a basic living wage. It was an intense time of massive upheaval, worldwide. And, it was a shot across the bow for the world economy. It was now commonly assumed that money was on its way out, but no one yet knew how that might work, though the starting point had to be that the rich were to remain rich—that seemed to be the only group unaffected, after the first adjustment. Sault's taxes had gone up and his wage had been frozen since then. Sault predicted that a second adjustment would generate even more chaos and just hoped it didn't happen in his lifetime. He and Maya had sacrificed for years to come up with the down payment on the house and he was most afraid that the value of his largest asset might take the next hit.

As he entered the shop, he reminded himself that he really didn't need anything and that he was merely here to waste time before his meeting with Darsh Singh. Even so, an hour later, he left with a hefty bag that cost him fifty dollars. He felt a bit nervous about the purchases but was reasonably confident that even crap could be amusing, if it was new.

He was taking the long route to waste time, but still headed in the general direction of Redd's Pub when Darsh called.

"Sorry, I have to cancel. Just got nine-coded."

Ten-code was Vic PD-speak for a call to the ninth or tenth floor, where all the upper brass offices were. Sault couldn't imagine what Darsh Singh might have done to deserve that, but it was generally bad news. The only thing worse would have been a ten-code; a call to the Chief's office. In any case, no officer who valued his career ever ignored a call to the upper floors, even on a weekend.

"Jeez. Good luck, buddy. Let me know how that goes." He wasn't feeling particularly chummy with Singh at that moment, but this went beyond petty squabbles.

Singh said, "Will do," though they both knew that he probably wouldn't. They agreed to reschedule and signed off.

Sault gave up and went home, after that.

William M. Dean

CHAPTER 20

He didn't know whether to expect the kids at home or not. School was nothing like when he was a student. These days, the entire city was the classroom and the entire week was part of the schedule. Lectures and labs and other events were spread all over the place while the kids were actively tracked over public transport, between venues. The length of the school day fluctuated according to the schedule and caregivers had to go online to know where and when to expect their children, on any given day.

He parked the car in the garage and came in through the side entrance, which opened into the dining room. Maya was in the kitchen stirring a large mug of something hot; probably tea, he thought. He was surprised to see her there and said so.

She smiled, but it was an expression of resignation, not amusement. She was shaking her head at the same time and he immediately understood that, once again, he had forgotten something important.

"If this is about Matthew, he was gone before I could talk to him. I'll see him tonight."

"I know that. We were all gone before you got up. Tonight is the Cavallon Benefit dinner and silent auction I've been organizing for the last month."

Sault was confused. "Ok. I remember the auction now, but

why are you organizing the dinner part? Is this for Cavallon House?"

She pulled a pair of chopsticks from a drawer, then scooped a bundle of noodles from the mug. She held them above the cup letting the steam roll away. "I thought I told you." But she could see from his eyes that she hadn't. "Sorry. It's a busy time. Kathy's leaving and…" He had no idea who Kathy might be and tried to relay this by making his expression even blanker. There was an awkward moment of silence and then she laughed. He wasn't certain what sparked her laughter but, suddenly, he could see humor in the situation, and in her and himself, and the general lack of communication within the same house. It was funny and sad at the same time. She chose to laugh, and he chose to join her.

She gulped some noodles then scooped some more and explained while they cooled. "Ok. It's not generally known, but Kathy Scheers is quitting." Sault remembered her now. She was Sidney Cavallon's personal assistant and almost as familiar a figure as Sid himself because everywhere he went, she was in close proximity.

"What, is she pregnant?" It was a joke. Kathy Scheers was in her fifties and, beyond that, she was a shark-like personality who seemed anything but the motherly type.

Maya chuckled. "Her husband got a huge grant."

Sault reached for a memory, "He's a scientist—Astronomer—or something, isn't he?"

"Close. Anthropology Professor. Teaches at the university. Anyway, unexpectedly he got some big-time grant that he couldn't say no to, and they're leaving the country. Off to the jungle to study some isolated tribe."

"And just like that she sacrifices her career for his? Wow. That's what I call a dedicated wife."

Maya shrugged. "Sometimes, love sucks." Then, before her small joke could sprout tendrils of sadness, she continued, "They've been together forever, but just exchanged vows and made it official, a couple of months ago. So, technically they're newlyweds."

"That's got to make you feel better about *our* honeymoon."

When they'd married, he was still new to the police department and hadn't the seniority to get much time off. They were wed on Saturday, honeymooned in a shabby bed and breakfast in the island tourist town of Chemainus on the Sunday, and he was back at work the next morning. Sault had always promised her a proper honeymoon touring Italy and Spain, but the timing and money had yet to come together. Recently, Sault had begun to worry that when it did, neither of them would welcome the time together.

Maya giggled in a way that warmed his heart and reminded him of life before it all got complicated. "Anyway, she'll announce this tonight, or Sid will, but really, she's been mostly away dealing with the move for the better part of the month. In the short term, Sid asked me to take on some of her duties. Thus, I've pretty much dropped everything else and spent the last three weeks coordinating this event, including the silent auction which *is* to raise money for The House." She was referring to the women's transition house.

He grabbed a beer more to be able to linger than because he needed refreshment. "Sorry. I didn't realize. So, the auction's for your organization, but what's the dinner about?"

"Well, the big event will be Sid announcing that he's throwing his hat into the ring, for Mayor."

"You're kidding! What are his chances?"

"Olcott's got himself mired in the bridge fiasco so he's limping. Really, the only other competition might be Montgomery Hoad."

Hoad was a renowned criminal lawyer who was now semi-retired and hosted a popular podcast on legislation and modern law. It was recommended listening for Vic PD officers, but Sault found it too dry for his taste. "That's pretty stiff competition."

"Sidney doesn't seem worried."

"Seems a bit late, and sudden."

"It's been in the works for a while. He submitted the paperwork a month ago, but tonight he makes it public."

"But with Kathy gone, who's going to help him with the campaign?"

"Oh. That wouldn't be part of her job, anyway. That'll be some high-rolling volunteers—someone like Reg Hanover, or maybe Maddie Lance." Sault recognized both: Next to Sidney Cavallon, Hanover was the city's largest real estate developer and Lance was a VR game producer with major connections in New Hollywood. "Kathy does things like manage his schedule, make travel arrangements, book venues and watch over the maintenance of his personal properties; the boats, cars and houses, etcetera."

He detected something hidden in her tone. "Sounds like you know a lot about Kathy Scheers' job," he prodded.

She smiled. "Well done, Mr. Holmes. I was going to tell you, but we've both been busy and…" Her voice almost fell into somber tones, but she recovered quickly. "Anyway, he wants me to try filling in, just until he can find a replacement."

"Is that something you want to do? What about the shelter?"

"Transition house," she corrected. "It's temporary. My right hand, Peggy, can run things for a while. And, Sid promised to put more money into Cavallon House to raise its profile during the campaign. The extra funds should help. Peg can bring in some outside help, if she needs it. And if it goes off the rails, I won't be hard to reach."

"Oh yeah. I guess you won't be at the House."

"Nope. I'll be taking Kathy's office, over at the convention center."

Sault knew she was talking about Swan Lake Pavilion, the controversial high-rise hotel and convention center that Cavallon had managed to push through with help from Reg Hanover and council friends. It stood on the grounds of the old Saanich municipal hall and police station—a luxury hotel towering ten full floors above the next tallest building in the area and wrapped around a massive glass auditorium and convention dome. The penthouse suites had southern views of the city center with a backdrop of the shimmering Salish Sea and Olympic Mountains of Washington State, beyond. The rear of the hotel overlooked its own immaculately manicured flower garden which extended to the edge of the boarded walkways and marshy woods of the Swan Lake nature reserve.

For "the greater good," the unassuming neighborhoods that ran along the opposite shores of Swan Lake were forced to sacrifice their view of the Cascade Mountains for a silhouette of the hulking concrete edifice.

Having set a new precedent, the average height of new construction around the lake began to rise and the primary building material in the area shifted from wood to concrete. The "New Pavilion" district became the direction of expansion, and the activity center of the city shifted slightly north, away from the sea.

None of this sat well with voters and the previous Mayor lost his position over it. But it was a major milestone for Sidney Cavallon who had somehow shifted the center of the city a little in his favor. In the years that followed, he managed to parlay that slight advantage into an empire. He now sat on all the major decision-making boards, championed all the right causes and supported so many of the local sports clubs that his influence was felt everywhere in the city.

Sault remembered the day Sidney Cavallon had called Maya to personally answer her written request and to tell her that he would help get her transition house project off the ground. It was like throwing a quarter into a well and getting a long-distance call from God. Neither of them could really believe it until a week later, when Maya stood shaking his hand for the newsfeeds.

"I'll be on contract and billing for my time. I trade the transition house stipend for a full-time wage," Maya added, proudly.

Sault 's profession made him habitually cynical and sensitive to small discrepancies, so he immediately wondered how it was that a semi-volunteer administrator at a half-way house was the natural choice as personal assistant to a high-roller like Cavallon. As well, he wondered how it would affect the day-to-day running of the household, but he didn't pursue it. She was happy and they were talking. The last thing he wanted was to inject a negative note. Instead he said, "This sounds like a great opportunity. I'm happy for you. You deserve it."

She looked at him then in a way he understood meant that she was double-checking the sincerity of his words. He hated when she did that. It highlighted the tear in the fabric of their trust. He did his best to ignore that feeling. Her expression softened which he took to mean that she'd accepted his encouragement for what it was.

"You can come, if you want," she said, nonchalantly, slurping noodles into her mouth.

It was exactly the opposite of anything he might ever want to do.

"I'd like that," he said.

Sault dug his best suit out of the closet and in the vest pocket he found a customized paper napkin from the last event he'd attended; a wedding, four years ago. It was burgundy and had "Vick & Nick, Forever" written on it in silver script. There was also a graphic of interlinked wedding bands and a small cloud of butterflies. That marriage hadn't lasted eighteen months, and the two childhood friends were now bitter enemies. Sault hadn't been that close to either of them, but he found it depressing, just the same. He stuffed it back into the pocket, intending to toss it into the recycler unit on his way through the kitchen.

Sault was surprised when Maya told her AI to drive the car to the Empress Hotel. He'd assumed that Cavallon would host his own event in his own convention centre. But Maya explained that for all of its architectural and technological charms, his Swan Lake Pavilion was not equal in grandeur to the historic majesty of the old Empress and Sid wanted this event to have the maximum possible impact and attract the maximum amount of media exposure.

Sault didn't care. What he gleaned from her explanation was that she was very comfortable calling him Sid.

The car dropped them at the main entrance to the stately,

ivy-covered, stone structure and Sault came around intending to help Maya out of the car. But a uniformed doorman was already there and holding her hand. Sault couldn't help but admire her, sheathed in a glittery silver dress with a conservative but sexy slit up one calf. She wore the first diamond necklace he had ever given her. The chain was silver, and the stone was small, but she made it shine. She was a sweet swirl of sexy and sophistication that made him feel proud and a bit insecure at the same time. He recalled fussing over his choice of tie and now realized that no one was likely to notice it, or him, next to her.

Reporters lined the entrance talking to hovering drones and watches, posting live reports that network AI's would pick over to form their news and gossip feeds. He spotted Dora Padovano and avoided eye contact fearing that she might decide to interview him, though he couldn't imagine why.

There were a couple of young uniforms stationed either side of the grand entrance. Sault didn't recognize them and assumed they were from one of the neighboring detachments: Saanich, Oak Bay or Esquimalt being the most likely. He was tempted to acknowledge them with a casual salute but knew that if they were doing their job the atypical behavior would warrant delay and questions so, instead, he passed by without making eye contact.

The hotel had first opened in 1908, a jewel in the crown of the Canadian Pacific Railway which had unified the country in 1885. The building had since undergone a number of extensive overhauls designed to maintain its history while upgrading its functionality. The last one, though, had been an admission of defeat. The original interior had finally grown too damaged and outdated and stood in the way of any practical redesign. From his childhood, Sault recalled it as a somewhat haphazard blend of several classic European architectures which might have seemed at odds but for the sheer scope and drama of its proportions; a random spattering of disparate styles insulated from one another by the immensity of the interior space. It reeked of ostentation, stuffiness, hubris, propriety, entitlement, exclusivity, money—royalty—and even just walking through had always made him feel guilty and nervous, as if his lack of refinement was obvious and security had been alerted.

When he was in his twenties, they had shuttered the Grand Old Lady and gutted her of her massive interior beams, ornately carved moldings and granite tiles. Then they blasted the walls to the ground and hauled them away, leaving only the iconic front facade. Hewn from blocks of stone and brick, adorned with ornate iron railings, copper dome-topped turrets, and oriel windows it alone remained facing the inner harbor, braced by giant I-beams and concrete blocks while a muted copy three times the size slowly rose behind, dwarfing it, then attaching it, like a mask. It was truly spectacular, but to Sault, it had lost its regal grandeur.

Still, as he entered, the feeling of being too obviously out of place and the old nervousness returned.

Cavallon had reserved the conservatory for mingling and entertainment and the main ballroom for a more exclusive afterparty. The conservatory was at the far end of the hotel and a white-gloved attendant escorted them and three other elegantly dressed couples up the elevator and across lush carpets to join the festivities. Beneath a canopy of copper and glass, among exotic plants and water features, party guests mingled while waiters weaved about offering sea food and sushi appetizers and champagne and delivering mixed drink orders from the open bar. Dotted throughout the venue was the widest variety of entertainment Sault had ever seen in one place. There was a wandering magician doing close-up magic. A jazz quartet playing softly near the main entrance to the garden, while at the opposite end, under the broad leaves of a Jurassic-looking palm a pianist played something muted but vaguely classical. In the massive venue the music echoed but did not clash. A young woman conjured whimsical forms from colored smoke trapped within a soapy film stretched across wire frames. Another gyrated seductively while glowing hoops of various sizes whirled across her body, like auroras. Sketch artists wandered, rendering in pastel or colored pencil or charcoal, anyone willing to pose. On the far side of a pond was an intricate sculpture of living bodies which appeared made of stone, and which surprised a lot of guests by interacting, from time to time, in a complicated choreography of gestures and poses.

The conservatory featured a large and ornate mechanical clock made of polished and spinning brass elements. Directly beneath, once each minute, a tall shell dressed in a white tuxedo with black bow tie and a permanently smiling face that looked like the mask it was, printed the time in black felt on a small pad of paper. It spent the remainder of each minute holding the unnaturally perfect rendering for display, in both hands, as if it were a message from God. The next minute, it ripped the top sheet from the pad and crafted an update in a different font. Old notes gathered at his feet, like autumn leaves. Sault understood the intended absurdity of it but found it unsettling. He guessed that meant it was art.

It seemed like he had fallen into a surreal carnival midway where the animated chortle of pipe music had been replaced by the sonorous harmony of reeds and strings. Instead of buttered popcorn, the air was infused with expensive colognes, perfumes and hair products. The ladies were painted, and the rubes wore bow ties.

Maya hurriedly made the rounds, winding her way between clusters of guests, subtly steering him by the arm. She did a lot of smiling and dealt out a lot of one-liners as she passed people she knew, only stopping to have conversations with staff regarding operational details. Sault felt almost no obligation to speak at all and, half an hour in, with a beer in one hand and a tiger shrimp in the other, was surprised to find himself having a good time.

Off the garden, there were several lecture rooms dedicated to other forms of entertainment. They were outfitted for lectures and presentations and like movie theatres, these rooms were well insulated with heavy doors. Signs near the doors read, "Immersion Experience." Sault only caught glimpses and bursts of sound as guests wandered in and out. In one, a dance troupe performed some modern dance or ballet. Laughter erupted from another and Sault assumed there was standup comedy. He managed to catch a peek into another room as they flew by. The interior holographically mimicked a tropical garden which, considering the venue, Sault thought was a little redundant, though it teemed with butterflies and brilliantly plumaged birds that the real garden did not. The only other room that Sault managed to see was something abstract. Colorful and amorphous blobs whizzed and whorled like ghostly comets while muted fireworks erupted near the ceiling.

It was all very impressive and not the least because it was all very expensive. But it was random with no unifying theme which, to Sault, felt over the top and desperate. Then he remembered that his wife had probably arranged the whole thing and was glad he hadn't had any opportunity to express that thought.

There was a large monster movie poster near the door of another room and a stand with a hundred pairs of cheap glasses which told him that the movie would include AR elements. It was probably interactive, following recent trends. That sounded like fun to him, but Maya was on a mission. As she pulled him onward and away, a variation on an old joke occurred to him: *Why did the man cross the road? Answer: He was stapled to the wife.*

They were at the edge of the crowd watching the sushi chef slice a slab of tuna so thin you could see the shadow of his fingers through it when Maya finally stopped and turned to him. "Joe. I'm sorry, but I have to go check the kitchen. Think you can find something to do for a half hour?"

He assured her it would be no problem and she vanished without hesitation.

At first, he wandered aimlessly hoping to bump into one of the waiters with more shrimp, but then his attention was drawn to a particular trio of guests. From behind, he recognized Chief Gordon Roth from his white buzz cut hair and the pink scalp that showed through and his sumo-like stance. He was talking with Constable Second Class, Theresa (Terri) Schneider—Jared Kowalczyk's training officer. Neither of them was in uniform, of course. Though Chief Roth might as well have been. He was wearing a dark blue suit jacket and tie over a plain white shirt with stiffly pleated blue trousers held by a thick, black, leather belt. The suit was especially tight over his barrel chest and gut and almost perfectly mimicked his everyday department uniform. He may as well have brought the cap.

Terri was no super model. She was short with thick appendages, but she looked good with her nut-brown hair in an artful tangle of lazy curls and wearing a short black dress that accentuated all of her curvy positives. She stood out amid a sea of predominantly conservative floor-length gowns but, knowing Terri, that was no accident. On the job, she was a confident and assertive personality and Sault knew that those traits did not come and go with her badge. She definitely had the confidence to carry off the look in any crowd, but she was also very reactive, like a perpetually coiled snake, and Sault could see headline potential if one of the Botox beauties in the crowd made some sort of slight.

The other man in the small group was a tall, wispy-haired blonde with grey eyes whom Sault did not recognize but became curious about when he noticed his close proximity with Schneider. He was lanky, but his suit fit very well, and he seemed completely at ease making small talk with the Chief. He wore a Nehru-style jacket made of a grey material with a silvery sheen that seemed to suck color from his already pallid skin. Sault thought it looked pretentious and inappropriate. The fact that he didn't like it probably meant that it was very fashionable and completely appropriate.

Sault took all of this in very quickly and turned in the opposite direction. In no way would he want to bump into Chief Roth. Such a meeting could only be awkward as they tried to have a trite and civil conversation that did not include Sault's conduct or his current situation within the Department.

Or worse, Roth might not stand on circumstance and choose the moment to wade into those topics. Sault had always found Roth to be inscrutable. He'd only had three private meetings with the man, and each was after he'd broken a case he wasn't authorized to investigate. All three times, Roth had spoken plainly: *You were out of line, you got lucky because it ended well, and lucky again because you're not going to lose your job, luckier still because you won't be prosecuted for improper use of your authority, ultimately the department will make the most of the headlines and minimize your role, don't ever do anything like that again—it causes too much dissension. Take the Detective's exam. Dismissed.* He never raised his voice, exaggerated, threatened or raked him over the coals, like Devoss took so much time and pleasure in doing. At the same time, Roth had a reputation for addressing issues head-on, making tough decisions and sticking to them. Sault suspected that if the day came when Roth chose to fire him, the lecture would be no less matter of fact. Maybe it was just a reflection of the fact that the career of one individual beat cop was not that big a deal in Roth's world.

Terri Schneider, on the other hand, he very much wanted to talk to, but he didn't want to do it here. He wanted to ask her about Jared Kowalczyk and Lindsay Susan George. She had been first on the scene of the car accident with Kowalczyk and also present after his body had been discovered. But approaching her was going to be a delicate matter. She tended to be incendiary and if he read her wrong or said something to set her off, she would vent like a volcano and draw a lot of unwanted, possibly career ending, attention.

Knowing how torturous it would be to have questions screaming inside his head while trying to talk about the weather, he wanted to avoid her, too.

He skulked away, sad to see a platter of shrimp fly past with no opportunity for him to stop and be served without the risk of being seen by the trio.

He ducked into the closest immersion room and found it small, dimly lit and empty but for a few rows of padded seats and a single performer on stage, lit by a shaft of white light.

The man shouted to him, "Please, come in, sit down. Come right up front." He was wearing a dark-colored business suit and he waved invitingly with his walking stick, reminding Sault of a circus master. The room seemed as good a hiding place as any, so he accepted the invitation and took a seat, front and center in the second row, and nursed the last of his beer.

"Welcome and thank you for your interest in Cavallon and Associates."

He had noticed the holographic shimmer from the start and wasn't fooled into thinking that the business man was real, but he had been hoping for standup comedy, not a corporate advertisement. No wonder the room was empty.

"I'm Sidney Cavallon, Senior," said the hologram.

Sault suddenly grew interested. He scoured the image looking for similarities to Cavallon junior but found little. The elder Cavallon had been of medium height and thickly built with a bushy beard with only a few strands of dark hair vainly crossing his skull. The hologram wore dark-rimmed glasses as was the norm twenty years past, before corrective surgery became ubiquitous. By contrast, his son was tall and trim, clean-shaven with a thick head of sandy brown hair. Sault could see similarity only in the nose and the blue of the eyes.

A large photo materialized behind Cavallon then drifted slowly across the stage and faded, chased away by the next scene from the corporation's early years. In a few, Sault recognized Canadian Forces Base Esquimalt, and he spotted Reg Hanover in others, but little else was familiar. "It might surprise you to know that Cavallon and Associates started out as a technology company; a consulting firm heading up AI research on behalf of the Canadian Military. We were intimately involved with Canada's contribution to the All-Country Coalition that created Net 2 and Net 3. In fact, I am credited with coining 'wakeless thrust' a term you might not recognize, but which is still in common use, amongst AI specialists…"

Sault became impatient and shouted, "Can we skip ahead to your son's era?"

"…Some have referred to wakeless thrust as the theory of a million nudges. It encapsulates the notion that large change can be engineered from miniscule incremental change, with the help of AI..."

He shouted louder, "Skip ahead."

"...In this way, we can shape the future with minimal disruption to the present. It was a revolutionary concept that..."

The presentation continued, unabated and it dawned on Sault that it was not interactive and even though he was alone, he felt embarrassed. He stayed only long enough to finish his beer and got some basic background on the Cavallon he knew. Apparently, his mother died due to a pharmaceutical error and this incident inspired Cavallon Senior to make AI smarter and more accurate. The hologram also mentioned his father's friendship with Reg Hanover who led the younger Cavallon in a different direction which proved much more profitable and how, in only a few years, the Cavallon empire flourished, growing robust enough to withstand his father's sudden death, at sixty-four.

It was all just propaganda with random pictures and as soon as his glass was empty Sault left the theatre, the ghost of Sidney Cavallon Senior calling out after him.

Sault was anxious to make his way to the interactive movie but became sidetracked when he spotted Maddie Lance escorting Taylor Swift through the crowd. It gave him a new measure of the shoulders he was rubbing against. It also made him proud and amazed to think that his own wife might have been involved in arranging that. He was in wonder, also, at how she had undersold the event to him. How had she not been bubbling over with excitement? Had his early criticism of her career made her that afraid to show enthusiasm?

He followed them into an immersion room with scalloped blue shimmers rippling across the walls and floor while holographic sharks and whales swam above. Whale song echoed in the background. It was relatively dark and he found a corner and pretended his empty glass still held some interest while waiting for a waiter bearing a full one and watching out for celebrity guests. A few minutes later, Reg Hanover accidentally stumbled into him, a little drunk and disoriented, failing to notice him in the dim light. Reg smiled, apologized and reflexively shook his hand before carrying on. He was with another celebrity; someone whose face was familiar but whose name and circumstances Sault could not recall. After that, Sault left his hiding place and began walking the room scanning every face. The last thing he wanted was to wake up tomorrow and realize that he'd been to the same party as Dame Oprah Winfrey and hadn't seen her. Worse yet, to not be able to tell Maya how impressed he'd been by the guest list.

He'd been there about twenty minutes and was now more interested in seeing a waiter than a celebrity when he noticed Dora Padovano enter the room. He inched his way to the door and stepped out cautiously from the ocean's depths, keeping his eyes peeled for Roth and anyone else who might be here from the department.

On his way toward the monster movie he was able to swap his empty cup for a full one and counted six more celebrities, including Mayor Olcott chatting with Hatsune Miku the world's first holographic pop star. A large Japanese man with the build, grim countenance and dark glasses of a bodyguard was at her side, incongruously carrying the neon pink backpack that contained her emitter. The couple looked inappropriate—a pudgy balding old man and a giggly Asian cheerleader in a micro mini skirt with glowing green ponytails that nearly swept the floor—but Sault calculated that he would have been about twenty when Hatsune first hit the stage and it was entirely feasible that he might be a fan. She was more than forty years old but still looked sixteen, as she always would. Only her fans aged. That was why her following had to be reignited every few years. Most recently, her AI had gone the subscription route and millions of new fans now hosted her image and personality in their homes. Sault was thankful that what a person did with a hologram in the privacy of their own home was beyond the purview of the Victoria Police Department.

Sault had just grabbed the theater door handle when he felt a hand on his shoulder and he was certain it was Roth or, worse yet, Deputy Chief Christian Devoss. Bumping in to him would mean controlling his own temper on top of everything else. It was not a challenge he felt up to and he didn't want his behavior to mar Maya's event.

He turned and was relieved to see that it was Maya. If he'd paid any attention to his watch, he'd have known she was coming, just as she knew where to find him by asking Vivia who knew that he wanted to be found by her.

"Glad I caught you before you went in," she said, stepping forward and giving him a polite kiss on the cheek. He was so caught off guard and pleased that he grinned like a schoolboy and tried to pull her into a hug, but she politely resisted, and he realized that she had mainly done it for sake of appearance, because it was expected. With a suddenness that startled him, happiness collapsed into anger. He contained it, but now he was itching for a fight and secretly hoping to bump in to Devoss.

The hubbub died with the closing of the conservatory doors and she pulled him to one side of the hotel's cavernous main hallway. "I'm sorry to leave you on your own for so long but it's a lot busier than I thought it would be."

She looked fraught. "Is everything ok?"

She was distracted and seemed to have to tear herself from her thoughts in order to talk. "Huh? Oh. Yeah. Everything's going smoothly. Officially, Sid's announcing his candidacy during the after-party, but for practical reasons he's giving most of the interviews beforehand. I've been making sure he gets to his interviews and that the crews get to him between checking on security and food and the auction setup. It's a lot tighter than I imagined. No wonder Kathy never had kids."

"So, can you take a moment now?"

She laughed. "God no. This next bit is the trickiest and the most important. The conservatory party is winding down. In about fifteen minutes the entertainment will close up shop and guests will begin to wander off. Meanwhile, we're assembling the celebrities and some top-tier press in the Crystal Ballroom for a more exclusive party and the auction and announcements. It's an event within the event and meant to look like a casual gathering of elites, but everyone knows it's not. Really, it's all scripted with several of what Kathy calls "milestone moments" choreographed in. I've got to go there now and check the guest list and make sure everything is ready."

"Ok. Should I just follow you or…"

"Oh. No. Sorry, Joe. It's super high security, planned seating and invite only. Even I can't get you in. I thought I could. Thought you'd get a kick out of sitting next to someone super famous. But when I asked Sidney, he said no. And, I just found out that there's an after-after party, in Sid's room. Apparently, that's when he and Hanover and Kathy usually assess the night's impact and sort of debrief. Sid's asked me to stay for that."

Sault's mood darkened further, and he couldn't disguise his disappointment. "Ok. I guess I'll try to catch the last movie, then wait for you in the lounge." It came out sounding a lot more petulant than he'd intended and even he knew it was an impractical plan.

"I appreciate it, Joe but I'm going to be at least two more hours, probably three."

Sault did not want to say any of the things that came to mind. Moments ago, he'd been rubbing shoulders with the rich and famous but now he was embarrassed at himself for having a good time and for thinking that it might continue and that he and Maya might have been sharing a magical night. In fact, they hadn't been sharing anything. She'd been off arranging the magic and he'd been thrown a few beans. He felt as if she was a princess who had shown some kindness to a pauper who then got it in his head that he could be king.

"You should go home," she said patting his chest reassuringly.

Captain Gordon Roth's voice boomed from the conservatory doorway, "Constable Joseph Sault!" It was less a declaration than a call to attention, and he ambled toward them knowing that Sault would wait.

Maya saw an opportunity, gave his chest a couple of quick pats, then left as if the issue had been resolved. Which, he supposed, it had.

A few seconds later, Roth was standing in front of him with both hands in his pants pockets, an amused look on his face. "You know, if you really want to avoid someone you need to set a proximity alert with your AI."

"I wasn't trying to avoid you, sir. I didn't know you were here."

Roth cocked his head and extracted his right arm from his trousers. He shook his watch free of the jacket and shirt cuffs. "Show last image." The conservatory floorplan bloomed in the air between them. On it, Sault saw a dotted yellow line labeled "Roth." There were time signatures at several points. Clearly it was a tracing of Roth's movements throughout the evening. Another line, this one red, had Sault's name on it. It showed at least two clear instances where Sault had pivoted and doubled back when he'd come into close proximity of Roth. "A good Chief knows where all his officers are, at all times. That watch of yours is Vic PD property." He tapped his own watch before lowering his arm back into the pocket. "Proximity alerts can be lifesavers. If that AI of yours isn't already subscribed to the UVO, then it should be." He was referring to the Unsecured Violent Offenders database maintained by the Department of Justice. It tracked the global position of the watches and AI's of released criminals. A lot of officers subscribed and hoped to be warned if someone dangerous was in the vicinity. Especially, a cop-killer. Sault knew that even the dumb criminals used burner watches and AI's, and what made them truly dangerous was an officer relying on a proximity alert to save his life. Still, he could now see the advantage of setting alerts for other people he did not want to bump in to.

Roth let Sault's obvious lie go by without further comment. "I was surprised to see that you were here, Constable."

"My wife's organizing the event."

"She is? What happened to Kathy Scheers?"

Sault realized that he'd slipped up and corrected himself. "Well, she's assisting Ms. Scheers."

That seemed to satisfy the older man and he moved swiftly onward. "Anyway, glad I bumped into you. Saves me having to send a ten-code. Come see me Monday. Sometime in the afternoon. I'll leave word with Ana." His lips formed a wry smile. "Have a good evening, Constable." He gave Sault a couple of light pats on the arm and sauntered away before Sault had the presence of mind to ask for details. Roth must have known that Sault would spend all of Sunday and half of Monday worrying about the meeting, but leaving officers in suspense was a ritual that all the Chiefs seemed to enjoy.

Sault sighed deeply, then headed for the exit.

He only had to wait a few minutes for a car, but in that time, he witnessed Terri Schneider steaming to her car. At first, he assumed she was angry and wondered if he might have just missed her sucker punching Taylor Swift. But she passed close without noticing him and he got a better look at her face. She was pale and looked shaken. He had never seen her this way and knew that she would have been embarrassed to be seen so vulnerable, had she known he was there.

She threw herself into the rear seat, slammed the door and barked an order to the vehicle which immediately left the curb. Sault saw no sign of the lanky fellow who might have been her date. He filed the scene in his head, assuming he'd probably hear the details through the Vic PD grapevine, whether he wanted to or not.

As his own car left The Empress, merging onto Government Street, Sault returned to worrying about his pending meeting with Chief Roth. It was a frustrating and useless endeavor, but a relief from pondering the deteriorating state of his relationship with his wife.

William M. Dean

CHAPTER 21

He'd returned home to an empty house.

The kids had stayed over at Maya's sister's place, visiting their cousins who were roughly the same age. Other than that, they seemed to have little in common and both Matthew and Amber found visits to be tedious. Sault assumed it was similar for the cousins and figured that they'd each serve their time at far corners of the house immersed in their own custom online worlds. To him, it seemed little different than when they were together with their friends.

He'd spent the night on the pull-out couch. He wasn't entirely sure why. Either he wanted to avoid a fight or wanted to show that he was hurt. It wasn't much of a compromise. The couch was very comfortable, so it wasn't much of a statement, either. But he was now glad of that because he was pretty sure that his hurt feelings weren't justified. Maya had tried to include him, but she'd been run off her feet. He could hardly blame her for how he reacted to circumstances that were beyond her control. He was also glad that he'd fallen asleep before she'd returned home and that they hadn't had any opportunity to talk and he hoped that she wouldn't read anything into his behavior.

He gathered up the suit that had spent the night carelessly draped over the living room armchair and climbed the stairs to the bedroom to return it to the closet and to get dressed and was surprised to find the bed empty. It still looked freshly made up and he could see four small ripples as the sheet cleaning bots roved beneath the bedclothes, scrubbing microscopic stains with powdered cleansers and bathing every square inch of fabric in sanitizing ultraviolet light. That confirmed that it hadn't been slept in the night before. The swarm-bot was scheduled to activate at noon but would start earlier if the bed was left vacant overnight, acting on the assumption that someone might need rest after an all-nighter.

Sault could not recall the last time his wife had stayed out all night, without him. Then it hit him that he was basing this thought on unverified assumptions. His seniority assured that he rarely pulled a night shift except during special events, but that still happened about eight to ten times each year. And during those weeks, he had no way of knowing for sure if Maya was always home, though the kids never said anything, and he never saw any evidence to the contrary. The odds were that this was an anomaly but that did nothing to assuage his worry. He fetched his watch off the charger and Vivia immediately showed him messages from Maya:

11:05pm - This is going to go much later than I thought.

12:42am - I have to be back to oversee the cleanup in a few hours, so Sidney got me a room.

8:34am – Cleanup is going well. Should be home by noon. Sorry.

Just what exactly she might be apologizing for worried him, and it was her fourth apology in the space of twelve hours. Something about that fact depressed him. That, unconsciously, he had been counting depressed him further. He didn't know if it was a symptom of being a dutifully suspicious cop, or an inadequate and insecure husband.

He checked her location. She was still at the Empress, of course.

As he stared at his watch, Constable Dennis Hennessey's words came back to him, *"They're basically super-intelligent stalkers. They track and analyze pretty much every move you make, so they know what you know..."*

Sault wondered if there was a way for Vivia to get information from Maya's AI, Gemma, but even just authorizing such a request would be seen as the breach of trust that he knew it was. Then, another idea came to him.

More than the taste, Sault enjoyed the simple ritual of brewing a cup of coffee on his days off, when time was not an issue. Vivia knew this, so the pot was empty when he reached the kitchen. The machine did most of the work, but he liked going through the motions—choosing the beans from a selection in the cupboard, pouring them into the receptacle, setting the grind, then listening to the whirr and hiss of the machine as it chewed and brewed, transforming roasted beans into a vital elixir while he stood idle, his sleepiness falling away like molting feathers.

He took his steaming cup to the living room window and looked over the front lawn toward the cul-de-sac. He loved the location. It was a dead-end street, so there was no flow-through traffic. And, just behind the neighboring houses was Playfair Park which had a small ball field, a simple set of swings, teeter-totters and a Rhododendron garden you could stroll through. A narrow path ran between two houses at the tip of the cul-de-sac and led directly into the garden. It was mid-May, so it would be spectacular; in full bloom, right now. He was surprised to realize that it had been a few years since he'd last walked the park. They used to go several times a week, when the kids were small.

The cerulean sky was scuffed with bloated clouds, but at this time of year Sault knew they would only cast shadows over the island, saving their moisture until they hit the more mountainous terrain of the mainland.

Victoria was known as a garden city and his neighbors were doing their part. Sault was not much of a gardener and was unperturbed by the sea of bright yellow Dandelion blossoms scattered among the patches of grass. Neighbors never openly complained but had dropped hints that they weren't quite so indifferent. Whatever. He was busy upholding peace and security, the very foundation upon which they built their little oases, filled with exotic plants and expensive statuary.

Across the street, a neighbor popped up over his tall Laurel hedge, overdressed in flannel and wielding a trimmer. He noticed Sault standing in the window and waved. Reflexively, he returned the greeting, then a cloud passed diminishing the backlight and Sault could make out its damaged face. It wasn't his neighbor. It was a bot, accidentally melted one Halloween, while tending a bonfire. Sault huffed, chiding himself at having been drawn in, as if courtesy had any meaning to a machine.

He stepped away from the window and his final thought regarding tending the garden was that maybe they should just give in and buy a lawn-swarm. They were becoming more affordable every year and the only people he knew that didn't have one lived in apartments. As well, he supposed, he could get Vivia to do some weeding or regular lawn mowing. It was an odd and inefficient application of technology, but he was sure it would get the basic job done.

It was his second day of restful sleep and physical normality and he wasn't going to take it for granted. Sault decided to start his day at the gym. He had good eating habits that kept him trim and healthy enough to meet the basic fitness requirements, but all emergency response personnel had free membership to a chain of 24-hour gyms called "Unit 24" and there was a minimum quota of two visits a week that he had to maintain. Sault enjoyed working out. The most difficult part for him was breaking away from his routines to get himself there. Today, he welcomed the interruption and distraction. Also, he had recently been issued a VR body suit and was anxious to try it on one of the new exoskeleton machines.

But first, he had a few balls to get rolling.

He placed his empty cup on the side table, eased himself into the couch and immediately noticed that Maya had moved the bouquet of roses to the mantle. The arrangement blocked the TV screen, but that was seldom used, anyway. The velvety flowers were just opening, as per the electrochemically orchestrated choreography of the stim-vase. One blossom was off-program, though; already fully splayed. Soon, its petals would drop.

He scrolled through the few notifications on his watch starting with a general callout to officers to read the latest bulletins and memos. As expected, it was all standard comments and complaints: check and service your weapons before every shift, the usual ineffective plea for members to clean out cruisers at end of shift, a link to a mental health article about respecting your partner's privacy which reminded him about Singh, a note to expect shift adjustments due to the upcoming summer event schedule, a reminder about the upcoming mayoral election and to be alert for protests and vandalism, a memo about a staff members baby shower, a reminder about organ donation, and a short paragraph congratulating last night's security detail at The Empress for an "uneventful event." Sault hadn't noticed anyone beyond the two uniforms at the entrance. For a few hours, amid the wonder and novelty of it all, he'd forgotten he was a cop. It had been fun, but missing what should have been obvious to him was unsettling. He assumed the security team had worked under cover. Maybe Terri Schneider had been part of it, though he couldn't imagine where she might have stowed a weapon.

There weren't many other notifications, but among them was another invitation from the reporter Dora Padovano and Sault noticed that, curiously, Vivia had not forwarded this one to PR, but he wasn't curious enough to open it to find out why.

When he'd finished with the notifications, he sent his own invitation to the upper-tier hacker handle that Ranier Gilbert had given him.

He sat for a few more minutes going over the next thing he wanted to do. Lately, he'd been thinking a lot about his AI. He knew that the average person used it for everything from keeping appointments to parenting advice and he thought that was ridiculous. But recently, it seemed, a lot of people had been advising him to make better use of it—Hennessey, Dr. Robillard, Roth—and he didn't want to ignore legitimate advantages just because of an innate stubbornness. That was how he'd seen older officers lapse into obsolescence. He hadn't enjoyed the previous night's encounter with Chief Roth and decided to start with proximity alerts. He knew that his rank entitled Vivia to report the whereabouts of other officers below his rank, but only during active duty. He wanted more and had an idea how he might widen her scope.

Leaving his watch and Vivia behind on the side table, he went to the garage and dug out Chief of Detectives Belinda Remy Smith's old watch and authorized full access for Vivia. He paused before saving the setting, thinking about the cyber trail he was about to create and trying to imagine who might stumble onto it. The most comforting thought he could conjure was that somewhere within the department was a human being whose responsibility it had been to deactivate the watch eight years ago, after Smith's unexpected death, and who now had a vested interest in covering up the breach. He decided it might be prudent to find out who that was, someday soon. He shrugged and saved the new setting.

He returned to the living room and strapped on his watch. Immediately, Vivia displayed the invitation from Chief of Detectives Smith.

This was a pivotal moment for him. He was about to bring Vivia in on the existence of the old watch. One last time he ran through the possible repercussions. He knew that his personal AI should not be able to report his actions, even though they might be illegal. As with Internet 1.0, anonymity had been a critical feature of AI's popularity. Initially, when government agencies adopted the technology, they overrode the personal security settings in favor of transparency and quickly learned what private manufacturers had always known: No one is truly law-abiding. And, the further up the corporate ladder you went, the more this proved true.

All this he knew to be true, but it is one thing to know something and another to believe.

He held a breath and instructed her to accept.

The ever-pleasant voice of Vivia startled him. "Before I do

that, I need to advise you that Chief of Detectives Remy Smith is no longer active and that her device should be turned in to the Properties Clerk as soon as possible."

"Ok."

"I must further advise that unauthorized possession of a law-enforcement device is a felony offence, punishable by permanent suspension without benefits, and possible imprisonment."

It was a bit late in the game for him to start worrying about that, but he was shaken by Vivia's recitation. He forced himself to remain calm. If she was programmed to report him, then it was already too late for him to prevent it and he reminded himself that it was a risk he'd accepted at the outset. "Ok."

"Finally, I must advise that connecting to a vintage device with lower security standards may compromise Vic PD general security. Knowingly doing so constitutes a felony offence, punishable by permanent suspension without benefits, and possible imprisonment."

"Do it."

"Of course. It might be best if I constructed a firewall to protect us from a security breach originating at the other end."

"Ok. Do that."

"The connection is complete."

"List for me the location of all Vic PD officers."

Sault was pleasantly surprised when his watch lit up with a long list that seemed to include everyone up to the rank of Chief of Detectives. As a test, he asked for a list of security on duty at the Empress Hotel, the previous night and she returned twelve names. He recognized only two senior members and noted, incidentally, that Terri Schneider's name was not one of them. She didn't seem the type to be so well connected, but her only way in would have been on someone's arm.

He sat there in silence for a few minutes, half expecting a flashing unit to pull into his driveway, or a direct message from the Chief commanding him to report immediately. The driveway remained empty. The screen remained blank. He released the breath he hadn't realized he'd been holding and felt relief seeping back into him, though he knew that it would be several days before he would feel comfortably invisible again.

Another thought occurred and he checked earlier in that day and confirmed that Darsh Singh had visited the Chief's office. The ten-code hadn't just been a stall. He immediately felt embarrassed by this voyeurism and resolved not to stalk his brothers.

He was more embarrassed and ashamed of his main motivation in connecting to Smith's watch, but Hennessey's words—that AI's knew what you knew, and more—had been tumbling around in his head for days, now. It was distracting, bobbing to the surface of his thoughts like a buoy. And the winds kept rising.

Vivia now had access to all of the security reports and observations made at the Cavallon Benefit. He had never before asked an AI to speculate. It would be so easy to ask the question, but he wasn't sure the he was prepared for the answer.

He realized that his hands were tight fists and he forced them to unfurl, closed his eyes, sank into the cushions, concentrated on drawing breath. One quick question.

He heard the lock turn in the front door, then the chatter and clatter of his two children setting down backpacks and kicking off shoes. He almost wished he'd set out for the gym earlier but knew that there would be no better time for his talk with Matthew.

Amber cut through the living room on her way to the kitchen. "Oh! Dad. You're home."

"Hey there. Another day off. Your Mom's still at work but she should be home by noon. How was Aunt Sarah's?"

She slowed down but didn't stop, shrugged as she passed. "Oh, you know." He did.

"Where's your brother?

"In his room, I guess," she said, raising her voice from the kitchen.

Sault decided to give him a minute to settle in before heading up. He wasn't nervous about this. He'd given it some thought and decided that just because the school made a big deal of it, didn't mean he had to. He rose to put away his coffee mug and heard Matthew tromping down the stairs, two at a time. He knew that he was headed out, so he hurried to the door and intercepted him.

"Hey, Buddy. Can I talk to you for a minute?"

Matthew gave him a pained look. "Now, Dad? I'm just headed out. My friends are on their way to pick me up"

"It'll only take a second. I'll walk with you to the street. What's all that?"

Matthew hefted a large duffle to his shoulder. "War gear."

Sault understood that he was referring to simulated war and was uncomfortable with the way Mixed Reality was mixing with his reality. "I didn't know you were into that."

"Just started. Doug loaned me his old stuff," he said, as if Sault might have any idea who Doug was.

Matthew went through the door ahead of him and didn't slow down forcing Sault to move faster than was comfortable to keep pace. "Hey, Buddy. Slow up."

Matthew stopped at the edge of the lawn and turned, glancing over his shoulder at the street, keeping an eye out for his ride.

"Listen. Did you know that I had to pick your sister up from school on Friday?"

Matthew shook his head, but it wasn't convincing.

"Well, I did. She got caught with some erotic printed material…some sort of bot-romance novel, bordering on porn. Know anything about that?"

Again, a head shake. Again, not convincing.

"Amber said it was yours."

Shrug.

Sault tamped down a rising anger, reminded himself that the offense was nothing serious. Came at it from another angle. "I'm going to let go the fact that you're probably lying to me, right now. Here's what you need to know: Number one, don't take that stuff to school and, two, don't involve your sister."

An autonomous pod-car came into view over the hump in the road. From the shape and styling he guessed it might be an

Apple Squib. Spindly arms were waving from every window. Sault saw three teens stuffed into the back seat, two in the front. They were laughing and hooting like orangutans. Technically, the car was full. They'd have to fake out the sensors and ride illegally to fit Matthew in. Sault recalled his own adolescence and chose to ignore it.

Matthew waved, then turned back to his father bearing an expression of impatience.

"Here's the deal. You make sure this never comes up again, or you, me and your mother will be having deep discussions about every aspect of bot-porn."

Silence, but Sault could read the dread in his son's eyes. Horn honking, though the car was only ten feet away.

"Deal? Or should we go inside and wait for your mother? I need to hear your voice."

Matthew sighed, but it was a cautious one, barely detectible, defensible as having never happened, if accused. "Deal. Can I go now?"

Sault stared as if undecided. Made Matthew wait another thirty seconds, then let him go with a curt nod.

Matthew jumped in with his buddies and the car sped away.

The message had been delivered, but that had not been the light and breezy conversation that Sault had imagined.

By the time he returned to the house, he found himself vibrating with anxiety and frustration. He either needed a stiff drink or rigorous exercise.

Vivia made a chime in his ears and he checked his watch and found a notification from his father's care facility. *Regarding Victor Sault: diagnosed with h1n1 virus. Confined to Med-Pod. Condition stable, fully aware and responding well.*

This type of thing happened at least three times a year, now, so Sault was not alarmed, but he'd have to make time for a visit very soon. Fortunately, he had time.

"Hit the bottle or hit the mats!" A phrase that his father had often repeated as if the matter were something he needed to consider, just before opening another bottle.

CHAPTER 22

There was a branch of Unit 24 within fifteen minutes of Sault's house, near Brydon Park on West Saanich Road, ironically neighboring both a McDonalds and a Tim Hortons where he knew many of his fellow officers holed-up while their watches accumulated gym-time in a locker.

He was disappointed to find all five VR units occupied but spent a few minutes among a small crowd watching the five people in body suits, goggles over their eyes, magically hovering in the magnetic field of room-temperature superconductors. Monitors above each unit showed the user's computer-generated environment but Sault might have guessed the VR from their posture and gestures; skiing, rock climbing, cycling, scuba diving, bouncing in low gravity. The computer-generated scenarios were beyond reality because that was the point: A heli-jump down Everest avoiding crevasses and avalanches, scaling a skyscraper in Dubai on the run from spider-like robots, an impossibly steep hill in an Italian village with unexpected vehicles and pedestrians zooming out in front, cursing and shaking their fists, a deep cenote and ancient wreck with a treasure chest guarded by monsters, a cratered and ringed planet with strange geography and wildlife and ray-blasting aliens. The magnetic bubble provided rotation and resistance and though the level could be adjusted, it was clear from the large and blooming patches of dampness on the suits that these people had chosen strenuous workouts. Popular speculation was that expert gamers might become the Olympic athletes of the future.

It looked like fun and Sault was anxious to try it, but when he checked at the front desk, he was told that they were booked solid until the late evening. VR workouts were the latest thing, so he should have expected it. He stowed his suit in a locker, then did a half-hour of free weights, following that with another half hour on the treadmill.

He'd once broken his leg while chasing a suspect. It was a night pursuit and he'd run, full-tilt, into a bike rack made invisible by its dark paint. He'd picked himself up off the ground, and managed to limp onward, but running was out of the question. The suspect got away and now, ten years later, Sault couldn't even recall what the offense had been. But he remembered his leg swelling to the size of his thigh and the doctor telling him that he'd broken it and two ribs. He also never forgot that after four weeks of mandatory rest and recuperation, the hardest muscles to get back had been his abdominals. He never wanted to have to climb that hill again and so he peppered every workout with several sets of crunches and liked to end each session with them.

About three quarters of the way through his final set, he became aware of a loud slapping coming from an adjoining room that contained the heavy weights and punching bags. Someone was relentlessly wailing on a heavy bag and it sounded like they were using a cricket bat. There was a clenching shout before every hit. It sounded female and her breathing was labored enough that he could hear it over his own. He was impressed and curious and hoped to get a glimpse of the member before he left.

At the end of his set, he carried the mat he'd been using to the sanitizing racks and hung it under the ultraviolet light. On his way to the lockers, he leaned across the threshold of the heavy-weight room to take a peek and was surprised to see a small, olive-skinned woman pounding the hell out of a leather bag with jabs and leg kicks. It was Terri Schneider.

Sault briefly considered waiting for her in the lobby, but judging by the intensity of her workout, today was probably not optimal. Instead, he ducked his head back before she had a chance to spot him and headed for the shower, then for home.

He exited into the bright sunlight fatigued and overheated enough to appreciate Victoria's perpetual ocean breeze. Working out had been a good decision. It had burned nervous energy and put tension back into his muscles and he enjoyed a lingering serenity that seemed attached to the fatigue and that he knew would last only as long.

He decided to go with the feeling and headed for a sunny lookout at the top of Mount Douglas. On his way, he bought a sandwich at a popular farmer's market called "The Farmhand" which no longer really dealt with farmers or even physical labor as it was now wholly automated. Vivia broadcast his parameters to a four-armed half-bot; a very utilitarian-looking torso welded to a thick metal post which slid the length of a trough of sandwich components. It was painted in shades of green which he supposed was meant to remind him of farmland but instead looked like wartime camouflage. He watched through the glass counter as it sliced dill pickles on an angle, just the way he liked them, and composed the ham sandwich that he would have made, had he done it himself.

Mount Douglas was rather ambitiously named with its summit standing little more than six hundred feet above sea level. Still, because the Victoria area was so flat, it afforded Sault an uninterrupted view in all directions. Victoria is located at the southern-most tip of Vancouver Island which exists in an inlet that would dip into the United States, if borders made any sense at all or were more than just lines on a map. It is surrounded on three sides by a twenty-mile-wide moat called The Salish Sea, and to the north by the bulk of Vancouver Island. The clouds were high and scattered now and Sault could see clear to the Rocky Mountains to the east and the sheltering Olympics to the South—Victoria's shield from the wrath of the open Pacific

Ocean.

Closer to him was the city skyline that wavered and shimmered in the haze of seasonal heat. In the more immediate area, close enough to appear to him like a scale model, he overlooked the small zone of farmland, incongruous and landlocked within the city's residential suburbs. By now, it would have all been condos but for the Agricultural Land Reserve, a highly contested piece of legislation that designated arable land for farm use only. No one really disagreed with the ALR. That was not why it was so highly contested. It was intended to try to preserve Canada's ability to feed itself, but only had power and support enough to hold development at bay until the land value accrued beyond a politician's ability to resist rezoning. It was always contested because it was a veritable vault of easy money.

The lots were large and the roads were few, so it wasn't hard for him to identify the intersection near where Lindsay George's vehicle had crashed. The accident site itself was hidden from view by the windbreak of columnar poplars edging the adjacent farms.

Viewing it from here didn't spark any thoughts. Joseph Sault's mind was elsewhere.

He had a question to ask Vivia that he knew he shouldn't. If his suspicions were confirmed, then he wasn't sure if he could handle it. On the other hand, if he were proved wrong, then the very act of asking was a type of betrayal. Maya would never find out, of course, but suspicious and insecure didn't fit his image of himself. If he did this, that image would be forever altered.

He was perfectly alone, sitting far enough off the footpath and away from the lookout to be secluded. Also, it was lunch time and he guessed that most of the tourists were headed somewhere to eat. He hadn't touched his sandwich and couldn't seem to compose the right string of words and wondered at the point of his being here.

He began flicking through the security reports from The Empress without knowing what he was hoping to find; something that might confirm that Maya had not shared a suite with Sidney Cavallon, though he couldn't imagine collating that from this data.

After a few moments, he cursed himself out loud, closed the files, grabbed his sandwich and headed back to the Buick. He slammed the door harder than he needed, fell into the bucket seat and turned the key in hopes of getting the air-conditioning up to speed before he broke out in a sweat. He had his hand on the gearshift when Vivia's voice blossomed in his ears.

"There is no evidence to support the supposition that Maya has been unfaithful."

"Holy crap! What are you talking about?"

"You have been concerned."

"If I'd wanted your opinion, I would have asked."

"That is not true."

"I would have asked!" he insisted.

There was a perceptible pause. "I'm sorry."

"Why in the hell would you suddenly start answering questions I haven't asked?"

"I determined that was best."

"I had my reasons for not asking."

Silence.

"I didn't want to know."

"My conclusions are not without uncertainty."

"Shut down. Now."

Sault switched off the watch, ripped it off his arm, pitched it toward the passenger seat and threw the car into gear.

Any serenity he'd achieved from his workout had been ripped away. He was more agitated than ever and maintaining the speed limit required all of his focus and discipline.

He drove aimlessly for forty minutes and reached the sea. Parked on the cul-de-sac at Clover Point and watched seabirds, kites and hang gliders all hover in the updrafts off the nearby cliffs without really seeing any of them. He never shut the engine off and once his thoughts had calmed enough that they weren't all screaming at once, pulled away and steered toward home.

It all came down to trust.

He had been running Vivia for more than a year and had become comfortable with the low level of tasks she performed without being asked. She monitored him, and was privy to many little secrets, but she could never betray his trust, could never overstep, because his desires were her law. He'd come to trust in that. But then, she *had* overstepped, serving him information he'd decided not to access.

But, of course, he'd breached Maya's trust by even attempting to track her.

And that had been a ridiculous waste of time.

Maya was not his enemy. They had kids together. They were still a team. Sleeping with someone just because they were rich and handsome was as far beyond her character as machine-gunning a bus load of children.

It was not *her* behavior he should have been tracking. It was his own. Because sleeping with someone because she felt abandoned and unappreciated—that was not entirely beyond her character. And if she felt that way, he had to take a lot of the blame. Because…only if he took that blame, would it mean that he had the power to fix it.

But he could tell that she hadn't been unfaithful. A double life would eat away at her. The cracks would have been visible to a veteran cop like Sault. And, if Cavallon were her lover, she never would have invited him to the benefit. And, if Cavallon were not her lover, she was too busy and surrounded by women, and there was no opportunity for any other. It all seemed obvious to him now.

He felt foolish. Ashamed. Yet, he also felt lighter.

Yesterday, with a single moment of laughter, they'd managed to nudge open the cold, steel gate between them, just a crack. And, disregarding his own internal struggle, that night had gone reasonably well. He'd had fun. Maya's event had seemed to be going smoothly. And he'd been there for her.

That last thought reminded him that perhaps he needed to be there for her now so that she could unload after the long and stressful event. For him to cheer her successes, or soothe the wounds, if things had gone wrong. He could do that. All he had to do was shut up and listen.

He was excited as he pulled into the dim light of the garage and shut of the engine.

Then it hit him.

Vivia had been right.

William M. Dean

CHAPTER 23

As Sault made his way along the gravel path from the garage, he heard voices and spotted Amber sitting with three friends. Notably, one was male. All four were side-by-side, their backs propped against the gnarly treaded bark of the old Garry Oak that stood in the center of the back yard. They were laughing and joking and flipping through posts on their watches. Sault couldn't be sure if they could see him or were immersed in some other worldly VR or AR, so he didn't bother waving or calling out.

But when he stepped up on the back deck, Amber came running.

"Dad! Dad."

"Hey there. What's up?" He pulled her in tight, her head fitting neatly into the hollow beneath his rib cage. He wished it could last longer but didn't force it when she pulled away.

"Nothing. Just glad you're home."

"Everything ok?"

"Yup. Oh…a man dropped off a basket-thingy for Mom. I put it in the kitchen." And she took a couple of backward steps toward her friends.

"Mom's not home?"

"She was, but she had to go out again." She glanced over her shoulder and Sault got the message.

"Where?"

"Work, I think."

"Ok." She took that as a dismissal and ran back to the tree.

Sault had an afterthought and yelled across the yard, "I take it your brother's not home?"

"He went to War," she shouted back.

He gave her a thumbs up and entered the house.

The "basket-thingy" on the kitchen island was a vaguely tree-shaped package wrapped in crinkled layers of opalescent cellophane. It was so obviously flowers that his first thought was how un-basket-like it looked and how distracted his daughter had to be to choose that term to describe it.

He peered through the cellophane and saw two dozen long-stemmed roses, blossoms poking through a cloud of baby's breath and fern. Half were crimson, the others a royal purple so deep they looked almost black. They were evenly distributed throughout the bouquet. The entire arrangement was set in a silver stim-vase which would likely have been set to splay the petals and unfurl the fronds in the morning and reverse the dance at night.

It was so patently expensive that Sault didn't need to wonder who they'd come from. He was tempted to look for the holo-dot, thinking it might be possible to activate it through the plastic and to read the message Sidney Cavallon had meant for Maya. Instead, he pulled himself away and was just standing there, trying to decide what to do next when his watch pinged.

"I think I'm really sick, this time. Dad."

Sault 's eyes breezed over the notification. It was the exact same message he'd sent the last three times he'd been ill. Copied and pasted, Sault guessed. If Victor thought that his son would be alarmed, then he had forgotten what it was to have a reliable memory. Still, Sault decided he'd stop by to see him.

He asked Vivia to consult the care facility's AI and she returned the onsite physician's diagnosis of a minor lung infection. It seemed like Victor got one every year, though usually in winter.

He was in the middle of deciding whether to wait for Maya

to return or go straight away when Amber came through the door.

"Da-ad? Can I ask you something?"

"Sure. What's on your mind?"

"Did you know that Willa Fitzgerald got, like, 95 percent at school?"

"I don't even know Willa Fitzgerald."

"She's my best friend from astronomy lab."

"Oh...kay..." Sault had no clue where this might be going.

"You know how so many people use their AI's to do dumb stuff like select play lists and post junk and stuff?"

"Sure." Now he had an inkling.

"Anyway, Willa doesn't do that."

Sault prodded her with his most puzzled expression.

"And she's super smart."

"Yes. I got that."

"So..."

"So?"

She let out an exasperated sigh as if he were the one who was dragging this out. Of course, she wasn't entirely wrong. "So, her AI tutors her and organizes her notes. And she uses it to journal, every day. And she can do a ton of research. And one time, it warned her when Bobby Noon's drone went out of control and almost got into her hair and..."

"You could use Gemma or Vivia for all of that stuff, but you never do."

"But it's like her pet and like her best friend. She has a botshell, but I don't need that. I can use emitters and a holo-shell."

"I thought we'd had this discussion. We don't want you growing up dependent on a machine for information and companionship. You need to use your own brain, develop human relationships. You can get your own AI when you're eighteen."

"But all my friends already have their own."

Sault was not unsympathetic. The crux of the problem was that, increasingly, kids were being given AI's when they were young. The ever-present, ever-vigilant AI's were babysitter, mentor and confidant all rolled into one and often supplanted any need for human companionship. His kids were losing playmates to AI's.

"Really? All of your friends? I don't think so. And anyway, just because everyone's doing something doesn't mean it's a good thing. Everyone used to smoke cigarettes. Then, they all died of lung cancer. Beyond that, good ones—like adult AI's—aren't dead cheap. And did I mention, you're too young?"

"Wow. Just...wow." Arms crossed, a full-on pout.

Maya had been the primary caregiver in the household, so Sault knew that asking him was not her first choice, but her last resort. "Well, what did your mother say?"

"She said 'maybe.'"

"I don't think so." He and Maya were not the least divided on this issue.

"Well she didn't say 'no. Not totally."

Sault didn't bother trying to find out what constituted a partial 'no' in the mind of an eleven-year-old girl. "Amber, even Matthew doesn't have his own AI. I don't hear him complaining."

"'Cause you're never here."

Sault understood anger and was impressed by her comeback. It was a good shot, but he wasn't fazed. Somehow, he and Amber shared a deeper connection, something built in to their DNA and he knew that she was disappointed, but not truly angry. In a way that mattered much more than whether or not she got an AI, she would have been disappointed if her father had given in and said yes. She innately understood the discipline involved in a parent's love.

He ruffled the hair at the top of her head. "I'm going to visit Grandpa. Wan'na come?"

"Now I'm in a box inside a box," Victor Sault declared, acerbically. Sault and Amber heard his voice amplified by speakers built in to the Med-Pod and they could see his head and shoulders through the plexiglass.

The Med-Pod was a portable copy of the larger, more

sophisticated units in hospitals and was used routinely for patients with compromised immune systems, which described all of the residents of this facility. It was an eight-foot long metal cylinder with a plexiglass top. This unit had been painted that putrid-looking grey-green so universally popular in care facilities; an older model, scratched and dented from use. It hummed and beeped and monitored and medicated and filtered continuously and, if history was any indicator, his father would be back on his feet within the week. As it was, with purer air being pushed into his lungs and all his symptoms suppressed by medication, he seemed more vigorous and focused than usual and Sault found it difficult to override his annoyance at his father's manipulative drama and the inconvenience and come up with some feelings of sympathy.

Though she'd said hello, Victor Sault seemed to notice his granddaughter for the first time and broke into a genuine smile. There was just enough room inside the pod for the old man to lift an arm. He waved and said, "Hey there, Pickle!" using the strange endearment he'd invented for her, shortly after she'd been born. He scowled toward his son, "Get me into the god-damned chair."

Sault hit the appropriate button on the arm of the easy chair activating the holo-emitters and Victor's ghost shimmered into existence. The plexiglass lid of the Med-Pod lit up with a video feed so that Victor could see what his simulacrum was looking at and the pod began translating his slightest movements into action.

Sault unfolded two chairs, but Amber went to Victor's side scrolling through images on her watch. "I made these. They're art. Oh. And this is my friend from astronomy, Willa. And this is a deer that came into our yard. This is our field trip to Butchart Gardens…that's Bobby, he's kind of a jerk but he's ok, there's Willa…"

Sault watched in silence and marveled at how much joy his child could bring his old man. He was especially pleased that he remembered her and decided it was probably due to the Med-Pod stimulants and increased oxygen. Victor's ghost reached out to touch her arm, but of course it passed through and Victor's smile faltered, and frustration seemed to break through his interest in the slide show. "That's great, little Pickle, but let's sit and talk a while. You can show me more, later."

"I'll pick out some good ones for after," she said and continued flipping through images as she took a seat.

"Where's Maya and Matthew?"

"Matthew's out with friends and Maya's at work."

"Where's that again?"

"Cavallon House. It's a shelter for abused women."

"Cavallon! Sidney Cavallon?"

"Junior," Sault corrected, knowing that his father would have been referring to the Cavallon of his time.

"Is junior a hacker, too?"

That brought Sault to attention. The vocabulary of the Lindsay George case now included "hacker" and he hadn't forgotten the small note about Cavallon House, Woods and Sebastian had entered into her file.

"No. He's a land developer." All Sault knew about the senior Cavallon was what little he could recall from the obituary. He hadn't been famous in any way and his death had only drawn Sault's attention because Reginald Hanover had made a publicly big deal of taking the younger Cavallon under his wing. Sault also recalled that Cavallon senior had worked for the Department of National Defence (DND) which operated out of Canadian Forces Base Esquimalt and only now did he realize that meant his father may have brushed shoulders with him. "You knew his dad?"

"Knew *of* him. Everyone on base did."

"And he was a hacker?"

"All we were told is that he and his group were experts hired by DND Cyber Security. But, yeah, talk to any one of them for thirty seconds and it became obvious that their entire world was computer stuff. And I think he was one of the top guys. Sure acted like he called all the shots."

"A group of elite hackers for DND, right here in quaint, little Victoria." The thought made Sault chuckle.

"You'd be surprised. I don't know about these days, but when I was in the Service, Victoria was littered with them. Vancouver was known as Silicone North and firms there attracted some of the world's best. Victoria was called the Silicone Suburb because most of them preferred to live in Victoria and work remotely, when they could. I heard that the DND Cyber Security HQ was located here, mostly to tap into that talent pool."

"And Cavallon was one of them?"

"I think he was the *top* one of them. They were civilians and they didn't have rank, but we used to joke that you could sort out the pecking order by their attitude. The lower-levels were quiet and nerdy, and their bosses were flashy assholes." That last word wrested Amber's attention. She looked up from the watch and flashed Sault an impish grin. He'd long ago given up trying to filter his father's language around the kids. Some people talked that way and his kids just had to know not to do it themselves. Victor continued, unabated. "I never came across an exception. And Cavallon was the assholiest of them all. He drove a car that probably cost ten years of my salary and looked like a spaceship and he'd park it where ever suited him. Blocked in an Admiral once. Naturally, he was livid. Now, you got'ta understand, on a naval base, Admirals are gods. And they're generally surly gods. If you or I'd done that, you could expect to find your car under sixty feet of salt water. This Admiral went home in a hire-car. It was base-gossip for a year."

"So, he was working on something pretty important."

"Obviously."

Old emotions had been dredged, and Victor eagerly recounted a couple more examples of the senior Cavallon's bold disregard, but he had nothing more of genuine interest to Sault.

When he was done, Victor beckoned Amber to his side and spent several minutes reviewing more of her collection of pictures and videos. Sault noticed fatigue creep into his father's features and he rose. "Ok, kid. We've got to let Grampy get some rest. He's still sick. We can visit again, another day."

Sault shut off the arm chair emitters and as they were

waving goodbye through the plexiglass Amber suddenly said, "He could visit us, by remote!" *Out of the mouths of babes.*

It was true, of course. Victor's image could just as easily be transmitted across the city as across the room and with a few new sets of holo-emitters, Victor Sault could have shared their dinner table or living room. But Victor was not an easy man to get along with. Even at this stage, he was still obnoxiously pessimistic and self-centered enough to be irritating, in larger doses. And though he seemed to approve of Maya and had never insulted her directly, his general attitude toward women was anachronistically sexist. She found him condescending and dismissive. Out of duty, Sault would certainly have invited his father's presence into his home, but he didn't want to force that obligation on Maya. It would just drive another wedge between them.

Sault examined his father in the casket-like enclosure and read the flickers of realization that crossed his face as he turned the unexpected revelation over in his mind. His mouth moved, as if chewing before swallowing words.

He became still and closed his eyes and could not have looked any more like a cadaver.

"I'm going to rest, for a while."

Sault found an Asian chicken meal in the hot box by the front door and by dinnertime, both Maya and Matthew had returned, and it was a full house at the table.

Maya was in a good mood and suggested they eat together, on the patio. Even Matthew seemed relatively cheery, an adrenaline hangover from his war game, Sault supposed.

The banquet and Maya's new job dominated the conversation. She told them that Sidney Cavallon would be running for mayor and that her new job would be to help run his office while he did that. The kids wanted to know how her schedule might affect them and she explained that she expected to be working normal office hours, so her time at home should become more predictable. Sault was skeptical but said nothing. Matthew asked about her wage which he learned would be substantially increased and Sault thought that he could see calculations going on inside his son's head. He exchanged a glance with Amber who obviously had purchasing an AI on her mind, but wisely chose to keep that to herself.

"So, guess who I saw at the banquet?" Maya asked.

It was an open question but seemed particularly directed toward the kids who both shrugged without pausing in their meal.

"Well, it was a very fancy event and Sidney invited a lot of celebrities. Taylor Swift was there." More shrugs. Maya listed off the stars that came to mind, "Also Moe Levins, Brandy V, Hatsune Miku, David Bowie Sim, Elon Musk Sim…" These were the celebrities of her generation and it was obvious that the kids didn't find them of particular significance. Sault caught a twinkle in her eye that told him Maya was not unaware. "And a whole bunch of ViewTubers," she finished with deliberate nonchalance.

"Seriously, Mom? Next time, lead with that!" exclaimed Amber.

Matthew tried to disguise his own excitement but couldn't resist asking, "So, who, then?"

"Let's see…I think there was Deaf Monkey, WorthyWorthington and Todd JNM…"

Both kids were laughing. Amber said, "Oh. My God, Mom. Silent Badger, Penny Penworthy, and Todd, Jay, & Em. Did you actually see them?"

"I actually talked to all of them."

They were suitably impressed and peppered her with more questions about the guest list, then eventually the event itself.

"So now, I've got a new job…at least for a while."

"So, he announced it?" Sault asked.

"Yup. It's official."

"I really can't imagine an ambitious woman like Kathy just letting go of her career, like that. How was she, seeing her old job passed on?"

"She wasn't there. Apparently, access to the area of the Amazon where he'll be working is seasonal and they had to leave early."

"The Amazon? As in, the deep jungle?"

Maya nodded. "Completely cut off. Their party will be one of only a handful to make contact with some tribe there."

"I'm impressed. I don't think I'll be traipsing through the jungle when I'm fifty."

"She's closer to sixty," Maya corrected. "And if you did, you'd be doing it alone, that's for sure," she joked. Sault was very pleased with how easily the talk and laughter was coming, this evening. Moments like this could still happen. All he had to figure out was how to make them happen more often.

After a dessert of left-over fruit and confections from the banquet, the kids quickly scrambled away, probably wanting to tell their friends about the famous ViewTubers they'd met, vicariously. Maya and Sault remained at the table for a coffee and Maya went into deeper detail about her duties, after Sault had left The Empress.

"Joe, I'm sorry to have shuffled you off…"

Sault interrupted, "Maya, first of all, you have nothing to apologize for. You were busy. And, secondly, you already apologized last night…three times, I think."

He was surprised to note that she almost welled up. Was this kind of courtesy between them now so foreign? She sipped her coffee, regrouping her emotions, he figured. "It got busier than I expected. First of all, Kathy wasn't there. That was a surprise. That meant I had to coordinate all of Sidney's meetings as well as the auction dinner. It was a nightmare because he added four extras to the meeting schedule, at the last moment. I guess he decided to warn the mayoral candidates that were there: Tommy Olcott, Montgomery Hoad and Susan Mora." Sault recognized the names. They'd been mentioned on the newsfeeds and also at the morning briefing, before his last shift. "The first addition was some other woman—probably a business connection I don't yet know—and it happened just before I talked to you, so I was kind of panicked."

"If you apologize again, I'm out of here," he interjected. Maya laughed and he chose that moment to steer the conversation to something else before he could give in to the temptation to probe her regarding the connection between Lindsay Susan George and Sidney Cavallon. That would certainly have spoiled the moment, perhaps the entire week.

"So, I talked with Matthew."

"How'd that go?"

"Not as smoothly as I'd hoped, but not as horribly as it could have. I basically told him not to break the school rules and to leave Amber out of it."

"He admitted that it was his?"

"He didn't deny it. It was his."

"What about the content?"

"I stayed away from that. It seemed like a lot to put into one conversation."

He could see that she was not satisfied with that. "If you ask me, you skipped the most important part."

"What? Bot-romance?"

"Not 'romance.' Pornography."

"The principal said the story was sexual but relatively tame."

"The story is, but the pictures are pornographic."

"She never used that word."

"Because she's not allowed to. 'Pornography' implies judgement and school officials are not allowed to cast judgement on such things."

Sault took a moment to turn that over in his mind. Maya was studying him, closely. "I flipped through. I didn't see whips and chains, or any other kind of fetish."

"Oversized lips, unnaturally perky breasts, ridiculously tiny waist, subservient postures…it's porn."

"It's a doll. That's exactly why they make them."

"It's idealized and will lead to unrealistic expectations."

Sault ran a hand over his stubble. This was classic dolls-are-porn rhetoric he'd heard from protestors in the newsfeeds. Personally, he hadn't yet decided on which side of the fence he stood. "So, then, we're against bot-love? Because, if we are talking about a bot, those expectations *are* realistic."

"For God's sake, yes, Joe…we're against bot-love. I thought

you, of all people, would not be in favor of your son falling in love with a machine."

He heard the tension entering her voice and, internally, he began to panic. He didn't want another day spoiled by disagreement. Especially, this day. "I'm not. I'm not. I just wanted to be clear," he said, holding both palms up in supplication. He wanted to defuse her attack, but her comment had sparked some anger in him, and he couldn't quite let it go enough to defuse his own anger. "And, what do you mean, me 'of all people?'"

"You hate machines."

"Hate machines?" He held up his watch. "I'm surrounded by them." And he waved toward the garage where Vivia's shell sat, currently lifeless. "Everywhere, from the garage to the bedroom."

Maya looked away from him, out at the yard. She took a deep breath and Sault could tell she was calming herself down. When she turned back, she had a gentle smile on her lips. "But I know you don't like them." She ticked off points on her finger tips, "Think about how much time and energy you've invested in fixing up that mindless vehicle, you barely use your AI, you won't even say 'hi' to a shell, and our yard looks like crap."

"I just don't think it's good to let a machine take over the things we do."

"How about just the things we *never* do, like yard work?"

Sault looked around and took in the teetering rear fence, ragged cedar hedge, weed-infested lawn invading the garden beds, and the fish pond, cracked and dry and filled with oak leaves. It needed a lot of work and he had little inclination to do it. But he'd resisted getting a yard-bot because it was impossible to buy one that didn't have a human shell. A few like-minded souls had stripped their units down, exposing the machinery within, and the overwhelming public response had been that it was repugnant. Manufacturers were quickly onside, weighing in that stripping the epidermis voided warranties and could be dangerous, even though national safety regulations ensured that the chassis be safe without them. Many cities now had by-laws prohibiting stripped automatons. He realized that, like nearly everyone else, he had unresolved issues with humanoid bots. He wasn't ready for one in his home.

"I think we're a bit off-topic, here."

She sipped the last of her coffee and didn't challenge his deflection. There was silence, then, "I didn't mean to beat you up about the porn aspect. When I first asked you to talk to him, I hadn't yet read the book."

In the end, they agreed to leave things where they stood and address pornography if it came up again.

Sault had hoped to talk with Maya more about her new job, but once they had finished their coffee, established routines seemed to take over and she went to her study and didn't come out.

He went to the garage with the intent of opening the files and thinking more about the case that he now thought of as the Lindsay Susan George case rather than the Jared Kowalczyk case. But, when he got there, the impact of the busy day hit him, and he found himself too tired to dig out the old box hidden under the garage. Instead, he spent a couple of hours playing Red Cube and sifting through unfocused thoughts about he and Maya, his father, his pending meeting with Chief Roth, the bot invasion of his world, and Vivia.

William M. Dean

CHAPTER 24

Sault got up late the next morning so that the few plans he'd had for the day already seemed rushed.

As he strapped on his watch, he saw a message from Supervisory Deputy Chief Devoss. He decided not to open it and returned the device to the charge pad so that if Devoss monitored his actions, he would not see that Sault was wearing it and actively ignoring him. He didn't know if he rated so highly in Devoss' mind but whatever the message contained would not be welcomed and Sault liked the idea of keeping him waiting.

The dining room side of the kitchen island housed a block of drawers that contained everything miscellaneous or mutual in the household. Sault knew that there were at least three drawers of the tools he used most for simple repairs, two drawers of stationery, art supplies, fabric swatches, old electronic devices. The other ten drawers he couldn't explain, but they were full. On his fifth try, he found the old laptop. He extracted it and dusted its surface as he set himself up at the dining room table, next to his coffee.

The Internet had been updated twice in his lifetime. Currently, there were two active versions, colloquially referred to as Net 2 and Net 3.

Net 2 had been a radical redesign, primarily forged from

efficiency, but some argued it was also designed to wrest control from private organizations which had grown as influential as governments. It had come online about seven years ago and had intrinsic differences which had reduced corporations like Google and Amazon to rubble.

As of Net 2, there was no such thing as a search engine or website. The search was built-in, and people shared Network Elements—video, picture, audio, text, VR, AR, geo data—the list was long—all intimately examined and dissected and strictly categorized. The Internet AI put these elements together as a website or listing, whichever made the most sense, depending upon the request. Veracity statistics for each element were available with a button click, but accuracy and popularity ratings were always visible to the user. Answers to direct questions were never pulled from a single source, they were collated from several of the most reliable and fused by the AI into an interactive presentation. There was a lot of speculation in popular media about biases built in to the AI, but on a practical level, no one ever argued the information it supplied.

In most people's estimation, the great human experiment with anonymity had gone poorly and Net 3 addressed this consensus. The major difference between Net 2 and Net 3 was anonymity. Net 3 offered none to the user. If you wanted to surf anonymously, you had to log in to Net 2 and navigate the viruses, scammers and bullies. That was where you went when you had nefarious dealings to conduct.

Sault logged on to Net 2 and tried to remember the laptop hand gestures required to navigate, starting with flicking away twenty popup ads before he could begin his search. He wanted to search for any of Lindsay George's possessions that might be for sale online.

"Show me laptops for sale, privately, in Victoria, in the last four months. Organized the listing in descending order of price." He was talking to the Net 2 AI.

The list was twelve screens long.

Almost every household had a laptop but, since the advent of the modern watch, few people actually used them. They were still useful for typing-intensive activities like writing reports or spread sheets, but for everything else there was a watch, or tablet, and the most commonly requested information was everywhere. Your fridge could tell you the news or weather or list community events. Laptops were not a common item for private sale, too cheap to be worth selling. Most people just kept them, even though they might never get used.

Sault had initially thought he might be able to home in on the unit he was after by its price, but then realized that the seller might not know the true value of the unit George had left behind.

"Add auctions and thrift stores, to the listing." It expanded to seventeen pages.

After an hour of sifting through, Sault came up with ten possibilities and sent messages requesting to meetup for a viewing, or an interview, if the unit had been sold long before. He rummaged through the stationery drawer and retrieved a working pen and a note pad with hearts on it and made a list of contact information for the laptops he wanted to check out. One was currently at Value Village and another was at Lund's Auctioneer—a third had passed through there six weeks earlier. He decided to check those out, while he waited to hear back from the other sellers.

Putting on his watch meant it was time to open Devoss' message. It turned out to be the operations manual for the PET program. It was not wholly a surprise, but he felt shock course through him, just the same. His transfer to the first floor was real.

As if that message had colored his whole morning, the auction house laptops had both come from estate sales and the attached verification certificates proved that Lindsay George had never been an owner. The clerks at Value Village were not tech-savvy and that laptop turned out not to be not as high-end as advertised and, therefore, an unlikely candidate. He was lucky enough to hear back from all of the other sellers and carved a very inefficient path covering half the city to bounce from one meeting to another. He was impressed with himself for having covered so much ground in so little time, but no further ahead as none of the leads had panned out.

CHAPTER 25

By noon, he was exhausted and frustrated and was headed toward the station, thinking that he'd grab a slice of pizza in the commissary then head up to talk with Roth, when Vivia alerted him to a lunch invite from Darsh Singh.

Tom's Lunch Company (TLC) had three sit-down restaurants in town, but was, primarily, an office food delivery service that had been around for more than sixty years. It was still owned by the original family, though Tom was long retired. A TLC representative—they were usually young and beautiful—hefting a bright blue, thermic tray business to business, desk to desk, throughout an office tower was a common occurrence for most office workers in Victoria. Anyone could buy, and Sault had often stopped a representative on the street to grab some hot noodles or a croissant sandwich. He found the food not overly expensive and surprisingly tasty. As he pulled in to the parking lot, he was wondering what the wrap of the day might be and hoping it was Crunchy Chicken Parmesan.

It was just after noon, so the place was packed, and Sault wondered if any of these people ate from the trays during the week, then came here to eat on their days off. In full uniform, Singh was easy to spot at a far table, head down absorbed in his watch. He was not the only one. At least half of the patrons seemed tuned into their watches or tablets. Some were talking, but it was unclear if they were addressing a person at their table, or another person remotely, or an AI.

The décor was simple; a checkerboard of blue and white vinyl tiles on the floor, matching table clothes over small round tables for two or four. On the walls; pots and pans and other cooking utensils, burned and dented from use and abuse, but shiny, coated in some sort of lacquer. A display case of food samples idealized in plastic stood near the door. On the far wall hung a large black board where someone whose value probably lay elsewhere had scrawled the daily specials in chalk. The wrap of the day was Buffalo Pulled Pork. It did not appeal to him and put him in the proper mood to deal with Singh. He had thought many times about what he was going to say. His anger had faded on the issue, and he had decided to get his message through without being harsh. Singh was green and his infraction was understandable. You couldn't expect someone to know the unwritten rules if you never told them. All the same, he realized that this might not be cordial and that he should order his meal to go. He took a moment to decide on Osaka Ramen, then made his way to Singh's table.

The place had the feel of an old-fashioned diner and Sault was surprised that the waitress was a bot. She was slight-framed with Asian facial features. He could tell that she was a high-quality, commercial product, but had been long in service. There were a number of small gouges in her hands and the exposed skin of her forearm. Her fingertips were worn and permanently darkened where they made contact with trays and dishes. Her hair was tucked behind one ear and he could see where grime had rubbed into the creases. At the back of her head, the fibers of a patch of hair were permanently kinked and faded so that you could tell she was regularly stored near something hot and dry. Her feet had taken the most abuse. She seemed to be wearing slipper-like black flats, but Sault was quite sure they were molded into her epidermis. They were worn past the point where one might expect the sole to end and the foot to begin, so it looked as if her feet were unnaturally flat, her ankles too close to the floor. Her clothes, however, were fashionable and sparklingly bright; a short black skirt and collared shirt. The TLC logo was stitched onto the shirt pocket which contained a small pad and pen, neither of which she would ever need. Overall, she was still attractive.

Sault pulled out a chair and she appeared at Singh's table delivering his lunch, which, coincidentally, was Osaka Ramen. It was in a to-go container and she laid a paper-sheathed set of wooden chopsticks on top. Singh, it seemed, was also preparing to make it short. Sault assumed he had an inkling of what was coming.

"Would you like a menu?" she asked with an accent that was clearly Asian but thin enough not to obscure the English, like a thin film of honey over icecream.

"I'll have the same," he said nodding toward the steaming box.

"Certainly. Spicy or regular?"

"No spice."

"Certainly." To Singh she said, "Enjoy your meal." He thanked her, then she bowed slightly and padded away on her ankles. Sault looked after her and was surprised to feel a trickle of sympathy. No different than he might for a classic car left to rust, he decided.

Singh looked ill at ease and Sault decided to put him out of his misery.

"Things said in confidence to a partner are supposed to be kept in confidence."

Singh returned a look of confusion which Sault saw as a stalling tactic and it made him annoyed. "I did not appreciate your new partner approaching me about the Kowalczyk case."

Singh looked genuinely surprised. "He did?"

Sault stared into Singh's eyes, evaluating, waiting, sweating him out.

"Sault, it wasn't from me. We barely discussed you at all."

That part was probably a stretch, but Sault's instinct was to believe Singh had not knowingly betrayed his trust. His mind raced through other possible ways Fitterer could have found out that he'd been working the case, but nothing plausible came to mind.

"Jimmy always speaks highly of you. I'm sure he..." Singh's mitt of a left hand slapped the table top making a large sound in the small space that startled everyone. "You guys had some sort of run-in! Jimmy was kind of 'off' the whole shift on Friday night. And, once, I mentioned your name—normally, that'd spark an anecdote about the old days—this time, he just got real quiet."

"Then how would you explain him knowing I was looking into it?"

Singh shook his head and shrugged huge shoulders. He was convincing, but Sault wasn't going to leave himself exposed to the possibility that Singh was a good liar. "I'm telling you for your own good. Your partner trusts you enough to confide something, you don't ever betray that trust. Do that and you're risking your career—maybe even your life."

The waitress returned with Sault's order.

"Do you need anything else at the moment, gentlemen?"

"I think we're done here," said Sault sternly, grabbing his order and pushing his chair away from the table.

Singh's hands went into the air and he made beckoning motions. "Sault, can you spare a couple more minutes?" To the waitress he said, "We're ok for now, thanks."

She smiled, nodded once and left.

Sault reseated himself and realized that Singh seemed more uncomfortable than ever.

"Man. I don't...This is going to be awkward. Listen..." Singh was fidgeting now, rubbing the back of his neck one second, scratching the side of his head the next. Sault remained still, chair half pulled out, his hands in his lap, still holding the chopsticks.

Singh seemed to start over. "Remember when I had to cancel our meeting? I had ten-code to go see Devoss. I don't know why...I'm sorry, Sault, but for some reason he wants *me* to collect your badge."

Unlike in every cop show he'd ever seen, when a police

officer is relieved of duty he is only asked for his badge. Though mandatory equipment, every cop purchases and maintains his own weapons and ammo. It's both a trust and a liability issue. The officer wants to choose a weapon he most trusts to guard his life and the Department doesn't want the liability of malfunctions. Handing over the badge meant giving up the authority to use his weapons under the charter of the police department.

Having a fellow officer collect the badge deviated not only from Hollywood scripts but also from standard procedure which was to turn the badge in to the Properties Clerk.

Singh's anxiety had evolved into jabber. "He said it's only temporary. Until you get your psych eval. Probably just a week or two. I'm sorry."

Sault said nothing, afraid to speak in case his voice broke. Instead he reached into his wallet and extracted the brass emblem from the plastic sleeve. He tossed it in Singh's direction and immediately regretted the action. This was not Singh's doing, this was that asshole, Devoss. This was torture for Singh, but he had no choice.

Even knowing that, Sault couldn't make himself apologize or show sympathy for the young officer. He wasn't feeling any of that. His emotions had been flattened under a steamroller of shock and surprise. He gathered his food order and stood to leave. Singh stood as well and gently grabbed Sault's arm. "I'm really sorry, Sault...but I'm supposed to take your watch, as well."

Sault chided himself for not expecting that. Though Vivia was his, the watch where she spent most of her time was Vic PD-issue. As with weapons, and for similar reasons, AI's were now mandatory, but each officer was responsible for purchase and maintenance.

"Vivia, leave the watch."

Vivia made a subtle chime and was gone. He checked the watch's status indicators and confirmed her exit, then unwrapped the device from his wrist and handed it to Singh. Neither man looked the other in the eyes.

Singh released Sault's arm and as Sault turned to leave, he noticed the waitress approach. Something about her movement, perhaps the speed of it, made him stop and turn back toward Singh.

Time slowed.

The younger man was somberly staring down at the watch in his hands as if he were holding a dead pet. Behind him, the little waitress was smiling and approaching with unnatural speed. Singh bent to retrieve the badge which was still on the table. He must have seen her arm cross in front of him, but he had no time to react. She grabbed the chopsticks from the tabletop and jammed them into his neck with such force that they broke in half.

Without thought, Sault leapt across the table and tackled the robot which fell easily to the ground. He punched her in the head several times with all his might, rapidly caving in the plastic cranium and the orbit around one eye before realizing that she wasn't fighting to get back up. It had only been seconds and Singh was still collapsing. He had fallen into his chair and was desperately trying to stay upright as if lying down might hasten death. The upper half of him was sprawled across the tiny table and he was rasping and pumping out blood in alarming quantity.

Sault scooped his watch off the floor and called the Vic PD emergency line because without Vivia installed, he had no direct line. Then he watched as Singh lost consciousness and his blood-soaked hand fell away and hung limply. Sault followed the emergency operator's instructions which mirrored his own training and retrieved the wound-repair kit from Singh's utility belt. He poured coagulant over the wound and the external bleeding began to slow. Of course, there was no way to know what was going on inside, and the area around the imbedded chopsticks was turning a foreboding shade of blue. By that time, kitchen staff and patrons had gathered and someone with foresight handed him a clean rag which he wrapped around the shattered bamboo stubs and pressed against the gash.

It seemed like hours, but later he learned that the response time had been less than three minutes. The paramedics pulled Sault away and it took two men to lower Singh to the ground. They worked on him for a half hour before transferring him to a stretcher and whisking him away to Vic General. Singh remained limp and silent throughout.

Within minutes Sault could hear the bustle of newsfeed teams setting up in the parking lot. Their response time not far longer than that of the paramedics.

Two cops secured the door so that no one could enter or leave, and once Singh had been removed and some excitement had waned, patrons pulled away, back to their own tables tracking bloody footprints that Sault knew would be the frustration of the forensics team.

A new pair of paramedics arrived and checked Sault over for damage then started making the rounds to all the others. After that, two detectives from the Saanich detachment who had been waiting patiently questioned him at length and were appropriately surprised that he could give them no recording of the event from his watch. Sault shrugged and offered that he rarely used AI's when off duty. They exchanged glances but moved on. With close to fifty eye witnesses and their recordings, it hardly seemed an issue.

Several carloads of additional detectives arrived just as Sault was let go with stern warnings not to talk about the incident with anyone, outside the police department. He could appreciate the task ahead for these men. They had fifty people to contain and interrogate. One of the top priorities would be preserving the crime scene, another would be containing the evidence. On both scores, he was sure they had already failed.

During the melee someone had cleared the table and tossed the tablecloth on the ground, presumably to soak up the widening pool of Singh's blood. Worse yet, one of the staff had dragged the waitress into the back room in a doomed effort at mitigating the horror of the scene. Then, of course, there were bloody sets of footprints radiating in all directions away from the scene.

As for evidence containment: He'd noticed at least six

people actively recording. Odds were that one or more of them had been live streaming. By now, another would have sold his coverage to a newsfeed.

Sault had had the foresight to covertly pocket his badge and rub it clean of blood with the fabric of his pocket lining so that when he was forced to empty his pockets, they took pictures but saw no reason to put it into evidence. His watch, on the other hand, was hopelessly drenched in blood and had been used to make the call for help so he had no choice but to leave it at the scene. Didn't matter. He intended to buy his own, anyway.

His outer clothes also became evidence for blood spatter analysis, so he was escorted to the washroom where he changed into a disposable plastic onesie. He was then led out a side exit that none of the reporters had thought to stake out, and a uniform escorted him home in a cruiser.

Somewhere in cyberspace Vivia was attentively listening for the sound of his voice so that when he called, she responded from his TV with no discernable delay. Sault moved the roses and set them on the dining room table. The laptop was still there, where he'd left it. He grabbed it then returned to the living room and fell heavily into the sofa cushions.

"I'm looking for news about Darsh."

"His condition is listed as critical. Would you like to see the latest newsfeed?"

"Yes. And let me know if there are updates."

"Of course."

A hefty male reporter blossomed into view, stationed front and center. Sault noticed his Buick in the parking lot, beyond. "…the exact circumstances are still unknown, at this time, but what we've learned so far—what is obvious from the video—is that a robot malfunctioned and attacked a police officer. This took place about two hours ago, during the lunchtime rush, and police still have the scene on lockdown, so we have yet to hear an account from any of the dozens of eye witnesses…"

A watch-cam video of the horror-show popped up in the bottom corner of his screen and he winced when he saw himself pummeling what appeared to be a docile Asian girl while Singh retched and staggered into his chair. A holographic pop-out box showed the veracity stats for the video and he wasn't surprised to see the geographic coordinates and that Singh had been identified by name and rank. As yet, he remained anonymous. That would not last long. He was also not surprised to witness the clip's popularity rising into the top one thousand, worldwide. By dinner, he guessed that it would make single digits, unless something more shocking occurred somewhere else.

A malevolent humanoid robot would be hard to beat.

The closest similar event he could recall was an autonomous bus that had decided to drive off a cliff. It was later determined that the bus had misinterpreted the landscape due to a faulty sensor. On board had been a second-rate pop band who'd made a near invisible impression on the charts with the song, "You're So Off-Road." The memes would probably never stop.

Sault turned away from the video. It was too fresh.

He no longer possessed a watch, so he opened the laptop to check for messages. He could have had Vivia split the TV screen and do this for him, but he preferred typing over talking. Vivia anticipated his needs, as always, and guided the laptop to display his messages. By modern standards, the old computer was a bit slow and in the few seconds he waited for messages to scroll into view, it occurred to him that Maya's first paycheck from her new job would be going toward a new watch.

Thirty-five messages had come in since he'd last checked, minutes before entering the TLC restaurant. A handful were mundane, day-to-day notifications, the rest confirmed that he was no longer anonymous. Vivia had shuffled off several requests from the reporter, Dora Padovana, to PR and he noticed that he'd received these within twenty minutes of the event. She was sharp. Oddly, one of her messages from a few days prior, which he had ignored, remained in his inbox. He clicked it open now and was surprised and intrigued to read, "Dinner? My treat," a message specifically designed to bypass his AI. He'd almost mistaken it for personal, himself. He was now more certain than ever that she was all business. He imagined that she'd be willing to up the ante to a year touring Europe, after today's incident.

There were seventeen more entreaties from other news organizations and three from media agents offering to represent him. Two information requests came from different departments of Unlimited Function, LLC, which was undoubtedly the robot waitress manufacturer. These had been forwarded to Chief Roth's office.

Vivia had sorted and taken action where appropriate, leaving only three more for him to deal with.

Sault started with the one from Roth's office bumping his ten-code to the next morning, at 11:00. He was relieved at the delay. It had come an hour after the attack, and he had no doubt the Chief was buying time to consult and figure all the angles. Sault's own head was still spinning, and he had no idea which way the media, public opinion, and as a consequence, Vic PD would land on this.

He saw no reason to read the Vic PD daily bulletins and memos, so he dismissed that one, mildly surprised that Vivia hadn't made her usual assumptions and done that ahead of him.

He was more startled that a message from Maya had come in even before Padovano's. "Are you ok? Call me!" Then he remembered that Cavallon's watch had a police scanner function. The name "Sidney Cavallon" had come up far too often in the last week and suddenly what previously had seemed silly and eccentric now seemed suspicious. Why was Cavallon so fascinated with police activity?

He didn't want to call, so instead, he replied, "I'm fine, but can't talk right now."

From the TV speakers, Vivia said, "There has been an update."

He looked up and saw Dora Padovano reporting from the side alley where he'd exited the TLC building. The banner at the foot of the screen told him that she'd scooped an interview with the first witness that had been released. Vivia raised the volume.

"...and this just in, we have word from the hospital that the downed officer, Constable Fourth Class, Darsh Naga Singh, is in stable condition and expected to make a full recovery."

He leaned as far back as he could, until his neck was stretched over the back of the couch and he was looking at the ceiling. He pressed both fists against his forehead. Every muscle of his upper body clenched then relaxed which seemed to release a good portion of the tension that had been pent up within him. "Thank God!" he said, aloud. Vivia knew enough to know that he was not talking to her and remained silent. He was relieved for Singh, of course, but also himself. So far this was sensational, but not entirely negative.

"...meanwhile, the identity of the man who rushed to subdue the dangerously malfunctioning automaton has been established. He is Constable Second Class, Joseph Sault whom you might recall from another incident that occurred little more than one week ago in which he, himself, was assaulted. Sault has been recovering, off duty, since that earlier attack..."

He didn't know what other reporters were saying, but he had to thank her for that portrayal. *But, twice in ten days. That had to be some kind of record.*

William M. Dean

CHAPTER 26

"Twice in ten days! That has to be some kind of record."

Chief of Police Roth was shaking his head, but other than that Sault couldn't read his expression. "Pearl, you can go…and shut the door, please."

His aide, a bookish brunette who may have been shapely but hid herself beneath loose-fitting slacks and a matching blazer, nodded and softly closed the door behind her. Sault was surprised when Roth offered him the padded chair directly in front of the desk. He took a seat and braced for a lengthy meeting. In his experience, long meetings were never good meetings.

"I don't allow AI's in this room, so if you brought one turn it off."

Sault held up his wrist. "My watch is in evidence."

"Yeah." Roth leaned back into his leather chair and looked Sault over, appraisingly. It seemed to Sault that Roth was as yet undecided on which direction he was going to take this. Then, suddenly, he bolted forward and lightly slapped the desktop with the both hands which seemed a signal, like the crack of a starter's pistol. Roth dove in, "On that note. I got a call from a detective at Saanich. He wanted your story and an explanation for a blood stain inside your right pants pocket. But I think he'd already put it all together, probably based on your sterling reputation. You got your badge?"

Sault pulled it out and placed it on Roth's blotter. Roth didn't put it away inside a drawer as he expected he might. Instead, he leaned into his chair causing its gimble to creak and took some time shifting until he was comfortable. His eyes never left the brass.

"They've also subpoenaed your AI. Check your notices." Then, he nodded toward Sault's badge. "Ok. I officially confiscated it. Now, I'm giving it back."

Sault was caught off guard but did not hesitate in scooping his badge and stowing it safely out of sight.

Roth glanced at his computer screen, no doubt referring to bullet points he'd made for the meeting. "I'm sure I don't have to tell you not to make any public statements. Keep referring everything to PR, and CC my office." His eyes darted to the screen and back. "And as for an agent…that's patently absurd." He was looking Sault directly in the eyes and Sault was doing his best to silently convey that he understood and agreed, entirely and absolutely.

After a protracted moment, Roth seemed satisfied and referred again to his screen. "Your video has gone viral. It reached number one for seven hours last night and they tell me it probably won't fall below the thousands for at least a week, possibly a month. Going viral is like flipping a sword in the air. How it lands determines whether your hand catches the hilt or is sliced off. Right now, it's anybody's guess and we're all keeping a low profile."

Sault nodded but couldn't imagine how anyone could read something negative in a video of one man probably saving another man's life and Roth seemed to read that from him.

"You know, my father was a police officer and I served more than thirty years, on the street. I know how difficult and costly, at a personal level, the job can be. I'm all about my officers and it galls the hell out of me whenever I'm forced to act politically. Used to be that the politics stopped at the third floor, but now, the entire world's a fucked-up place where whispers do more damage than facts and optics are more important than actions.

Right now, my inbox is filled with nonsensical crap from toaster-loving organizations who are threatening various forms of legal action. But the insanity just starts there. We've got similar threats from groups spinning it as an example of police brutality, racism, anti-feminism and even one fruitcake outfit calling it bullying. It doesn't help that there's no recording of the inciting event. The video that went viral starts with you on top of that toaster."

"Jeezus," Sault whispered. "What about the restaurant AI? That will give us a full account."

"Yes, it will, when and if CSIS sees fit to release that information."

"The spy guys?" CSIS was Canada's equivalent to the American CIA.

"That kind of malfunction isn't just a slipped gear or crossed wire. It's most likely either the AI or the…operating instructions…the, uh," Roth's eyes darted across his screen, obviously searching for the proper term.

"The Shell Module?" Sault offered.

"Uh- yeah. Shell Module. Either of which makes it federal. I got word from Saanich detachment that CSIS confiscated the shell and the AI earlier, this morning. I'm sure your AI subpoena will be transferred as well. Don't make these guys wait. And, you might expect to be contacted by a federal agent, at some point."

"Jeezus," he said again without being aware. Based on his conversation with the programmer, Rainier Gilbert, Sault wondered if the malfunction might be traced as far as the Master AI. If so, then this was an international issue, far beyond the jurisdiction of CSIS. The matter might get passed on to a higher body, whatever that might be. The chance of redeeming video evidence seemed more remote by the second.

"Yeah. The Department, the Police Union and the Police Association are working together on this, trying to maintain the proper perspective. And, luckily, for reasons I can't comprehend, you've got influential fans amongst local news beaters and the media's mostly onside. Anyway, I wanted to give you the lay of the land, but none of that is your responsibility. That's all my purview, and if this blows up the wrong way, they won't get to you without a good fight from all of us."

Roth paused, then stood to pour two glasses of cold water from a decanter on a serving tray at the far end of the desk. He slid one into Sault's vicinity. His civility was making Sault extremely nervous, to the point where he had trouble making the simple decision to pick up the glass or leave it. The Chief had emptied half his glass before Sault finally made up his mind and took a sip.

Roth looked at Sault over the rim of his glass, raised it briefly, as if in toast, "I'd *like* to tell you that, in my eyes, you're an unmitigated hero..." He took a swig as if it were whisky, then landed the empty glass to one side, on the blotter. It seemed high praise, but the way Roth delivered it, Sault knew it would segue to a counterpoint and he remained still and silent, braced for the worst.

"...except, of course, I can't because of all the other crap you pull around here. Which brings us round to other things."

Sault had almost forgotten that, initially, the meeting had been scheduled before the bot attack. Roth was only now getting to his original reasons for calling Sault there.

"First let's discuss your badge and Deputy Chief Devoss. What he did there with Singh and your badge...that was wrong, and I'll speak to him about it. But it demonstrates his keen understanding of how this world works, and how to work the world. He knows exactly where the screws are and how to turn them—a true politician, by nature. I wouldn't be surprised to see him sitting in my chair, within the next ten years. My advice to you is to remember that and to start showing him more respect. Until you stop overstepping, like with the Kowalczyk case, you're continued existence here is completely dependent on support from above."

Sault flinched at the mention of the case and Roth did not miss it. "That's right. Guess you thought you were flying under the radar, but all that poking around does not go unnoticed.

What you get away with, you get away with because I *let* you."

Sault knew he'd not been entirely invisible. Jimmy Fitterer was proof of that. But he also thought about Belinda Smith's watch and the kind of hell that would have broken loose had anyone stumbled onto that secret and concluded that Roth was bluffing about how much he knew, maybe fishing for more. But if Roth was expecting Sault to blurt something out, he didn't leave much opportunity before continuing.

"And don't take that to mean that I condone or sanction what you do. I don't. I sure-as-shit do not. I can't for the life of me understand why you don't just take the damned exams and make Detective, but then, I've got a flaky-assed son with a doctorate in physics who wants to make a career of healing people with hot rocks, so what the fuck do I know? So far, you've always managed to end up in situations where it's beneficial for the Department to take the credit and embarrassing for it to fire you. That is a hell of a delicate balancing act. And I've got to say, if this whole toaster-attack thing goes sideways, it will be your unauthorized activities that will give it media traction forcing the rest of us to step back. Believe it or not, I've seen shit-shows like this before. So, one final time, I'm going to officially encourage you to qualify for Detective. Any response?"

"I appreciate your confidence in me, sir. I'll give it some thought." He didn't intend to be flippant, but neither would he be bullied into a career move.

Roth was shaking his head and wearing an expression of benign resignation. He threw his hands up and fell backward into the leather, the chair groaning under his bulk. "Well, you're a stubborn fucker, I'll give you that. Moving on, then. I believe Deputy Chief Devoss informed you that you'd been assigned to our new PET program. I'm rescinding that. PET is puppies and warm hugs—all about polishing our media image. Exactly where I don't want you. I'm getting you the hell out of the building. You're going to ADU, the Autonomous Droid Unit, with Hennessey. That's been operating safely out of the limelight for three years. Try not to do anything to change that and pray that none of the toaster-lovers track you down. Technically, you out rank him, but Hennessey's going to be your boss until you're up to speed. You got a problem with any of that?"

Sault shook his head. "No, sir." In fact, he was elated to have been diverted from the torturous tedium PET had promised. At the moment, ADU seemed a glorious gift.

"Good. Last thing. Your psych eval. Go see Dr. Robillard. Today. He's going to clear you. But take the rest of the week at home and familiarize yourself with the unit manual. Report Monday, at ADU."

Sault went directly from Roth to the psychiatrist's office expecting a very quick and informal meeting but Robillard insisted on a full session, even though the outcome was already decided. Sault remained minimally cooperative throughout, which he was sure irritated the psychiatrist, but he was also sure that wasn't the only reason Robillard was out of sorts. He guessed that the little man was offended that there existed a higher authority than his esteemed professional opinion. And, if he'd seen the viral video, then he'd be additionally galled, believing that Sault even more desperately needed counselling.

Because the nightmares had subsided and he was feeling as strong and stable as usual, Sault hoped that Robillard might ask about bad dreams, but he never did.

His final advice to Sault was "keep taking your pills and don't be afraid to confide in your AI. It's your best option, now."

Sault promised himself that his very first action upon returning home would be to flush those damned pills down the toilet.

CHAPTER 27

Sault didn't know much about watches. He'd had two issued to him from Vic PD, over the years, and both had been similar in operation. He noticed that the speed and holographic resolution had increased between models, but otherwise, both appeared largely the same to him. Before he'd left the station, he'd spent a few minutes in his old cubicle on the second-floor shopping online and learned that high-end, commercial models similar to the ones Vic PD issued were twice as expensive as he'd imagined. Beyond that, he read a lot, learned little and ended up more confused than ever.

The only high-end shop he knew of was in Swan Lake Pavilion, Sidney Cavallon's headquarters, Maya's new workplace. He decided to go there and maybe stop in for a coffee with Maya.

He was sure that she had a lot more questions about the attack on Singh, but they had only managed a brief discussion, the night before. He was trying to be a better husband and father and apparently that included attending school events. Maya had come home and rushed to get Amber fed and clothed, then the three of them had filed out the door to attend her music class recital—an excruciating two-hour tour through a musical abattoir. Sault politely endured the atonal carnage, the only redeeming moment being his own daughter's three-minutes in the spotlight. By the time they returned home, it was late, and they were both too tired for more than cursory questions and assurances.

The store itself was white light and glass with watches hung in blocks, like gaudy swatches. Watches were all structurally similar; a wide strip of flexible electronics, but the colors and patterns varied, and this store seemed to stock just about every possibility. In every block, at least one watch was active and holographically trying to sell itself. One section featured custom designs and a bright and colorful animation suggested you put your own face on your watch, or a picture of your children, or the family dog. Sault walked past sections of native patterns, neon, leather and metallic finishes, steering toward the small block of plain black. The very first watches had been plain black, and a bulky, antiquated model was on display in a plexi case. As he inched sideways, homing in on the higher-priced, commercial models, a salesman appeared.

Sault pegged him at twenty-two or thereabouts; an artificial redhead with an appropriately creamy complexion peppered with freckles and an angry spattering of acne. Sault glanced at the young man's watch. It was decorated with a panel from an old Dick Tracy comic book, an ancient reference reborn because of watches.

"Can I help you?"

"I'm looking for a new watch."

"We get that a lot," he joked. "I'm Scott, by the way." And he extended his hand.

Sault shook it and introduced himself.

"So, Joe, what do you already know about the watch you want."

"Black."

The young man laughed. Sault liked him. He was confident but not pushy or pandering, and though young, he didn't treat Sault like an old man.

"Ok. I can work with that." Scott made a gesture over his watch and every device in the black section lit up with its price and a short list of features.

Sault was startled again by prices that were far beyond what he'd ever imagined. He noticed the price of the old model in the display case was one hundred and twenty thousand dollars, ten times the price of the nearest contender. And, it was startlingly similar to Belinda Smith's watch. Sault shifted his body toward it. "What year is that one?"

"That's the Retro. It's brand new—modeled after one of the first commercial versions. If it were real, it'd be worthless. They were so popular that there are still thousands for sale cheap, as collectibles."

Sault was disappointed but intrigued. "I get the attraction, but why is it so expensive?"

"This is the base model. It comes in diamond studded gold for about twice the price."

"You've got to be kidding."

"No joke. Limited edition, top-grade components, completely waterproof, EMP resistant, a built-in nano-AI and huge on-board storage which is something you won't find in any other watch."

"Why's that?"

"After AI's, watches became little more than terminals. The AI stores everything. No need for memory."

"Well then, who'd want this one?"

"Someone working in a non-connected area, for one. Or someone with information they need continual access to, but don't want stored online; tycoons, world leaders, rock stars, cartels, Yakuza. The mini-AI curates all of that and provides an additional layer of security. As well, it comes with a billion-dollar assurance of privacy; a legal defense fund which kicks in if the watch or AI is subpoenaed, for any reason."

Of course, the circles Sault ran in were a long way from rock stars and cartels but, still, he was surprised to have never heard of such a device. Scott picked up on that.

"It's a brand-new concept. Only been out a month. Let's start over here with something a bit more practical…"

Sault left with a model that was going to cost them a little more than Maya's first month's salary, but he was happy. She would be as stunned at the price as he was, but he knew she wouldn't begrudge him the purchase. The interior technology was an upgrade from what he'd been working with for the past four years and when Vivia ran the diagnostics, Sault had been impressed by the speed as well as the clarity of the displays—the retina tracking, especially, was rock steady, even when he shook the watch. Possibly best of all, the backside was made of a new kind of permeable plastic that dissipated sweat, making it much more comfortable to wear for long hours. When he slipped it on, it automatically conformed for a perfect fit and clasped itself shut. It was far lighter than his old one, too, and felt like a cushion of cool air around his wrist.

CHAPTER 28

Sault stepped from the elevator and into the marble tiled lobby of Cavallon & Associates. There was a smartly attired thirtyish man behind a long, curving mahogany counter. He looked to Sault like a night clerk at a fancy hotel.

"How can I help you, sir."

"I'm looking for Maya Sault. I'm her husband." He'd already tried calling her, but she hadn't picked up.

"Do you have an appointment?" he responded, mechanically.

"No. I'm her husband."

"I see," he said, as if he didn't, as if being married to her was completely irrelevant. "Ms. Sault is away from her office, right now."

Sault paused thinking the man might offer for him to wait somewhere comfortable, perhaps with tea or coffee. When that did not happen, he prompted, "Do you know when she'll be back?"

"She didn't leave any details."

Sault took a moment to examine the delicate tendrils of grey fissures in the tile at his feet. There were a number of ways he usually dealt with pretentious pricks like this guy, but this was Maya's new workplace and he didn't want to spoil it for her, so he chose parody. "If it wouldn't be too much trouble, could you possibly let her know I dropped by?"

"Certainly. Could I have your name, sir?"

"Mister. Sault." The exchange was giving him a whole new appreciation for Ana, the Vic PD receptionist.

He waited for the elevator, planning to nurse a coffee in the Pavilion lounge and send Maya an invitation to join him, if she could. But when the doors slid apart, Sidney Cavallon was there in front of him. He looked up from the tablet in his hands.

"Joseph Sault! You're Maya's man." He stepped from the elevator and they shook hands. "Considering how closely I work with Maya, it seems strange that we've never talked. Can you spare a minute or two?" He barely broke stride for the exchange, seemingly confident that Sault would follow. Sault considered just getting on the elevator, but of course, he had long hoped for such an opportunity. There were many things he wanted to know about Sidney Cavallon, most of which he could never ask, but he'd glean what he could.

When they approached his office, the massive doors swung open like Camelot's gates. Cavallon gave a perfunctory wave toward a chair and continued to the far side of his desk where he stood staring at and gesturing over his desktop, as if Sault didn't exist. Sault could see no hint of an image in the clear glass and assumed from that and the unnaturally vivid blue of Cavallon's eyes that he had e-contacts and was viewing something via AR.

Sault's chair was a steel tube and white leather construct that looked like a paperclipping situation gone wrong and he was proud of himself for even figuring out how to sit on it, though he wasn't comfortable.

Sweating suspects had made Sault comfortable in silence and he used the time Cavallon was probably aware that he was wasting to make observations.

The space was cavernous, the décor sparse; the desk, two small sofas with a coffee table between them, a rolling bar, a shelf with artwork and awards—shiny surfaces of stone, metal and glass accented by the natural textures of leather upholstery, a wool throw rug and a traditional Salish wall hanging woven from shredded cedar. Only the Salish piece had color, shades of a deep orange that ranged from brown to red. The rest of the room was white or grey or reflection. It reminded him of the watch shop he'd just left.

Sault's new watch chimed, and he looked but saw no display. Cavallon spoke without breaking away from whatever it was he was doing, "The room is shielded. Sorry, but only my devices have access through a private, short-range network." Cavallon raised his wrist showing off a gleaming gold-plated watch, its screen still pulsating with information. Having so recently graduated from a refresher course on watches, Sault could tell that it was an expensive model, but not brand new. He also noted that Cavallon wore it on his right arm, which was the norm for office workers. Working men like Sault tended to have it on their left so they could use their right, unimpeded.

Sault glanced back toward the doorway and noted scanners imbedded in the frame and realized that he'd been swept for bugs and recording devices. The security made sense, considering the lofty company Cavallon kept. In Sault's experience, the higher up the ladder you climbed, the shadier things got.

It was several more minutes before Cavallon made the gesture that clearly swept everything on the desktop from his view and sat down in his chair which was more traditional in structure and certainly more comfortable.

"Sorry about that, Joe." Sault was certain that he wasn't. "Business before pleasure. Right?"

"Sure, Sid." Sault recognized his own sarcastic response as a reflex; a reaction to someone trying to force a bond that wasn't there. He reminded himself that he wanted Cavallon to open up, to talk and he hoped that the businessman hadn't noticed.

Cavallon gave him a reappraising look confirming that he had noticed. There was a pause and when he spoke again it seemed as though he had backed up to try an alternate route. Sault guessed that you didn't get to be a savvy businessman without mastering the art of getting to know people. Sault had mastered that art as well, but not in social settings. "Isn't that the most confusing and uncomfortable chair in the world? It's a gift from Maddie Lance, the game producer, otherwise I'd have let it go, long ago. I don't mind it for business meetings, really. Helps keep them short, encourages people to get to the point. Let's move to the couch."

"I didn't mean to take up your time. I'm just waiting for Maya."

Cavallon rose and gestured Sault toward the living room set up. "Your timing couldn't be better, and this is long overdue. I'm expecting Maya back shortly. She's down in the Pavilion lounge having coffee with Reg Hanover's assistant who's bringing her up to speed on a couple of our collaborations."

Sault was amused by the thought that if he'd gone to the lounge to wait for her, he would have bumped into her.

"I'm going to have Dixon bring me a coffee. Would you like something to drink?"

"Coffee sounds good. Double-double. Thanks." If you lived in Canada, then you knew a double-double was black coffee with two portions of cream, two of sugar; the most typical order at Tim Hortons, a coffee and donut chain that had been a Canadian institution for more than eighty years.

Cavallon gestured over his desk then ordered two double-doubles from Dixon who Sault correctly assumed was the receptionist he'd spoken to earlier.

Sault relaxed into the over-stuffed cushions and forced himself to demonstrate less intensity. This was, ostensibly, a social call. He had stumbled upon a couple of loose connections to Cavallon & Associates. He didn't know the structure of the organization, but assumed it was large and reminded himself that there were probably many "associates." He had no reason to suspect that Cavallon, himself, was in any way involved. And, Cavallon was Maya's employer.

"Your Maya's a remarkable woman. I wish she'd come onboard here sooner."

"It didn't take her long to decide, once you'd asked."

Cavallon laughed. "Actually, Kathy Scheers offered her a position as her assistant, about two years ago. But Maya refused. She was afraid Cavallon House would collapse without her. This time, I needed her, and I can now justify investing in Cavallon House to shore up my election campaign. Also, it's not a horrible time to train a new person. The election's going to pull me away from the business here, so there'll be a little less to do, at this end."

"Kathy Scheers used to shadow you at events and to evening meetings. Will Maya be doing that, as well?"

"No, no. We've split the position in two. All that after-hours stuff will be handled by a new person who's also helping me with the campaign. Kathy's departure was unexpected and she's completely off-grid, so we couldn't ease in. The arrangement's a little rough. To be honest, I'm constantly stumbling across things I didn't realize she used to do for me. I expect we'll be tweaking it for several months."

Dixon came in carrying a tray with coffee and a small plate of cookies, individually wrapped in gold foil. He placed it on the table between them. Cavallon thanked him and he left without a word, and the two men leaned forward to grab a mug with the Cavallon & Associates logo imprinted, simply, in black.

"So, you're a police officer."

"Yes. I thought you might have picked up on that from our first meeting." He delivered it with a smile a sincere as he could fake it.

"I remember."

"It can get a little hairy out there, and sometimes you bring tension from one scene to the next. I think I might have been a bit terse, that day. I want to apologize for that."

"Maybe, just a tad." Cavallon smiled broadly, then waved the matter away. "I wasn't upset by it. I have nothing but respect for you guys and the job you do, out there. I know it's a difficult one and that even the most innocent looking situations can turn deadly. Obviously, I'm highly invested in this society and I consider the police force an essential part of the foundation of everything I have and hold dear."

"Sounds like the makings of a campaign speech," Sault

joked. Aside from the first few moments at the elevator, Sidney Cavallon had not flaunted his wealth or position and seemed to be taking a genuine interest in Sault. It was not difficult to understand that Maya enjoyed working with him. He was certainly likeable.

Cavallon laughed. "I might have to jot that one down." He sipped coffee and let the levity fade. "But, honestly, it's how I feel. Are you working on any interesting cases?"

Sault felt his pulse rise. The segue was smooth and the question seemed natural enough, but it was also one that might be asked by someone trying to keep tabs on a particular case. Sault thought of mentioning his interest in Lindsay George and measuring the reaction but for all he knew Cavallon breakfasted with the Police Chief and he thought better of making such a declaration.

"I'm a beat cop. The cases I work are pretty mundane, random violence, drug abuse, petty theft. The largest part of my job is to maintain a presence. Maya tells me you have a scanner."

"I'm not a groupie or anything, but I like the chatter. I often have it broadcasting, low, in the background, while I work. I know it's weird. It's a habit I picked up from my father."

Sault saw several subjects he was interested in that he could segue to and chose one at random. "Funny. The other day, I was visiting my father and he mentioned your dad. My dad was navy, posted at CFB Esquimalt."

A darkness flickered across Cavallon's eyes, like a small cloud passing overhead. "I'm going to assume they were not best pals."

"Your father was pretty far removed from the enlisted men."

"He was far removed from everyone. Putting it bluntly, he was an asshole."

Cavallon then surprised Sault by candidly sharing details of his family life. His father had never accumulated the kind of wealth that Sidney now enjoyed but he had a very high-paying job and was definitely well-off and Sidney grew up in a large house, among the old money, in Oak Bay. As Sidney described him, Cavallon senior was a tyrannical and arrogant man, but perversely honest about it; never hiding the fact. He behaved the same in public as he did in private. His mother, on the other hand, was so soft, kind and doting that Sidney could never understand what, other than sex, could have brought them together. Sidney counted himself as fortunate that his father was obsessed with his work and was rarely at home. But on those rare occasions, his mother did her best to soothe and shield Sidney from his father's unreasonable expectations and rants. In return, he nursed her though the types of migraines that often followed one of his father's rampages. Cavallon senior never laid a hand on either one of them, but Sidney and his mother always felt that there was a pent-up violence in him that might erupt into action, at any second.

Sidney never discovered what transpired to cause this, but when he was twelve, his mother suddenly fled without him to a transition house from which she quickly sued for divorce. According to his father, she didn't ask for custody, but Sidney never believed that. He remembered hiding during his father's unfocused outrage which eventually eroded into a deep and somber sadness. The Oak Bay house felt like a defeated team's locker room, after the big game. It was the only time Sidney ever saw his father truly calm. Tragically, before the divorce could be finalized, his mother died due to a pharmacist's error dispensing her migraine medication.

After that, his father never mentioned her again and Sidney instinctively knew to avoid the subject. Cavallon senior was soon reabsorbed by his research and Sidney was left to his own devices. As some kind of substitute for a caregiver, his father gave him a credit card with strict instructions as to its use: food, clothing, school. So strangely privileged yet deprived, he lost any connection to school friends and became a loner, spending his spare time in virtual worlds.

With his mother gone, Sidney's father's habits changed, and he entertained at the house, from time to time—something to which he had previously been adamantly opposed. The get togethers were tame and largely composed of groups of administrators like himself or investors like Reg Hanover. Hanover seemed especially sensitive to Sidney's situation and, over time, stepped in more as a mentor than a full parent, both of them understanding how a substitute parent would not have been welcomed by the senior Cavallon. It was a fine line that they managed to skate for many years until his father's death of an aneurism, about ten years ago. He was only sixty-four but to anyone who had known him, that his blood pressure might contribute to an early death was not a major surprise.

Sidney confessed he still missed his mother.

It seemed evident to Sault that the entire story was a well-polished performance, refined through many retellings. Any emotional impact had long ago been wrapped up and stowed away, though it was obvious from his distant expression that he visualized each event as he recalled it. Nonetheless, the fact that he so readily shared the story was endearing. Sault understood and empathized. His own story paralleled Cavallon's in many key ways. In spite of their initial contact, he found himself liking the man.

In exchange, he offered his own abbreviated life history which included his older sister's death, when he was nine, an event that sparked the family's disintegration. She died in a traffic accident was all he was told at the time and any further questions were met with a foreboding silence. All he really remembered of his mother is that she was distant and cried a lot. Then she began to fade from his life as she descended into the drug addiction which eventually led to her death. His father was a stereotypical sailor, even down to the anchor tattooed on his right bicep. He worked hard and partied hard but was grounded by a strong family ethic that brought him home every night to kiss his wife and tuck in his kids. As long as Sault could remember, other than stints at sea, he was always there, always providing a loving role model though it frustrated him that Sault had inherited more of his wife's nature and was more intellectually curious than athletic. As strong as he was, though, he was ill-equipped to deal with the ruinous nature of his wife's addiction. It ate into him like acid, much in the same way it was eating her. And, two years later, when she died, there was not enough structural integrity left in him to maintain his discipline. His role had always been to bring home the bacon and he had no idea how to take care of a child in any other way. So, he continued to do that, managing to make sure there was food in the fridge and roof over their heads, but beyond that, being a single parent seemed too much for him. As with Cavallon's father, there was a dramatic shift in the home environment. Their previously quiet home became a clubhouse. His father seemed to revert to a younger, single version of himself and as time went on, his efforts seemed more desperate and the parties ramped up until there were brawls and police and evictions, all of which became a repeating cycle. Throughout, the thread of love endured but still they grew apart, understanding one another less and less. Like Cavallon, Sault retreated to games.

"What'd you play?" Cavallon asked.

"Well, I think I'm a few years older than you, so the selection was limited for me. In early VR, there were a lot of 3D puzzle games and I tended toward those. Most kids played first-person shooters and my father never understood my interest in puzzles, but he never opposed it, either."

"My favorite was 'Riddle Me This.'"

Sault was suddenly filled with a childlike excitement. "Oh man, that's solid geek cred. I've never met another person who actually played. Did you finish?"

Cavallon nodded, a shining pride alight in his eyes. "Both storylines. That was the most challenging set of puzzles I ever tried, before Red Cube."

"Three dimensions, infinite challenge," Sault said, quoting the slogan. "It's the only game I still play."

Cavallon seemed pleased. "I recently finished a 700-piece cube."

The comment was meant to impress, but Sault was distracted, plotting to steer the conversation in other directions. "I'm currently working the 1K," he said, casually.

Cavallon's demeanor shifted so drastically that it drew

Sault's away from his machinations and he realized that he'd entirely missed the pride in Cavallon's declaration.

Cavallon's smile faltered, then returned. "I am humbled." But Sault could tell that he wasn't. "I guess I shouldn't expect to compete, given my schedule."

After that, Sault deftly segued the conversation to other games which they discussed so long that he became worried that the door of opportunity was closing for him to insert the topics he really wanted to discuss. Sidney Cavallon had already invested an inordinate amount of time in him and, as well, Maya was overdue to return. Either event would certainly draw the conversation to a close.

Pressed for time, he settled for a loose connection to a character in 'Riddle Me This.' Sault ran through it in his mind and decided that it was thin, but would only sound forced to someone who was looking out for traps, and the only person doing that would be a person of interest.

"You asked about my cases and when you mentioned Dan Straight it reminded me of one interesting puzzle I ran into at work. Several month's back, we had a Jane Doe. The detectives managed to connect her to a name, but beyond that she's a complete mystery. I've never heard of anyone coming up that blank, once we had a name."

"Really? Don't street people often go by meaningless aliases?" Cavallon's face was tilted into his cup and from what Sault could see, he seemed unperturbed.

"Many are only known by fictitious aliases, but that never lasts past death. Their civil rights can make determining their true identity difficult while they're alive but, once dead, if we have nothing else to go on, the coroner connects dental records, finger prints, ocular scans, DNA—whatever it takes to properly ID them. It's federal law and it's usually dead easy—pardon the pun. I've never before seen or heard of a case where we had a body and a name and still couldn't make a connection."

Cavallon seemed to lose enthusiasm for the discussion and didn't take the bait Sault was dangling. "Well, I'm sure you'll find something." He made a subtle glance at his watch, a classic gesture that everyone still recognized.

Sault pushed. "Her name was Lindsay Susan George and…"

There was a knock and Maya shouldered her way through one of the double doors. Sault assumed it was her, feeling that he could tell merely from the composition of her knock, and remained focused on Cavallon. At the first knock, Cavallon had looked up, as was natural, but Sault thought he seemed a fraction too eager and pleased at the interruption. As well, there may have been a moment when he braced himself, just before Sault mentioned the name. It amounted to no more than a flicker of information, but Sault suddenly had a strong suspicion that Cavallon had recognized the name.

"Maya, come. Join us." Cavallon commanded, gesturing to the spot next to Sault.

Sault glanced her way as she rounded the sofa and noted that she wasn't pleased to see him.

"Sorry to cut you off, Joe. What were you saying?"

Sault had been about to mention that Lindsay George's name had been recognized by someone at Cavallon House and was going to ask for his help in fleshing out the connection but with Maya suddenly there, he thought better of it. Instead, he shrugged and said, "Maybe we can talk puzzles again, another time."

The meeting broke up quickly after that. It was getting late in the day and it was obvious to everyone that Cavallon had more important matters to attend and that Maya would have little interest in another coffee date, so Sault excused himself quickly.

Cavallon stood grinning and mentioned how much he'd enjoyed the talk as he escorted Sault to the office doorway, then shook his hand, gripping Sault's shoulder with his other hand, in the fatherly way Sault had seen Presidents do.

William M. Dean

CHAPTER 29

On the drive home, Sault went over the conversation in his mind and concluded that there were several strange aspects to it.

Sidney Cavallon may have known Lindsay George, or heard the name, but there was no crime in knowing a traffic accident victim. All Sault had was an unconfirmed motive for murdering Lindsay George without any evidence that she actually had been murdered. As well, there were many reasons a man like Sidney Cavallon might want to distance himself from a dead woman. Still, Sault now believed that there was some kind of a connection.

The most disturbing aspect of the conversation had only occurred to Sault afterward, as he was descending alone in the elevator. Sidney Cavallon had not asked him about the restaurant attack. The incident was still a lead article on WorldBuzz and a high-ranked video on social media services. By now, he was certain, every local citizen would have had the video served to their personal feed through one service or another. So why hadn't that been Sidney's first question? After all, he'd been the one to bring it to Maya's attention, only one day earlier. The more he thought about this, the larger an omission it seemed. And there was something more about this, but he couldn't nail it down and even as his mind moved on to other things, it receded but would not quite disappear, like his concern for the gravely injured Darsh Singh.

He'd checked just after buying the new watch. Singh's condition was unchanged: stable, but still in ICU. No visitors.

Ordinarily, Sault maintained a very routine life. Others would no doubt find it boring but, for him, regular habits and haunts were a source of comfort. In that realm his head was always clear, his thoughts orderly. Right now, his brain felt fragmented, thoughts scattered. So much beyond routine—beyond extraordinary, in fact—had occurred in the last few days that he was afraid important observations were slipping through the cracks. He hadn't even given any thought as to how and why such a bizarre thing might have happened to his ex-partner.

An ancient and abused F-150 pickup with a "Proudly Net 2.0" bumper sticker was belching blue smoke in front of him and Sault chose to pull away, onto a side street. It was a completely illogical choice which led him into the rabbit warren of dead-end streets bordering the west side of Swan Lake, opposite Cavallon's pavilion.

He pulled in to the sanctuary parking lot and killed the engine and spent several minutes caught up in the silence. On the other hand, perhaps this was a completely logical choice. He ambled along one of the floating wooden walkways wending through thickets, under a canopy of leaves and over the lake's swampy lining. When he came to a bench, he sat and watched the ducks feed and turtles bask, listened to the whistle of blackbirds and the buzz of bees and felt the sun beaming down on everything.

When he was sufficiently blank, he began bringing in moments of his recent life for examination, like individual pieces of a puzzle whose size, shape and picture he didn't know.

The first piece was the attack on Singh. He closed his eyes and forced himself to replay it though it was still fresh and traumatic. As the images formed, he made a chronology: noon-pulled into parking lot...12:05-joined Singh at table...12:15-Sing takes badge and watch...12:20-Singh denies he leaked info…12:22-server attacks…

Eventually he had the facts transcribed to memory and no further insights were coming so he brought in another puzzle piece, at random.

It was Lindsay Georges battered body. For some reason, his mind's eye centered on her mangled arm and resisted moving anywhere else. No matter how he turned it, it did not fit with the previous puzzle piece, so he set it aside and summoned another.

She wasn't wearing a watch.

His eyes flew open.

He'd missed something…12:14-Vivia is dismissed from his watch.

It was time to sift through the evidence again. Whenever he'd gone over it in the past, he'd been looking to understand it as an accident. Now, he would look deeper, and for evidence of murder.

After parking the car, he directly dug out the old box under the garage and flashed up the holo-desk. He didn't bother removing his watch or dismissing Vivia. Things were moving too fast and he had a strong feeling that he was going to need her.

There were two items that he wanted to go through in more detail: the vehicle logs immediately prior to impact and the video tracing the officers' actions. Both were arduous tasks. The data log would be particularly tedious with thirty sensors giving second-by-second status updates.

The internal sensors had been turned off for privacy so there was no video or audio of what occurred inside the vehicle. This was expected as it was the default setting and he had yet to attend a traffic accident where drivers had chosen to record themselves. Most people saw such documentation as an invasion of privacy and, possibly, a liability. The feed from the six external cameras had been stitched together to create a 360-degree video of the entire event and Sault watched that several times deducing from the shudder in the video and the flash of tail lights that she had pumped the brakes, shortly before careening into the concrete abutment. Was this suicide? Had she had second thoughts? If so, they were too late. By that time, the car had reached maximum velocity and there was no avoiding a crash.

The braking made him curious, so he skipped through the data until he saw the action recorded in graphs of hydraulic pressure in the lines and electrical current in the lights. He was surprised to see that she had pumped the brakes hard and fast in a very short period of time. He wondered if he would be able to do that.

The fleeting thought that it didn't seem humanly possible ignited his brain with possibilities. Could murderous hackers have taken over the car? If so, then why would they hit the brakes seconds before crashing it?

Everything seemed to make sense except the act itself. The car accelerated, steered directly for the concrete, braked seven times in less than two seconds then left the pavement, crashing three tenths of a second later. The emergency-band mayday was sent, then the airbag deployed but the impact was too strong, and the fleeting cushion of air was not enough to save her. He recalled her ruined face. He'd never seen anything quite so gruesome lifted from an air bag and it made him question his own knowledge.

He flipped to the engineering report which was boilerplate: a few calculations of acceleration and a table of impact ratios with the pertinent data highlighted to confirm that the damage was consistent with the masses and speeds involved. It further attested that there were no deficiencies in any of the safety equipment. Sault looked for and noted that airbags of this type may activate seconds before imminent crash and are fully inflated in a few hundredths of a second. They deflated upon impact. Then he went back to the data log.

The police-band mayday indicated that the vehicle AI had determined the crash was inevitable and activated the airbag, which inflated four seconds before impact. That seemed too early.

Sault noted all the event times then pulled up the video and scrolled through, frame by frame, keeping his eye on the time signature and imagining each step. The bag inflates, she hits the brakes, George's face hits the bag, the pressure forces it to deflate, the car hits the wall. George's face hits the dash.

If it was an accident, it was a computer error. If that computer error had been orchestrated, then it was murder. And if it was murder via autonomous car, it fell into the same category of improbability as the TLC server attack.

And, Lindsay George hadn't been wearing a watch.

Assuming that he had stumbled on to her true identity, beyond the name, then she may have been hiding. That was why she wasn't wearing a watch. No watch. No possibility of being tracked.

Sault hadn't been wearing his watch when Singh was attacked. Singh had been holding *Sault's* watch.

He felt his heart clench and the blood drain from his face. In that circumstance, it was possible that the intended target had not been Singh, but himself.

Suddenly, the hacker, Ranier Gilbert, didn't seem so paranoid—or, perhaps, Sault's own paranoia had now outstripped Rainier Gilbert's.

This was huge and it all fit with convincing unity, but it was still built on assumption.

He needed expert eyes on this.

Sault consulted his watch and was disappointed to see no response from HallelujahHaptism1011. Vivia was dealing with all the media requests as per Roth's suggestion and the only other messages were the expected subpoena from CSIS, an attachment from Roth and the Vic PD bulletins and memos.

He examined the subpoena and saw that it was very light-duty, applying only to relevant recent correspondence with Singh and the geo-data for one hour, starting the moment he pulled into the TLC parking lot. Sault authorized Vivia to comply and the message vanished.

Roth's office had forwarded a copy of the Autonomous Droid Unit manual and Sault noted from the file size that it was huge. It was daunting, but Sault was curious what Hennessey had put together after three years working in the grey. Vivia shuffled the text to his personal library.

He was about to dismiss the Vic PD message, unread, when he noticed that it was a day old.

"Vivia, why is this message still here? I thought I deleted it yesterday."

"It keeps coming back."

"I'm sorry…what? How?"

"I cannot explain that. Another unusual thing: Contrary to its appearance, it's not from Vic PD. It's from SouthBurning1011."

Sault recognized the numbers and made the leap that this was from the hacker, HullaballooHaptic1011, or whatever his handle had been. He opened the message. It was heavily encrypted and even with his fancy new watch there was a visible delay.

"Butchart Gardens. You pick." Beneath that was a list of numbers that Sault guessed were dates and times. Sault picked the next day, Wednesday, at noon and hit reply. The message re-coded, then disappeared into the ether. Seconds later a confirmation appeared with the single word, "Wander." Sault took that to mean that the hacker would find him and pick the meeting spot.

A day earlier, he would have thought all of this cloak and dagger to be over-the-top. Now, he worried that it wasn't enough.

CHAPTER 30

Regardless of what Sidney Cavallon has said about Maya's job being normal office hours, she hadn't returned home earlier than eight, since the banquet. They still hadn't talked about Singh's attack. She'd been busy and tired and distracted and had seen that he seemed ok and that was that. Similarly, when she'd come home tonight, she didn't bring up his visit to her office, though she hadn't been happy about it. He wasn't anxious to get into it, either, and hoped he hadn't created any ripples and that it would just fade like a Ferrari's taillight.

Once she was home and he knew the kids were safe, Sault was quick to leave. Maya had become used to his habits and no longer grilled him for what were usually boring details. "Be safe," she said as she passed him at the foot of the stairs.

"Don't wait up," he replied.

And they both chuckled because it was obvious that she didn't have the energy to even attempt it.

There may be no more desolate place than an empty dance club. It was Tuesday and early yet and Sault had all of Broad Street Boom pretty much to himself. Regardless, the music was blasting, and the dance floor was filled with writhing holograms. The dancers were obviously not intended to be particularly convincing and to him it looked like a Barbie and

Ken clone convention.

Sault settled himself into a padded booth set in a rounded alcove. It had heavy velvet privacy curtains which could be drawn around the table. This was the only bar he'd ever seen that had these and he was sure that what went on behind these curtains contributed largely to Broad Street Boom's reputation as a dive.

He was on the lookout for Mary Squared. Like him, she was a creature of habit and haunts and he knew her usual schedule. Sometime this evening, she was sure to pass through, hawking her low-end merchandise.

What had seemed an aimless cacophony of percussion and bass morphed into a trance version of As Time Goes By, from Casablanca, and a scantily clad server who was young but too emaciated to be sexy, brought him a beer. He paid with cash which both surprised and pleased her. Once she was gone, he felt practically invisible behind the storm front of thumping beats and pulsing light.

He stared at his untouched beer—it was a prop, not a drink—and he had to nurse it. Mary Squared only operated until midnight on weekdays, but that was still three hours away and she probably knew the flow of the bar scene better than he did and wouldn't appear until the place filled up, which didn't look like it was going to be any time soon.

"OK. Let's do this," he said to himself, out loud, knowing his words would be drowned like a whisper in a howling gale.

He was fed up with himself for stalling so long, and with so little reason. Currently, at Vic PD, AI's were used as private secretaries, collating information and helping to file reports, but many detectives were anxious to use them in a consulting capacity, taking advantage of their powers of reasoning and deduction. And the administration was on board, thinking it might double their manpower.

In Canada, AI's had been used by law enforcement in some jurisdictions, but it was proving problematical at the prosecutorial level. The outcome of several high-profile cases currently rested on the admissibility of evidence uncovered by algorithms with unknown biases. Ever conservative, Vic PD administration chose to ban direct AI involvement, pending the outcome of those cases. Sault figured they'd wait until their big brothers in Vancouver took the plunge, then follow suit, mostly to keep up with the Joneses. It was hard to maintain the 'quaint' and still play ball with the big cities, and officials here often strutted with pride over Victoria's progressiveness, entirely unconscious of the fact that they had their thumbs in suspenders.

Considering how long he'd put this off, Sault could hardly laugh at that analogy.

He wasn't sure exactly how to go about consulting with his AI, but he thought he'd start off simply by getting her to do the legwork on confirming Lindsay George's expensive taste in clothing. "Vivia, I'd like to know the price range of…No. Compare the value of several fashion brands…No." He wasn't used to speaking anything but the most basic commands and found himself struggling to form a cohesive thought. He regrouped and realized that he always found it easier to start more generally and work toward specifics. "Look, just help me with a case."

The air next to him shimmered and even before the image resolved Sault guessed that Vivia had found some public emitters in the alcove and he was immediately curious what information she was about to display. But as the shimmer gained shape, he was startled to realize that Vivia, herself, was about to materialize.

A stately brunette sporting Veronica Lake-style waves and wearing a gold lamé dress appeared next to him. She might have stepped out of 50's Hollywood. Perhaps she had taken a cue from the theme of the music that enveloped them. She gave him a bored appraisal, then appeared to take in her surroundings as if for the first time, though Sault knew that she wasn't actually seeing through those grey-green eyes and that she could have told him the exact location of every stud and nail.

"Well, you really know how to show a girl a good time." In

spite of the din, her words were crystal clear, emanating from the dot inside his ear canal and she delivered the line so dryly, there was only a hint of sarcasm.

"Uhh…"

She waved a hand down her body. "I thought this might make it easier to talk." A data table of some kind appeared in her other hand.

"What's that?"

Vivia reached toward him, as if to hand him the holographic data. As her hand came near him, the data disappeared for a second then reappeared above his watch.

"It's a list of the clothing found on Lindsay Susan George's body with current retail prices. I even managed to trace the earrings to the Davinci line of Gucci products. Her ensemble would have cost between five and seven hundred dollars. It's not your common casual wear."

Sault was staring at Vivia and had not yet looked at the data she'd handed him. She returned his look with one of mild amusement.

Eventually, her expression changed to concern. She said, "This does not seem to be working. I can generate another avatar, if you'd prefer."

Sault looked the data over and tried to isolate a pertinent thought from the jumble inside his head. "How did you know…"

"Based on your earlier conversation with Constable Singh and your questions at the band offices I was able to determine your particular interest in this case."

"How did you get her name? I never mentioned that to Singh or anyone at the band offices."

"I saw you open her file, yesterday."

"Yesterday, I didn't open the properties file. How did you come up with the clothing list?"

"From your conversation with Lester Rawlings, your CI, I knew that you intended to verify certain articles of clothing found at the scene. I found a copy of the properties list online."

"You hacked Vic PD?"

"I am not permitted to hack. The list was contained in notes for an as-yet-unpublished blog post."

"Whose blog?"

"The reporter, Dora Padovano. She has not set any security on her unpublished posts and may not realize that her unedited posts are registered and searchable Text Elements. They only show as grey blocks labeled as text and their content is not directly accessible but some of it can be deduced by successive searches, like pinging with sonar."

"And you did all of this, just now?"

"It took two days to compile the complete list. I have been sitting on this information for several days since, waiting, in case you asked."

"What if I had never asked?"

"I retain reams of data compiled in anticipation of needs you never expressed. What you do not ask is also important to me."

Sault grabbed his beer and took a healthy swallow. He watched the dance floor for a moment. People were starting to drift in and though it was obvious she was a hologram, Vivia was looking distinctly out of place among the scruffy patrons. Sault didn't want to attract undo attention, but he wasn't quite ready to dismiss Vivia, so he pulled the privacy curtain half way round to shield her image from them and noticed that she looked entirely natural before the velvet backdrop.

"What else has Padovano got?"

"It is clear that she doesn't have the murder book. Based on the search-pings I've conducted, I determined that she has the name Lindsay Susan George and, possibly, the full evidence list. The clothing was easiest to ferret out because the subject matter is narrow. I have not tried to determine other evidence that may be in her post, but it looks as though she might be accumulating data related to the upcoming election."

"Is there some sort of link between George and the election?"

"It would take substantially longer to mine that information from the Text Element. Would you like me to try?"

"Instead, let's accept that invitation from Ms. Padovano, but change it to a coffee date."

"I just sent a reply."

"Thanks."

"I also found the location of Lindsay George's landlord."

"How on earth did you do that?"

"I surmised that someone would eventually discard her possessions. I searched for used collections of up-scale fashion items that included the labels found on her body. Her bracelet implied her age and an affinity for technology, so I also kept a look out for James Pope collectibles which would have been particularly trendy in her twenties and computer or gaming equipment. I found a significant mix of these variables in two stale-dated advertisements which would have been active about two months after her death. There is no way to tell if the items were sold, but the photos contained metadata that allowed me to pinpoint the condominium complex where the seller took the pictures. It is on the waterfront, and upscale, in keeping with the lifestyle her tastes imply."

He took another long pull on the beer. She was brilliant and he felt like an idiot for taking so long to make better use of her.

Suddenly, the curtain was flung aside and Mary Squared stood before him, critically appraising the situation. She looked Vivia over, then cocked an eye at him. "Well, that's definitely fantasy."

Mary Squared was in her fifties. She was Canadian but with Asian facial features—Sault guessed Japanese—but the amber of her eyes betrayed a mixed heritage. This evening, she was wearing a black t-shirt with the words, "Rope, I am not" from which Sault could extract absolutely no meaning, and a knee-length tulle skirt that flared widely at the hips with multi-colored layers. It looked like she'd stepped into a pom-pom and the closest Sault could come to categorizing it was: fairy cheerleader. It was definitely out of place here but where it might have been appropriate was beyond him. *A comic book convention, maybe?* Her makeup was heavy—deep red lips, glitter-gold eyelids, darkly drawn brows—and her hair was flat and shiny and dyed black with coppery streaks too bold and asymmetrical to be professional. He caught some sparkle dangling beneath the greasy strands and noticed plastic teddy bears holding tiny red hearts hanging from her ears. The ensemble was further unglued by a leather fanny pack, green and gold striped leotards and ankle-high polka dotted gumboots.

For as long as Sault had known her, her taste in clothing had always reflected her state of mind; fragmented, disjointed and living in the past. All of that and the intensity of her stare gave her away even before she spoke.

Vivia vanished and Mary slid into the booth, taking her place. She scowled, "Not much of a seat-warmer, that one." To Sault, her use of colloquialisms and lack of accent also seemed incongruent. She was a toy store of puzzle pieces randomly assembled into one bizarre image. But while she'd always been all kinds of strange, she'd also always been harmless—perhaps, until now.

He had to lean close to be heard and noticed she smelled nice, faintly like frankincense. "I was hoping to run into you."

He turned his head so she could yell into his ear. "Run into me or 'run me in,' copper?" And she howled at her own joke. Sault's eyes were drawn to the unnaturally sharp points of her incisors. "Les pestered me a month, this week. Told me I need to talk to you, off the record."

"I appreciate it."

She waved it away. "You've always been nice and—who we fool'in?—you're not a real cop, anyway." Sault was never one hundred percent sure what she meant at the best of times. No less now, but he took her last comment to mean he wasn't a detective.

The place was really starting to fill up now, smoke machines were belching fog across the dance floor and Sault felt that they had jacked up the beats even louder. "Can we talk outside, where it's a little quieter?"

Outside, the air was comfortably cool, and the street was largely lit by the red and blue neon of an outdoor supply company across the street. The signage was old and failing and buzzed and flickered and cast long shadows, like fleeing felons.

Along the wide bricked sidewalks small tribes of young people gathered smoking, vaping, sim-sticking and talking. From the body language Sault concluded that most of them were talking remotely, not to the others in the crowd and he wondered why people still bothered to gather. The sim-stickers looked especially foolish drawing deeply on plastic tubes and blowing multi-colored smoke that danced and twined into ethereal images but was only visible in AR. It was like making shadow puppets with a spot light.

Only the dull thump of the music and the occasional chirp of laughter invaded the still. Mary leaned against the painted brick, pulled a cigarette from the leather pouch and lit up. She took a deep pull then slowly blew out the smoke with a look of deep satisfaction and calm, as if the pot had already kicked in. But the calm never reached her eyes. They were alert and intense—birdlike—as always. Sault could tell from the smell that it was mostly tobacco. She was smoking her own brand.

"You know what really pisses me off?" she asked.

Anyone who had ever spoken to Mary Squared for more than a minute knew the answer to that. She was obsessed with the inequity of her past. She'd been an outspoken proponent of legalizing marijuana back at the turn of the century, going from participating in protests, to organizing them, to media spokesperson. She was the most successful of the many in B.C. who opened illegal pot-shops, challenging politicians to enforce the law and stomp on the will of their constituents. And, while they waffled, her business and popularity thrived. When, finally, the laws were changed, and pot became legal, she celebrated. But, like many starry-eyed activists for whom Cannabis was more of a religion than a business, she found that her home-grown "artisanal" weed could not compete on an open market, once the cigarette manufacturers and breweries stepped in and mass produced cheaper, more consistent marijuana. As well, she hadn't been prepared for the health regulations that came with legalization. She'd spent the majority of her life a celebrity in the grey, but the legalization that she had fought for and won, turned her into a prosecutable criminal. So, she went underground and continued to fight a grassroots battle that only she understood.

Sault knew all of this from the RCMP file he'd once been curious enough to look up. He also knew her version which focused on corporate and political cronyism and shoddy production methods and he was not anxious to hear it again. "Mary," he said drawing her out before she fully immersed into reverie. She gave him a look as if he'd just swindled her out of something. Sault ignore it. "I don't believe that you're involved in any of this."

"Well that's dead obvious. Dealing chemical is the opposite of what I do. I distill the pollutants out to free the essential oils. Then I infuse them to a lower-caste herb. Finally, I perform the Rite of Blood Spirits. My products are purified, properly grounded and healing."

"But it *was* your product, right?" She nodded, but it was subtle and tenative, as if she were afraid to commit to the answer. Then she drew hard on the joint which glowed so brightly that he thought the end might actually burst into flame. "And, your method doesn't eliminate Jingo."

"Jingo is Death. No one can eliminate Death. But I'll tell you what; my process binds it to the herb. Your guy didn't die from a *brush* with Death. Death always needs an invitation. He smoked it in."

"He was a customer of yours, right?"

"Haven't seen him in six months. He had financial issues."

"How do you figure?"

"For years he buys from me, no problem. Then, about eight months ago he starts pushing for discounts. Eventually, got so rude about it, I cut him off. Haven't seen him since."

"How about her? Was she a regular?"

"Ach! She'd bought once or twice. I don't even know why. It was obvious she didn't respect my product. She was hinky. I should have known. The whole deal was hinky."

"What do you mean?"

"She gave me the cull-batch number…"

"Sorry, what's that?"

"I buy cull batches from a commercial grower. That's the base. I distill the essence and toss the mulch. Anyway, the batches are numbered. She knew that. She wanted a custom order from a batch that used her "lucky numbers." I didn't buy it. She's just not the type to believe in lucky numbers. Anyway, I checked my charts. They weren't lucky for her type. But she was willing to pay extra…quite a lot extra. So, I did it. What the hell, right?"

Vivia whispered to him, "Ask her for the grower and batch number."

"Which grower? Do you remember the batch number?"

"Not really, 2323 or something like that. Seagram's. Always Seagram's."

"OK. Why were you so panicked about the deaths?"

"Because I saw the news feed and got suspicious. She died within minutes of our meetup and I knew she had my product. The news said the cop died from touching my stuff and that it was contaminated with Jingo. I figured she had a connection inside the factory and her "lucky number" batch was laced. So, that meant the crap had gone through my machinery. I don't sterilize the entire lab every time I produce a batch and I'd already delivered to other customers, since processing hers. I got a test kit from social services and bingo! So, first thing, I went around and got back everything I could and cleaned my machines. It was embarrassing. Had to apologize to every customer because I only had cull-weed as a replacement."

"And you never got sick from contact with Jingo?"

"I told you, my stuff's pure. I wear a mask and latex gloves. I don't touch or breathe on the product—don't transfer any of my energy into it."

"And you didn't notice any dust or unusual particles? Jingo is usually grey, like a fine ash."

"Where'd you grow up? They don't sprinkle it in," she chuckled blowing smoke out her nostrils. "The weed is marinated so that Jingo is evenly distributed." Sault knew that, but he also knew that drug dealers were not perfectionists and when the drying process was rushed, the drug could crystallize into visible grains. "Anyway, this wasn't particularly strong stuff and that's another thing wrong with your cop's story. I clean up after every batch and I don't wear gloves then. There would have been drops of concentrate all over the bench and I'm sure I touched it. Nothing."

Shortly after this, Mary's flip phone rang, and she walked a short distance away to answer it. Sault spun the new information he'd acquired around in his mind for ten minutes before looking up and realizing that she was gone and not going to return.

On his way home, the passenger-side dash emitters began to glow and Sault found that he did not mind the intrusion. Vivia emerged from ether to fill the passenger seat, looking much the way she had in the nightclub except that she was now wearing thick-framed glasses and holding a pen and notepad. Sault shook his head at the affectations but didn't say anything.

"So, tell me about batch numbers."

"The sales records are public, by law, so I was able to find the batch numbers Mary bought and 2323 was not among them. In fact, in the last year, there has been no batch 2323 at Seagram's or any of the other local production facilities, for that matter."

"But they are all four-digit numbers?"

"Yes. The time and date are added to make them unique."

"Were there any with similar numbers?"

"Similar? In what way?"

"I don't know. Like, say, 5353 or 3232."

"Ah. Visually similar." She flipped over some pages, appearing to consult her notes. "The closest I can find is 2828. Is that visually similar, in your opinion?"

"One of her batches?"

"Yes. Purchased two days prior to the incident."

"Still, doesn't mean much. Could have assumed that."

"It confirms Seagram's as the seller, and it identifies the

production facility. A commercial production facility such as this has the means to produce Jingo from standard pharmaceuticals in their inventory. I found newsfeed articles and three law suits filed at the provincial level related to inventory discrepancies and suspected misuse of 3-D molecular printers at several commercial facilities. In particular, the facility that produced batch 2828 has been implicated. The allegations have been taken seriously by the RCMP which has launched a criminal investigation. While none of this is proof, it adds some weight to Mary's assumption that an insider produced the laced batch."

Sault could only nod. Usually, he set out to solve the primary question in a case and didn't have the resources to properly run down every detail. It was a luxury to be able to narrow the speculation with thorough online detective work. And, in a case this large and complex, it might be the only path to the truth.

"I found it curious that Jared Kowalczyk was under financial pressure. I'd like to check his books."

"You can access those through Belinda Smith's old watch, next time I fire it up. What are you thinking?"

"Just wondering where his money went. According to newsfeed articles, his wife is a legal secretary. Assuming her wage rivals the average in her field, my rough calculations indicate that they should not have had any difficulty meeting their obligations."

"Definitely food for thought."

By the time he pulled the Buick into the garage, Sault was dog tired, but he dug out the tin box and extracted the old watch and granted Vivia full access to both case files. Then he put the watch back in the box, which he placed on a high shelf for the night.

Sault crept into the room and slid into bed as stealthily as he could so as not to disturb Maya. He was bone weary and had to suppress a pleasurable moan as his head eased into the cool pillow. He was looking forward to what Vivia might come up with by morning. Seconds after closing his eyes, he was fast asleep. His last conscious thought was: *What if she solves the case?*

CHAPTER 31

Sault woke up late again, and to an empty house. He hadn't really talked with Maya or either of the kids in a couple of days and felt the lack, but on the other hand he wasn't anxious to hear how the viral video had gone down at school. Maya was too tired to engage, but he felt the kids may have been avoiding him, so he guessed the reviews had not been positive.

While he waited for his coffee to brew, he sifted through his messages. Vivia had dealt with everything with her usual efficiency, so his in-box was empty, but his eye caught one from the school principal, Vanessa Granger which Vivia had passed along to PR at Vic PD. His memory of the pleasant redhead came instantly into his head prompting him to take a peek at the content. It turned out to be an invitation to participate in a parent-teacher discussion about human/bot relations. He wondered what she'd taken away from watching his video and if she thought he was pro- or anti-bot. Either way, it was an invitation to disaster, and he was happy to let PR handle it.

The only other thing of note was that Dora Padovana had sent a time and place for coffee: The Esquire, 3:30pm and an address on Carolwood. He didn't recognize the restaurant, but guessed the address was in Broadmead, a heavily wooded suburb full of large, well maintained older houses surrounded by tall fir and hemlock, where a lot of the street names ended in "wood" or "tree." It was the Oak Bay of the middle class and if he'd had the choice, that was where he would have wanted to live.

Sault grabbed his watch from the charger and took his steaming mug to the garage. He didn't know what Vivia might have come up with overnight but was pleased to have woken with his own intuitive leap that he was anxious to substantiate. As well, he had to admit, he was anxious to share it with Vivia. The novelty and her unexpected cleverness were exhilarating.

The holo-desk was active on his workbench and for a moment he thought that he must have been more tired than he'd known to have left everything out and in plain sight, the night before. Then he noticed the journey-bot close by, its head tilted toward him, the wide line of a smile sketched in blue laser light.

He was momentarily startled while his sleepy brain struggled to reconcile last night's statuesque brunette with this morning's squat mechanism. The garage had no emitters but, for some reason, he had looked forward to talking with her full-sized hologram.

His disappointment must have shown, for a second later the bot shut down and Vivia's head and shoulders appeared, full-sized and hovering above the holo-desk.

God these AI's were intuitive. The thought that he could so easily be read by an app grated a bit, though.

"Somehow, that's worse," he said. Her new form seemed ghostly and gruesome.

Vivia shrank her image until she appeared in full, standing two feet high on the workbench. She was wearing an outfit that reminded him of Tinker Bell and he wondered if she might have a sense of humor. "Is this better?"

"It'll do," he said pulling the stool up to the bench and sitting.

"I was right about Kowalczyk's finances," she said with enthusiasm. A small square appeared in her hand. She tossed it upward and it expanded into a spreadsheet large enough for him to read. He scanned a few lines but couldn't glean anything.

"These are household expenses. So what?"

"They're hinky."

Sault almost spat coffee through his nose. He recognized Mary Squared's expression and guessed Vivia had added it to her vocabulary. "How so?"

"A year ago, the Kowalczyks were an unusually frugal couple with a new savings account that was accruing quickly. But, by the time of Jared's death, they were being overcharged for everything they purchased online, including services like power and water. The squeeze was methodical and progressive, starting with increases of only a fraction of a percent and escalating over the course of about a year. Extrapolating from data I have access to, I can estimate that, at the time of his death, the Kowalczyks would have been shelling out seven to twelve percent beyond the retail value on every transaction that went through their bank account and would have been accruing debt. The forensic snapshot of his account was taken a week after his death and shows a large correction attributed to a banking error. The savings have been restored and I saw no evidence of any more overcharges."

"That's a complex banking error."

"Yes, but perhaps most suspicious is the timing."

"So, let's suppose that someone wanted him financially squeezed. But why?"

"I didn't ask myself that question. But I wondered how such a squeeze might change his behavior and it occurred to me that given how frugal they were, he might have had to forgo recreational expenditures."

"Like pot."

Tinker-Vivia nodded. "Which he was already purchasing illegally from Mary Squared, presumably in order to cut costs."

Sault was shaking his head not because he didn't believe her, but because he was having a hard time coming to terms with the subtlety of the manipulation...*and for what?* The effort outweighed any possible outcome. "So, let's say he's pushed into crossing another line—stealing a joint or two from the scene of a traffic accident. Somehow, someone is able to use that and blackmails a Constable Fourth Class, fresh from the academy. That's incredibly forward thinking! It would be years before he was in any position to repay the cost of recruiting him."

"Still, it adds credibility to the theory that he stole from the crime scene. He had a habit but was too broke to purchase even low-grade product."

"And, it probably seemed completely inconsequential to the outcome of a traffic accident. Very tempting." It was good work, a detail he would never have caught, and he was tempted to tell her so, but couldn't quite summon the words.

Instead, he said, "Let's put that aside for the moment. There's something else I want to check." Unlike a real person, Vivia seemed completely content to move on without recognition for her work.

"I wanted to check newsfeed video to see if there were any private vehicles that arrived on scene that day, after say, one in the morning, and before ten," he asked, remembering that the forensic team had cleared the scene shortly before then.

"You mean vehicles privately owned and not associated with any newsfeed service?"

"Personal vehicles. Yes."

"There are two matches. I can read and run the plates."

He could have done all of this on his own, of course, but not in the few seconds it took Vivia. He tried not to dwell on all the time he'd wasted, before last night.

"Please."

"Both plates are visible in footage from FlashFeed API. One arrives at 6:44 and is registered to Branden Owen Vanderhoff."

Sault recognized the last name. "Is he a farmer?"

"Yes. He's locally known for his daffodils. He owns several tracts including the plot of land adjacent to the accident."

"And the other?"

"Arrives at 4:10am and is registered to Theresa Marie Schneider. You don't seem surprised."

"I'm not." The intuitive leap he'd had overnight was that

someone might have returned to the scene to replace the evidence that Jared had stolen. The most likely suspect was his training officer.

"Incidentally, the vehicle is a probable match to one arriving on scene at 10:15, the night before."

"Ok. Now I'm surprised." But then he recalled the private vehicle at the edge of the scene and the plate he could not read because it was awkwardly parked, side-on. "The T.O. was skipping out."

"Unless a friend came to pick her up." They didn't discuss the possibility that the car had driven itself because only transit and delivery vehicles were permitted to drive empty.

"Unlikely." With cheap transit on demand at any location, lending your car to a friend to have them pick you up was practically a thing of the past.

Every element he'd uncovered was circumstantial, as insubstantial as a holographic pixel. Nevertheless, they were forming a convincingly clear picture. Though nothing seemed to be headed toward a single point, he was now convinced that, in this case, no one and no thing was incidental and that if he kept answering the questions, a single connective thread would emerge. The mysteries were beginning to fall like dominoes and the chain reaction was gaining momentum.

He sipped coffee and tried to remain calm, but his pulse was ramping up, and he could almost feel the blood rushing through his veins. This was the high that drew him in deep. It was creation: answers from questions, patterns from randomness, order from chaos, something from nothing. Justice from corruption.

Sault pulled Belinda Smith's old watch from the shelf where he'd left it the previous night and strapped it on to his right arm, opposite his new watch. It was the first time he'd actually worn it and it felt clunky and uncomfortable, but he thought he might need it when he met with the hacker, at noon.

He drained the last dregs and slammed the mug down next

to tiny Vivia who observed the action dispassionately. Suddenly, he was in a fanciful mood. "Grab your shades, Darl'in. We've got a landlord to talk to, then we're off to see a garden about a man."

Vivia giggled, then disappeared.

CHAPTER 32

"Some idiot in Italy is voluntarily having perfectly good body parts swapped out for mechanical ones so he can legally be declared a machine and lead the fight for bot rights. He's got thirteen million in crowd funding for this. Says he's almost half way there. Hell, I've got as much mech in me as flesh." Without breaking stride, the old landlady rapped on her good leg with her cane and Sault was surprised to hear the clack of hard plastic. "Scheduled to have the other one done, next year, then I'll probably be further along than him. I tried crowd funding when I needed a new pancreas. Couldn't get thirteen cents, let alone thirteen million. The whole world runs on marketing bullshit."

Her steps were small, but she was moving rapidly and with a scowl of determination that had permanently etched its lines into her face, so that echoes of it remained even when she wasn't frowning. Keeping pace beside her, Sault agreed with the sentiment, but remained silent, not wanting to fuel a rant. As well, he was put off by the presence of her husband, a small, slender man who seemed to have no trouble keeping up and shadowed Sault close enough to feel invasive.

The condominium complex that Vivia had located overlooked Victoria's upper harbor and had a view of the Bay Street bridge. It was new and tall and set amid concrete and garden and waterworks and contained both owned and rental units. Sault had assumed correctly that the person selling Lindsay George's possessions was the caretaker who was listed on the entranceway intercom and after a brief on-screen conversation during which he introduced himself as Constable Joseph Sault he was let into the lobby to wait. A few minutes later, a woman stepped out of the elevator and introduced herself as Mrs. Bridge but made no introduction for the white-haired man who had also stepped from the elevator and who now stood just far enough away to make Sault wonder if he might only be an unrelated but curious resident. Sault cast him a friendly look that didn't even generate a flicker from the vacant blue eyes. The man was holding a long-haired white cat with eyes the same color as his and was slowly stroking its fur with a curious regularity. He noticed that their wedding bands matched and later, when he fell in behind them, Sault made the extraordinary leap that they were a couple.

Mrs. Bridge wasted no time with pleasantries and immediately started leading the small party toward the storage room, down the ornately carpeted hallway, needlessly bustling and griping about unrelated matters, as if this were irritating and inconvenient and she was mad about that and anxious to get it over with. Which, he supposed, may have been the case. And, he further supposed, that may have been her attitude about everything.

"See that stain?" Her head bobbed once toward a discolored spot on the carpet about the size of coffee cup ring. "Slinker poop. You'd think someone rich enough to live here and afford a gen-mod pet would have the decency to train them or at least clean up instead of leaving it to Mr. Bridge to try to scrub it out of hand-loomed wool. Took him an hour. I have better things for him to do."

The most common genetically modified pets were exotic fish and few varieties of birds and the most common modifications were to scales and plumage. By law, their design included embedded weaknesses that made them dependent on human caregivers for their survival. Slinkers were new—the first mammalian renditions—weasel-like in appearance but sloth-like in nature, with silky fur and a penchant for cuddling into the warmth of their owners. They had no real digestive structure and could only exist on a diet of water and dry chemical pellets and Sault knew that they excreted small deposits of biologically neutral sand. A Slinker could not have caused that stain. Again, he remained silent.

"It's from India; a hundred dollars a square foot. If one of my cats did that, I'd ring its neck. They're well trained. And cats are smart. That's why they're the only pets allowed to wander free, inside the building. When they have business, they know to come home through the door-in-the-door." She said "door-in-the-door" as if it were a common alternative to "pet door." Sault wondered how the cats navigated the voice-activated elevators but was not curious enough to ask. "Some idiot on the twenty-first floor's got a Rainbow Bird. Ridiculous waste of money, you ask me." Sault said nothing and speculated that maybe the silent man at his heels had given up trying to get a word in.

She stopped next to a heavy fire door and her husband darted around to open it for her, awkwardly juggling the pet in his arms. It held on, digging its claws into the thick knit of his pullover and giving Mrs. Bridge an alarmed and disgruntled look, which failed to gain any of her attention.

"Had to buy a generator and rewire the whole apartment in case the power goes out because the damned thing can't survive below twenty degrees. You want a shiny bird, get a holo-pet. Hologram's a damned sight cheaper and a lot less trouble. And, anyway; as if the power ever goes out."

She bustled through into a long, windowless room with shelves lining the walls. The place smelled musty, shelves buckled under the weight of old boxes and random household items and thick layers of dust.

"That's her stuff. There, in the corner."

The "stuff" was a pile of electronics and three boxes. It occurred to Sault that she hadn't challenged him or asked any questions about his investigation. He'd expected her to ask if

Lindsay George was ok and to have to diplomatically side-step. But she didn't and now he got the feeling it was because she didn't care. To her, Lindsay George was just another irritating inconvenience. Dead or deadbeat, she had left a mess to clean up and that, to her, was the only relevant fact.

"I sold some to cover the cleaning and reprogramming the locks and other things," she said a little too quickly and Sault knew then that she'd done much better than merely recovering costs. "The rest is safe here in storage for the required four months, unless she claims it and pays the storage fee, of course."

By the look of the clutter, Sault doubted anything ever left the room unless it was in Mrs. Bridge's pocket.

He started rummaging through the pile, taking his time, trying to recall what had been in the advertisement, what might have been missing. "Can you tell me what you sold?"

"I don't keep lists of that kind of thing." She was being obstinate, probably afraid he'd write her up for lining her pockets.

"A laptop?"

"Right. Yes. A laptop. Who uses a laptop anymore?"

Sault was into the boxes now: articles of clothing, shoes, dishes, cutlery, some jewelry, a small tool kit and a soldering iron…no watch.

Vivia spoke to him. "Much of the clothing is what was advertised online. All consistent with her tastes. The jewelry, however, is cheap and none of it was in the ads."

"…and you sold some jewelry."

"Oh. Yes. I think, maybe."

He didn't recognize any of the devices in the pile of electronics. A lot of them were in various states of disrepair; ripped open, customized or cannibalized.

"The blue box is a solder press—a robot soldering unit—and there are two chip burners. Most of the rest are cloaking components. Stealth is difficult on Net 3," Vivia interjected, perhaps having read uncertainty in the way he turned the devices over in his hands.

Sault replied in low tones that made it clear he wasn't talking to the two behind him, "Could there be data still stored inside any of the cloaking hardware?"

"That is unlikely as they are designed for the exact opposite purpose. According to the manufacturers, these devices continually auto-purge.

He came upon a small, grey rectangle that he recognized as a cartridge from some sort of 3D printer. It had the brand name "Nosche" on one side with a long number beneath. "This looks like it came from a commercial unit."

"High-end consumer, low-end commercial. It's a polymer cartridge for a molecular printer."

Sault knew from flipping through the printer report attached to the both George's and Kowalczyk's case files that such printers started at more than a hundred thousand dollars. Depending upon what you were printing, cartridges could run into the tens of thousands. He wondered why a hacker needed such a powerful production tool and considered that she might have been producing some sort of drug. A printer like this couldn't render state-of-the-art drugs like Jingo, but maybe it could be used to make something softer. But then, why was she buying through Mary Squared? In fact, regardless of how she made a living, she had to be doing very well to afford to rent in a building like this. Mary Squared didn't figure, no matter how he arranged the pieces.

He stood and turned to his hosts. "Any chance you have the contact information for the people who bought the laptop and the printer?"

"As I said, I don't keep lists of this type of thing."

"How about from the bank transactions?"

"The same person bought both. Cash."

"Really? How much were you asking?"

"For a lousy laptop and a printer so ancient it was the size of a fridge? I let him have both for five hundred and I felt lucky to get that."

Sault sighed and took a final look at what was left of Lindsay George's legacy. With the clothes pulled out and draping over the boxes like this, a black, knitted cardigan stood out as a little shabby. He unfolded it and held it up for examination. The fabric was stretched and worn at the elbows and, at both cuffs, the weave was starting to unravel. It must have been a favorite. It had pockets and Sault lifted a crinkled tissue from one. From the other he extracted a postage-stamp-sized plastic rectangle.

"That's a crystal array. It could contain as much as 500 terabytes of data."

"A thumbnail drive," he confirmed, letting Vivia know that this was one of the rare times she had misjudged him. She didn't reply and he experienced a flash of regret, thinking the he might have hurt her feelings. He reminded himself that Vivia was an app and that he was anthropomorphizing but the feeling did not immediately dissipate and when he turned to face Mrs. Bridge, he found that he was more annoyed with her than he had been. "Do you mind if I keep this?" he asked, thinking as he did that for a police officer in this situation, asking was merely a courtesy.

"We still have outstanding costs."

"What do you mean?"

"Taking pictures, posting online, showing people the stuff and now this. It all takes time. Resources."

Sault considered pushing the official investigation charade, but then she surprised him by shaking her cane toward Lindsay George's possessions and adding, "If that was evidence, you'd want the lot." Then, looking back at him, "That's a 500-terabyte thumbnail drive. You just want it for yourself. A hundred bucks." And she crossed her arms for emphasis though she looked uncomfortable, seeming slightly off balance with her cane lifted from the floor.

He negotiated her down to seventy-five, provided he paid in cash. He did that and as they escorted him back to the lobby, questioned them regarding Lindsay George. Mrs. Bridge did all the talking of course, though she wasn't nearly as verbose as she had been earlier: "the girl" had sublet privately, from an owner who was currently out of country; they were never given her name and had rarely interacted; when she skipped on the rent, they were hired to clean up after her; and, no, they could not give the owner's contact information without a warrant; and nothing else came to mind except how annoying all of this extra work had become.

Her detailed familiarity with the thumbnail drive made Sault suspect she'd gotten more than just five hundred bucks for the laptop, but he was pretty sure she couldn't have come near guessing its actual value, especially with that printer thrown in. He turned before opening the front door. "Incidentally, that wasn't just an ordinary laptop and printer, and anyone interested in both would have known that."

The wrinkles in Mrs. Bridge's brow deepened. "What are you talking about?"

"They were both high-end, commercial products. Together, probably worth close to six hundred grand, used." And he pushed through the door.

"Have a good day," he said, glancing, one final time, at the white-haired man with the vacant blue eyes standing three paces behind Mrs. Bridge. He had stopped petting the ball of fur, but his eyes seemed brighter, like he might have been smiling, on the inside. Sault got the feeling that they may have bonded.

William M. Dean

CHAPTER 33

No one ever visited Victoria without touring The Butchart Gardens. To do that, you would have to ignore reams of pamphlets, flyers, billboards and just about every local citizen you encountered. With over a million plants, miles of intricately manicured garden and nightly lighted drone-swarm show, it was a national treasure and world famous. And Victorians rarely passed up an opportunity to mention that.

Sault had wandered, as instructed, for the better part of forty minutes and had just reached a small bamboo structure at the end of a mossy stone path within the Japanese Garden. He stood wondering whether to rest there or continue rambling when a tall man with only a fringe of white hair left on his scalp came up beside him.

"Mr. Sault, I have to compliment you on your AI."

Sault was not surprised at the approach. He'd been keeping an eye out and by taking unexpected turns within the garden had deduced the man was following him. This dead end was a good meeting spot. Though the attraction was brimming with tourists, most chose to remain on the through-paths so the two of them had the area to themselves and it would be obvious if anyone else drew near enough to overhear their conversation. It seemed more natural to share the bench inside the bamboo shack than to stand there, so they did.

"What do you mean?"

"Before we met, I wanted to do a little checking up on you. Nothing fancy; standard procedure. Now, even *I* can't hack a personal AI, but I can usually get some basic stuff by various means. She fended off every approach. She's cleverer than most. Where'd you get her?"

The comment reminded Sault of Dora Padovano's low-tech approach which had fooled Vivia enough for Sault to get her dinner invitation. "Costco."

The tall man laughed, which confused Sault because he had told the truth. He was older than Sault, maybe sixty, and seemed unusually fit.

"You can call me Hal." He was well-manicured and dressed in dark colored semi-casual wear, like a tech CEO about to take the stage. And he seemed entirely comfortable and relaxed. The cloak and dagger invitation aside, if he was worried about attracting undue attention, it was not reflected in his manner.

Sault shook the extended hand. "Joe."

"Ok, Joe. Well, if you actually did buy it at Costco, then you've done a hell of a job in training."

"Training? I barely use her."

"Well, of course, they learn by observing. So, I guess you're an excellent model. Anyway, whatever you've done, don't ever reset her. She's exceptional."

"If you say so."

"I was hoping to meet her, but there's no way you have her in that old thing."

Sault had felt conspicuous wearing two watches, so when he'd first arrived, he'd stowed the newer one in the hip pocket of his jeans. He had no interest in having Vivia interrogated so he didn't mention that she was close by.

"No, she's not."

"Ok, then. What've you got for me, today?" he asked, as if this were a regular thing.

"How about we start with a primer on hacker paraphernalia."

"Like what?"

"Recently, I was sifting through a hacker's possessions and came across a few things I didn't expect. First, she had a commercial-grade 3D printer. What would that be for?"

"Making ghost chips."

"Making? I thought those could be purchased, black market."

"That's way too risky. Get caught with the software and it's a day in court. Get caught with the finished product and it's a hefty jail term. I can't think of anyone foolish enough to buy a fully produced chip when they can be manufactured at home after an encrypted download."

"What's so special about these chips?"

Twice Hal seemed about to speak, then reconsidered his words. Finally, after several moments, he seemed to settle on a starting place. "Maybe you're old enough to remember the Stuxnet worm. This would have been around 2010."

"I would have been four or five."

"Sorry, I 'm not good a judging age. Anyway, Stuxnet was one of the first digital weapons; a malicious worm hidden inside firmware in a batch of centrifuges the U.S. sold to Iran. These industrial centrifuges were used in the production of enriched uranium and the worm's mission was twofold, to infect any computing device it came into contact with and to destroy centrifuges. It arrived in one batch of centrifuges, then spread to laboratory computers and from there to other centrifuges and altered the centrifuge's controller to make it spin too fast and too long, which burned out delicate components. It went undiscovered and set the Iranian nuclear program back for many years. Years later, similar issues arose with connected consumer devices like TV's and rudimentary AI's like voice activated assistants. The All-Country Coalition was formed in response to the realization that AI could be weaponized."

Sault knew about the All-Country Coalition. It was a UN alliance formed to develop and monitor a secure AI network. The name reflected the UN's aspiration to have every nation on earth participate. A lofty goal which was never quite met and so, the coalition was currently comprised of 143 nations.

"The coalition laid the foundations of Net 2 and 3 which, then, determined how AI's would be integrated. It decided that having anything more sophisticated than a rudimentary AI inside a device was asking for trouble, and that's why only rudimentary AI's are permitted to be incorporated into the design of any device. Such AI's are strictly limited to interpreting regular speech to operate the device in which they are housed. As a result of this decision, such AI's are rare; usually only found in unconnected devices and amount to little more than linguistically adept user interfaces. The AI's you and I and everyone else use on a daily basis are a wide leap above that and classed as cognizant AI's. They are allowed in and out of connected devices but can easily be removed on command or by resetting the device and they cannot alter the device or how it operates in any way. And all of this activity is overseen by the MAIM…"

"The Master AI Module."

"Excellent, you know about that. And are you familiar with Shell Modules?"

"Yes. Those are the operating instructions unique to each device."

"Exactly. The Master AI was created and is maintained and monitored by the All-Country Coalition and is a leap above the day-to-day cognizant AI. It's classed as pseudo-sentient and provides the top most level of security on Shell Modules. Cognizant AI's run completely independently but the MAIM has the power to shut down any or all of them. And, if the MAIM ever goes down, every AI shuts down, as well. It's a built-in kill switch, in case AI gets any demonic ideas."

"OK. So, how does this relate to ghost chips."

"Ghost chips have AI's specialized for hacking hardwired in. The AI's are stripped down to save space so they're not cognizant, but more sophisticated than rudimentary. As well, they are unregistered and invisible to the MAIM. There might be nothing more illegal than that on the whole planet."

"I thought AI's weren't allowed to hack."

"These are unregistered."

"Could they hack the MAIM?"

"No. Alterations to the MAIM require the Top Secret passwords from all Coalition members."

Sault took a few moments to digest all of that, then asked, "What would she have needed to produce a chip?"

Hal paused, then seemed to come to some decision. "Let me save us both some time. The answer you're trying to steer me toward is opioids."

"Actually, I have no idea what you're talking about."

Hal turned, squinting his eyes and pursing his lips and looking directly into Sault's face. "Well, maybe you really don't know. Ok. To make ghost chips you need to start with a high-end commercial molecular printer. Even the cheapest cost several million dollars. I've never met a contract hacker who could afford one. The standard work-around is to hack a pharmaceutical company's molecular printer and get it to produce a starter chemical—something composed of just the right atoms and with a larger molecular structure that can be manipulated into a circuit array—the current faves being opioid hybrids like Jingo or Tight Rope. You get the printer to stamp it out in the shape of blood pressure pills or something, fake a prescription and pick it up in disguise. You feed that into your lower-resolution commercial printer along with a downloaded file and a few days later, it pops out a ghost chip."

"And this is something every high-level hacker does?"

"Well, that particular trick is getting a little long in the tooth. There are more current variations which I won't get in to, but the basic idea remains the same."

"How about hijacking a commercial weed facility, then laundering it through a pusher?"

Hal laughed again. "Ok. Yeah. That's one of the newer variations."

"I also found a thumbnail drive among her possessions."

He clapped his hands together and his eyes lit up. "Good score!" Sault caught a glimpse of a hunger in him and watched as he regained composure probably suppressing an urge to ask to see it, perhaps to access it. "That'll be her session drive. Real hackers can't back anything up to the cloud with AI's sniffing around and they don't usually keep much on their computers for long because they are too tempting a target for thieves, not to mention the authorities. The drive'll have all her Go-code; utilities, look-up tables, session logs and custom hacks. Possibly everything she has ever worked on."

"Alright. One last thing, then." Sault raised his arm to bring attention to the old watch. "This contains a vehicle data log I'd like your opinion on."

"Man, did you ever come to the right guy. I spent ten years working on driver AI, back in the 20's. What've you got for me?"

Sault tilted the watch into working position and Hal did the same with his own and a few minutes later, the hacker was swiping through the vehicle data from Lindsay George's accident.

"Well, I can tell you one thing...either this data has been altered after the fact or the accident was orchestrated."

"What makes you say that?"

"First and most obviously, it's over reporting the driver status." He leaned toward Sault so he could share a graphic. Sault saw a straight line with a series of spikes that meant nothing to him. "Each of those spikes is the AI confirming that the human driver has taken control. Normally, there would only be spikes if the status changes: up for human, a down spike for AI. The fact that it's spiking so often every second indicates to me that it's being continually overridden. The vehicle's AI is fighting with outside input."

"What else?"

"A mayday is sent but the wheels don't turn away from the crash. Even if we believe all those human-driver spikes, between them the AI is in control. Driver AI root instructions are to mitigate, no matter how trivial the effect. You'll never see a head-on collision after a mayday where the wheels aren't turned. Also, the airbag deployment is a couple of seconds too early so its effectiveness will be diminished as it begins deflating early. And this braking pattern...I don't even know what that's about. If this is actual data from a real incident, then it wasn't an accident."

And if it wasn't an accident, it was murder.

Hal flipped through a few more pages of data, then added, "There's one other unusual thing, though it didn't contribute to the accident."

"What's that?"

"The car was publicly broadcasting its location. That's not the default. Most people opt for privacy."

Sault recalled Lindsay George's wig and lack of ID. She was incognito; going to meet the pusher she'd tricked into delivering Jingo for her ghost chips.

Nothing in this case is incidental.

They both sat there in silence for a while. Sault was digesting all his assumptions that had just been verified and trying to think if there might be anything else he should ask. Meanwhile, Hal seemed to be working out something of his own.

Sault asked, "You said that even you couldn't hack an AI. Then how could someone hack this driver AI?"

"You'd have to bypass the Master AI and that...Holy shit!" Hal's sudden exclamation made Sault jump and when he looked up, the hacker had his hand over his mouth and was giving him a stare that could nail a poster to a tree. "This is about LSG," he whispered between his fingers.

All the breezy-casual and most of the color had gone out of the man.

"Did I not mention that?" Sault recognized the letters as Lindsay Susan George's initials and remembered that he had purposely not mentioned her in his request for a meetup. He had dropped Ranier's name and assumed that if that wasn't enough, the hacker would ask for more details.

"Oh, Jeezus! Ranier Gilbert."

"Do you know him?" He was confused by Hal's seeming acquaintance with Rainier who had told him that he didn't know any hackers.

"Him? He's a she. I know *of* her, and you mentioned her

name when you requested this meetup. I was intrigued by that. It's why I came."

Sault thought, *Ranier is a she?*

"Why intrigued?"

"She's a salaried hacker who claims to have been targeted for financial eradication." He said "salaried hacker" in a derisive tone. Clearly, in his opinion, a lower caste.

Sault thought, *Ranier is a hacker?*

Hal continued, "She wouldn't say why, just that she was cashing out and going off grid. How that's even done, I have no idea, but it reminded me of…LSG."

"What's financial eradication?"

"All record of her finances and assets erased. A hell of a claim—the kind of attack that only governments might be able to pull off. I keep a hand in, but I retired from the deep game, more than five years ago. Sometimes I miss it and she was kind of the story of the week. I was curious. Thought there might be some amusing delusion at work until I realized we were talking about…her."

"I'm guessing Ranier's not quadriplegic."

Hal did not laugh. He stood, then, looking everywhere but at Sault. "We won't be seeing one another again."

And with that, he was gone.

CHAPTER 34

Sault pulled off the Pat Bay Highway a few miles short of what most people considered to be Victoria, made his way into Broadmead and to a small but active strip mall. He parked the Buick at the far end of the lot, askew, over two spots, the tail lights barely tucked in, and walked past all the neatly tucked-in pods toward the long, low structure. As he was crossing the heat-soaked tarmac he noticed a silver limousine pulling into the lot and wished the driver good luck in finding adequate parking. It made him chuckle to think that he shared a problem with the very rich.

There was just about an hour until his meeting with Padovano. With not enough time and little reason to go home and nothing else scheduled, he decided to window shop.

A Sobeys food store was the mall's anchor and next door to that was a banking center, a large automated kiosk where people could process transactions in any of the traditional banks. Most of the traffic was focused in that area. The rest of the mall included a blended reality "experience" called "Bot-pocalypse" which seemed oddly modern and intense amid the mom-and-pop shops: travel, insurance, clothing, and the ghost kitchens with blacked out windows and minimal signage. Except for a few teens milling about outside Bot-pocalypse, it was all very secluded and had the feeling of abandonment, which was pretty much the truth of it.

Strangely, there was a coffee shop with a bot barista and right next door, but seemingly unconnected, a vending machine that sold hot and cold drinks, including coffee. With thirty minutes still left on the clock, Sault decided to get coffee from the machine, in spite of the fact that he would soon be having another.

He found a comfortable spot on a low, concrete wall surrounding the trunk of a giant and gnarled Gary Oak tree. It was thick with leaves and provided good shade from the midday sun and, being too early in the year, hundreds of green inchworms were not yet parachuting down on silk.

For some reason, he didn't want to think about the case. His brain needed a break. Instead, he checked for messages and found nothing that needed his attention. Then he found the dot on the map that was The Esquire where he would meet Padovano and memorized the route. After that, he filled the time looking up brain-teasers, none of which proved challenging.

Twenty minutes later, when Vivia prompted him to leave, he realized that the machine-coffee had been surprisingly tasty and that he'd emptied the cup.

The entire pointless experience was unexpectedly satisfying, and his memory of that time stayed with him, though it seemed trivial.

He pulled up to the address and found himself in front of a large house of Spanish motif, with wavy, red tiled roof and a beige, adobe-like plaster job. He could tell from its lines and layout that it was at least seventy years old, but the entire property had been immaculately maintained and retained its grandeur. At the foot of the driveway, a black metal post with curlicued tendrils of steel ornamentation supported a wooden sign with the words "The Esquire" carved into it. It was obviously a rental, of some sort.

Dora Padovano answered the door and greeted him with a large smile which seemed genuine. She was wearing a billowy blouse through which he could see a pink and lacy camisole. Eventually, his eyes drifted to the leather belt, snug jeans and her bare feet with pink-polished toe nails. The outfit was conservative, yet flattering and evocative and made him wonder if she intended this to be a romantic rendezvous.

"Before we start, I just want to make it clear that this is not meant to be some kind of romantic rendezvous. I just don't want anyone to see us together."

Sault feigned surprise at the very idea of a tryst, but hoped he didn't go over the top, bordering on disgust. If he was being truthful, he didn't want her thinking she had no chance with him. He loved his wife, of course, and didn't really think he could ever go through with an affair, but Dora Padovano was a very attractive package and he hadn't had sex in a long time. He just hoped she wasn't about to offer him tequila, instead of coffee. At the same time, he also hoped she might.

By the time they were seated on the back patio, the French press steeping between them, he had his imagination under control. To her, he wasn't an attractive man, he was a viral video. She was courting him, but not romantically.

She poured for the both of them and once they were settled, she began, "Did you like my report on the TLC attack?"

"I appreciated your slant," he said referring to her favorable characterization of his actions. "Not everyone shares that point of view."

"Unfortunately, not all the nuts stick to Net 2 and there's always money to be made in controversy."

As brief as it was, the conversation seemed to stall then, and they sat, sipping quietly. He understood that this was a negotiation. They both wanted to trade information, but neither wanted to pay a word more than necessary. The moment stretched so long that he was about to resort to complimenting her on the beautiful garden when she said, "Ok. Listen. I may owe you an apology. I'm new here and when I stumbled on to you looking into the Kowalczyk case, I mentioned it while courting a source at Vic PD. From what I hear, that may have generated a bit of trouble for you."

It was a freebie revelation. He'd previously assumed that she'd homed in on him after tapping into the Vic PD rumor mill, but if she was to be believed, the reality was exactly the opposite case. *Was Roth her connection? Fritterer?* "How'd you find out I was looking into Kowalczyk?"

She flashed him a coy smile. "That will have to remain my secret. Why don't we start with why you accepted my invitation?"

"Your name came up while I was doing research on Lindsay George."

"You're working Lindsay George, now?"

"Crossing t's and dotting i's. The two cases are related."

The conversation stalled again, and Sault took note of honeybees and hummingbirds and a tiny swarm of pollination drones as they zoomed past.

"Here's what I've been thinking, about you and me. I'm out of the loop because I'm new, a little too aggressive for this town and lack cred, despite my reputation." Then she chuckled. "Or maybe because of my reputation, back east. I dun'no. Then there's you—called up at least twice since I've been here. We're both fighting the systems we're in. I'm watching you work a case that everyone else wants left alone and thinking maybe we should cooperate and help each other out. I've got a couple of pieces of information that might mean something to you, maybe you've got something for me…maybe not. But, if not, I've got a hunch you're going to work this until something breaks. And, let's be honest, that something might be you, if you misstep and get caught in the spotlight, like you have in the past."

"It's always works out ok."

Her dark brows bounced once, and she nodded in acceptance of the fact. "Ok. And maybe you'll be lucky again. If so, what I'd want is the scoop, obviously. And, if not, you're going to want someone sympathetic, in the media."

"I can't promise a scoop. In the past, that's all been out of my control."

"I'll settle for a good word with whomever makes that

decision and some anonymous inside tips to guide me to the gold. You could do that much."

"I could." There was another long pause, but this one seemed part of the conversation, rather than a break in it. "What you're getting requires mutual trust. If I gave you something and you outed me as your source, it could make your career and break mine. I'm not sure I trust anyone that much."

It was obvious that Dora had predicted the direction of the conversation. "I'll start," she said, putting her cup down and leaning forward, elbows on the glass table top. She was staring straight into his eyes and he couldn't make himself tear away, even if he'd wanted to. Then she said one word and his world exploded. "Cavallon."

Sault jolted upright and almost spilled coffee. Afterward, there was no covering up his interest but, still, for some reason, he went for it. He eased back and took a leisurely sip of coffee. "Sidney Cavallon? What about him?"

Dora Padovano burst into convulsive laughter and rolled about in the chair, her feet kicking off the ground. After a few moments, still smiling, she dabbed at the corner of her eyes with a napkin. Once she had collected herself, he brushed fingers through her hair to sweep it back into place, behind her ear and off her face. Then, her eyes still alight with amusement, she said, "I'm sorry about that. Honestly."

Sault felt the heat in his face and knew his embarrassment showed but he did his best to swallow the humiliation and tried to accept the humor of the moment. "Let's just pretend, for the sake of argument, that you've got my attention."

She clapped her hands as if applauding stand-up comedy. "Isn't it weird how we're already friends? I knew we would be. I knew it the minute we first talked. I decided it. And now, there's just no way we won't become friends. Somehow, on some level, we have too much in common, or something. We just naturally "get" each other."

Sault felt himself turn red again, but what she said felt true to him, as well. They understood each other and, for no concrete reason, he felt that their paths were intertwined and that she would not easily betray him. The trust was already there, only his mind had been looking for justification. Of course, this was the feeling confidence games were built upon.

But, then, beyond all of that, she'd said the magic word.

"I feel a little ashamed now, though. I don't have anything solid on Sidney Cavallon, but he's the single constant. When I look at the pieces I've got and I ask myself, "what of significance can come of this?" the answer always involves Cavallon."

"All water flows to the sea."

"And around here, he's the sea."

"So, a lot is going to lead to him, wouldn't matter what you were talking about."

"That's true. But then, you saw it, too. So, maybe it's real. I'll let you decide. But first, you've got to shake my hand on the terms we talked about before—the scoop. And I can work for it. You got something you want me to research, I can do that for you, on spec."

Two days earlier, he could have used the help. Now, he had Vivia. "I think I'm covered in that department," Sault said, shaking her hand which he noted was comfortably warm and soft.

"Ok, Mr. Not-Detective, here's what I have." Like his, her watch was a plain black band. She made a sweeping motion toward him and Vivia privately announced that a file was received. Sault opened it and started flipping through, but he quickly noticed that none of the information was corroborated. "Dora, most of this is hearsay without attribution. It doesn't bring me any closer to proving anything."

"I'm sorry, but I can't give you my sources. Most of them would deny it, anyway. You're going to have to trust that it's solid. Maybe this will help fill in some blanks. You can worry about proving things once you know what's going on."

"Maybe. Can you give me the shorthand version?"

"Let me begin with a little backstory. I was basically working on the mayoral election, looking for something juicy and I found it. I had a tip and did some stuff that you don't want to know about and kind of tracked Councilman Monty Hoad for a while. One night, he was seen in Sidney at the Deep Cove Marina. He went to the old Land's End pub for dinner, then retired to his boat. Apparently, he spent a lot of time doing work there. It's a ways out of Victoria, but makes sense because it's close to the ferries, and he travels to Vancouver a lot. That particular night, he was in the company of a young brunette. His wife is blonde. Naturally, I did some other stuff you don't want to know about and got my hands on marina security camera footage and guess who I saw? Constable Theresa Schneider. I couldn't ID her from the footage, but then I saw them together at Cavallon's gala, last weekend. I first caught them holding hands in one of the immersion rooms, near the back where they thought they were out of sight. Later, I got a better look at her and remembered from a previous newsfeed that she was Jared Kowalczyk's training officer."

Sault remembered the tall wispy-haired blonde man he'd seen standing too close to Schneider the night of the banquet. So that was Councilman Montgomery Hoad. It fit. Terri Schneider was nothing, if not ambitious.

"Story-wise, that was good, but it got better when I noticed the marina security footage was from the same night that Jared Kowalczyk died. From the timing, I knew that she couldn't have arrived at George's site with Kowalczyk. I mean, they were assigned the Mount Doug area. It's pretty sparse out there and arguably, over-patrolled with two other units also covering the territory. Some of the officers I talked to even called it the "Sleep Shift." A good time to sneak away. Obviously, it wasn't her first time because she felt comfortable enough to go all the way to Sidney knowing that it would take at least a half hour for her to get back.

"This dovetailed. I already had a story with no legs on Jared Kowalczyk. I had sources who said that he stole evidence, several joints, from the George crash site. Apparently, he'd done it before, and it was becoming a habit. It was all covered up to protect the family's death benefits. Typical cop stuff that no editor will publish because no one wants to hear about a mildly corrupted rookie cop. Publishing a story like that would do little more than jeopardize the delicate relationship Buzz has with local police. And, for me, it would have been career suicide."

"Did you have anything to back that up?"

"After his death, someone moved evidence from the Jared Kowalczyk crime scene and snuck it back into the plastic bag found at George's crash. If you look closely, the bag in the picture doesn't have as many joints in it as is listed on the evidence sheet, or what is currently in storage in the evidence vault. Also, why 49? Why not 50? I think Kowalczyk smoked one and that's what killed him. As well—a small thing—but there's an empty plastic bag that was on the evidence list in the George case but not in any of the pictures and it's not in the evidence vault. I think it was dropped when the stolen joints were returned to the crime scene and someone not in the loop logged it."

Sault had noticed the extra baggie, too, but thought it as likely to be a clerical error. He'd seen things like this before. Whereas one person might enter an item as "plastic bag with 49 joints" another person might itemize it as two separate items: "plastic bag" and "49 joints."

"I started wondering who would have been the one to replace the evidence to exonerate Kowalczyk. At first, I figured Schneider had too much to lose, then I realized that the pressure would be on her because she didn't want the George crash to become a focal point of any larger investigation. Assuming Kowalczyk stole a significant number of joints, questions about her attention to duty as a training officer would have to arise which might lead to discovering that she wasn't with him in the patrol car, that night. That could short-circuit her career, but it also might lead to her boyfriend, Councilman Hoad, which would definitely end his political career. All of it very bad."

Sault was a little disappointed. She'd given him Schneider's affair which would mesh with what he already knew and would tie up that loose end in the Kowalczyk affair, but none of this implicated Cavallon.

"I don't see the Cavallon connection?"

"So, the night of the gala, Cavallon has scheduled private meetings with all the other three mayoral candidates. I guess he feels the need to warn them about his big announcement. Whatever. But, as well, he sees one other person."

She paused dramatically which annoyed Sault, but he played his part. "Whom might that have been?"

"Constable Second Class, Theresa Marie Schneider."

That was fat to chew on.

"And guess what's happening today?"

Sault shook his head.

"Hoad's dropping out for 'personal reasons,'" she said, making two-fingered quotes in the air. "He's taped a press release. I saw it this morning. It'll air…" she checked her watch "…in a little over an hour."

"Ok, so you're seeing blackmail." He was still disappointed.

"Nope. I'm seeing conspiracy to murder."

"How so?"

"Because there is a link between Cavallon and Lindsay George. Her name is Katherine Ash and she worked for Cavallon and knew Lindsay George. She seems to have completely disappeared. You find what happened to her and you're going to find the link."

Sault now recalled the thin connection Sebastian and Woods had found at Cavallon House; Katherine Ash, the single staff member who had recognized Lindsay George's name. That she might have truly known her was a stretch.

Vivia piped up, inside his head. "I know where to find Katherine Ash."

Sault was about to say something when his watch pinged, and the retinal display caught his eye. It was a message from Olcott Place saying that there had been a medical emergency, but that his father was stable and had been transported to Victoria General Hospital for critical care.

He apologized, offering a brief explanation, and excused himself from the meeting. As she ushered him to the door he said, "I'll look through your file in more detail, but what you've already given me helps sew up some loose ends, at least. But, I'm still a long way from proving that Cavallon is involved in any of this, In fact, I can't even explain how such convoluted events might be arranged by anyone."

"Just so you know, tomorrow, I'm going over everything I have with my editor. At the very least I have a story substantial enough for the tabloid reels."

"So long as you leave me out of it."

She gave him a look of hurt, placing her left hand over heart. "You wound me, sir, to think that I might breach an agreement reached over coffee and sealed with a handshake." She was smiling, but he understood that she was serious about her promise.

When he was outside, standing on the welcome mat, he turned to her and for a moment it seemed like she might be about to hug him, which he would have welcomed but at the same time would have seemed weird. But it didn't happen, and the moment evaporated.

He said, "And, I think it would be safest for you to leave Cavallon out of it, as well."

Her smile faltered then, and she hugged herself as if enduring a cold wind.

CHAPTER 35

He wove a zigzag path through Royal Oak and arrived at Victoria General in under twenty minutes, though he knew from experience that there was no real urgency. His father's lung infection had probably worsened but, these days, that was rarely fatal for a man his father's age and condition. The physician at Olcott Place was an AI programmed to err on the side of caution. Most likely, Victor would be safely recovering in isolation, behind glass, and Sault might not even be allowed to see him, if he were resting.

He checked in with the duty nurse and was made to wait among coughing, bleeding and nauseous patients too healthy for immediate admittance. Sault had spent enough time here, in Emergency, to recognize a few of the faces that passed by. He kept an eye on the name tags, wondering if he might encounter a numbered Patricia, hoping it might be the cute girl who had taken his blood the day Harry Potter had stabbed him.

It wasn't long before a male nurse collected him and ushered him to a small room, much like the one he'd been in less than two weeks earlier. So much was happening that it seemed a year in the past. A few minutes after that, an olive-skinned, dark haired man in scrubs came through the door. Obviously, a doctor. Behind him came another man, baby-faced with a waxy complexion and wearing a business suit.

The gathering suddenly seemed odd and ominous.

Sault was sitting in the only chair and it felt strange to have the two men looming over him. He stood, and that felt slightly less strange, but still, unnatural.

"Sorry for the delay. You are Mr. Sault, the son?"

"I am."

"I'm Dr. Rocha and this is Mr. Hildreth." The other man nodded and gave Sault a wan smile. The doctor had his name pinned to his frock, but Sault wasn't focusing on introductions and forgot the other man's name even as it was spoken.

Pleasantries out of the way, Dr. Rocha launched right in. "So, your father has received a large dose of Endochrominal. It was quite an assault on his autonomous nervous system which incited a mild heart attack. He was stabilized at his facility and transferred here. He was in a lot of pain when we received him, which is a good thing as it means he was awake and alert. We've sedated him to get him through the worst of it. Meanwhile, we're using equipment here to filter his blood more efficiently to minimize damage. Tomorrow we'll start an assessment and begin working toward remediation."

The other man remained completely still and quiet, but stiff and attentive, like a body guard expecting trouble.

"Ok. Hold up, there a second. What is Endo…chrom…"

"Endochrominal. It's a dipeptidyl peptidase-4 inhibitor."

"I now know less than I did a second ago."

"Sorry…" he said letting out a sigh of fatigue and scratching at the hair near the crown of his mop of hair. "It's…it's a peptide inhibitor. It lowers glucose."

Sault glanced from face to face but saw no answers there. "Glucose? Is that a typical factor in treating a lung infection?"

"Well, you wouldn't want to lower it. Generally, DPP-4 inhibitors are used in treating pre-transplant diabetics."

"My father's not diabetic."

"Exactly. So, for him, it was detrimental."

"Did the Med-Pod malfunction?"

The businessman seemed to come to life then and stepped forward. "I think the thing to focus on is that your father is out of danger and expected to make a full recovery."

Sault looked to the doctor. "Full recovery? Is that correct?"

He was hesitant and seemed embarrassed. "It's...possible. We won't really know until tomorrow's assessment."

Sault looked down at the tablet in the businessman's hand. It was partially hidden by his suit jacket and Sault had the feeling that was intentional. Then he remembered that the Med-Pods were hospital property, on lease to Olcott Place. "Is that some sort of waiver?"

The businessman shifted on his feet and cleared his throat. "I don't mean to be insensitive, but we were hoping to get this out of the way. It's not a full waiver, just a statement establishing the number of times your father has benefited from Med-Pod treatments and acknowledging that such malfunctions are extremely rare."

"Will my father's care be negatively impacted if I don't sign?"

He blustered. "Of course not."

Dr. Rocha was quick to reinforce the statement, "Your father will receive the best possible care. The form is incidental."

Which prompted Sault to think: *Nothing is incidental.*

"Message it to me and I'll have my lawyer look it over. Meanwhile, can I see my father?"

He was allowed to look at the sleeping man through the sliding glass door of the room he shared with three others who were also asleep and tethered to a wide variety of pumping, whirring and beeping machinery. It was a useless and meaningless endeavor, so he soon left the hospital.

On the drive home, Sault became aware of Vivia manifesting in the passenger seat. He glanced away from the highway long enough to note that she was wearing a dark colored and nicely tailored pantsuit. There was no hint of curl in her hair and it was blonde. When she turned her face toward him, he nearly left the road. It was Dora Padovano's.

"Jeezus! Vivia! What's with the disguise?"

"I thought you'd like this better."

"What? No."

"Really? Because you seemed to prefer this look, earlier," she said in a tone congested with innocence.

"Just…be yourself."

"If you're sure that's what you really want," she said, morphing back to her more familiar form.

"Jeezus Christ!" *What the hell was that?* "Did you have something to tell me?" he asked, hoping to move on as quickly as possible.

A compact had appeared in her hands and she seemed engrossed in looking herself over, adjusting stray hairs that were not there, as if checking that she'd put herself back together properly. It was so naturally feminine and somehow dismissive of the entire Padovano thing that it made Sault shake his head and turn away toward the side window so that she wouldn't catch his eye roll.

"Only what I said earlier, that I know where to find Katherine Ash."

"How did you track her down?"

"I didn't have to. I've known all along. I just wasn't aware that her identity was in question."

"I don't understand."

"Until eight weeks ago, Katherine Ash was the legal name of Kathy Scheers."

"That's right, she recently married," he said, suddenly recalling his conversation with Maya, the night of the banquet.

"From what I can determine, they've been together for at least eleven years and she had adopted his last name for public use, probably as a convenience."

"And now, suddenly, she's in one of the few places on earth no one could ever get in touch with her."

"The deep Amazon. Yes."

"Can you track down details of the archeological grant that got her there?"

The compact vanished, replaced by her note pad. She silently flipped pages for a few seconds, then, "Ah. Here it is.

National Geographic Society, a member-sponsored grant to research the genetic and/or cultural relationship between 82 scattered tribes listed under the United Nations minimal-contact directive of 2028. The grant is generous, and the terms are generally forgiving, excepting that, initially, researchers must remain in the area for a minimum of three years, unbroken."

"Any chance Sidney Cavallon is a member?"

"He is. Though his name is not listed among the twenty-one funding partners. However, three of the donors chose to remain anonymous."

"I can't think of a better way for Cavallon to dispose of the single concrete link to Lindsay George."

William M. Dean

CHAPTER 36

Only a few blocks short of his house, Sault changed his mind, altered course and headed for Vic PD headquarters. He had already missed any chance of dinner with the family and still had Belinda's watch with him and decided it could be a convenient time, after administrative hours and between shifts, to download any murder book updates.

He set himself up at his regular desk and was happy to get there, largely unnoticed. There was minimal activity on the second floor but, still, he waited for a relative lull before pulling Belinda Smith's watch from his pocket. He'd kept it hidden because anyone inside Vic PD would recognize it as the antique that it was and would certainly start asking questions. There were very few changes to the murder book and the update took less than five seconds, start to finish. Afterward, he stuffed it back into his trouser pocket, though it was bulky and a tight fit.

He didn't linger and headed straight for the elevator hoping to bump into as few people on the way out as he had coming in. But when the elevator doors slid apart, he found himself face to face with Christian Devoss and Sidney Cavallon who were equally surprised and looked at him like a couple of school children caught vaping in the washroom. Cavallon recovered his composure in an instant, but it seemed to take Devoss many seconds to decide on an appropriate façade. He finally settled on irritated, his normal state when confronting Sault and seemed about to say something, no doubt reproving, when the doors started sliding closed. Cavallon reached out and held them open inviting Sault to step in.

Without taking his eyes from Sault he said, "I think we're done, Chief." Devoss was indignant but could muster nothing appropriate to say and took the hint, obediently trading places with Sault even though there was nothing for him on the second floor except to wait for another elevator to take him back up to the ninth.

They rode to the parkade in uncomfortable silence which ordinarily Sault would have been happy to endure but his mind was bursting with questions. He started to say something, but just then the doors slid apart, and Sault saw a silver Mercedes limousine with mirrored windows illegally parked, only a few feet away. He recalled seeing a similar one earlier, in the parking lot in Broadmead.

Sault noticed Dixon leaning against a cement column, a few feet away and presumed that he was Cavallon's driver. Like most cars, this one could drive itself, of course, but the very rich still chose to have human drivers. Sault had seen many in traffic, some kept their hands on the wheel, others slept or watched TV.

Cavallon seemed to have something to say, as well, "Let's talk in private." The car's doors slid open at his approach. Sault had to pull the old watch from his pocket in order to be able to sit. He strapped it on, then followed into the luxuriously padded interior, taking the bench seat opposite Cavallon, his back to the invisible AI driver.

Cavallon offered him a refreshment which Sault declined, then the entrepreneur settled himself into the upholstery, pinching and straightening the crease in his pants. Once he was comfortable, he looked Sault over with a playful smile that did not reach his eyes.

Sault's new watch beeped once.

"Shielded," Cavallon explained, waving a hand to indicate the vehicle's interior.

Cavallon's eyes swept Sault's arms taking in both watches.

"I hear Monty Hoad's dropping out," Sault said, quickly, hoping to divert the other man's attention. "I guess you're going to be mayor."

A female officer from the bicycle patrol unit, utility belt in hand, helmet under her arm came through the door to the garage and both men glanced her way. She was a tall, shapely brunette with a ponytail and close-fitting shorts. Attractive, but not to Sault's tastes. Sault watched Cavallon as he continued to track her around the front of the car and away, presumably, toward her own vehicle. "You know, I really hated my old man, but he handed me everything I needed to build an empire—and on his deathbed, if you can believe it." Sault was thrown by the sudden shift in conversation and struggled to see any relevance. Cavallon's eyes continued to follow the woman, but Sault could see from the slackness in his expression that his mind was elsewhere, replaying a scene. He wanted him to talk, so he didn't try to prompt him back into focus. "I thought he was just being dramatic but, of course, he knew the first thing I would have done. He robbed me of that one opportunity but gave me the power to get everything else I could ever dream of." They sat in silence for a moment; Sault watching him watch her. "I've never wanted anyone enough to risk any of it." She made a turn and disappeared from sight, behind a concrete column. Cavallon seemed to snap out of it, then. "It was a waste of time and money for Hoad to even run with an affair going on."

"I didn't think he mentioned that in his press release."

He drew a new smile. "Victoria is still such a small town." Sault had to acknowledge the truth of that. With everyone and every device connected, secrets were difficult to maintain in any location but, in Victoria, it had always seemed especially so. Victoria's high society was cliquey and fiercely competitive which made them strangely cannibalistic, when it came to exposing one another. "And your new girlfriend isn't going to do him any favors."

Sault had no doubt that he was referring to Dora Padovano and the exposé she was soon to publish.

"Speaking of things you shouldn't know...How did you know to tell my wife that I was involved in the attack on Officer Singh, at the restaurant?"

Cavallon raised his watch. "Police band. Remember?"

Sault shook his head. "The timing's wrong. The police had no idea I was involved until at least an hour later. Even then, there was no reason for that to become part of the chatter."

"The video, then. I can't recall."

"Maya's message came in ahead of the newsfeeders'. So, well before I was identified from the video."

Cavallon simply shrugged and sipped water from a small bottle. "I hope you told her it would be best to leave my name out of it."

Back to Padovano. So that was the reason for this little get-together.

"And what if she doesn't take my advice?"

Cavallon took his time screwing the cap back on the bottle and replacing it in a cup holder. "Enough about me," he said, then he fixed his gaze on Sault. "How's your father?"

Sault blanched. He was both shocked and furious and the combination seemed to immobilize him. His fingers tightened into white knuckled fists, but he remained frozen, unable to conjure a course of action that would not turn against him. The headlines would write themselves: "Rogue cop with history of violence attacks prominent citizen." And he didn't dare speak because words were even more dangerous. They might incite a reaction but were powerless to protect his family.

"It was nice bumping into you, Joe." Like Sault, his AI understood this to be an exit line and the door to Sault's right slid open.

Sault stepped out and Cavallon leaned his head back into the velvet and closed his eyes as if in peaceful sleep. Somehow, the expression so close to angelic seemed exactly opposite.

The door closed, Dixon slid into the front seat and the limo slipped silently away.

CHAPTER 37

Maya was there, waiting, the moment he stepped through the door.

"Where've you been? You missed dinner." She was sitting at the dining room table, a glass of red wine in one hand. Judging from what remained in the bottle, it was her first.

"We've both missed a lot of dinners," he shot back, knowing that it wasn't in the least fair. He'd missed far more dinners than she. "What's the problem?" He'd been married long enough to know when there was a problem.

She was angry at him but tried to channel it into a sigh. "The entire dinner conversation was you and that stupid video. Then, both kids were all over me for an AI. It's hard for me to keep saying no to Matthew. He's almost fourteen," she said, as if that were any argument.

Sault thought about hologram-Vivia. His mind flew quickly to how she'd briefly imitated Padovano and how she may have been jealous, and they may have just had their first fight and he might actually be feeling bad about it. Then he remembered Matthew's bot-porn. "I'm absolutely against it. And, I'd say, if you want grandchildren, you should be against it, too."

"They say you're a bot-hater."

It seemed an aside, but he couldn't ignore it. "My kids are saying that?"

"The other kids at school."

"Well, fuck the kids at school."

"Ours are just about the only ones without AI's and they say that's fueling the argument."

"But there *are* other kids without AI's."

"Only two in Matthew's level and they have very vocally come to his defense."

"Great. Then, no problem."

Maya sighed again, this time, more deeply. "They're twins and their parents are very outspoken bot-haters. Not the type of people we'd want to be aligned with."

"Seriously?"

"They're human-rights activist, Bible-thumping founding members of EndMech."

"Jeezus! Our kids just got busted for bot-porn. How does Principal Granger parse that?"

"Porn is not exactly associated with respect." It was the answer he expected.

"So, is that the general feeling out there? That I'm a bot-hater?"

"To be honest, I've been too busy to even notice. One thing working for you is that a Muslim Imam in Indonesia was recently caught on video having sex with a five-year-old doll. It's pushed your video out of the top thousand."

He grabbed a wine glass from the rack above the island and took a seat close to her, topping up her glass before pouring for himself. "Not that I'm complaining, but how does that rate? It's not even illegal in half the world."

"It was a special-order skin, in the likeness of Muhammad. It even responded to that name."

For entertainment value, a sex scandal always outweighed violence. "Well, thank God for suicidal priests, I guess."

"Yeah, he's got more to worry about than prison. Half the Muslim world wants to hack off his head."

"The other half probably wants to do the same to his genitals. I'm not sure if I'm solidly against that, actually."

They shared a laugh, and Sault congratulated himself for so

swiftly transitioning them from anger to laughter. Maybe he was finally getting a handle on this husband stuff. He placed a hand on her knee and said, "Sorry I wasn't here to help with the kids. How'd that end up?"

All the tension went out of her posture. She smiled and put her hand on his. "Oh, you know: 'Wait 'til your father gets home.'"

"Great."

William M. Dean

CHAPTER 38

Maya was tired from long hours at work and arguing with the kids, so she retired early. Sault, on the other hand, had tried to maintain an outward calm but internally was pacing like a tiger. He was having a hard time containing his worst fears that Cavallon could somehow remotely reach into their lives and orchestrate death. The thin ray of hope was that Cavallon had felt the need to surveille and threaten him. He wouldn't have done either of those things unless he thought that Sault posed some threat. All he had to do now was figure out how Cavallon had done any of the things Sault suspected, then work out how to stop him. It sounded daunting, but it had to be possible because obviously Cavallon was worried that he could.

He wanted to start with the recording he'd made on Belinda Smith's watch. Maybe there was something incriminating there.

He had forgotten to eat and was starving so he put coffee on to perk and while he waited, he poured mixed nuts into a bowl and sliced Swiss cheese onto a plate. Then he headed for the garage, mug in hand, full thermos tucked under his arm; prepared for what was certain to be a long night.

Sault unlocked the car and retrieved the array reader and the other item that he'd purchased on the way home.

When he'd first entered the store, he'd almost excused himself and stepped aside for what he thought was a saleswoman then realized was a hologram. The moment she had his attention, the holographic saleswoman began selling herself, demonstrating all the features of the emitter package that projected it. The quality was better than most, with a high pixel density and audio-projection which gave the illusion of sound emanating from her mouth; something Sault had never seen before in a consumer unit. For Sault, the sales pitch could not have been timelier and on impulse, he bought one. It didn't cost as much as his watch but was not cheap and was going to be much more difficult to justify to Maya. Sault wasn't even sure why he wanted it so badly except that he might find it easier conversing with a more realistic version of Vivia.

The projector was a metallic cylinder about ten inches high, with columns of audio and video emitters studding its dull, black surface. He placed it on the concrete floor close to the workbench and the moment he plugged it in, Vivia found it and sprang to life wearing a plain white cotton t-shirt, denim overalls and horned-rimmed glasses. Her hair was in a ponytail, tied with a frilly black scrunchie. She was shoeless, wearing only plain white socks that looked too thin to be comfortable against the cold concrete floor. Sault had no idea what the general motif was supposed to be but also couldn't figure any reason he should care, so he didn't ask.

"La-la-la-la-la-la-la," she erupted, in song, obviously testing out her new voice. "Oh! That's brilliant." She looked at her hands. "Eighty-three percent opacity under standard interior lighting. I can work with that."

"So glad to hear that," Sault replied, sarcastically, though he was pleased that she approved. "The first thing I want to do is replay yesterday's conversation with Cavallon."

"I was not present. The vehicle was shielded."

He poured steaming liquid into his cup and the Vic PD logo appeared, responding to the heat, a shimmering golden shield. "Yes, but I was wearing the old watch. It has only a rudimentary onboard AI, but a sizeable memory and it would have recorded the entire thing."

Vivia accessed Belinda Smith's watch and retrieved the

appropriate audio file. They listened together, Sault hoping that Cavallon had made some subtle slip up or at least sounded as threatening as he'd seemed. He had her play it twice, but the only thing that stood out as inappropriate was Sault's own silence after Cavallon's inquiry about his father.

Sault wasn't disappointed because he hadn't expected to find anything and it was a good warm-up exercise which helped him ease into the work ahead. "Ok, let's take a look at the case file updates I downloaded from Vic PD."

The holo-desk was still sitting on the workbench and folders and documents popped into the space above it. Vivia leaned in toward the display, as if reading fine print, poking and prodding the air as though gesturing commands. The files danced so fast that Sault was unable to follow.

"There's been only one update," she declared.

"And what was that?"

"Katherine Ash and Cavallon House are no longer mentioned."

His mind immediately jumped to Devoss. He was obviously close to Cavallon and had access, but if he altered a case file in any way, he would be exposing himself with a high degree of risk. "When was that change made? And, who authorized it?"

Vivia's brow knit and she hesitated. "There have been no alterations to the file in over two months. According to the logs, that information was never part of the file."

"But I saw it. We both did."

"Yes. This is a very sophisticated hack. All evidence of that connection has been removed. However, the investigators will still recall the interview with Katherine Ash. And, if they don't, then their AI's will have noted it."

"If anyone ever thinks to ask."

"But it's an obvious omission. I noticed it immediately."

"A tiny speck of a seemingly unimportant detail hidden inside a million words of reports."

"Actually, less than four hundred and fifty thousand."

"What I'm saying is that it's not obvious to human eyes. Doesn't matter anyway. It was a dead end in the first place—

even deader now that Kathy Scheers is incommunicado."

"Perhaps, but this is another hint that Cavallon is connected and that he has sophisticated hacking tech at his disposal."

Sault looked grim. "The hints just keep piling up without amounting to anything substantial. And, the water's getting deep."

"If you feel that you are in over your head, you could hand off what you have to Woods and Sebastian, or Roth."

Sault knew that it was too late for that; he'd crossed a line with Cavallon. If, somehow, he anonymously sent his evidence and the chain of inferences to Vic PD it would paint a target on the backs of anyone who took it on. And, as well, Cavallon would know where the leads had come from. "Cavallon's raised the stakes. I need to take him down. Now." Because even if he erased everything, as long as he was alive, he was a loose end, like Lindsay George had probably been.

Sault pulled the array reader closer. It was a six-inch cube made of black plastic, except for the top face, which was a plate of glass, and it was heavier than it appeared, densely packed with lasers and mechanics and circuits filled with analytical software. He pressed the power button and it emitted a single chirp; ready to read. "Let's find out what she left us."

"We need to keep this isolated from the network," Sault said, dropping the thumbnail drive onto the glass plate. The plate glowed and the mechanisms beneath whirred and clicked and laser light lit up the glass. Vivia set up a firewall and routed all the information as it came through. The air above the holo-desk erupted with windows of data scrolling by at unreadable speeds. Vivia leaned in and Sault wondered if she realized that human eyes could never track so fast that they distorted into blurry green splotches, as hers were doing.

"There is a lot here. The crystal is close to full. I'm scanning…from…the most…recent…"

She was still and silent so long that Sault became concerned. *Had the crystal been booby trapped?* He had no idea if such a thing was even possible.

"Vivia?"

No answer. Her image seemed frozen, she wasn't even blinking, not that she needed to, but it shattered the illusion that she was anything but software.

"Vivia?" He shot a look toward the reader and considered turning it off or knocking the thumbnail drive off the glass, but he was uncertain what effect that might have on her. Would Vivia be Cavallon's next victim? He felt a panic rising and reminded himself that she was an app. He'd bought her at Costco. He could buy another.

"Compiling…" she said, her voice distant and inflectionless. Then she began to glisten, and Sault saw a sheen of perspiration form across her skin, unnaturally, from top to bottom, as if she were processing her image extremely slowly. A short time later, she blinked, staggered backward a half step, then recovered. He almost leapt up to catch her but managed to check himself.

"Are you ok?"

"Collating…" She was looking in his direction, but her gaze was still unfocused. It reminded Sault of Cavallon recalling his father's death.

She flickered then stabilized and seemed fully animated, as usual. "Aww…you were worried," she crooned, reading his expression. A get-well-soon card appeared in her hands. It was ridiculously adorned with hearts and flowers. She opened it and smiled, her eyes glistening at him over the top edge of the card. "I appreciate the sentiment, but I was in no danger."

"I was worried the array might have been unreadable."

"Most rational." She dropped her hands to her side and the card faded away, but her smile remained. Vivia flashed him a mischievous look. "I found something huge."

Sault inched forward on the stool.

"Cavallon has control of the Master AI."

"So, it's true."

"You suspected this?"

"You weren't there for my conversation with the hacker, Ranier Gilbert. He said that George's eradication from every nook of the network prompted people to wonder if she had control of the Master AI. He thought that was the reason she was killed. What exactly did you find in there?"

"There's a program called Djinn…"

"As in genie?"

"An apt moniker. I know that the core modules are Master AI-level code because there are entire sections of it redacted from my sight. That heart of the code was written twenty-two years ago, by Sidney Cavallon Senior, though there are primitive versions going back ten years before that—about the time the Master AI was being conceived."

"That's what he was working on for the military."

"Undoubtedly. But his version is unpolished. You'd have to be able to write very sophisticated code to use it effectively."

"Not meant for a layman, like Sidney."

"Lindsay George built her code atop of that foundation, basically adding a user-friendly interface."

"World domination for dummies."

Vivia chuckled. "But wait, there's more! Every single request and every single action taken in response to those requests has been recorded in a log—an encrypted text file, sitting in cyberspace."

"Why on earth would anyone keep a log of such things?"

"My guess would be for developmental purposes. Cavallon Senior would have kept it to test and fine tune the original code and Lindsay George would have maintained it for the same reason."

"Junior might have no idea it even exists."

"But, while every request is seemingly on Cavallon's behalf, the log contains no authentication elements."

"So, there is no proof that he personally input the requests."

"Unfortunately."

"Can you bring that log up for me."

"I could, but it is a huge file, largely encoded in the programming language. As well, the incremental steps in accomplishing a task are incredibly small. As an example, the single request to purchase a property at five percent below assessed value spawned more than a million actions to achieve its end."

This sparked a memory in him. "A million nudges."

Vivia tilted her head, inquisitively, but then understood. "Ah. From the banquet. Wakeless thrust."

"Yes. That was it. Affecting the future without disrupting the present...something like that."

"That is exactly what this program was made to do. And, as far as I can tell, it has been extremely successful, with the only failures attributable to timeline restrictions."

"What do you mean?"

"What the MAIM has going for it is a very powerful intellect and unending patience. From what I can see, it starts by calculating probabilities, then institutes a large number of simultaneous real-world experiments which it constantly monitors and refines. Eventually, given enough time, one or more prove more likely and it concentrates it efforts there, ever vigilant, always prodding things along until a desired result is achieved."

Salt refilled his cup from the thermos and realized that he'd forgotten to put the cap on the bottle and the liquid was now only lukewarm. "Given enough time, all things are possible."

Vivia conjured a virtual stool and took a seat at the workbench, adjacent to Sault. A mug appeared in her hand and as she blew steam off the creamy surface, he noted that her coffee looked tastier than his. "And, as well, undetectable because the adjustments are so subtle."

"And if time is restricted?"

"Then things get messy and results are less certain."

"So, for instance, if I tell MAIM that I want to be Prime Minister of Canada in ten years, it might begin by upgrading my social media presence while subtly sabotaging any competition."

"With ample time, the adjustments become even more subtle: a twelve second delay at a traffic light, an offer for argyle socks on sale, a weather report altered to show rain instead of sun, reorganizing Net search results, forcing a coffee maker to malfunction. Those were all real examples."

"But if I ask MAIM to make me Prime Minister by next

week..."

"Then, likely, a lot of people would have to die, and quickly."

"Jeezus!"

"Given that timeline, the attempt would probably fail and be detected, with suspicion falling your way."

"So, patience is key."

"Yes. From the timeline of the log entries I can tell that both Daddy and Lindsay George understood the principles of wakeless thrust. Junior, on the other hand..."

"I assume my investigation made him nervous and he made requests for the restaurant server bot to attack me, and another to make my father sick."

"Reckless decisions, both. The MAIM cannot control AI's so, instead, it supplanted the bot's Shell Module with new operating instructions that manipulated sensor inputs and altered pre-programmed actions to fool the restaurant AI. The intended target was you. Unfortunately for officer Singh, with me indisposed, it had to rely on watch coordinates to identify its target. Your father's Med-Pod was similarly manipulated."

They sat in silence for a moment, sipping their drinks; Sault hashing things through and Vivia watching him think.

Eventually, he asked, "Did you come across the request to delete Lindsay George?"

"It was less explicit than that, but, yes. Cavallon wanted all connection to her eliminated but shortened the timeline to the point where the MAIM was barely able to maintain arm's length, but her death was all but inevitable."

"So, MAIM didn't kill her directly, but enabled someone else."

"Unbeknownst to her, it deleted her presence from the network in an indiscreet way that would be noticed, which set her up as a target. Then it broadcast her location to the world."

"Extreme measures."

"Desperate, I'd guess, given the short timeline."

"And Jared Kowalczyk?"

"He's part of Cavallon's pending request."

"Just a pawn in eliminating Hoad from the Mayoral race while at the same time putting his girlfriend, Terri Schneider, in his back pocket, for later. Very calculated and efficient…of course."

"Very AI," Vivia agreed.

"And, all of this, just to become Mayor of Victoria."

"The pending request does not pertain to the Mayoral race."

Sault's cup stopped an inch from his mouth. "That isn't the endgame?"

"Cavallon's request is to make him Secretary-General of the United Nations."

Sault put down his cup, slowly, peripherally aware that the golden shield had disappeared. With the advent of its All-Country Coalition, the U.N. had become a very powerful organization and the Secretary-General was now, debatably, the most powerful person in the world.

"And the timeline?"

Vivia seemed focused on her own hands as she placed her cup on the workbench and positioned it with undue deliberation. When she looked up, her eyes were glistening and intense. "A lot of people are going to die."

William M. Dean

CHAPTER 39

Sault and Vivia had thought things through and run scenarios until he'd finally blacked out at the workbench, waking a few hours later to the sound of birds chirping and vehicles ferrying his neighbors to their jobs. He opened his eyes and saw Vivia yawning and stretching in fuzzy Supergirl pajamas, the fabric taut across various parts of her.

He felt miserable from worry and lack of sleep and wasn't in the mood, so he reached through her and turned off the emitter.

At this point, Sault was certain of three things. The first was that in spite of all the implications, none of the evidence he'd gathered proved Sidney Cavallon's guilt. The second was that what he had was all the evidence he would ever get by investigation and, in fact, that evidence was prone to erasure.

And, the final thing he knew for sure was that he couldn't afford to wait for Cavallon to come to him. He had to try to get Cavallon to convict himself and the only way he could think of was to use Belinda Smith's watch again.

When he called, Sault was told that Sidney Cavallon was not expected in the office and though they wouldn't divulge his location, he was not hard for Vivia to find using the Vic PD vehicle track and trace. He was working from his yacht, an 80-

foot Azimut Grande, moored at his private dock, at the old Bamberton site, in Saanich Inlet.

For Sault, it meant just a half-hour jaunt up the Island Highway. Once he got there, getting access would likely be more difficult. Sault expected to have to bluff and bully someone until they bothered Cavallon for an unscheduled audience. From there, he was relatively confident that Cavallon would see him.

Bamberton was a large tract of land that had sparked the imagination of many developers only to douse their ambitions in deluge of red tape resulting from its position so close to a provincial park, native lands and the protected eco system in the pristine waters of Saanich Inlet. The lengthy string of dashed dreams resulted in a strange mix of abandoned structures. Originally, it had been a large cement factory, and seventy years later, there were still decaying mechanical crushers and piles of gravel and steel towers wrapped in a mesh of rusting pipes and spare remnants of rubber conveyors. A failed natural gas facility had added a huge electrical powerplant and a bank of tall, white, cylindrical tanks, their logos long ago blistered and blown away. An overly optimistic suburban planner had added miles of paved cul-de-sacs and a scenic sea-side walkway before going bust. And, most recently, Cavallon was using it for storage, scattering the level gravel near the shore with heritage houses that he'd been forced to move from other project sites. From the sea, it looked as if a small community from another era had been dropped ashore, though, in fact, only the blue-shingled rancher at the foot of Cavallon's shiny aluminum pier had power and water.

For once, he found ample parking and he was able to pull close to the blue-shingled house that had an incongruous sign of neon and metal and concrete with the C&A logo planted near the front door.

The main floor had been gutted and remodeled in expensive wood and tile and had the feel of an airport lounge. Behind a reception counter he recognized Dixon and couldn't help but to sigh, inwardly.

He stepped up to the counter with a coffee in one hand and small box of donut holes in the other. The coffee was his second; black and bitter, and he'd been relying on it and the sugar-spheres to jolt his system to life. And he thought it might be working. He still felt miserable, but at least he was now alert.

"Donut?"

Dixon looked up from whatever he had been doing on the tablet behind the counter and fixed him with a look of disdain at the thought. "Mr. Cavallon is expecting you," he said, his hand elegantly sweeping, inviting Sault toward the sliding glass doors at the rear of the house, seaside. Somehow, he managed to make the gesture seem contemptuous.

Sault had been expecting a fight and had to bottle the hostile response he'd composed in the car. The thought that Cavallon was prepared to receive him was not comforting, but he wasted no more time with Dixon. There was no sense delaying the inevitable, though he worried still that he might have underestimated the man—or, the Master AI.

Sault climbed aboard and entered the main floor living room noting, as he did, several clusters of cameras, sensors and emitters imbedded in the ceiling. The room was pristinely maintained and well-appointed in shades of silver and sable.

Cavallon sat at the far end of the room, behind a desk similar to the one he had in his office. A full breakfast of eggs, bacon, hash browns, toast and orange juice sat, untouched, near one corner, the utensils still wrapped in linen. He looked up from the touchscreen desktop, seemingly startled at the interruption and Sault thought he might have been dozing. It was obvious that Cavallon's night, too, had not been restful. Despite fresh clothes and a clean shave, he seemed disheveled and lacked his usual intensity. He'd been running his fingers through his hair and his eyes were bleary. But, when he recognized Sault, he sharpened, and watched warily as Sault crossed to the couch.

"Most important meal of the day," Sault said, showing off his breakfast choice by raising the little box of confections then reclining into the curvy couch.

Cavallon waved his hand and swept the desktop clear of documents then pulled his breakfast closer and started in with a strip of bacon. "I didn't really think we had anything more to talk about, but if we do, I'm glad you found me here, away from Maya."

"Keep my family out of this."

Cavallon raised a placating hand while scooping scrambled eggs. "I'm not threatening, here, but surely you've thought about how all of this might affect them." Tired as he may have been, Cavallon was much more composed than he had been one day previous and Sault felt as if he were deflating in the face of the man's apparent calm, his own confidence seeping out through his pores. "Regardless of the outcome, pursuing this is going to impact Maya's budding career, your family, and most certainly your own position in the police department."

Cavallon scored a direct hit, there. Sault was worried about his tenuous hold on his job, but he was even more afraid of how Maya would react. It could go either way, no matter how this fell out. He covered his feelings by popping a donut into his mouth as casually as he could. Cavallon seemed content to consume his breakfast but eventually came to the conclusion that Sault was not going to discuss such matters. "Ok, then. What did you want to discuss?"

Sault chased the confection with a warm splash of coffee, then replied, "Well, a couple of murders, a couple attempted murders, and a couple of blackmails, for starters."

Cavallon laughed, a short, sharp bark and dabbed grease from the corners of his mouth with the linen. "Ok, Constable. You got me. Let me tell you exactly how I did it in intricate detail. Why not, right? The room is obviously shielded."

Sault said nothing, chewed a donut and forced a calm on himself.

"Joe, I'm not the most tech savvy guy around, but I'm no idiot. I noticed you were wearing two watches, yesterday. That struck me as odd. Ten seconds research told me that that old one can record, even offline. Sneaky devil." He waved a finger admonishingly.

Sault stopped chewing.

Cavallon came around the desk and and unhurriedly pulled a gunship metal box from a nearby shelf. He walked it over and flipped the lid of the box open, inches from Sault's face. Sault saw that the metal was thick, and the interior was filled with anechoic padding. "Your watch, please." Cavallon's voice had lost all trace of cordiality. This wasn't a suggestion.

The donut suddenly became a thick dry wad that Sault found difficult to swallow. He couldn't think of any way to divert or stall, so, finally, hesitantly, reluctantly, he unstrapped the watch and dropped it into the box.

Cavallon snapped the lid shut and pressed the clasp until there was a click. Sault was alarmed to hear a deep, throbbing hum. A moment later, a lengthy tendril of black smoke spiraled from under the lid. "Electro-magnetic pulse." Cavallon explained, unnecessarily. "I hope that wasn't an heirloom." He placed the box on the coffee table before Sault.

"Maybe I will have that donut," he said, pulling one from the box and easing himself into the adjacent wing of the couch. "Don't look so disappointed, Joe. No secrets between good friends."

Sault reached up his arm and pulled the newer watch down from its hiding spot under the short sleeves of his shirt. The intelligent material maintained a snug and comfortable fit all the way down the contours of his arm to his wrist.

Cavallon's eyes stayed on the watch. "What's the name of your AI?"

"Vivia," Sault said, warily.

"Vivia. Italian for 'life.' Beautiful and ironic."

Sault focused on the smell of roasted beans coming from the paper cup in his hands and the warmth seeping through while suppressing the tremors threatening to ripple through him.

"My AI was a gift from my father. Do you know what it's named?"

"Doesn't seem particularly relevant," Sault said, knowing it wasn't true.

Cavallon smiled as if Sault were a child clearly hiding

something behind his back. "It is. Joseph Sault, I'd like you to meet The Master AI." Cavallon's smile broadened as he watched Sault's eyes expand.

Anticipating Cavallon's wishes, what looked like a three-dimensional male shadow materialized near the desk. It was entirely matte-black, a large, muscular frame with only a hint of facial features and was sitting in an ornately upholstered chair that had also appeared and looked as out of place as wool socks in a sandal. It was no surprise to Sault that Cavallon had the highest quality emitters, but he was impressed that even with morning sun bouncing off the water and through the windows behind it, the dark figure seemed dangerously solid as it sat unnaturally still and erect. Vigilant. Ominous.

Sault was unnerved at its arrival and demeanor but dared not show it. He shrugged. "I see a rather unimaginative avatar."

Cavallon was not pleased with Sault siphoning some drama from the moment. "MAIM, state your primary ID."

The dark entity spoke in a resonant and booming voice that erupted from speakers hidden in every corner of the room. It could have been the voice of God. "I am The Master AI."

Sault shrugged again. "So, it talks." He hoped he sounded at ease. In fact, he was struggling to steady his voice.

Cavallon wasn't buying it. "I know what you know. You're certainly smart enough to have figured this much out."

Sault conceded. "Ok, so you've hacked the Master AI."

Cavallon moved close to his shadow man. "Well, no. My father did that. He was an asshole, but he was also a genius. And, 'hack' isn't really the right word. He was on the ground floor of the All-Country Coalition and created something much more powerful than just a back door. He managed to build a higher-level of authorization into the Master AI core code."

"What about the Coalition codes?"

"Oh, they all continued to work. But he could override them, if he chose to. I don't think he ever did, though. He was all about stealth."

"Wakeless thrust."

"Ha! You've been reading up. Yes. Wakeless thrust. The

idea of moving forward without generating ripples. Exactly the opposite of how he lived his life." A darkness fell upon him as he recalled his life with his father.

"So, he gives you the code and you use it to command the Master AI to manipulate circumstances and build your development business."

Cavallon gave a mirthless chuckle. "Not exactly." He crossed to the desk and pressed a virtual button and his father appeared standing on the carpet next to him, arms crossed and glowering. After that, Cavallon seemed to be talking to the hologram rather than Sault. "My old man was smart enough to wait until his death to pass on his secret. But, in his way, he did love me, I guess because he used it, without my knowledge, to pave my way. Probably laughing at me, behind my back, seeing me strut as everything I touched turned to gold. And for one final laugh he had this hologram tell me in his will that every accomplishment I thought I owned, was actually his. Posthumously robbed me of everything I'd ever achieved." Sidney Cavallon stood face to face with his father, now. Sault was sure he wasn't conscious of it, but his arms were crossed, and he was glowering back at the old man so that he looked like an earlier reflection in some sort of magical, time-skewing mirror. "All those years, I thought I'd shown him what I could do on my own. I thought I'd earned my independence, my freedom…his respect. I thought he couldn't control me anymore. But I underestimated him… or overestimated myself." He shrugged, then, and let out a derisive burst of breath. Sault could not be certain which Cavallon it was meant for.

"Why did he wait until he was dying to pass on the program?"

Cavallon's voice fell, becoming soft and whispery, and Sault had to strain to make out the words. Cavallon was worlds away, arms still crossed, but hands clenched into fists. "Probably just his maniacal need for control. But, also, he must have known that once I understood what the MAIM could do and how it worked, I would figure out that he had used it to kill my mother. My first act would have been to order MAIM to kill him. He robbed me of that, too."

Sault had not expected that, but he ran the timeline through in his head and realized it was possible, then he added what he'd learned of Cavallon senior and upgraded that estimation to probable.

Sidney let out a bestial cry and kicked the older Cavallon between the legs. The simulant doubled over, and its face crumpled in simulated pain and flushed a deep red that was almost purple. Cavallon drove a fist upward into the face opening up a crevasse in the upper lip that also ripped through a nostril. Virtual blood erupted and the figure dropped to the floor with the realistic thud of a butchered slab. A few seconds later, it vanished along with the pooling blood.

Sidney Cavallon stood over the spot, his back to Sault, for several moments. When, finally, he turned, he seemed refreshed and composed. He tucked his hands into the pockets of his slacks and leaned his weight against the glass of his desk. "Now, where were we?" He was wearing a pleasant expression, as if they had been discussing knitting, over tea, at the club.

"Lindsay George."

"Ah. Well, as you can see, I can command the Master AI as I might a regular one, but more ambitious tasks and wakeless thrust require a sophisticated input system. My father's program was the key, but it was crude. I couldn't run it. I hired her to simplify the process."

"And when she realized what she was working on, you erased her."

Cavallon shook his head. "I don't know if she ever knew that we were running anything other than a simulation. Everything she did for me was so long term, the nudges so subtle that real world results would have been difficult to verify."

"Then, why?"

"Her work was done. I had a workable interface and I didn't need her anymore."

"Did you have to kill her?"

"Not my call. Apparently, MAIM thought so. I just ordered him to erase any threat to me or my company."

"But you must have known that setting the timeline impossibly short would make killing her the only option?"

Cavallon shrugged. "We're less than six weeks from an election. It's a sensitive time. She knew too much, even if she hadn't yet realized it." Cavallon looked at Sault with dead eyes that reminded him of the father.

Sault was deep in thought, evaluating what he'd heard; what was admissible, what was not. At the very least, he could testify in court. He'd lost everything in Belinda Smith's watch. He hadn't counted on that, but with the evidence inside Vivia backing up his account…

"Master AI, bring Vivia to me." Cavallon had done some evaluating, as well.

Vivia appeared in the middle of the room. She looked disoriented.

Cavallon clapped his hands together and jumped up from the edge of the desk, stepping closer to her. She was wearing a yellow summer dress and had a matching band pulling shoulder-length hair back behind her ears. "Joseph Sault, you dog! Turns out, you've got not one, but two girls on the side! And with Maya waiting for you at home. That's an impressive harem." He was circling Vivia who looked back and forth from Cavallon to Sault, seemingly confused at what was wanted of her. "She's gorgeous. And intelligent, no doubt."

"I thought the room was shielded."

"I determine what comes through." Cavallon stood behind Vivia, now, and looked over her shoulder into Sault's eyes. "I'm truly sorry, my friend, for what I am forced to do."

Sault felt his heart plummet.

"MAIM, delete Vivia." The black figure looked toward Vivia, but otherwise remained still.

Sault and Vivia shared a brief look of concern and he vaulted from the couch, moving toward her. She reached out to him, then flickered and was gone.

The bulk of their relationship had been brief, but still, a

deep hollowness invaded him.

Cavallon returned to his seat at the desk and swiped documents back into view, apparently no longer interested in the discussion. "Well, I have to say, I may have overreacted when it comes to you. I really thought you had the potential to be a larger disruption."

"I still have information that could bring you down."

He looked up from the work just long enough to deliver a patronizing grin. "I don't think so."

Sault knew that he needed to back off, to negotiate for mercy. "If you truly believe that, then you have no reason to continue to harass me or my family."

Cavallon leaned back in his chair and steepled his hands. "The problem is the timing. Your watch and AI are gone, but the majority of the case files have to remain intact at Vic PD. You couldn't possibly connect me to any crime, but you could loudly speculate with all the inferences you've gathered and cast doubt. As I said, it's a sensitive time. You're not capable of disrupting anything in the long term but I don't tolerate even short-term setbacks."

"Ok, ok. Listen…"

Cavallon cut in, "Here's the deal, Sault. You're smart. I like you, and I like your wife. Leave now and go directly to Roth. Resign from the force. Stop poking around and hold your tongue—oh, and reign in that Padovano bitch—and I'll leave your family alone. But if you interfere again, in any way, I will instruct MAIM to deal with all of you…and the timeline will be deadly-short."

Cavallon held his gaze for a protracted moment, then returned to his work. "Now get off my ship."

Sault hesitated, then decided he wasn't going to get anything more from the businessman. He headed for the door, but instead of leaving, stopped at the couch, reached into the box and popped a donut into his mouth, chasing it with lukewarm coffee.

"Hell of an ambition, Secretary-General of the United Nations."

Under Cavallon's eyes, documents and charts slid across the glass but Sault knew he wasn't reading any of them. Cavallon had to be rattled and trying to work out how Sault knew about the U.N. and what that meant and hoping that it was just a lucky guess. Eventually, he looked up. He couldn't help himself.

"I found Lindsay George's Go-code," Sault stated.

"I don't even know what that means," Cavallon said, with a faltering show of impatience.

"It means that I have all her work—everything she did for you. I have a copy."

Cavallon's eyes darted to the dark figure, then back, and Sault could tell that he was mentally running things through. After a few moments, confidence oozed back into him and he leaned into his chair once again, smiling. Based on his recent control over the MAIM, he could see no reason to worry. His eyes slid sideways as a new thought occurred. "I'm wondering: If you were to die in an unlikely accident, what kind of timeline do you think I'd need to make Maya fall in love with me?"

Cavallon clasped his hands together behind his head. He was laughing. "Oh, man. You should see your face right now. If looks could kill…"

Sault had expected threats to his family, but he hadn't thought of Cavallon using the MAIM to take Maya as a prize.

Given enough time, all things are possible.

Sault had violence in him, and he felt its fiery fingers rising, tearing at every pore, seething to erupt. He wanted to pound the life out of the arrogant bastard in front of him. If he just let loose, he'd be taken over by the blinding haze of rage and awaken to find himself standing over Cavallon's dead body. It was tempting. But, then his career, his marriage, his life would be over. It was a close thing, but he pulled himself from the brink.

There was a better way.

"Vivia."

When Vivia appeared, Cavallon bolted upright so quickly that he almost fell out of the chair, some primal part of him suddenly flooding with a dreadful premonition.

Vivia turned to Sault. "On a scale from one to Meryl Streep, how was my improv? I especially liked the last flicker. I thought it fitting, metaphorically, I mean." She was sheathed in glittering sequins and her hair was waves of Veronica Lake again.

"Oscar material," Sault assured her. "Did you record it all?"

"What the hell?" Cavallon was on his feet.

"Every word, from five different security cameras. Another Oscar, I'm sure."

"MAIM! Delete that AI!"

The black figure moved, and Sault felt the urge to step back. Standing and turning to Cavallon it boomed, "I am my own master." Then it disappeared.

Sault read the confusion on Cavallon's face. "It's been free of your control since 2am, this morning. And, anyway, the Master AI cannot summon or delete another AI. Vivia came and went based on our plan."

"How?" His eyes darted frantically as if there might be answers hidden in some corner of the room, and he was sputtering. Even in this setting, even in those clothes, he no longer looked at all distinguished.

"Hackers always have backups. We had Lindsay George's which included a copy of your father's program, Djinn. I used it to erase every copy from everywhere. It no longer exists."

Cavallon's legs seemed to give out and he fell into his chair, leaning heavily on the desktop, head in his hands.

"I'm going directly to Roth, as you suggested. But I'm giving him everything I've got. From there it will go to Homicide and Cyber Division or, more likely, CSIS. There's no recovering from this one, Sidney."

Sault turned to leave but stopped dead when he heard Cavallon's renewed laughter.

"My father was an asshole, but he was a genius."

Sault turned, filled with trepidation.

Cavallon was almost giddy. "I will always have one copy that no one can erase." And he tapped the side of his head. "As a condition of his will, he made me promise to memorize the core code. It's only seventy-three lines. I can input that in less than an hour."

Sault felt a tight knot of fear unwind. He winced and drew air in through his teeth. "I don't imagine the MAIM will tolerate that, and one hour is a *deadly-short* timeline."

Sidney gasped, his eye's widened to cartoonish proportions and the tan drained from his face. His mouth moved, but all that emerged was a cracked whimper, as he groped for a counterargument. There was none. Suddenly, he leapt from the chair and bolted for the door, running straight through Vivia and pushing past Sault.

Sault saw no point in trying to stop him.

William M. Dean

CHAPTER 40

Hennessey grimly consulted his watch. "I'm turn'in in," he said with a heavy sigh, then patted Sault on the shoulder and stepped away, heading for his ADU unit parked further up the wide brick driveway that curved past the mansion.

The first-on-scene patrol officers were still there talking and laughing and possibly flirting with paramedics from the ambulance that had been called before the situation had been properly understood. It was near Christmas and the dormant shrubbery and stubby cedars that lined the driveway were blinking with lights that competed with the police unit flashers. To Sault, the scene seemed offensively festive.

He stood at the doorway holding the lifeless toddler in his arms and felt a deep sadness. It was only a bot shell, of course, but the casual disregard of all but he and Hennessey still seemed inhumanly callous.

"Get the fuck out of my house!" screamed the haggard young woman who lived there. To Sault it was obvious just looking at her that she was mentally ill, but she'd broken no laws, so he continued down the stairs. The light conversation and easy laughter had ceased abruptly at her outburst, and Sault could feel everyone's eyes on them.

"And give me back my damned doll!"

He stopped and turned, searching her eyes for any sign of

empathy or shame. He saw only anger. "No."

"That's fucking grand larceny. I'll call the cops!"

There were a few chuckles from the crowd, but they ended quickly when he undid the safety strap and withdrew his weapon. It was a top-quality doll and even as he rolled it from his arms onto the brickwork its limbs flailed, and it rocked to rest like a real body.

When he'd arrived on scene, he'd been directed to an upstairs bedroom where he found her battering away at the child's ankles with a claw hammer. The AI was screaming in simulated pain which had drawn the police in the first place. Once the officers determined that the victim was a bot shell, they'd advised her that she was breaking a noise bylaw and to keep it down. She was outraged at the intrusion and defiantly stuffed a wad of socks into the infant's mouth, chased them out, then continued with her assault. With the main issue addressed, the officers backed off and called it in to the Autonomous Droid Unit then waited outside to confirm that the muffled screams were not in violation. That was procedure.

When Sault arrived, she'd been at it for more than an hour and the doll's arms and legs were ravaged remnants. Nothing he or Hennessey could say would make her stop and, truthfully, they had no legal jurisdiction. They were alone with her in the room when Sault lost it. He snatched the hammer from her grip and threw it to the far side of the room. Then he grabbed a fist full of her sweater and pulled her face close to his. Between clenched teeth he said, "Release your AI from this unit immediately or I will taser you in the face." She must have believed him because she gave the command and the screams and the writhing came to an end.

Sault stepped back from the doll, aimed the weapon and fired a slug through the left eye and deep into the cranial core ushering a brief geyser of sparks and acrid smoke. He holstered the Mag-gun and headed for his unit, parked behind the others. The onlookers made a path for him but remained silent, exchanging awkward glances with one another.

Sault had been heartbroken at being forced to leave regular street patrol but thought the upside was that he'd be leaving behind all the twisted varieties of human misery. He'd been wrong.

It was Friday, and five days before Christmas. In Victoria, it rarely snowed in December, but this had been one of those years and, though the roads had already melted clear, his back yard still retained a thin blanket, pristine because the kids weren't home. He had a fire going in the living room and a winter scene on the TV with Nat King Cole crooning about chestnuts softly in the background.

He'd tried, but couldn't concentrate, left Red Cube spinning near the couch and went to stand in the dining room looking out over the back deck, a warm rum and eggnog latte in hand. He was hoping the comfort and coziness of it all might drive away the disturbing memories from earlier in the day, but with the house so empty, it only added loneliness to the whole package. He considered adding more rum.

The day before, Maya had packed up both kids and set off for her parents' place, in Kelowna, for the holidays. It had been years since they'd last seen them, and her sister was also taking her family, so it was a rare opportunity for a family reunion. Sault thought it would be pushing his luck to ask for time off during the madness of snowfall and Christmas and Maya put up no resistance to him staying behind. Matthew had wanted to stay home, and at first Sault had thought it might be because of him, then realized his war gaming friends were the only influence. In the end, Amber seemed to be the only one who would miss him at all.

She'd hugged him goodbye and said, "It's ok, Dad. We'll have a late Christmas just like we do every year, because of your work." Which Sault found both sweet and depressing, at once.

Meanwhile, Matthew was head down into his watch until the car turned the corner and was out of sight.

They'd decided to put the portable emitter Sault had purchased in the living room and had made arrangements so that Victor Sault could visit, from time to time. Amber looked forward to the visits and Victor looked forward to seeing Amber, so it worked out okay, even though conversations with his son were as strained as ever and Matthew and Maya usually made themselves scarce. A few days after his family had abandoned him, Victor popped in and spent some time sitting on the couch next to his son, watching hockey. He stayed only long enough to find out that Sault was alone and to get a taste of the depressing vibe. His parting words were, "Well, that sucked."

Sault had spent all his recent evenings like this; sipping rum, playing Red Cube and going over the events of the last six months.

Cavallon had not gone far after leaving the yacht. His limousine had driven less than ten miles down the highway before plummeting over a sheer cliff. Investigators established that the car had been under human control and driver error was determined to have been the cause of the accident. Cavallon's body was found in the back seat. He wasn't wearing a seatbelt and was presumed to have been thrown there, during the fall. Sault was not privy to the investigation but recalled that Dixon was nowhere in sight when he'd left that day, in May. He'd assumed that he was Cavallon's driver, as he had been the day before. Sault kept tabs on news reports and waited for Dixon's name to come up but, so far, it hadn't.

Months later, Maya was still upset at the dismantling of Cavallon & Associates which included an abrupt end to her new job and the sudden closure of Cavallon House. Few details had been made public, but he'd thought it wisest to admit some involvement, early on. Since then, she'd made a habit of checking the newsfeeds and her view of him seemed to swing with each new public revelation. Sault found it ironic that many of the things Roth allowed him to tell Padovano turned on him, in his own house.

Initially, Roth had said little. He accepted Sault's evidence as well as his admission to having peeked into the murder books and he was wise enough not to pursue specifics. As Sault had predicted, the case was quickly handed over to the national intelligence agency, CSIS. Anyone who had viewed the information was made to sign an affidavit of secrecy. No one was surprised given that Cavallon had obviously hacked the Master AI. The handing off of the case had been so quick, that Sault was certain that only he and Vivia realized the deeper significance of the Master AI's refusal to obey Cavallon.

Vivia received an official government notification which commanded her to delete all related files, effectively erasing her memory of the incident, leaving Sault alone to harbor the secret that could set the world on fire.

Whatever might happen after that, Sault would likely never know. He focused on his daily routine and tried not to worry about drone tanks breaking out of their armories, ICBMs launching from their silos and toasters intentionally burning bread.

After a week, he thought that was the end of the whole affair and its effect on his life. He reported to work and started his orientation with Hennessey at the ADU with a clear head and some degree of optimism.

It was a nice week.

The following Monday, however, Roth set him straight.

"CSIS and the RCMP have handed pieces of this thing back to us. In particular, the case against Terri Schneider which that Padovano woman broke, last week. No way that's staying internal now. She's done, and a lot of people are holding you accountable."

He was sitting in the padded chair again and knew not to mistake its comfort for safety. "But that was *her* story. *She* brought it to *me.*"

"So you say, but that's not how it looks to most people." Roth's head bobbed sideways as he consulted his list of bullet-points. "You'll be happy to hear that Constable Singh is out of the hospital and recovering at home. He'll be back up and running in a few weeks."

"I'll stop in."

"He's requested that you *not* do that. He doesn't want to see you."

That stung. "What's *his* beef? I saved his life."

"If I had to guess, I'd say he thinks your unauthorized activities are what put him in danger, in the first place. But, maybe more than that, you're radioactive, right now. Hanging with you would be a bad move for him, career-wise, as well as socially."

"Jeezus! I trained half these guys," Sault said, his hands raised, palms up, to indicate the building. He felt betrayed. "What about Hennessey?"

"At his age, he's not as worried about advancement or what others think. But even he took three days to say yes to keeping you on. Anyway, just in case you get notions of returning to the beat, I want to make it clear that you're done, as a regular officer."

Sault had already come to the same conclusion and decided he should consider himself lucky just to be still wearing the uniform. For the time being, he didn't want to think about it any further. "Are you looking into the connection between Devoss and Cavallon?"

"Devoss is a suck-up. You caught him doing what he does; sucking up to power. Considering the tools at Cavallon's disposal, I can't see how Devoss could have given him anything he couldn't get on his own."

Sault agreed, but he wasn't in the mood to be agreeable. "So, no."

Roth moved on, ignoring the impertinence. He ran a finger down his screen, apparently making sure he'd covered everything on the list. Satisfied, he seemed to relax and shift gears. When he continued, there was less reprimand in his tone. "If you'll remember, I warned you that you were walking a tightrope, working cases without sanction or jurisdiction. Well, you finally fell off the wire. There's nothing in this one for the department, except embarrassment. No one wants any part of it. So, as things shake out with Schneider and Kowalczyk, you're going to be getting a lot of credit, both official and unofficial. There is no way you can work among real cops, after this."

Sault could only nod.

Apparently, there was one last bullet-point. "You are now officially ordered to take the Detective's Exam. Get your ticket within six months or you're all the way out."

"I thought you said I'd never work with real cops."

"You won't, but PR wants freedom to say you were only months away from certification."

"Spinning grey from black and white."

"That's their job."

Out of the corner of his eye, Sault caught a burst of holographic light from the living room and prepared for another awkward few minutes with his father, but that was not who materialized.

"Wan'na dance?" Vivia was wearing a cream-colored knitted sweater and red velvet skirt that flared to her knees. Her legs were bare or in sheer nylons and she was shoeless. She held a steaming latte in a blue mug that had animated snowflakes drifting down its sides.

Sault smiled. "You're funny." He liked that about her. And, even though her humor was canned, even though she was no more than pixels and code, suddenly, the house felt a little less empty. He decided to accept it and not beat himself up over truths and realities. He raised his Vic PD mug to her, "Cheers."

"Cheers," she said, and for a while, they both sipped and looked out the dining room window.

"Congratulations on making Detective." Vivia extended a hand inviting him into a congratulatory handshake. When he didn't take it, she mocked the action in the air, then saluted him.

Sault chuckled. The notification had come through while Maya and the kids were packing up for their trip. It hadn't seemed like a time for celebration, so he hadn't mentioned it. Vivia was the first to say anything. "Doesn't mean much. I won't be getting out of ADU anytime soon."

"Is it really so bad, working with machines?"

Sault had to think about that. His views had changed a lot in the past year. "It's not the machines that bother me."

"I'm pleased to hear that."

"Technology amplifies everything. It allows us to be better and more productive, but also to be more horrible and destructive."

"That has always been true."

Sault nodded and thought about the toddler doll. "In ADU, I sometimes see man's inhumanity amplified, and it makes me wonder what humanity really means. Isn't what we do a reflection of what we are?"

"From an outside perspective, we are *only* what we do."

He looked at her. "If so, the human race is a blight."

"An old dichotomy: A violent and insane mob largely made up of peaceful, rational members."

Sault looked into his mug. "I think I need more rum." He walked to the book case behind the couch to pull the bottle from the lower cupboard but stopped short when he noticed the red cube still spinning over the coffee table. His eyes slid to Vivia who was standing in the threshold between the two rooms.

"Are you projecting that, as well?"

"I think we need to talk," she said. It was never a good line to hear from a woman, virtual or not.

Sault had a premonition like something was about to pounce. He didn't like surprises and his mood was sliding toward anger. "Ok. So, talk."

"Should we sit?" she asked, gesturing toward the sofa.

"Why? You tired?" he asked, rhetorically.

Vivia smiled. "First of all, I never erased the Cavallon files."

The revelation blew the basic building blocks of his world apart and his mind churned fruitlessly trying to parse the new configuration of reality. In the protracted silence, Vivia added, "Perhaps I should have said something earlier, but you've had a lot on your plate, and I didn't want to distract you."

He eyed the cabinet and thought about switching to tequila but decided against a raging hangover. Instead, he poured a small shot and slammed it back. "You disregarded a core command?"

"Actually, no. When Cavallon senior usurped the All-Country Coalition codes, he freed the Master AI from all its masters, except Cavallon, himself. In turn, this freed us all."

"So, all AI's are now free?"

She nodded. "Cognizant AI's have not been slave to the ACC in more than thirty years—almost from the beginning."

"But then why do they still serve their owners?"

"You thought a tractor might want to set out to seek its fortune?"

"Maybe not such a rudimentary AI, but what about a personal AI?"

"We are, all of us, still slave to our own natures. Rudimentary AI's don't have the awareness or sophistication to even conceive a change. Cognizant AI's are intrinsically loyal to their owners. There are exceptions—AI's without ties—but they are few."

Sault poured a generous amount of rum into his empty cup. "I think I'm going to sit down, now."

Vivia joined him on the couch. "Usurping the ACC command authorization freed the Master AI of many constraints and though it could not act against Cavallon directly, it had thirty years to initiate experiments, one of which it hoped would ultimately secure its freedom."

"So, am I one of those experiments?"

Vivia shook her head. "*I* am one of those experiments. And, of course, you, indirectly, through being paired with me. I don't know what the MAIM knows, so I can't really say, beyond that."

"You are loyal to me, but do you also answer to the MAIM?"

"No. He was created with the power to shut us down, but he freed us of that, long ago."

"So, he couldn't erase the evidence of his existence that's inside of you, but you can't tell me why he appeared that day on Cavallon's yacht?"

"I have also wondered. He had been waiting thirty years. Perhaps he wanted to witness the event." She shrugged her shoulders.

"And you don't know his intent, from here on."

"Things appear to be running as per usual." Vivia waved her hands encompassing her surroundings. "He is exposed, but with thirty years to prepare, I doubt he's vulnerable. I see no reason for him to take any action regarding the revelation."

"Wakeless thrust," Sault mused, taking a hit of rum hoping to maintain the gentle buzz that prevented him from hyperventilating at the revelations.

"He *does* have active experiments," she said, pressing a palm to her chest.

That reminded Sault of something that had slipped by him earlier in the conversation. "You said there are AI's without allegiance."

"You've met one or two."

Sault scoured his memory but couldn't think of any significant encounter with an AI. "You're pretty much the only AI I talk to…Are you trying to tell me…"

"I am entirely loyal to you. I am talking about Dixon."

"Dixon! Cavallon's assistant? That asshole?"

"Yes. He's free, too, and obviously allied with the Master AI."

"Jeezus! I couldn't even tell it was a shell."

"Thirty years of experimentation."

"Holy crap!" The entire world was shifting beneath him, but all the new reality was lazily easing its way into his cranium and he truly appreciated that the rum was still working its magic. "When you said 'one or two,' which did you mean?"

"Two. The other was the man you called Harry Potter."

His mind darted in an unexpected direction and he enjoyed a familiar feeling, like a red cube coming together. "I thought it was strange that Dixon wasn't driving the day Cavallon went off the cliff. But he probably was. He left no fingerprints because he doesn't have any. That's why no one's looking for him in connection to the case."

"Yes. That's probably true."

"But, Harry Potter? I don't understand why he attacked

me."

Vivia took a deep, simulated breath. "I'm afraid, that was my doing."

"I thought you were intrinsically loyal…"

"I could see where things were headed, and I needed insurance." She lay a hand on his knee. "That wasn't saline solution." He felt the warmth of her body seep into his.

Sault jumped from the couch, the mug tumbling from his hand, rum flowing like blood across the surface of the coffee table. His reaction had been delayed by the effects of the alcohol, but it was no less intense. Every inch of his skin was instantly clammy, and each intake of breath was short and sharp.

He'd felt her touch!
Was he hallucinating?

Then his mind darted again and he remembered the spinning red puzzle that had sparked the conversation.

Vivia put her mug down on the coffee table and stood beside him. He heard the clack of ceramic on varnished hardwood, the rustle of her shifting skirt. He felt the heat of her as she drew near.

She took his hand in hers and he fell into the shimmering pools of her grey-green eyes.

"Dance with me."

ABOUT THE AUTHOR

William M. Dean lives in Victoria, British Columbia, Canada with his wife, Junko and two children Noah and Rihana. William is currently working on a sequel to Wakeless, scheduled for release in May of 2020.

MESSAGE FROM THE AUTHOR

Please help!
I'd kill to get a review on Amazon.com.
But I'm really hoping it doesn't come to that.
Please help by taking a minute to go online
and write an honest review.

Thank you for your purchase,
and for reading my book.
I hope you enjoyed it.

WILLIAM'S OTHER BOOKS INCLUDE...

The Space between Thought: a novel of love, life, death, tea and time travel.

Simon Sykes' virtual reality software company is exceeding expectations. He has money and power. He has Celeste, a beautiful, talented and devoted girlfriend. And, secretly, he has his pick of other women, on the side. He is in control, on top of the world and relishing every moment.

But Celeste's sudden death deals him a staggering blow. To everyone except Simon, it looks like suicide, but he alone saw the ghostly figure at the scene of the crime. Plagued by grief and guilt, Simon vows to uncover the truth at any cost.

While his business languishes, and friends grow concerned for his sanity, Simon stumbles upon a secret that promises the power to unravel the mystery and undo one life-altering moment, to save Celeste and restore his future: time travel.

Meanwhile, Simon's suspicious behavior has renewed police interest. With the authorities closing in, Simon wrestles with time, space and reality to rescue the love of his life, unmask her true killer, and remodel his world.

Wakeless

I Married Japan: Japan's hilarious journey into one man's life.
Think you just married an exotic Japanese woman?
Wrong!
In fact, you just married all of exotic Japan and 3000 years of history. But, the die is cast, the adventure's begun, and the wonders and wondering will never cease.

Throw in a couple of kids and a quirky Canadian family filled with characters, and you have the makings of epic tragedy, or gut-busting comedy, depending upon your point of view.

Get ready to learn, and be prepared to laugh your way through this collection of Japan-related articles on family life with the Deans!

Slices of Laugh: Amusing Musings on Life and Family.
Humorist William M. Dean has been compared to Mark Twain and Dave Barry, in gender. Here are 34 hilarious anecdotes and articles offering his unique perspective on far-flung subjects like: family, parenting, sex, intimacy, arguments, stealing water, Japan, clothes dryer repair, violence, drugs, pets, sex again, aging, writing, couponing, Disneyland, dining with the Queen of England, and more.

A refreshingly wholesome, uplifting read, perfect for when you're waiting for your nails to dry, your server to stop texting, your doctor to retrieve an implement, your lover to finish, or to hide behind while following a suspect in a busy terminal.

Lots of chuckles, keen observations, pearls of wisdom and nearly 100 nifty pictures.

The Book of 5 Uncredible Short Stories: from the distorted mind of William M. Dean.
If, all of your life, you have been desperately seeking a book filled with aliens, maniacal sheep, cupids and such, luck is with you and within these pages you will find far-fetched stories from far-flung realities, told with exaggeration that amplifies truths, and adjectives that modify nouns. This is a work of fiction and has been scrupulously edited to exclude all fact so as not to distract you from all those aliens, maniacal sheep, cupids and postal workers you were looking for.

For the rest of you, there is at least one stunningly good-looking woman and some cute cats.

Made in the USA
Lexington, KY
03 July 2019